I0738617

JUMP TECH

Book 2 of the Jump Light Chronicles

AJ Kilgore

Jump Tech Copyright © 2020 by AJ Kilgore. All Rights Reserved.

All rights reserved. No part of this book may be reproduced in any form or by any electronic or mechanical means including information storage and retrieval systems, without permission in writing from the author. The only exception is by a reviewer, who may quote short excerpts in a review.

Cover designed by Lae Klinger
Cover Logo designed by Rick Magyar
Cover image Energy or matter © rolffimags / Depositphotos
Edited by Josiah Davis – JD Book Services

This book is a work of fiction. Names, characters, places, and incidents either are products of the author's imagination or are used fictitiously. Any resemblance to actual persons, living or dead, events, or locales is entirely coincidental.

AJ Kilgore
Visit my website at www.ajkilgore.com

Published in the United States of America

First Edition: September 2020
Penny Candi, www.pennycandi.com

eBook ISBN-978-1-7327829-2-1

Library of Congress Control Number: 2020919395

CONTENTS

"Conscience is the inner voice that warns us that someone might be looking."

H. L. MENCKEN

CHAPTER 1

Hot Seat

Christian Meadows was ready to be fired. Or expelled. Maybe even shot by the campus cops if it came to that. Anything to get out of the university president's outer office, off the damned uncomfortable visitor's couch, and as far away as possible from the president's high-strung executive assistant Doreen. She was having a bad day, to put it mildly—much worse than Christian's, which was saying something.

Christian had been called to the president's office to answer for the small matter of his PhD advisor's treason, but Doreen had the much harder job of thwarting the incessant phone calls from reporters inquiring about the scandal. Though Christian expected an unpleasant conversation with the president—full of accusations culminating in his termination and expulsion—he much preferred that to the odious task of talking to the press.

But the waiting was killing him. He'd gotten there on time and had been shunted to the couch, forced to wait while the president dealt with some other participant in the whole ugly business. Five minutes. Ten minutes. Thirty minutes passed. At a quarter till the hour, he'd considered gnawing his leg off, sure that the crunch of bone and gristle would be loud enough to drown out Doreen's saccharine-sweet voice as she answered call number ten thousand in the same passive-aggressive sing song. The tick in her jaw belied her pleasant tone and Christian wondered how many more calls she could take before she stood up and quit.

On some level, she must have realized the calls were inevitable. When the university's director of commercial development gets arrested for treason, questions were inevitable. As the guy who hired the traitor, President Hayman moved to the front of the line. But poor Doreen, his stalwart gatekeeper, suffered Hayman's indignities first.

Christian, the traitor's graduate assistant, was the next logical interrogation target. The feds had already put him through the wringer the day before, but the university's legal department wanted a whirl, resulting in his appointment with the president today.

Their mutual unfortunate circumstances should have been enough to engender in Christian a feeling of sympathy, perhaps even camaraderie, with the put-upon secretary. But damn... her voice.

He searched the outer office for any distraction from her sour expression and helmet hair. A beam of light caught his eye. It had landed on the dimpled wells of the outer door's frosted glass, forming shiny reflective pools. His eyes shifted to the pools. The longer he stared at them, the more they seemed to transform into tongues of white fire. The illusion was so strong he could almost feel the heat from each tongue penetrating his jacket. Pulsing. Multiplying. Drawing him in, calling his name...

"Mr. Meadows? Christian. *Young man!*" Doreen punctuated each word with a whack of her pen on the edge of her desk.

Christian looked up at her, startled. He'd gotten lost in the dappled light. *Odd.* And the tongues of fire calling his name, that was just... strange. Suddenly, he felt disjointed and sweaty, like he shouldn't be there—like needed to run. He shook himself. *Snap out of it.*

Doreen, losing patience, tapped her pen at him once more. "Meadows!"

"Yes, sorry," he said, shifting his full attention to Doreen and flashing what he hoped was an ingratiating smile. It wouldn't do to get on the bad side of the president's gatekeeper. His path to tenure began at her desk.

Doreen glared back at him, all impatient eyes and thin lips. "Dr. Hayman will see you now," she said with a sharp gesture toward the inner office door.

"Thanks."

The waiting was finally over. Christian felt so relieved he almost kissed her. But as he gathered his backpack, the phone rang again and the volcano of frustration that was Doreen erupted ever so slightly into tightened fists and a strangled "Grrr." That's all she would allow herself. Taking a deep breath, she switched on her headset and said through clenched teeth, "Colorado School of Mines. President's office. How may I help you?"

He could just make out the brash talker on the other end asking about yesterday's incident and hoping for "a comment from Dr. Hayman." Doreen covered her eyes, but still spoke sweetly as she gathered the reporter's information and apologized yet again for Hayman's lack of availability. Her discomfort with the situation was palpable.

Christian nodded sympathetically. After all, the whole mess was his fault. He'd been the one who had ratted his advisor out to the feds, a fact nobody else knew and one he wasn't interested in revealing. And despite all the trouble it seemed to be causing, he sure as hell wasn't sorry.

He knocked, then opened the inner office door.

The president's office was huge. Bookcases filled with the university's publications and a variety of scientific tomes lined the wood-paneled walls. Hayman's relatively small oak desk lay directly across from the door. It was near the large bay windows that offered a breathtaking view of South Table Mountain's Castle Rock, a sprinkling of snow visible near the base of the mesa and along the trail leading to the top.

"Christian." Hayman stood up to greet him. "Thank you so much for coming." The president shook his hand; to Christian it felt like he was touching lightning.

Dr. Leland Hayman was a spry older man—thin, graying, and in his upper sixties. He was shorter than Christian by an inch and impeccably dressed in a brown, tailored suit. He'd been the university's president for the past decade, but before that had spent twenty years as Dean of Physics, guiding the department into a period of immense growth and innovation. His tenure as president was similarly distinguished and had been largely free of controversy until yesterday when Hubert Wilkins, his successor as Dean of Physics, had been carted away by federal police for selling technology to foreign spies.

Christian studied him now, his first direct encounter with the man. Hubert had always derided Hayman as a bland, senile tool, propped up by the board as a smiling figurehead. "His best days are *far* behind him," Hubert always said. As usual, Hubert was dead wrong. The eyes that locked with Christian's now twinkled with good humor and deep intelligence. Hayman's handshake was firm and warm, suggesting an inner strength and a breadth of experience Hubert would never attain.

Christian had sensed all of that in an instant, at the moment of contact between them, like an electrical shock. When they separated, the impressions lingered and played softly at the back of Christian's mind.

He began to sweat. Every nerve in his hand, every hair on the back of his neck, came to attention. And as he stared wide-eyed at Hayman, he swore he could feel the president's brain waves pulsing. He blinked twice, hard, and the sensation dissipated, but he still felt rattled. What was happening to him?

Hayman's welcoming eyes filled with concern. "Dear boy, are you alright?"

Across the room, a sarcastic voice said, "It's okay, kid. You aren't in trouble. Yet. Sit down."

Christian jumped. He hadn't noticed the other man—a stranger, younger than Hayman, with slicked-back hair and dressed in an even more impressive, three-piece suit. The man stared haughtily up at Christian from one of the two chairs in front of the president's desk. His legs were crossed, and his hands rested in his lap so that the thumbs touched. His whole demeanor screamed *lawyer*.

"Yes, please, take a seat," said Hayman kindly. "This shouldn't take long. We just need to confirm some information." The president reached out as if to guide him to the remaining chair. Christian pulled away, not wanting another shock, and wondered, *Did Hayman feel a jolt too?* The old man acted as if nothing had happened. Christian surmised it had been one-way—whatever "it" was.

As he stood in front of Hayman's desk, pondering, Lawyer Man sighed loudly and tapped his thumbs. Christian took the hint and sat down.

The president went back to his desk, then inclined his head toward the other man. "This is Carlos Rabel."

Christian turned to the man. "You're an attorney."

Rabel nodded. "And your ex-boss is a traitor. Tell us what you know about that."

Ah, a complete asshole. Christian almost sighed in relief to be back in a situation he understood. Three years of abuse from Hubert had made Jerk Town familiar territory. It was a welcome place he could regain his footing after the last disconcerting five minutes.

"Nothing," he said, focusing on Mr. Three-Piece Douche like a laser. "He didn't consult *me*, his lowly lab tech, before committing treason."

"Come on. You must have known *something* was up," said Rabel, curling his lip in disgust.

"I only knew that he'd had meetings with a rep from a Korean company. But since meeting company reps was, like, his job, being the commercial development director and all, I didn't give it much thought."

"So, you never knew that he was peddling the school's intellectual property? That the 'rep' he was talking to was actually a North Korean spy?"

"Well, the moment the rep held me hostage and tortured me, then broke my arm just to make a point to Dr. Wilkins, I started to have my suspicions."

"Pfft. We're supposed to believe this kidnapping and torture actually happened?"

"Rabel," Hayman warned.

"Come off it, Leland. It's a valid question. Nobody saw him abducted, he has no cast, and his arm looks fine. Where's the proof?"

Unconsciously, Christian flexed his left hand. His palm itched and the skin on his arm felt flaky where the cast used to be. *Used to be? It had been there yesterday. When did it come off?*

Now he was truly rattled. *What's wrong with me?* He'd woken up feeling terrific, but as the morning wore on, a fog had descended. At the back of his mind was a vague memory of... something happening. His light experiment...

The disconcerted feeling returned. He looked at his arm. Broken yesterday, fine today. *There must be some explanation.* It frightened him that he couldn't think of one. Something had happened yesterday, after Hubert's arrest, back in the lab. But what? Why couldn't he remember?

"Ch-check the hospital," he stammered. "Or student insurance."

Rabel picked up a file on Hayman's desk and thumbed through it angrily. "There's a bill here from St. Anthony's, but not a lot of details, and it's for an outrageous amount. Is that your game, Meadows, to extort the university? Frame Dr. Wilkins for you own unfortunate scheme, scam us for money while you're at it, and then pick up where you left off with North Korea once the dust clears?"

"Rabel! That's not what we discussed!" said Hayman, eyes blazing.

"I—" Christian began without knowing what else he would say. The cast was gone; his arm felt strong; the bruises on his hand had disappeared. As he stared at it, the light from the fixture above him collected in his skin just as it had in the frost wells of the door. And in his palm, there appeared a tongue of fire. It was just a flicker, but it was there nonetheless. He made a fist to hide it and looked up, panicked. *Had anyone else seen?*

Apparently not. Hayman and Rabel had forgotten him for the moment, intent on arguing a point of order that had probably started before Christian had entered the room.

"We're supposed to be *debriefing* Meadows. Not badgering him and making unfounded accusations."

"Maybe so, Leland, but what else fits? Hubert's not smart enough to have handled this operation alone. *Somebody* tipped off the feds. The kid faked the injury to avoid indictment. Broken arms just don't heal that fast."

"Look at his face, Carlos. Can't you see he's traumatized? And I was there yesterday. I saw the cast, watched the agents examine it. I can't tell you where it went, but he was certainly *not* faking it. Forget the embarrassment to the university for a minute and try being human, for god's sake."

Rabel deflated and ran a hand through his hair. "Sorry. It's just that this is such a mess."

"You're not making it better. Meadows is clearly a victim. The feds released him. Have some compassion, man."

Rabel chucked the file back onto Hayman's desk and got to his feet. "I need some air."

He walked over to the curtains and slid them aside, revealing a bank of tasteful casement windows amidst the unrelenting executive wood paneling. He cranked open the largest window and let in a cold blast of air that smelled of pine sap and wet snow. The room flooded with light from the midday sun, and when the window swung out on its hinge, Christian was seated at just the right angle to catch a glimpse of his reflection in it.

"Gaah!" The tongues of white fire covered him—his face, arms, torso, everywhere—like bright drops of dew. Within each drop he saw a full-on image of himself, screaming and pounding against the white fire prison.

"Do you see them?!" He held his arms out in front of him and examined them. They looked normal. But when he looked at himself in the window, the tongues of fire were there once more. "Gaah!"

Hayman shot out of his chair and was back by Christian's side. "See what, son? Calm down. You're not making sense." Christian tried to get up before the old man reached him, but the chair got in his way.

Hayman's steel hands landed on Christians shoulders, which sent another lightning bolt coursing through him, carrying the waves of the president's mind into his own. Like a drowning man, he grabbed hold of the strongest wave Hayman projected, one that conveyed logic and calm. Touching that wave brought him sudden clarity and he remembered *exactly* what had happened to him the night before.

He pushed Hayman away. "I've got to go."

"Now wait a minute," said Rabel. "You still have to sign—"

He ignored the lawyer, grabbed his backpack, and ran out of the office. The weight of the backpack should have been confirmation enough, but after he stumbled out the front door of Guggenheim Hall and down the stairs, he unzipped the main pouch and looked inside. The beaker was still there, filled to the brim with bluish-white pearls that flickered and pulsed and for all the world looked like encapsulated tongues of white fire. *I have to get back to the lab.*

He stepped out into Illinois Street, intent on retrieving his car from the CASE building parking lot, still staring at the impossible contents of his backpack. Too late, he noticed the pickup truck backing up toward him, its driver craning his head out the window looking like he'd missed a turn. Christian thrust out his left hand stupidly as if that were enough to protect him. "Stop!" he shouted.

Time slowed. From the middle of his still-itchy palm leapt a tendril of light that pierced the empty space between him and the truck. Within the widening rift, he saw the inside of his lab—not as he'd remembered it from last night, but the way it might look that very minute, illuminated from the skylight by the midday sun. He didn't know how it had happened. Couldn't tell if it was even real. But the truck was still coming. He closed his eyes and leapt—

CHAPTER 2

Fresh Start

Christian squeezed his eyes shut, fully expecting the Toyota Tundra to smash him to the pavement, smear his body into paste, and crush his beaker of plasma balls into a coruscant fireball. None of that happened. He wasn't exactly sure what *had* happened. Only that the mid-morning chill and smell of wet snow had been replaced by a warm numbness and the faint scent of curried lime. And though he had sprung forward, he still hadn't landed. His body had stopped falling but hadn't yet touched the ground. *Maybe it would help if I opened my eyes.*

He did, but whether that helped was debatable. He was back at Hubert's off-campus lab—Unit 411, at the corner of Violet Street and Corporate—in a small warehouse four miles away from campus. The warehouse was vacant except for a workbench and the remnants of his dinner from the night before. The scene looked the same as it had in Christian's memory at his moment of clarity back in Hayman's office: empty containers of coconut soup and brown rice, scattered equipment, his over-turned toolbox, a gash like a lightning strike in the far cement wall, and at the center of the warehouse, blast marks from the explosion that had created the beaker's contents. *But how did I get here? Did I really open a portal? Why does everything look fuzzy? And why haven't I landed?*

He dared to glance down, then wished he hadn't. His feet were floating above the warehouse floor, supported by a curved band of white that spread out in a faded sheath up and around his body like a giant soap bubble. He must have created the bubble the moment he'd jumped, forming it around himself like a protective shell. It reminded him of the plasma coating surrounding the photons—the "tongues of white fire"—in the beaker. *How did I do that? Why can I do that?* His eyes drifted back to the blast marks. And his earlier memory returned like an electric shock.

*****

The previous night, he'd replicated one of the last student projects Hubert had stolen, following the steps outlined in an article the student had written to protect his invention. It was an utterly amazing piece of technology, a device that converted light beams into portals that transported you from one point to another in a literal instant.

But the student, a freshman named Mitch Campbell, was a clumsy builder. The device was clunky too large, and awkward. Campbell had called it the Canopy, an apt name given that it covered its nearby space with a sideways umbrella of azure blue. Light portals were embedded in the big blue matrix, hundreds of holes dotting the artificial sky. The Canopy was a beautiful miracle, but thoroughly impractical for everyday use. Though Hubert had found a buyer—the North Korean spies—for the average consumer it'd be a hard sell. Few people had a whole room they could devote to just one device, no matter how incredible or innovative it might be. But people *would* appreciate a hand-held device. And Christian knew that he could adapt the freshman's tech to make not just one but a million of them.

So, on his way out of the CASE building following his government interrogation, Christian discreetly slid Campbell's article off Hubert's stack of stockpiled projects and vowed to use his newfound freedom to remake the freshman's invention according to his better vision.

That night, at the warehouse, the experiment succeeded beyond his wildest imaginings. When he'd flicked the switch, the light portals formed, embedded in the same azure matrix. Instead of being stuck like flies in amber, however, each portal was encapsulated in its own plasma skin and dangled from the matrix like drops of dew, ready to be picked and pocketed, as portable as pearls. He'd done it!

Before Christian could celebrate his victory, something went wrong. Through one of the dew drops, he witnessed a cataclysm that expanded from its point of origin until it violently rocked the surrounding matrix. His version of Campbell's Canopy exploded. The plasma-coated dew drops rained down like meteors from their artificial sky. They landed on Christian, piercing his skin like white-hot nails, searing his muscles and flowing through his extremities, out to the tips of every nerve. He was everyone, then no one; everywhere, then nowhere; splintered across an infinity of dimensions, but simultaneously dimensionless. He screamed and screamed in a multitude of voices, a chorus of Christians howling across an infinite series of interdimensional voids. At the height of his immolation, he passed out. While he slept, he dreamt of a million suns.

*****

That had been yesterday. He hadn't remembered coming to and driving home, nor floating to his bed flush with a fever that seemed to radiate from his bones. He did remember waking up this morning feeling oddly euphoric as he'd dressed for his meeting with the president. He'd instinctively avoided the mirror in his closet, irrationally afraid of what he might see. Now here he was back in the lab, transformed, floating in a bubble of his own inner light and, just at the edge of his perception, hearing whispers of the multitude that voiced the pain of his immolation. *Oh god, don't let me see my reflection again.*

A futile thought, for the door to the warehouse bathroom was open, the mirror above the sink clearly visible, and in the mirror he saw the faces of the multitude—*his* face repeated over and over, trapped in portals from ever possible dimension. He yelped and shook his head, but the faces didn't disappear.

An army of Christians, yelling at him as they pounded their fists against their plasma prisons, had through some quantum anomaly of the Canopy's explosion become embedded in the dew drops inside of his body. All but two of them yelled the same thing as they fought to get out of their plasma shells. [*It should be me! It should be* me!]

The other two—embedded in his gut and forehead—were even more unnerving. Forehead Christian, unlike the others, stood quietly in his portal, staring at him intensely but aging with each passing second. Not shouting or fighting, just silently contemplating while slowly becoming an old, old man.

Like the others, Gut Christian raged, but he struggled against his prison with focused, hateful purpose. [*It* will *be me!*] he shouted, punching his shell. [*You're weak and stupid! I* will *replace you!*]

And in that moment, this dimension's Christian felt real danger. Each whack from Gut Christian echoed like an earthquake and he knew that over time Gut's shell would break. The realization filled him with terror, and he could almost feel the splintering and the disassembling of himself that surely would follow once any of the subsumed portals were breached.

"Noooooo!"

His eyes burned, his body shook, and a pressure like fire built in his chest. He felt on the verge of losing control.

[**Don't**,] said a new voice unlike the others. Forehead Christian? [**You are Prime. Stay in control.**]

He closed his eyes and concentrated, willing the pressure to move from his chest and into his hand. He stretched out. A tendril of light leapt from his palm into the bathroom and vaporized the mirror. The multitude of voices fell silent.

His protective light bubble burst, bringing him to his knees on the warehouse floor. He set aside the beaker of dew drops and tentatively felt inside himself. He'd bought some time, but the danger of splintering was still there. For the moment, however, he had it under control. If he strung together more of these moments, he might never splinter at all.

Christian's analytical mind took over. The key to keeping control was learning about everything his newfound power could do. He refilled his toolbox, righted the workbench, cleared the smart board, and then wrote "Christian 2.0" at the top of it.

His body continued to shake as he wrote, but several deep breaths steadied him. He stepped back from the board. "Alright, Prime. Let's see what you can do." Carefully, he opened his hand.

CHAPTER 3

Backwards

"Prepare to be *dazzled!*"

Larry Knight tapped the computer lab's smart board and couldn't help but smile at the collective "Oohs" and "Aahs" that rippled through the class as a large, shimmering cube materialized above their heads. He tapped the board again, and the same shimmering light erupted from its stylus and encircled his hand. *Now for the true pyrotechnics.* He stepped onto the sensor array directly beneath the ceiling projector. Immediately, the glow from the stylus spread up his arm, to his head, then all around his body until he was engulfed in bright, yellow, virtual flames. A nearby student gasped.

Turning his mic up to full volume, Larry flung back his head and let loose a wild laugh that reverberated through the room.

"Behold!" he said, wild-eyed. "I am the Sun! And I give you... *Light!*"

With a dramatic flourish, he stabbed the stylus at the cube. A fake bolt of lightning shot out that pierced the box's side, then exploded into a brilliant cascade of colorful waves before coalescing into a single pulsing-white dot. The light particle zipped randomly around the inside of the cube, dragging a cloudy-blue vapor trail that soon obscured its path.

"See how the Sun's essence seeks to hide?" he asked, still affecting a theatrical tone. "Who among you dares to find it?"

He dangled the stylus in front of them like a prize, and a dozen hands raised into the air. He'd barely gifted it to the closest eager student before she pushed him away from the sensor array and began furiously waving the stylus at the cube. Soon, other students rallied around her, shouting encouragement and suggestions. Larry found himself squeezed into the back of the room, edged out by the students' fervor.

Fantastic, he thought. *Just the reaction I wanted.*

The "Particle in a 3D Box" problem could not be drier. Even as a freshman physics geek, Knight had fallen asleep when Dr. Forbus taught it. Now here he was, Forbus' teaching assistant, still geeky enough to love the topic and vain enough to not want to be dull teaching it. With the old man out sick, he'd reworked the lecture, adding interactive visuals and motion capture. Cheesy as they were, the theatrics and graphics had everyone in the class on their feet and engaged—a vast improvement over the usual reactions to Dr. Forbus' stale delivery. Each student was completely invested in solving the problem, and Larry was sure they would. Just as soon as someone remembered what a smart board stylus was for.

"Let me try!" Dean Chambers, one of the more technically savvy students, forced his way to the front. The latest failure, Billy Hoag, gladly handed him the stylus.

This should be good, thought Larry. *Chambers is pretty sharp.*

Dean's innovation was to add jumping and slashing to all the stylus waving. Larry shook his head and laughed.

"Not workin'," said Billy.

"Maybe we need magic," said Steve, Billy's bench mate. "Try a spell."

Dean grunted and continued jumping up and down and waving. "Don't know any. *Oof!* Yell some at me."

"Aparecium!"
"Revelio!"
"Wingaridum Levi-OH-sah!"
"No, Billy," Maggie Heinz said with a giggle. "That lifts things. Duh!"

They spent the next ten minutes alternating between faux Latin phrases and quotes from *Harry Potter* which, to Dean's credit, he repeated unironically but without result.

"My turn," said Maggie with a grin. She hip-checked Dean off the sensor array.

"Try the spells with a British accent," Billy suggested.

Try thinking. Larry stopped himself from saying it. The point of the exercise was for the students to solve the problem on their own—a feat this crew should be well-equipped to do. They were Gabriel Bische's Innovation Program superstars after all: the up and coming cream of the crop: the smartest of all the freshman classes. Surely one of them knew that smart board styluses were meant for *writing*, not just waving. From there, the solution should present itself—just write the 3D wave function and voila! Problem solved.

Seconds later, as if reading his mind, the ever-astute Maggie shouted, "Guys! I think we can write with it!" She held down the button on the side of the stylus and with a flick of her wrist, drew the sigma for a calculus integral in mid-air. "Yippee!" she squealed with delight. Her success inspired a fresh round of shouted suggestions from the class. Soon, the blue vapor faded as Maggie deliberately wrote out each part of the wave equation. Larry took a moment to pat himself on the back. *Nobody's sleeping today.*

Then he heard a deep sigh behind him and felt less joyful. He had completely forgotten about the lone hold-out still seated and staring glumly out the window. Mitch Campbell, normally one of the more engaged students, had withdrawn into himself a few weeks ago, and had remained that way since. Oh, he turned in assignments and scored well on tests. But the ebullient Mitch from the start of term had devolved into a pensive, taciturn worrier, fretting over minor mistakes and apologizing for less-than-perfect scores.

Old, happy Mitch would have been the first to raise his hand, and probably would have solved the problem in the first five minutes—he was the sharpest of this bunch. Today's Mitch just sat completely lost in thought, and not in a good way. Whatever this quiet was that had descended on the boy could only have been born of some unvoiced distress. *Should I bring it up with Dr. Bische? What's eating the kid?*

"Hey, Larry?" Maggie's voice brought his attention back to the larger group. He turned around and saw the nearly completed equation hovering beneath the 3D projector.

"Looking good, guys." He cleared his throat and said with Gandalfian flare, "Finish it and the Light will be yours!"

"That's the problem," said Billy. "We're stuck. What next?"

"I bring Light, not Answers, young mages. The information you seek is... within yourselves!"

Dean rolled his eyes. "Alright, let's get Mitch. Hey, Mitch, buddy!"

Campbell jerked his head away from the window. "Huh? What?" He looked around the room as if only now noticing everyone else was otherwise engaged.

Larry dropped the act and said, "'Particle in a 3D Box', Campbell." He pointed at the equation floating in front of the green cube. "Your classmates are stuck. Would you have a suggestion?"

Mitch squinted as he studied the box and the equation. Then he said, "Oh, yeah. Just take the product and normalize the integral."

Maggie smacked her forehead. "Duh!" After a couple of additional strokes, she double-clicked the stylus' button. The fog in the box completely cleared, revealing the light particle suspended in a far corner.

"Hooray!" The class clapped, and there were calls of "Thanks, Mitch!"

Bische's protégé smiled feebly, but soon his eyes drifted back to the window. Larry stared at him, amazed. *Solved the problem without breaking a sweat. But, man, what is eating this kid?*

*****

Mitch had arrived at class determined to pay attention and just lose himself in the schoolwork. He'd spent the past two weeks making that vow at the start of every one of his classes, but every time it turned out the same regardless of how hard he tried to focus. His mind would drift away, back to Cheyenne Mountain and the photon gateway, to the blue plasma grid with its bright, orange-ringed portals, and to the joy he'd felt riding on the backs of photons to new, exciting places via a device he had built with Dean and Wayne.

But with the flip of a switch, the gateway was gone—shut down by its original creator as a necessary step to save the world from a madman. His great invention, the Jump!GO—a miniaturized version of the Canopy—should have brought him fame and improved the world. Instead it hurt his friends, got him imprisoned, was stolen by an assassin, and nearly triggered a war with North Korea. Whenever Mitch's mind reached that memory, his stomach would knot, his strength of spirit would evaporate, and he'd find himself dropped inside a well of sorrow, to a place no lecture could reach.

Before long, whatever class he was in would end and he'd shuffle on to the next one, vowing again to pay attention, only again to start to drift, his depression on repeat.

Today, Larry Knight nearly disrupted his funk. Big, broad, and booming, Larry was a magnetic speaker and hard to ignore. Though it was the end of the day, Mitch had managed to stay with the lecture up until Larry "magically" captured the particle. Beside him, Dean had laughed then, with a scoff, he'd leaned toward Mitch and whispered, "Try riding *that* to Cheyenne Mountain."

And just like that, Mitch's descent down the stairs of his mental basement had begun anew. Dean had been trying to make a joke, but his underlying anger since their return from Colorado Springs made every word out of his mouth sound like a prelude to a fight. At least they sounded that way to Mitch. So, he'd returned to the window, letting the voices of his classmates fade into the background while he thought back on better days.

He could smell the nachos and burgers of Sutter's Pub in Seattle, the musky oil and exhaust fumes from the New York subway, the moldy pier platforms on the Embarcadero, all images and sensations to warm his heart. Then he made the mistake of closing his eyes, and the assassin, Geomi, was there, firing his gun at Dean. The burning husk of the North Korean spy headquarters filled his vision; the soot-covered faces of their friends Jin and Chung appeared; and though he was happy to see them alive, he felt like he would drown in guilt. He longed for those early days of the Jump!Go, when firing up the plasma grid meant good food, fun times, and only a little adventure. It had been exhilarating and frightening. He'd felt both powerful and powerless. He wanted so badly to go back with his friends to the good times but was too scared to consider how they ever could. He missed it and hated it. It was too much too much. *Will there be no end to the pain?*

"Hey, Mitch, buddy!"

Dean's voice cut through the fog in Mitch's mind. He jerked back to the room. "Huh? What?"

Maggie held the smart board's stylus and a familiar equation hovered near her head. Mitch looked at Dean and shrugged.

"Particle in a 3D Box, Campbell," Larry prompted. "Your classmates are stuck. Would you have a suggestion?"

Mitch blurted out the first thing that came to mind. Maggie tried it, the photon appeared, and the class cheered.

Billy said, "Hey, Campbell, jump through that photon to Sutter's Pub and buy me some nachos." Most of the class laughed, though Dean glowered. Maggie poked Billy and said, "Not funny."

"Come on," said Billy, undeterred. "These guys made a big deal out of their 'instant travel' machine. They took everybody's money, but then suddenly it didn't work anymore?"

"If it ever worked at all," said Steve.

"We gave the money back!" shouted Dean. "And Billy, you helped test the Canopy. You *know* it worked!"

Billy folded his arms and got into Dean's face. "I know you guys set something up and made it *seem* like it worked. Sutter's Pub was awesome and all. Best nachos I've ever had. But I never stepped outside. How do I know I really went to Seattle?"

Somebody in the back of the room said, "I heard some guy even died."

"Nobody died! That's a *damn* lie!" said Dean, his face red and his hands balled into fists. He scanned the room for the offender, but no one revealed themselves. The whole class collectively backed away from him.

"Okay, everybody, that's it for today." Larry stepped between Dean and Billy. Dean was tall, beefy, and imposing, but beside Larry he looked like a ten-year-old. Billy got the message and backed down.

Larry nodded and smiled at the rest of the class. "Good! Be sure to write up your analysis and rationale for today's solution. Dr. F expects you all to submit those, so be sure to get 'em to me by Thursday's lab. See y'all then."

Everyone gathered their things and headed for the door. Dean cursed under his breath and picked up his backpack. "Thanks for the help," he said to Mitch, his voice dripping with sarcasm, then turned to leave. Mitch stood and trudged after him looking miserable.

"Hey Campbell, Chambers. Hold up," Larry called out to them, beaming and beckoning them to the podium.

Mitch veered toward the door, hoping Larry would think he hadn't heard him, but Dean grabbed his arm. "Come on. Won't be that bad."

Larry motioned for them to wait while the last of their classmates left, then said, "Sorry about that, guys. Billy was way out of line. I have to tell you, I finally read your paper last night. Great work. Fantastic stuff."

Mitch's blood went cold. "Our paper?"

"Yeah, the plasma Canopy paper from last semester. 'Big Blue is calling you.' Hilarious."

"How'd you get a hold of that?" asked Dean.

"Downloaded from the internal network."

Mitch panicked. "But we withdrew the paper after some... problems surfaced." *Shit!* Bische had told them to delete the paper completely. Mitch thought he'd caught all the copies. *Which internal site did we miss? Oh gods, what if someone else stole it again?*

Larry looked sheepish and said, "Oh, it's probably gone now. See, I downloaded it *last* semester. But with work and classes and writing my thesis defense, I only just now read it. You've got me curious, though. The protocol in the paper seemed fine to me. What kind of 'problems' surfaced? "

"Short-sightedness," said Dean bitterly.

"Actually, we found a safety issue," Mitch corrected him. "Worked otherwise." *It's not exactly a lie,* he thought. Misuse by assassins could certainly be considered a "safety" issue.

"Ah," said Larry, nodding his head. "I can see that. Pretty radical discovery. Bound to have some kinks. Too bad. I was hoping you could tell me if Bische needed more help on the team. What better job for a particle physicist, right?" He pointed to himself and smiled broadly. "I mean, I like Dr. Forbus and enjoy teaching and what not, but there's nothing like applied work in the real world, you know?"

Dean hung his head. "Sorry, dude. Like Billy said, project's cancelled. There is no team."

Larry's face fell. "Wow. Guess I really did miss out. But... with that knowledge out there, there'll be other chances." His smile returned. "My moment will come. As will yours again—I guarantee it. Chins up, gentlemen." He clapped them on their shoulders.

Reluctantly, they nodded their heads in agreement. Mitch stood up straighter and tried to look sincere, hoping Larry would think he'd gotten the point. Dean followed suit and Mitch chuckled inwardly. *Posture pals.*

"Good!" Larry beamed at them. The ruse had worked. "I gave that same speech to your buddy. Popped him out of his funk too."

"Which buddy? You mean Wayne?" Mitch asked.

"Yeah, Wayne Hirano. Seriously, who else hangs out with you guys? You're the Three Musketeers. I'm kinda surprised he's not here today, but I figure he just has his head down working on you all's idea."

"Our idea?" said Dean. Mitch caught his eye, but Dean seemed as confused as he was.

"For the Tamblyn Intern Mentoring competition. He needed the rule pack and was gonna ask Bische for it, but Dr. B was out, so he asked me. I printed the packet and he left. That was last week, though."

Mitch smacked his forehead. He'd been moping so much he had completely forgotten they were supposed to be applying for TIM. From the look on Dean's face, he'd forgotten too. *What self-centered jerks we are*, Mitch thought. No wonder Wayne had stopped talking to them.

"He seemed really excited. Said Tamblyn interns are auto approved for the Rising Stars forum at the Tech Convergence Conference in a couple of months. Rising Stars attract plenty of angel investors. If I had a team, I'd apply for TIM too. Smart move on your part to go for a spot."

"Yeah, that's us. Always thinking ahead," lied Dean. "Um, we haven't seen Wayne all day." It had been more than a day, but after the Three Musketeers remark, Mitch understood why Dean was reluctant to share that with Larry. "Do you know where he went? "

Larry shrugged. "If you're not in class, I don't track you. Wherever you are, that's on you. But he did say he'd fill you both in." He stared at them, incredulous. "You're the Three Musketeers... you haven't talked?"

Dean looked away. Mitch shook his head and said, "We've been pretty busy the past couple of—uh, I mean today."

"Huh. Well, I'd suggest you find him. Seemed like he was on to something hot. You make a good team. I bet you'll get selected for TIM, fix your problem with the Canopy, and rock the world." Larry looked at his watch. "Whoops. Gotta go start Dr. F's next lab. Remember what I said: try again. You'll never find gold unless you dig. Bye!"

Larry ran off, leaving Mitch and Dean alone in the classroom to ponder. Dean was the first to break the silence. "So, you think Wayne just forgot to tell us his grand idea? Or do you think he intentionally ditched us?"

"If he ditched us, would you blame him?" Mitch stared glumly at his friend. It was the first time he'd looked Dean in the eye since they'd returned from Cheyenne Mountain. "Neither of us have been a barrel of laughs lately. Hell, *I'd* ditch us if you weren't my roommate. The only reason I don't is cuz you'd sell my stuff."

"Already tried it. Dude, even the thrift store doesn't want your stuff." They chuckled quietly together, some of the tension between them finally dissipating.

Standing on his toes, Dean wrapped an arm around Mitch's shoulder and in a fair approximation of Larry said, "Chin up, Campbell. Let's go find the third Musketeer."

Mitch laughed. "Now say it like you're British."

Dean cleared his throat and switched to an exaggerated, English falsetto. "Cheerio, Campbell. Let the Wayne Hunt begin!"

The computer room door snapped shut on their laughter.

CHAPTER 4

Health Check

"Call him," Dean said as they walked out of Brown Hall.

Mitch dialed Wayne's number and tapped the speaker so that Dean could hear as well. After three rings, Wayne's terse voice answered, "Wayne Hirano," followed immediately by the mechanical "... is not available right now." After a short pause, the mechanical voice said, "This mailbox is full. Please try again later." *Click.*

"Crap. Clear out your phone, Wayne!" Dean yelled into the speaker.

"I know," said Mitch. "He's always doing that, not deleting his messages. And who the hell else is calling him anyway? It's not like he has friends besides us."

"He might now. We were pretty famous after the Canopy party last semester."

Mitch felt a fresh wave of melancholy. "I shut down the light gateway. Squashed his dreams pretty good. Maybe he decided to find new buds."

"Aw, shut up, will you? Just shut up. Your pity party's the absolute worst. Not everything is about you and your damn decision."

"Well, what else could it be? He's off lying dead somewhere?"

"Geez, what's wrong with you? You're either being fatalistic or morbid anymore. Snap out of it!"

Dean threw his hands up in frustration, then stomped off a few paces before turning back. "Look, we both know how Wayne gets sometimes. Head-down, ignoring everybody. If Big Larry says he was all excited about something, then he's probably holed up in the machine shop or at Bische's or the dorm working it out. We've been friends too long. He wouldn't ditch us. 'Kay?" Dean was red-faced, breathing hard, and still clearly frustrated, but he was reaching out.

Mitch shook himself. *Get it together, Campbell.* "Okay," he said.

"Great." The Guggenheim bell tower chimed the top of the hour. "It's dinner time. Let's text him, then get something to eat. Wayne's gotta eat. He might be at the food court and we'll bump into him there."

Mitch sent the text as they walked to the student center. They arrived and scanned the food court, but Wayne wasn't there. They headed out back to the food trucks, stopping at Wayne's favorites—Poke Bait and the Murli's Curries—but still found no sign of their friend. Neither proprietor had seen him all week. They bought a couple of naan burritos from Murli, with extra mint chutney, then walked to the library.

Mitch checked his phone—no answer to his text. Hardly anybody was at the library, likely because it was dinner time. But that just made it easier to see the total absence of Wayne. Even though Dean harangued him for being morose and fatalistic, Mitch couldn't help but feel a kernel of worry.

Pop!

He glanced at Dean and saw him cracking his knuckles, something he only did when he was anxious. Dean was worried too.

The CASE building was their last stop before the dorm. They started in the basement at Dr. Rebar's machine shop. Not there. Next, they went upstairs to Bische's lab. Dr. Bische, head of the Innovation Program, was also their unofficial mentor. The three of them had known Bische since middle school and were always welcome in his lab whether he was in class or not. The lab was Bische's sanctuary and he was almost always there, working on one thing other with students or alone. But today, surprisingly, the lab was locked and dark.

Cupping their hands over their eyes, they peered through the front window. Wayne's bench was way over in the back and on the other side of the lab. Each bench had a small light tacked to the wall for close-up work. "Is his light on?" asked Dean. Mitch couldn't tell. They pounded on the door regardless. No one answered.

Lainie Troy, the building manager, had the office next door to Bische's lab. Mitch tapped on her door. "Excuse me, Ms. Troy."

She'd been deep in conversation with a member of her team. When she saw Mitch and Dean standing at her door, she rolled her eyes and said to the guy, "Oh, lord, it's that Campbell boy. Goodness."

She called out to Mitch. "One second, young man." Then to her employee said, "You just know this is gonna be some kind of mess. This boy and his *friends*. Always up to something strange, like that business last semester with the radiation leak that Dr. Wilkins had to clean up before he got fired for selling secrets *supposedly*, but probably *really* 'cuz he threw out whatever radioactive thing Campbell left *lying* around, and then *both* of them tryin' to blame Dr. Bische for their *own* foolishness. Hmmph."

She finally got up to greet them at the door. "Whatcha need, young man?" as if there was no way for Mitch to have heard every word of her diatribe.

"We're looking for Dr. Bische, ma'am. Have you seen him?"

"He had some place to be and left early. Can I help you?"

Dean said, "If you can open up his lab, we'd appreciate it. A friend of ours is working on something with him and we just need to check it."

"Oh, no, uh-uhn. Not happening." She pursed her lips and advanced on them, hands on her hips. "Not after last semester with the *loud* music and y'all *trashing* the lab and then causing some kinda *hazardous* leak in the back room and poor Dr. Wilkins nearly havin' a nervous breakdown tryin' to find it and then *him* all of a sudden *landing* in jail 'cuz of *y'all*, probably. No. Never again. Checkin' on something 'for a friend'? Not today. You can call Dr. Bische if you need to, but the door's staying locked."

She'd backed Mitch and Dean clear out of her office, then said over her shoulder to the employee, "Just like I toldja. Some kind of mess." She slammed the door shut.

"That could have gone better," said Mitch.

"Let's hit the dorm. Wayne might be there, and we can drop off our backpacks. I'm tired of lugging this thing around." Dean grimaced and flexed his shoulders. "Jump!GO'd be nice right about now. Just hop through a light hole to the dorm. Be there in a second." He sighed. "I miss that."

Mitch stayed quiet. He missed using the Jump!GOs, too, but was too embarrassed to say as much. They'd argued hard after returning from Colorado Springs, Dean blaming him for siding with the feds and letting them turn off the QEP—the quantum entanglement processor that powered the light gateway and made the Jump!GOs possible. "We could've put restrictions on it. Blocked the bad guys. Figured it out," Dean had said.

"Too dangerous," Mitch had countered. "And whether we wanted them to or not, they were going to pull the plug. You know that."

"But you gave up on it! You gave up on *us*! You didn't even try!"

The argument stopped at that point but hadn't ever really ended. Dean's continued snide comments since their return only proved to Mitch that the decision still angered him. For a while, Mitch hadn't cared, so sure that he and the feds had been right. But as the weeks had passed, he'd begun to feel a regret so intense he couldn't concentrate on anything else. Still, he'd be damned if he admitted it to Dean.

At the dorm, they gratefully shed their backpacks. Wayne's room was catty corner to theirs. The door was closed, but like Bische's lab and their own room, it shouldn't have been locked even if Wayne wasn't there. The three shared everything: snacks, books, tools, coffee. Wayne's Kona beans, gifted to him by his aunt in Hawaii, were particularly prized. Unfettered access to his stash was a must. They'd secretly created pass keys at the beginning of the semester, but the RA had found out and confiscated them. So, they'd gone low-tech and simply blocked the latches on their locks with thick rubber bands. They only removed the rubber bands if they'd all planned to be off campus.

Mitch pushed on Wayne's door, but it didn't budge. *Damn.*

Dean pounded on it. "Wayne! Dude, you there?" No answer. He put his ear to the door and his brow furrowed. "Mitch, come listen. Do you hear that?"

Mitch listened and for a second he couldn't quite place what he heard, but then it came to him: a faint creaking, followed by a soft bang, silence, and then more creaking.

"What does that sound like to you?" asked Dean.

"Kind of sounds like Wayne's closet door. It's got a mad squeak."

"What about that thump?"

"I don't know. Maybe something's on the door, like a—" Mitch stopped suddenly. Dean's face went white. Obviously, the same thought had crossed both their minds. "No, Dean, it's not that. It's not like your dad."

"I'm getting Tina," said Dean. He sprinted to the last room at the end of the hall, the one reserved for Resident Assistants. Mitch trailed behind him.

Tina had the door propped open, her earbuds were on, and she was dancing around her laundry basket as she sorted and folded clothes.

"Tina! Wayne won't answer his door. You gotta orange key his room right now!" It all came out of Dean in a tumble.

Tina took the earbuds out of her ears and with a quizzical look, asked a sensible question.

"You sure he's there?"

"We don't know. Haven't seen him for a few days. Kinda worried."

"Health check, huh? Okay, sure."

Health checks were common at the university. The engineering program was demanding, and some students had been known to barricade themselves in their rooms toward the end of term, completely wigged out... or worse.

Tina pulled the orange master key out of her drawer and said, "Hirano doesn't seem like the type to crack, though. If I had to choose one of you three to survive the first year without problems, I'd pick him. He's probably just out and about."

"We wouldn't ask, but you took our spare keys, so there you go," said Mitch.

"That'll teach me. Come to think of it, haven't seen him much myself this week. You sure he's not off campus? Like you guys were a couple months ago? "

"No, that didn't work out."

"For you two, yeah. But maybe *he* landed a new gig. Happens a lot with the intelligent ones. People find out you're smart and that you built something hot, so they nab you. That Jump!GO thing was pretty hot, and Hirano's off-the-charts smart, so he might've gotten sniped."

"Come on, hurry up," said Dean, hopping from one foot to the other.

"Alright, alright."

They trotted back to Wayne's door. Tina held up the orange master key but covered her nose with her hand before swiping.

"Whatcha doin' that for?" asked Dean.

Tina shrugged. "You said it's been a few days. He might be kinda ripe."

Dean gulped, but Mitch immediately spoke up "Don't play like that, Tina."

"Wow, you guys are seriously worried. Sorry. Let's check our boy." She opened the door.

Wayne's closet door swayed on its hinges, but the only thing hanging on it was his bath towel. The window was open, and it was a windy day, which explained the swinging door. Tina peeked into the closet, then opened it all the way. "Corpse-less."

Dean bent over in relief. "Oh, god. Thank goodness."

Mitch sniffed the air. Normally, Wayne's room smelled of spicy curry and excellent coffee. But all he smelled was dust, like Wayne had been gone for a while. He went to the coffee pot and looked in. "Bone dry."

"His backpack's gone too," Dean observed. "*And* his Jump!GO," he said under his breath, only just loud enough for Mitch to hear.

"We done here, guys?" asked Tina.

"Yeah, I guess," said Mitch.

"Since he had it locked and it's his room, gotta close it up again. Out you go."

"We'll keep looking for him. Thanks, Tina."

"Sure thing. Stay sane, boys." She returned the earbuds to her ears and bopped back to her room.

Without thinking, Mitch said, "Friend!GO'd find him in a minute." Friend!GO was the social media app Dean had built into the Jump!GO. It helped you find your friends with Jump!GOs and opened a light hole to their location. Dean had been particularly proud of the app.

He frowned at Mitch, and Mitch immediately regretted having brought it up. He braced himself for the snide comment that was sure to follow, but instead Dean said, "Not a bad idea, Mitch. Gimme your phone." Dean pulled out his dead Jump!GO and attached it to Mitch's phone.

Mitch shook his head. "You *know* that's not going to work."

"Not the way it used to. But watch this." As soon as he attached the Jump!GO, the faintest blue swirl appeared at the fob's center.

"How are you making it do that?" asked Mitch, his voice low and hushed, as if talking louder would reveal a dreadful secret they'd been keeping all this time.

"I didn't make it do anything. It's been alive this whole time, Mitch."

"What?!" He stared in disbelief at the fob. "Why didn't you say something?!"

"I tried!" said Dean, clearly exasperated. "But every time I'd start talking about the Jump!GO or the Springs, you'd just bite my head off. Wayne was hardly around, and you were barely talking to me. I... I just didn't want to argue. And since my phone's still busted, I couldn't test it, so what was the use?"

Huh. All this time, Mitch had blamed Dean for their bad blood, but maybe the problem had mostly been him? He took a deep breath and protested, "Sorry. Sore point, I guess. So, can we jump with it?"

Dean relaxed. He pushed the button to bring up the plasma grid. Nothing happened. "But something's still alive in there," he said. "That tells me we might be able to use it to pinpoint Wayne. You got your fob on you?"

He did. Even though it had all gone to hell, pocketing his Jump!GO was still part of his morning routine. Phone, fob, wallet, complete. He felt almost naked without it. For some reason, he just couldn't leave it behind. For all of his protestations, a part of Mitch wanted to believe he could still figure out a way to make it all work.

He pulled the fob out of his pocket.

"You sly dog," said Dean with a slow grin. "And here you had me convinced you were done with jumping and everything associated with it."

Mitch blushed. "So, what's your idea?"

"There's a GPS backdoor in the Jump!GO app. I added it as baseline tester for Friend!GO's location feature. If we switch a couple things on the fob's internal board, then modify a setting in the Friend!GO app, we should be all set."

Dean pried off the back of each fob. He swapped a couple of jumpers, snapped the covers back on, and then laid them out side by side to see the affect. The blue swirl on both got noticeably brighter.

He linked the fobs together and sent the test ping. *Boom!* Wayne's fob immediately answered, transmitting the coordinates from the ping to the Friend!GO app and it pointed to... "Sam's? Really?" said Dean.

"He's at your sister's. Interesting. Why would he be there? You don't think—" Mitch had been going to say that they were dating. Which would have been amusing if it weren't also kind of, well, weird.

Dean snorted. "You know that's unlikely." Then he went back to fuming. "Damn it! I bet she roped him into a project and didn't want to include us. It better be that. I think I could stand that better than them being together."

They headed out to Sam's.

CHAPTER 5

Reunion

Walking through Sam's backyard felt to Mitch like coming home. Everything good that had happened to him over the past three months had happened in Sam's garage. *And everything bad, for that matter*, he reminded himself.

Then Dean unlocked the garage door, and it was like he'd unlocked every memory Mitch had been desperately trying to repress ever since their grand plan to revolutionize travel had gone to hell and back over a month ago. Every decrepit thrift store table lining the garage's walls dragged a bittersweet scene to the front of Mitch's mind. In that corner, he'd burned his fingers pulling the first Jump!GO casing from the 3D printer. At that bench, they'd whooped in triumph at the first video feed from a Jump!GO harness. On that shelf, the collection of state-by-state tchotchkes were still arranged in jump order.

His eyes landed on their mugs from Sutter's Pub, and he could almost smell the nachos, taste the burgers, and hear the janky house band as they joked, debated, and planned out their bright future and their ascension to entrepreneurial greatness. But then he spied just beyond the mugs Dean's battered cell phone, turned over to hide the assassin's bullet still lodged in its screen, and Mitch felt a longing for their Sutter's hangout that went beyond thirst and hunger. It was a desire for good times, happiness, and a sense of hope that he thought he would never feel again.

"What's all this junk?" said Dean, drawing Mitch's gaze away from his navel. All around them, on every workbench and table, lay small piles of equipment attached to Jump!GOs in a variety of odd arrangements.

Dean was examining the bench where their game console should have been. The console had been disassembled, its drive, controllers, and headsets squeezed onto a nearby shelf on top of Sam's gardening tools. In its place on the table was a hodgepodge of parts, haphazardly connected to a breadboard. Data scrolled by on an adjacent monitor, likely generated by the collective parts, but without context Mitch couldn't tell what the data meant.

A couple of steps away, a smaller breadboard was taped to the handle of Sam's electric lawnmower. A Jump!GO fob was soldered to a junction on the breadboard, the blue spiral at its center flashing once a second. "Power Pill" had been scrawled on the breadboard with a marker in thick black letters.

The lawnmower had displaced their packaging table which Mitch realized had migrated across the room and currently sported a router, another Jump!GO, research papers, and a jumbled host of equipment plugged in to the breaker box that powered both the house and the garage. The router didn't seem to be attached to anything, yet it clearly appeared to be on. *That's odd*, thought Mitch.

The breadboard Wayne had used to collect the rest of the equipment was labeled "Power Slab." A journal article about cold plasma and Rydberg atoms Dr. Bische had given them as a reference for the original Canopy paper sat atop a stack of notes on the table. Mitch wondered if the article somehow explained the heaps of mashed-up electronics. On the surface, it all looked like a jumbled mess.

And there was Wayne in the center of the mess, his eyes half-lidded and his hands resting on his keyboard but snoring loudly. His swivel chair was surrounded by snack wrappers, noodle cups, and overturned soda cans. His Jump!GO lay to the left of the keyboard, the only one of the travel fobs left in the garage that wasn't in some state of disrepair. Strangely, unlike the other devices, Wayne's Jump!GO glowed brightly, pulsing the way Mitch would expect for a device running through its normal slate of diagnostics.

A quick glance over Wayne's shoulder confirmed Mitch's suspicion. "Dean, come look," he whispered.

Dean hurried to the monitor, then smacked his fist. "I knew it! He's running tests on his fob."

There were ten diagnostics. Unsurprisingly, green success bars appeared next to the top five, which focused on mechanical integrity—did the fob have power, had they seated its board right, could the phone send it data, was it hot, were the apps synced?

The last five tests were tougher, revolving around photon filtering and light beam trapping. They required connectivity to the light gateway in the Springs, but with the QEP turned off they would fail. Wayne's fob seemed stuck on diagnostic number six.

"Do you think it'll pass?" whispered Dean. Mitch detected in the question an undercurrent of excitement.

"It can't pass," Mitch whispered back. "The main gateway's shut down."

"It's been three minutes. It should've failed already."

"Don't worry, it'll time out," said Mitch, trying to sound confident.

Dean's eyes gleamed. "Betcha it won't."

The progress bar inched forward. 30%... 60%... 85%... 100%. A spinning icon appeared while the diagnostic crunched the final bit of data, then the black bar flickered once... and turned green. A new progress bar appeared next to diagnostic number seven, inching ever so slowly forward.

Dean pumped his fists into the air above his head in silent celebration, then leaned into Mitch's ear and whispered, "He figured it out!"

Mitch gaped at the monitor. "But... but *what* did he figure out?"

"I don't know. But as soon as he wakes up, I'm gonna kiss him. Then I'll kill him."

"It won't pass seven. It's gotta trap a photon to pass seven and it can't do that. The gateway's gone."

"It'll do it."

"How?!"

"I don't know how! Just watch."

Mitch's heart thumped against his chest; he wasn't sure if it was from excitement or panic. Seven's progress bar crept forward as confidently as six's had. 40%... 65%... 90%... 100%!

Dean was jumping up and down now, quietly urging the bar to turn green. When it did, he threw victory punches at the screen.

Mitch couldn't take it anymore. He reached over Wayne and clicked the diagnostic off.

Immediately, as if his sleep cycle were tied to the program's run time, Wayne snapped to attention and squinted at the screen.

Dean pushed Wayne's swivel chair around to face them. "Wayne, dude, what the hell?" he said, his expression at war between excitement and anger.

Wayne stared at them blankly, then said, "Guys," as if reminding himself of who exactly they were. A huge yawn overtook him. "Sam called you, right? Told you to come over? I had some ideas about TIM and stuff. What time is it?"

"6:30," said Mitch.

"Man. You sure took your time."

"What's that supposed to mean?" Dean demanded. "We had class all day and so did you. *You're* the one ditching school. And us."

"Class? Wait... on Saturday?"

"You've been here since Saturday? Dude, it's *Wednesday*."

"Wow," said Wayne. "I really lost track of time."

"And here we were worried about you, but turns out you're just workin' behind our backs!"

Wayne sighed. "Dean, brah, you're killing me. I told you, Sam was supposed to call you."

"Well surprise, she didn't. Or maybe she couldn't. My phone's busted, remember? I wouldn't know if she did, which is great for you. Thanks for having a breakthrough and not telling your buds. We'd just bring you down, I guess."

Wayne looked confused. "What are you talking about? This junk—" He waved at the piles around the room—"it's kids stuff. If you guys had stopped moping around for ten minutes, you coulda probably made most of this too. Heck, Mitch would've built twice as much stuff."

"Don't lie," Dean persisted. "Your fob is right there."

Wayne rolled his eyes. "Like you don't carry your fob around everywhere too. Every time you check it, my fob pings. And he checks it a *lot*, Mitch. Like about twenty times a day, and because my fob is a master fob, I see it. Every. Single. Time."

"I may carry my fob around, but I'm not *using* it. I'm not *studying* it. We saw the diagnostics. We know you fixed the gateway. *You're* working on it behind *our* backs. I thought you were dead, but you just ditched us! We had to sneak up on you to find out. Is Sam paying you to be here? Are you sick of us?"

"Geez Louise, Chambers!" Wayne staggered to his feet and got in Dean's face. "Every day since Colorado Springs, you've been jumping down my throat for one reason or another, especially if it has anything to do with the Jump!GOs, so excuse the frig out of me for not immediately sharing." They stared at each other, breathing heavily, like bulls pawing the ground before they charge.

Mitch cleared his throat. "So... what we saw with the diagnostics. How'd you get that to work?"

The question broke the tension and Wayne shifted his gaze toward Mitch. "Pfft. It's not working. I just plugged it in out of habit. Nostalgia, I guess. Are you like Mr. Mental, here? Do you think I built a quantum gateway out of... what... Snickers bars and ramen noodles?"

"It passed the first seven tests, Wayne," Mitch said.

Wayne took a step back. "Now I *know* you're mental." He plopped down into the swivel chair and examined the diagnostics. The program had stopped running, but the results from the last run remained on the screen. Wayne's mouth dropped open. "That can't be right."

"Yeah, it might've been a fluke," said Mitch, but if he was honest with himself, he hoped it wasn't.

"Hmmm. Only one way to find out," said Wayne. He shifted the pointer to diagnostic number eight and opened the command window to restart the job.

"No! Don't!" Mitch tried to reach past Wayne, but Wayne was too fast. Eight's progress bar proceeded across the screen. With the test underway again, Mitch found himself unable to stop watching, mesmerized by the progress while simultaneously dreading the results.

Number eight passed. Nine—passed. And then came number ten, the Home Point diagnostic which, if successful, connected them to Sutter's Pub in Seattle. Could their base of good times once again be in reach?

50%... 75%... 90%...   There the progress bar stopped and turned red. The bar blinked and displayed an error message: "Endpoint not found. Click here to view log."

Dean's shoulders dropped. "Damn it." He whirled away from Wayne's monitor, smacking the other swivel chair out of the way.

Wayne leaned into the screen, fully awake. His eyes glittered. "Nine out of ten. Not that bad. Something I built must be helping the Jump!GO somehow. If we find it and fix it, we are back in business."

He jumped out of his chair and started scanning the scattered piles of equipment. "Which one is it?" He went from table to table, examining one jumbled mess and then another. "Guys, help me find it."

"Oh, *now* you want our help," said Dean.

"Will you stop it with the anger and the blaming? I'm sorry Sam didn't call you. I'm sorry I worked on TIM—on *our* team entry—while you two moped, so that *we'd* be selected. Emphasis on *we*, not me, you big dope. Now help me figure out which one of these things I built is miraculously a quantum gateway."

Dean glowered at Wayne's back, but said, "Guess I can't stay mad at you. I'd flunk out without your Kona beans."

He walked to the nearest pile and examined one piece of equipment after another, becoming more enthusiastic as he warmed to the task. "Would be cool if you actually did make a new gateway and got the Jump!GOs working again. We'd be smart about it this time. Build controls, block the crazies... order chili with the nachos at Sutter's

Pub. Everything would be great again." He picked up a box of springs and shrugged. "Might help if I knew what I was looking for, though."

"Not really sure myself," said Wayne. "Something's not acting the way we'd expect. Look for something glowing or vibrating or inexplicably cold. Anything weird like that. Mitch, a little help here?"

Mitch was still at Wayne's workstation, studying the diagnostic log in one window and the Jump!GO code in another. He was dying to know what Wayne had done, despite his trepidation about the consequences of activating a new gateway. The question piqued his curiosity and strummed the chords of hope that made his heart long for what Dean had articulated—everything being great again.

Maybe Dean's right: I gave up too soon. Maybe we can block trouble users. If we put some time into safety, maybe the gateway will be okay.

He wanted that to be true with every fiber of his being, to bring back the good times, the freedom, the *fun*. Identifying the hardware was only part of the equation. The other part had to be in the logs. That's where they'd find the failure. Whether the problem lay with the hardware or the code, they couldn't fix it until they knew what "it" was. *I'm on the right track. I can feel it—*

"Hey, Mitch, stop dreaming. We need a hand," Wayne insisted.

"One sec," he said.

He scrolled to the line in the log that contained the error message: "Endpoint not found." What did that mean? The coordinates for Sutter's Pub were logged, but the markers for photon trajectories were missing. They'd never had to calculate trajectories before. Once the coordinates were laid in, the plasma grid simply appeared.

Thinking about it now, Mitch realized the QEP at Cheyenne Mountain must have handled the trajectories in some way. But with the QEP shut down, how could they compensate on their own?

For no obvious reason, he pictured Maggie under the 3D projector, carefully writing the integral equation formula, and he chuckled. *That's too good to be true.* He keyed in the calculation anyway, folding it into their locator routine as a new final step. He hit enter, and somewhere at the back of the garage, a piece of equipment thrummed to life.

"Found it!" called Wayne excitedly. He trotted to the table by the breaker box. "Mitch, what did you do?!"

"He's got his flash face on," said Dean. "Mitch, buddy, you did it!"

Mitch brought up the command window and restarted diagnostic number ten. Wayne and Dean scrambled to his side, and, collectively they held their breath as the progress bar walked across the screen.

50%... 75%... 90%... 100%!

An azure blue slab of plasma, no thicker than a textbook and as wide as a window, sprang out of Wayne's fob into the center of the room and embedded in its upper-left corner was the light point for Sutter's Pub, burning bright and true.

It took only a second for the reality of the situation to sink in. The grid was back, their favorite hangout in reach. Spontaneously, joyously, the three friends roared.

"Wayne?" Sam's voice cut through their celebration. The inner door to the kitchen of the house opened.

"Crap!" said Mitch. With a quick flick of his wrist, he disconnected Wayne's Jump!GO from the diagnostic. The plasma grid disappeared just as Sam's face, so much like Dean's, peered around the door.

"Hey there," she said, all smiles, until her eyes landed on Wayne' junk food trash. "Wow, Wayne. I was going to ask if you were back, but it looks like you never left."

"Uh, yeah. Got caught up building prototypes for TIM," he replied.

She turned to Dean and slapped his shoulder. "Did you get my messages? I called you at least three times but only got your recording. Clear your ding-dang voice mail once in a while."

Dean flushed red, then pocketed his phone, careful to keep the bullet side down away from Sam's view. "Sorry. I guess I left my phone here."

"Ah, that explains it. At any rate, glad you all made it," said Sam. "Wayne told me about the Power Pill. Pure genius. You guys are amazing."

Dean looked at Wayne perplexed and mouthed, "Power Pill?"

Wayne ignored him. Turning to Sam, he said, "I guess Dr. Bische taught us right."

"Bische has been a great influence on you three." She picked up Wayne's Jump!GO and turned it over in her hands to admire it. "Your design is fantastic. Sleek, practical, just the kind of thing we look for at Tamblyn Tech. When Cecilia sees it, I know she'll love it. Good job!"

"That's not the only thing she'll love," added Dean. "We've got something else that'll completely blow her mind."

Mitch ducked behind Sam, waving at Dean and frantically slashing his hand across his throat. "What?" Dean mouthed.

Sam raised an eyebrow. "Takes a lot to blow her mind these days. She sees all kinds of amazing tech proposals. Even thinks up some of her own. She used to work for DARPA, you know."

"Well, *our* tech—"

"—is great just like you said," Mitch interjected before Dean could continue. Dean glared at him.

"Pretty sure she's gonna love all our prototypes," said Wayne, purposely drawing Sam's attention. "We can give you a demo if you want to see?"

"Great! I bought groceries on the way home from the airport. Let me put them away first." She disappeared back into the kitchen.

Dean waited for his sister to close the door, then rushed over to Wayne's Jump!GO.

"Let's get the grid back up and surprise her when she walks back in. She's gonna flip out when we take her to Sutter's. This is gonna be good. Hey, what are you doing?"

Mitch took the Jump!GO out of Dean's hand. "We're not gonna tell her, Dean." he said. "Not Sam. Not CC Tamblyn. Nobody. We keep this to ourselves until we figure out those controls you talked about."

"Can't put the genie back into the bottle, Mitch." sighed Wayne. "For all we know, right this minute somebody else is working on the exact same thing. They'll go to market with our idea, and *then* who would we be? The suckers who didn't strike while the iron was hot."

"You heard Sam," Dean added. "CC Tamblyn's jaded. To get on her radar for TIM, we need something major. After that, if we she chooses us, we'll need something *killer* for Tech Convergence. The Jump!GO works for both situations. CC and the angel investors are gonna eat it right up."

"Damn it, can't you just do this for me? Can't we just leave it alone until we can figure it all out? We moved too fast last time and people almost... I mean... Chung and Jin... they almost died. We can't start talking about jumping again until we get a handle on how to control it."

Dean frowned, usually a prelude to protest, but Mitch could tell his heart wasn't in it. Mentioning Chung and Jin had taken the wind out of his sails. Still, looking to have the last word, he opened his mouth to reply, but Wayne was quicker: "Alright, Mitch. We'll do this for you."

"What?! Wayne, you can't be seri—"

Wayne raised a hand for Dean to stop, then turning back to Mitch continued, "But you gotta do something for us. We can't hide the Jump!GOs forever. The cat's out of the bag. As soon as we come up with a way to protect the gateway from loonies, you gotta let it go. You gotta let us put it out there. Because if we don't, someone else will, and they might not be as ethical about it as we're gonna be. Agreed?"

Mitch could think of no counter argument. "Agreed," he said with a sigh.

Sam returned. "I ordered pizza and wings. Figured Wayne would like a change from corn chips and ramen."

"Thanks," he said.

"You betcha. Welp. Ready to have my mind blown. Show me what you got."

Wayne went to the lawn mower. "How would you like to never buy gas, plug in a cord, or recharge a battery whenever you had to mow?"

"With Dean mowing the lawn, I've already sorta got that."

"Keep paying me so little, you might sorta lose that."

"Keep eating me out of house and home and maybe I'll sorta let you go."

"Hey, don't blame me for all this trash. This was Wayne—"

Mitch let Dean and Wayne talk to Sam. He had to admit, Wayne might be right. Just like Chung, someone might already be out there building their own version of his device. The thought made him shudder.

Maybe our best bet is to get into TIM, he thought. *Then we can quietly mention the problem to Sam, or even CC Tamblyn herself.*

Things might go better with corporate backing and lawyers. It couldn't be worse than going it alone. With CC Tamblyn on their side, what could possibly go wrong?

CHAPTER 6

Confidence

Christian woke up happy. Today was a big day. He'd spent the past month learning, testing, and building, and he finally felt ready to reveal his plans. Luckily, Dr. Hayman's schedule had an opening and the president had agreed to a second meeting, granting Christian a full hour to speak with him and the other Physics Department heads. An hour was more than enough time to make his proposal. Christian was certain that once they experienced his presentation, everything would change—not just for him, but also for the School of Mines.

Smiling, he climbed out of bed, conjured a bubble of light beneath his feet, and glided into the shower. He loved gliding when he was alone. Gliding was easier than walking, and the buzz of electricity around his toes made him feel strong. He turned up the hot water, luxuriating in the steam, and thought back on the last month.

He'd called in sick the first week, spending the time stress-testing his newfound powers instead. Then he'd returned to CSM and played the victim card for all it was worth, fanning the flames of the board's worries about a lawsuit and discussing his distress with sympathetic faculty members at every opportunity. He'd even added some theater, grabbing his forearm and grimacing in pain during lectures, staring off space during conversations, and generally giving the impression that despite his pain, he was soldiering on with a courage that deserved acknowledgement.

The ploy had worked. Carlos Rabel came to visit soon after, bringing a letter from the board expressing how "*deeply* sorry" they were about his ordeal and offering what they hoped he'd view as "fair compensation." They offered to elevate his position from teaching assistant to postdoctoral fellow and to cover any remaining medical bills. Much to Rabel's relief, he'd agreed, and was given Hubert's classroom, office, lab, parking space, and even a shelf in the faculty refrigerator. Life was good.

But it could be better. What Christian really wanted was a seat at the Physics Department's table, complete with the authority to make decisions that steered the department's direction. He wanted what Hubert had promised him: a full professorship, with money and minions and respect. With a little luck, today's meeting would grant him all three.

The key was his prototype, a box that generated the very dew drops his body now made. The box could only make one plasma-coated photon at a time, but it didn't need to make any more than that for the demo. If they wanted to see more, he could discreetly pop another out of his palm. It was still an impressive demo, and the presentation would play on everyone's sense of university pride. "Light tech is the future. We're miners. Let's lead the way and mine light."

A simple pitch, but layered with ideas for tech spin-offs, the innovation program, and new areas of research based on the dew drops. The prototype would lay the foundation for a greater transformation. And every good thing Hubert had tainted would be fixed. Christian wouldn't rest until he'd made everything right. Dr. Hayman would have no choice but to see him for what he was: the Physics Department's future, the university's savior.

Christian packed his tablet and the prototype into his backpack and laid it by the door, being careful to avoid the full-length mirror nearby. He hadn't looked at himself in any mirror since his first meeting with Hayman; his sense of control depended on it. He had no idea which version of himself he'd see—or whether seeing a different Christian would make who he was right now disappear.

The voices of his alternate selves had drifted to the background, muted but always there. At their worst, especially when he was tired or stressed, the whine would become unbearable and he'd feel his very molecules... drifting. It took every ounce of his strength in those moments—both physical and mental—to keep the cells of his body and his psyche from splintering.

Today was too important. He couldn't chance triggering an attack with even a quick glance to straighten his collar or comb his hair. Casting his eyes to the ground, he glided into the kitchen to make breakfast. *Who needs mirrors? Just smile and be confident. People will ignore the rest.*

It was nine o'clock. The meeting was at ten. *Might as well use the hour to practice again, maybe rerun the diagnostics on the prototype, just to be sure.* He grabbed his backpack and with a wave of his hand conjured a portal that led to the loading dock just behind the CASE building. Portals had become his main mode of transport. They were faster and, like gliding, decidedly more fun.

A gentle breeze blew in through the hole, the scent of it filled with new grass and the freshness of spring snow. Christian inhaled deeply enough to taste the brisk morning air. *Oh, that's good. Too good to miss.* He closed the portal and decided to walk.

It was gorgeous, the nicest morning in weeks. Last night's snow still covered the ground, but the sun shone brightly, birds chirped happily, and beneath the crispness flowed a warmth that would soon melt the snow. Christian decided to help the breeze. He conjured a tiny ball of energy in the palm of his hand and with a casual flick swept the path before him, volatilizing the snow at every step into thin wisps of vapor, revealing the occasional dandelion and the first blades of spring grass breaking through the late winter sod. *Christian the liberator*, he thought, grinning at his efforts.

The other walkers around him seemed oblivious to the greatness of the day. They huddled in bulky coats, rushing about campus and dashing into buildings, desperate for shelter from the cold. But Christian felt comfortable in his light jacket. He reveled in the bite of the frosty wind; his newfound senses were tickled by the trembling of freshly sprouted grass, the citrusy aroma of trampled clover, and the raw energy of the beaming sun. He felt it all in every nerve ending, every scent receptor, every cone in his retina, every ossicle in his ear. It was glorious, invigorating, like falling into a vat of cold water infused with spearmint. He gasped at the intensity of the sensation. His sinuses were open, but so was his mind. He felt so clear, so aware, so *alive*. How could things *not* go his way on such a glorious day?

Hayman would give him all of Hubert's responsibilities, including the rest of Hubert's academic assets. Once he had those in hand, he could announce himself to Hubert's business contacts. Not the weapon-hungry crazies. Just the ultra-wealthy angel investors looking for the next new thing. He didn't intend to make Hubert's mistakes. He'd go legit, build a reputation for excellence, and change the world. He was certain he could do it, thanks to the dew drops.

His arms swung loosely by his side as he walked, generating the slightest arc of electricity and sending a thrill up his spine. He suddenly felt a surge of power leaking out near the tips of his fingers; it was desperate to be let loose anywhere, onto anything. He'd reached the walkway leading up to the CASE building. It was lined with bushes, a thin layer of snow covering the tops of each. *Those should do*, he thought. He lifted his hand to release the energy into the neatly trimmed hedge. *What's a few burnt branches. Maybe it'll just melt the snow.*

A bud on a nearby branch caught his eye and suddenly he was drawn to it, to the potential energy lying dormant within it. *I could touch that*, he thought, entranced. The plasma ball in the palm of his hand transformed, became a tendril that licked the bud, pierced its outer shell, and wound its way down, down into the very heart of the bud's atoms. The branch sang to him then, and the tendril curled around the sound, amplifying the song until the tiny bud bloomed.

Christian yanked his hand away, surprised. At the back of his mind, the most antagonistic of the voices bubbled up from its hiding place. [*Why the parlor tricks, Prime? Clearing snow, tending hedges. Are you the groundskeeper? Is that the extent of your power?*]

A group of students approached on the opposite side of the path, their giggles drawing Christian's attention. [*Have you no influence beyond inanimate objects?*] the mocking voice egged him on.

He shook his head, trying to ignore it, but the question had made him... curious. He hadn't expected to influence the energy of the bush, much less cause one of its buds to bloom. *Can I do the same to a person? I wonder...*

Christian focused on the group, tentatively sampling their individual energies. Then, feeling more confident, set to manipulating their mental wavelengths, tuning them to a single frequency compatible with his own. Once he had them hooked, he projected his best, most charismatic self into their minds.

Time slowed, and as one the group turned toward him, their expressions full of favor and longing. [*You could have any of them,*] the mocking voice purred. [*Make them do your bidding. Bend them to your will.*]

Emboldened, Christian closed his fist on the collective's string, drawing the group more tightly into his energetic web. He moved them together farther down the path, to the crosswalk and the edge of the busy street, but then suddenly the murmuring in Christian's head grew louder. The mocking voice was drowned out by another, stronger one. [**You're being used. This isn't power, you fool. Wake up!**]

Pain flared through him, as hot and intense as the fire that had consumed him the night of his accident. The voices screamed, and in that moment, Christian felt the mirror of himself, his facade of power, shatter into pieces. The jagged shards pushed against his skin and threatened to shoot out. "Gah!"

He stumbled, losing control of the group, which stopped just short of the morning's rush-hour traffic. The crossing light changed, and they walked on, unaware of what had almost happened. Christian was left bent over and panting, his arms wrapped around his chest, desperate to contain the fragments of himself. *Losing it. Gotta get inside.* He turned back toward the CASE building. *Just a few yards more.* It might as well have been miles away.

"Hey, Christian! Hold up!"

Larry Knight ran up behind him. "Good morning!" He clapped Christian on the back. "Thanks for waiting. Whoo, it's cold. No heat on the bus. Started running to stay warm. Hey, are you okay?"

The clap on the back had set Christian coughing. *Got to get it together.* He gritted his teeth and swallowed hard. "Fine. I'm fine," he said between coughs. With an effort he straightened up took a deep breath, and said, "Just swallowed wrong." He started walking again, feeling steadier with each step. "Heading to Hayman's office?" he asked. *That's it. Just act normal.*

"Heck yeah. So excited. I'm thinking he'll give me a new assignment. Maybe something permanent now that Dr. Wilkins is gone. Wow, *that* guy, right? I mean, I don't have to tell *you*... "

Christian nodded weakly as Larry prattled on, his enthusiastic chatter drowning out the whines of Christian's own internal distress. The conversation, though one-sided, steadied him, and he grew stronger as they walked. One by one, he gathered the fragments of himself, carefully rebuilding his internal reflection. Breathing was key. He inhaled and exhaled slowly, each breath sealing up a crack in the mirror and turning down the volume on another panicked voice. He was whole again by the time they'd climbed the CASE building stairs.

He was closest to the door. Unconsciously, he curled a tendril of energy around the glass handle and pushed it open for them to enter. Larry looked on in surprise. "Some wind," he chuckled. Christian just smiled. *That's better. Why was I so upset?*

"Don't get me wrong. I really respect Dr. Forbus," Larry continued his side of the conversation. "He gave me a shot as his TA when no one else would. I'm grateful, really. But it's not like the work he throws my way is... taxing. There's enough of it, especially since he's been sick, but grading papers and rehashing old lectures is, I don't know. Slow? If Dr. Bische is at the meeting, I might ask him if he needs help."

"Bische?" Christian scoffed. "You'd still be babysitting undergrads. That's no better than Forbus, really."

"You kidding me? What about last semester with the Campbell kid and his crew? Very impressive. That travel canopy was completely next level."

"If you call a fluke 'next level.' It's clear they didn't understand their own tech. But Bische pushed them anyway, and then they crashed."

"I'd take that. Seriously. Sign me up. At least Dr. B. *tried* to make them geniuses. He cultivated his people, gave them a shot. No chance of that with Dr. F. Me, I'm not a kid like Campbell and his friends. Give *me* an opportunity like instant travel? No stopping me."

A tiny burst of irritation rolled through Christian. *Bische and his glorified grease monkeys.* People constantly fawned over the kids in the Innovation Program when there was nothing particularly remarkable about Bische or his "special" students. He was all flash and no substance.

"Bische is small beans," he said, more casually than he felt. "If it's a challenge you want, why not come work for me? I'm already doing Wilkins' job, and to be honest was doing 90% of it before he was arrested. It makes sense for me to take over his position. As the Director of Commercial Development, I'll oversee work on all viable projects. You'd get your hands on all the cutting-edge tech before anyone else does. Once I've settled into the job, there will be lots of opportunities for my doctoral candidates. Especially the talented ones, like you."

Larry raised an eyebrow and laughed. "Can't fault you for being confident. That'd be some feat, getting a full professorship less than a year out of post-doc. Personally, I'd think they'd want an established PhD to handle all that responsibility. No knock against you, of course."

"My presentation today should prove to everyone how responsible I can be. Then President Hayman will make my new position official." *Whether he planned to or not,* Christian thought.

The failure with the giggling students showed him the current limits of his power. With too many people, he'd lose control. But one person could be tuned to his frequency, coaxed into accepting his ideas, just like the bud of the holly bush he'd coaxed to grow. *Not a parlor trick*, he told himself. *More like research and development.* He waited for the Others to object, but they stayed quiet. His inner light surged in anticipation.

They arrived at Hayman's outer office. Doreen acknowledged their arrival with a curt nod, seemingly preoccupied with the task of sorting the president's mail. *Time for another test.* Christian reached out, gently tap-tapping on her energy and projecting his light into her brain waves. "Good to see you again, Doreen," he said. Even to his own ears he sounded suave as hell.

With an impatient sigh she looked up from her work, but her expression changed immediately from irritation to warm admiration. "Oh!" she said with just the hint of surprise. "Goodness, Christian. I didn't notice it was *you*." Still looking at him, she pushed the intercom button on her desk. "Christian Meadows is here, Dr. Hayman."

"And Larry Knight," said Larry, leaning over her desk to speak directly into the intercom.

Doreen blinked and shook her head a little, color rising in her cheeks. Looking at Larry as if he had just arrived, she said, "Oh, yes, Mr. Knight also." She took her hand off the intercom button and whispered, "My apologies, young man."

President Hayman's voice emanated from the intercom. "Excellent, Doreen. Send them right in."

Christian winked at Doreen, then led the way into Dr. Hayman's inner sanctum. A cart festooned with bagels, fruit, pastries, and coffee sat in the middle of the room. Off to the side, taking up most of the remaining space, was a larger, round table with copies of Hubert's old development plan stacked in the middle. Hayman, Dr. Bische, and Dr. Rebar occupied three of the six chairs around the table. The president rose as Christian and Larry entered the room, extending his hand in greeting.

"Ah, gentleman, good morning. So glad you could join us."

Hayman smiled at them, warm and cordial, his positive energy enticingly palpable. He clasped first Larry's hand then Christian's in both of his own, like they were old friends. Christian's confidence swelled. *This could go extremely well.*

"There's breakfast on the cart over there if you like. Help yourself and have a seat. We have much to discuss."

"Fantastic, thank you!" said Larry, eying the spread in appreciation. He had enough grace to shake hands with Bische and Rebar before launching himself at the cream cheese and muffins. Bische and Rebar joined him at the cart, replenishing their food and drink, and engaging in a bit of good-natured banter with Larry.

While the three of them chatted amiably, Christian set up his tablet and portable projector, thankful for Larry's gregarious distraction. *Larry may be the opening act, but Hayman knows I'm the headliner. And I'm ready to kill.*

The president appeared at his shoulder and said quietly, "Christian, thank you for arranging another meeting. Good to see you recovering and I'm glad we have another chance to talk. I trust our insurance team has contacted you regarding your medical expenses?"

"Yes, sir," said Christian. "Very kind of the university. All taken care of."

"Good, good. And how are you feeling... well, emotionally?"

Christian detected true concern in Hayman's tone. *He really seems to care*, Christian thought, but the mocking voice returned. [*Don't fall for it. He fears a lawsuit. He doesn't care. No one does.*]

Christian shook away the intrusion. With a conscious effort, he tapped into his own energy, fanning it into confidence until the heat of his inner light tickled the edges of his fingertips and the surface of his skin.

He smiled kindly at Hayman, and replied, "Every now and then I catch myself looking cautiously around corners. Not as much now that some time has passed."

"Splendid. If at any time you feel distressed, just ask and we'll gladly arrange for counseling or whatever help you need." said Hayman.

"I appreciate that, sir, but lately I've been feeling fine."

Larry joined them at the table, a full plate of fruit and a cranberry-orange muffin topped with a schmear of cream cheese in hand. Hayman stepped aside to include him, cleared his throat, and said, "Let's get started, shall we?" He took the seat next to Christian. "I want to thank Christian and Larry for taking on the extra load of Dr.

Wilkins' and Dr. Forbus' classes since both are out for... a variety of reasons. And while we expect Dr. Forbus to return, Dr. Wilkins most decidedly will not."

"Here, here," said Dr. Bische, raising his cup in salute.

Christian smiled and lifted his own to join the toast. "I'll second that."

They all laughed, then Hayman continued, "Which leaves us with the task of how best to fill the unexpected vacancy going forward."

Here it is, thought Christian, *the moment of truth.*

"After internal deliberation and a discussion with the board, we've decided to promote you both. Larry will be made a predoctoral fellow until his doctoral defense is completed, at which time he will be offered the position of full doctoral fellow."

Larry's eyes widened and he nearly dropped his muffin. "Really? You're not just shifting me over to help another professor?"

"Of course not," said Hayman. "You're far too valuable to leave to simple TA work. Your re-imagining of Dr. Forbus' lectures has elevated his classes to 'must attend' status. You've got great potential and we want to cultivate that. Your promotion is well earned, young man."

Larry sat speechless, his plate of goodies forgotten, but then he burst out laughing. He stood up and shook everyone's hands again. "Spectacular. Thanks for the opportunity. Can't wait to get started!"

"As for you, Christian," Hayman continued, "we're prepared to offer you an entry-level research assistant professorship, a step up from your current status as a postdoctoral fellow. The promotion would be effective immediately and extend through to the end of next year, at which time you'd be eligible to apply for an associate professor position, putting you on the tenure track. The board sees this as an acknowledgement of your demonstrated expertise while assisting Dr. Wilkins as well as covering his classes after his arrest. They also see it as a way for the university to show its faith in you despite resulting ugly business that followed. What say you to that?"

Christian maintained his external calm, but inside he seethed. Was that all? After everything he'd gone through, after doing Hubert's job for the better part of a year even before the "ugly business," Hayman and the board couldn't bring themselves to, at minimum, make him tenured?

[*Insulting! Disrespectful!*] the strident voices called out. His pulse quickened and, involuntarily, under the table a ball of plasma formed in the palm of his hand. He knew with deep certainty that unleashing the energy would incinerate everyone in the office, including Doreen. He could roast them easily, let their ashes blow out the window, open a portal to a new place, and give himself a new identity. No one would be the wiser. *Sorry, Larry.*

But the stronger, saner voice rose above the others. [**Try persuasion,**] it told him. [**Scorched Earth will ruin you. Keep your cool and salvage the situation.**]

His gaze landed on the pile of Hubert's reports and his anger receded. He knew what to do.

Standing up, he squelched the fireball in his palm, retrieved the stack from the table, and said, "These are Dr. Wilkins' projections for commercial development next year, right?"

"Why, yes," said Hayman. "I had Doreen print those out so we could discuss."

"I'll save you some time." Christian walked over to Hayman's recycle bin and pitched the stack into it.

Bische guffawed. "Gotta give him credit, Leland. He knows trash when he sees it."

Christian turned on his projector. "I know even more than that. If you can't grant me tenure, then make me your new Director of Commercial Development. Let me guide the university into the future and I'll spin Dr. Wilkins' trash into gold."

The presentation flowed out of him as power and confidence surged through him, each slide building upon the next with research ideas, student initiatives, and tech development proposals beyond anything tried by Mines' faculty in the history of the school. "All of this is innovative. None of it requires stealing from the university or its students. None of it is tied to foreign investments with hostile nations. I present to you a development slate of which Mines can be proud."

Bische regarded him thoughtfully, while Rebar, Larry, and Hayman seemed astonished.

"Impressive," breathed Hayman. "Extremely well thought out, I might add. The breadth of your ideas and planning will surely be a great asset to the Physics Department in the coming years."

"Talk about next level," said Larry. He flashed a thumbs up at Christian, new respect in his eyes.

Christian smiled. *Successfully salvaged.*

Turning to Bische and Rebar, Hayman said, "Photon mining. Light technology. Perhaps the world is ready?"

"Is that the right question, Leland?" asked Dr. Rebar. "Excellent presentation, Christian. The potential of it all is very enticing. But Leland, given the recent experience with Mitch Campbell, can the school safely take the challenge on?"

"Good point, Reba. We'd need to consult Carlos Rabel, obviously. Gabriel, your thoughts?"

Dr. Bische stared at Christian with an intensity that would have been unnerving prior to his transformation. Now, filled with power and confidence, Christian used it to add fuel to his considerable fire. *Bring it on, Dr. Bische. Who's the real innovator now?*

But the good doctor merely said, "Meadows seems to have taken Campbell's work in a different direction. Might be interesting to see just how far it goes."

Hayman nodded. "Yes. I totally agree. Christian, these proposals are excellent. I'll happily present them to the board."

Christian beamed. "Then you'll convince them to make me the new Commercial Development Director?"

Hayman's expression grew solemn. "I'll recommend they include you as an *advisor* to the director, given your passion and demonstrated expertise. But I'm afraid the board will not approve a first-year post-doc to be placed in that role."

Christian couldn't believe his ears. *How can he be turning me down?*

"Dr. Rebar will be named the Dean of the Physics Department. Along with that promotion comes the Commercial Development Director's position. As for innovation, until his contract is up Dr. Bische will continue in *that* position. The board recognizes his unique ability to mine talent from our students while teaching them the merits of mining."

Christian felt a heat rise within his chest and spread out into his extremities. A light built behind his eyes and the voices applied their pain again. [*Hayman's a fool, but we'll make him see it our way.*]

As with Doreen, he took the flare of his inner light and projected it out at Hayman. The quantum wavelength of Hayman's mind sang to him as clearly as buds on the branch had. Christian grabbed hold, twisting the wave in his direction, dragging the thought pattern into alignment with his own. Unlike Doreen, Leland Hayman was no mental lightweight. His mind resisted, but Christian pressed on, pulling the wave tighter until finally he'd made Hayman's wavelength his own.

The president's face went slack, then slowly transformed. He looked up at Christian and in his eyes was nothing less than admiration and deep, unfiltered appraisal. It had taken only nanoseconds. He opened his mouth, no doubt ready to agree to Christian's demands.

"Leland, are you alright?" Bische suddenly interjected.

Christian's tendril to the president snapped. Hayman shook his head and laughed to himself. "Curious. I seem to have lost my train of thought. Where were we?"

Dr. Rebar said, "You just explained how our duties will be divided now that Hubert is gone."

"Ah, yes, yes. Any questions?" Hardly any time had elapsed. In the quantum realm, nothing took long at all. Christian felt Bische's eyes on him. He couldn't possibly know what almost happened. Christian glanced at the doctor, hoping to steal more fire, but Bische's eyes pierced into him. He winced and looked away.

Larry saved the moment. "Sounds great to me, Dr. Hayman. Whatever gets me to defending my thesis sooner than later." He laughed. "Seriously, thanks for the opportunity. Can't wait to get started!"

As a group, they turned to Christian, waiting for his response, but he said nothing. He'd been defeated. *I don't know* what *to say.*

The strong voice guided him. [**You don't need them. Time to leave.**]

He nodded to himself. A calm washed over him. He'd been thinking big in a small space. Maybe it was time to branch out.

Turning on the charm, he said, "I'm sorry, but an associate's position is not what I expected. Honestly, it isn't even close to what I wanted. Given my track record, a full professorship is the only valid position."

Hayman put out a placating hand. "Christian, that is definitely in the cards. But we'll need to consider it in a year or two. Just not right now."

"Hmm." Christian disassembled the projector.

"I'm still very interested in adopting your ideas," said Hayman. "Surely we could build an implementation team for them with Dr. Rebar's help—and the board's approval, of course."

Christian shook his head. "Sadly, no. My ideas are far too detailed for anyone else to execute. And they are *my* ideas. I wouldn't trust them in anyone else's hands. Not even Dr. Rebar's. No, President Hayman, I will take these elsewhere. Someone will be willing to invest in my ideas and in me. Thank you for the meeting."

He walked out the door. His calm solidified around a new idea, one born of freedom.

"Oh my, certainly looks like things went your way," said Doreen, appearing to still be in the grip of his previous influence.

Quite by accident, he caught his reflection in the outer-office's glass door. The Christian that stared back at him was not unexpected. His reflection seeped power, and his visage virtually glowed. Christian graced Doreen with another smile, sure this time that it *was* suave as hell. "They will now," he said.

Life is indeed good. It can only get better. A little light leaked out the corner of his eye. He felt a slight tremor, but it passed.

CHAPTER 7

Meet the CEO

"Where'd Mitch go?"

Dean stood in front of their prep pit at Tamblyn Tech's exhibit hall, sipping Kona coffee from his monster-sized travel mug and scanning the area for any sign of his friend's distinctive mop of curls.

Mitch had disappeared twenty minutes ago in search of a bathroom. Before he'd trotted off, they'd spent most of the morning eating donuts and drinking coffee, waving at people they knew, and making bets on which weird prototypes might edge them out of the TIM competition. More teams had arrived since then, and now the hall was crammed wall-to-wall with so many students, partitions, and gear the top of Mitch's head was about all Dean expected to see. *If* Mitch ever returned.

"He's got fifteen minutes," said Wayne. He'd stepped behind their partition to run another check on their equipment. "We're still looking good. Don't worry."

"Not worried, just curious. I know we're good."

We've got this, he thought. They'd arrived early thanks to Sam, who'd needed to be there before everyone else to coordinate registration, and so they'd had plenty of time to prepare. The presentation hadn't changed much from Wayne's original impromptu pitch back in Sam's garage, but over the past month they'd improved it by de-junkifying the components, creating an animated slide deck, and adding talking points—polished by Sam—that emphasized each unit's convenience and marketability. The demo was short and sweet, and, unlike some other teams, their prototypes looked professional and they worked. Even Bische, always their harshest critic, had liked it. Dean grinned at his coffee. *I'd select us if I were CC*, he thought.

It surprised him a little how much he was enjoying being there. The atmosphere felt like any other science fair or maker competition they'd participated in over the years. And as Bische's protégés, the good doctor had made sure they participated in a *lot*. He should feel jaded, maybe even kind of bored. What made today so enjoyable was the feeling that he was in his element with other like-minded people. He could *taste* the excitement. More than that, he could feel something the three of them had been missing for weeks: pure, simple fun!

And the part he'd liked best was being back with his buds, creating and building like before the mess in the Springs. Ever since clearing the air that night at the garage, they'd settled into a happy groove, attending classes, working on TIM, and, when the mood struck them, opening a light hole or two. The router wasn't strong enough yet to maintain a gateway for longer than ten minutes, but that was enough time to grab nachos from Sutter's Pub or pop over to one of their other old haunts, reminisce about the good times and remember all the fun. The past month had been great.

And now they were about to meet one of the most famous CEOs in the country, a woman who might just help them bring the Jump!GO and its re-imagined tech alive. He danced a happy dance inside. *Things are better than great*, he thought. *They're just about perfect.* All they needed now was Mitch.

"Maybe he got lost?"

"Unlikely," said Wayne. His voice was muffled as he leaned over the cart with a voltmeter, re-checking every appliance's Power Pill connection. "Knowing Mitch, he probably stopped at a pit to help somebody out."

Just then, a commotion broke out near Metro State's pit, which was directly across from their own but until then had been blocked from view by a sizeable throng. White smoke and a loud, sizzling *Pop!* scattered the crowd. A familiar laugh sliced through the bedlam. "Bingo," said Wayne without turning around.

Dean craned his neck to see. Through the gap in the horde, he spied Mitch with members of the Metro State team, fanning away smoke and grinning from ear to ear. Some piece of equipment on their cart sputtered then purred until finally track lights along the edge of its container flickered on. Everyone around the cart cheered.

"Thank you! Thank you!" Members of the Metro State team took turns shaking Mitch's hand. Surrounding teams enthusiastically applauded. Several students Dean recognized from Mines pointed proudly at Mitch and slapped him on the back.

Wayne paused in his equipment checks, looked up, and shook his head. "Making new friends as usual. Mitch Campbell, The Great Uniter."

"That's our boy," said Dean. He cupped his hand to his mouth and yelled, "Hey, Mitch!" then pointed to the big digital clock on the wall. "Time's a-wastin'!"

Mitch glanced up at the clock. "Yikes! Guys, I gotta go!" He pushed his way through the mob back to their pit.

Dean spread his arms in mock exasperation. "You run off to the toilet then disappear. We thought you fell in!"

Mitch blushed. "Sorry, but that Metro State guy was freaking out in the bathroom cuz he dropped their machine on the way in from the parking lot, so I went over to help. Fixed it, though! Ha!" Dean high-fived him.

"Just in time," said Wayne. "We're up."

The clock hit half-past the hour. On cue, the event announcer called "Team Jump Tech, School of Mines" over the sound system. "Please proceed to conference room number two."

They hustled their carts out of the pit and made their way across the exhibit hall to the bank of prefab modules lining the wall. Teams called out to them as they passed by.

"Go Mines!"
"Die, Frosh!"
"Break a leg, guys!"

Sam poked her head around the conference room door. "*Psst!* Dean-o. You ready?"

"Just about." Confidently, Dean tapped his tablet to cast its display to the presentation monitor. Nothing happened.

"Crud puppet," said Wayne. "I did all those checks but forgot about the monitor."

"It's okay. I got it," said Dean. Quickly, he reached behind the monitor and examined its tangled mass of wires. Suddenly, he couldn't seem to get enough air and every finger on his hand felt like a thumb. *Now you're nervous, goofball? Calm down.*

Sam ducked in again, "What's up?"

"Need a sec," he called over his shoulder.

"Too late. Here she comes. Do good!" She popped out. From the other side of the door, they heard her say, "The next group is ready for you, Cecilia. Team Jump Tech from the School of Mines."

"Keep working," said Wayne. "We'll cover 'til you get it hooked up again."

The door opened. Behind him, Mitch and Wayne introduced themselves, then scrambled to arrange two chairs strategically around the carts. "Thanks, guys," said Sam cheerfully.

Then the voice of Dr. Cecilia Cassandra "CC" Tamblyn rose above the others, no nonsense and commanding. "Gentleman. What've you got?"

"Whoa," said Mitch under his breath.

"Interesting," Wayne whispered.

What's with them? Dean wondered absently. *And where've I heard that voice before?* He immediately dismissed the question. Of course he'd recognize the great CC Tamblyn, arguably the most famous tech figure in Colorado. She'd appeared in every Tamblyn Tech ad. There wasn't a month in high school when some Tamblyn-narrated video wasn't shown as class filler or shared ironically on the net. It was silly to wonder why her voice sounded familiar. Yet... something about the deep, husky cadence tickled a memory as he fumbled with the monitor's connections. If he hadn't been freaking out, he might've been able to put his finger on it.

The sudden silence behind him was a swift reminder that Mitch and Wayne could only vamp for so long. He had to fix things fast. *Maybe if I swapped these inputs...* The monitor sprang to life, and the title page of their presentation scrolled across the screen.

"Huzzah!" he exclaimed. He turned around and did a double take. *Marion? No, that's ridiculous*, he told himself. Why would CC Tamblyn remind him of the government agent from the Springs? He was so nervous he was seeing things.

"Spoken like a true Renaissance man," Tamblyn quipped. "Shall we begin?"

"Yes, ma'am." Dean forced a grin and gestured toward Mitch. "Hit it."

Mitch just stared at Tamblyn, slack jawed. Dean smacked his arm and hissed, "Dude. Time to start."

Mitch shook himself. "Right. Sorry." He tapped the tablet and advanced past the title slide to an image of him at the lawn mower. "Mowing's fine when you've got gas or a plug. But what happens when you lose one or the other?"

The presentation flowed smoothly from there. They progressed from powering a blender to a lawn mower to a scooter; they projected 3D diagrams and explained the Power Pill innards; told jokes and role-played a retail transaction; they even enlisted Sam to connect a Power Pill to a microwave to demonstrate ease of use.

Through it all, Tamblyn nodded and chuckled at their jokes, raising an eyebrow occasionally as the Power Pill activated bigger and more energy-intensive equipment. But toward the end, she sighed and glanced at her watch. *Not good*, thought Dean. *Maybe this last bit will get her.*

Mitch unveiled the pièce de résistance—their Power Slab. Wayne had managed to remotely align it with the prefab module's circuit strip. He hit a switch and plunged the room into darkness, then flipped on the Power Slab. The fixtures came to life and the three of them raised their arms triumphantly. "Voila! Let there be light!" Dean declared.

"From Leonardo to the Almighty," said Tamblyn. "Very impressive, gentleman, especially given that you're just freshman. I'm glad to see that CSM continues to develop good minds."

Mitch high-fived him. Wayne clenched a fist and whispered, "Yes."

"But," she continued, "Tamblyn already has quite a few energy initiatives. This year, we need interns with transport engineering experience. So, I'll pass. If you think of something more along those lines, feel free to apply to the next intern cycle." She got up to leave.

Dean couldn't believe it. "Now, wait a minute," he said, following her.

Sam intercepted him. "Hold tight," she whispered as she followed Tamblyn to the door.

But Dean was having none of it. "What do you mean hold tight? We worked really hard on all of this. She can't just half listen, act bored, and then walk away."

Tamblyn cocked an eyebrow. "Your brother's a feisty one."

"Damn right I am—"

"Dean," warned Sam.

"—and for good reason," he continued. "We demoed quality tech and we're a quality team. I wrote every line of software that connects every piece of equipment in here. All these devices? Wayne made them—using *your* 3D printer, by the way—in less than a week. He's a brilliant engineer. And Mitch is unbelievable. The Power Pill came from his mind. He made energy from thin air. He's a mad genius."

"Your point?" said Tamblyn.

"We deserve better."

"Oh, you do, do you? All I see here are glorified batteries. You got what you deserved, which was more than enough of my time. Good day." She headed toward the door.

Sam was mortified. "I'm sorry, Cecilia."

"Not a problem. They're welcome to try again next year."

Mitch picked up his backpack and thrust it at Tamblyn. "There are other applications!"

Dean exchanged a surprised look with Wayne. They both knew what Mitch had in his pack. *Is he really going there?*

Tamblyn sighed. "Young man, unless it can move a communications satellite from here to California in less than a day, I'm not interested."

"How about in less than a second?" Dean's heart skipped a beat. *Mitch went there!* But how much further would he go?

"Pfft. Impossible." Tamblyn opened the door and said to Sam, "Who's next?"

"It's not impossible," said Mitch, speaking quickly. "You just need a quantum entanglement processor to open the gateway." The words tumbled out all at once, leaving him breathless.

This stopped her. "Where did you hear that?"

"I didn't hear about it. I experienced it."

"Unlikely, young man. The QEP is a fairy tale—a nice theory that never worked. I should know. I was the one who went down the rabbit hole looking for it. Came up empty... and burned."

"It exists," Mitch insisted. "We used it." He gestured toward the Power Pills like they were evidence.

"And you expect me to believe your batteries are some kind of proof? Or are you hoping to lure me back down the rabbit hole? Either way, I'm not biting. Nice try, though."

"For crying out loud," said Dean. "Didn't you hear what Mitch said? We don't have to *try*. There is no rabbit hole. We've *done* it already. It works!"

"A little too well," added Mitch. "We..." His face fell and he looked ready to launch into the whole story of Jin and Chung, Dear Leader, and the assassin.

That's not gonna help, thought Dean. "Mitch, don't—"

But Wayne jumped to Mitch's defense. "If we want Tamblyn's help, Dean, she ought to know what happened."

"I already know what happened," Tamblyn said. "Mr. Software here hacked into the DARPA archives, found my name on the QEP specs, and convinced the rest of you to pretend like you had magically found a way to bring it to life, hoping to impress me. Did I get that right?"

"Only if you meant to insult us," said Wayne.

Dean threw up his hands. "Unbelievable. You are so wrong, and so full of yourself."

Sam's eyes blazed. "Dean, please!"

"Sam, she called me a hack. She's dismissing us outright. It's no use talking to her, guys."

"Then why don't we show her instead," said Mitch. He opened his backpack and pulled out the router.

Wayne regarded him somberly. "Mitch. No going back after this. Dean and I are good, but... you sure about this, brah?"

Mitch nodded. "Yeah. Thanks for asking, though." He attached the router to the Power Slab, then hooked his Jump!GO fob to his phone. Turning back to Tamblyn, he said, "Here's your proof."

Dean held his breath, worried that with Sam and CC Tamblyn as witnesses, the router would fail—awful payback for his boasting. But just as it had in those secret moments of joy they'd stolen throughout the month, the plasma grid flared to life beside Mitch: big, blue, and bedazzled with thousands of embedded jewels of light.

Mitch zeroed in on the San Francisco quadrant of the grid and triggered the nearest light hole. As it expanded, the Ferry Building at the Embarcadero came into the view. The salty smell of the wharf wafted through the hole as did the clacking of an approaching streetcar across Market Street.

Sam's jaw dropped. Leaning toward Dean she said, "Is *this* what you guys worked on over winter break?"

"Uh huh," said Dean, beaming with pride. "Not such a screw up now, am I? Ow!" Sam had punched him hard in the arm.

"My god," Tamblyn whispered. She closed the door and slowly walked over to the plasma grid, reaching out to touch it, but stopping short and eying it suspiciously instead. "Sam, turn the projector off."

Dean rolled his eyes. "You still don't get it. Go on, Sam. Flip the switch. Watch it not disappear."

Sam disconnected the monitor from Dean's tablet. The plasma grid held strong.

Tentatively, Tamblyn held her hand in front of the light hole, the opening expanding wider the closer she got to it. "It's... it's not a projection," she breathed. "It's actually there."

"You can even step through," said Mitch. "See?" He jumped into the light hole, landing easily on the sidewalk in front of the Ferry Building.

Wayne tossed him a headset and activated his own. "I'll verify stability." He closed the forgotten presentation, replacing it with the Jump!GO's standard monitoring software. The stability graph spiked at the connection, then a timer displayed on the screen. "Okay, you've got nine minutes," said Wayne.

"Time enough to visit the Donut Farm," Mitch said. He stretched his arm through the light hole, beckoning Tamblyn. "Come on over. I'll buy you an apple fritter."

"Can people see me standing here talking to you?"

"As far as we can tell, no one notices anything as long as we stay close to the light hole. They won't see us until we move away from it. Then it's like we were always wherever the hole dumps out. We think." Wayne waved at him from behind Tamblyn and pointed at his watch. "Wanna come over and test the theory?" Mitch asked.

She ignored him and inspected the opening instead as if hoping to find a hidden wire or trick mirror. When neither appeared, she shifted focus to the Power Slab.

Mitch shrugged. "Suit yourself."

"Hey." Dean passed some bills through the hole. "Buy me a matcha fig donut?"

Mitch waved away his money. "My treat," he said with a grin and trotted off.

Shaking her head impatiently at the Power Slab, Tamblyn reached for the router.

Wayne gritted his teeth. "Don't touch that, please." He said it politely, in the flat, "Wayne" way that Dean had always interpreted to mean "Step the frig off." Dean didn't blame him. Mitch was in transit and they had no backup router. If she messed it up, Mitch would be stuck.

Tamblyn must have recognized the undertone. She raised an eyebrow, then picked up the router anyway, bringing it close to her face and examining it from different angles. "This is nothing like my design," she said, almost to herself. "Yet you managed to create the same effect, though clearly it's unstable. That you even *know* about quantum processors is suspect."

"Why would it be?" asked Wayne. "Dr. Bische talked about quantum processing as if it was an industry standard." He stared daggers at her hands.

She smiled a little and put the router down. "Dr. Bische?"

"Their academic advisor," said Sam.

"Never heard of him," she said, turning to Dean. "Is he a hacker like you?"

"I'm not a hacker," Dean said defiantly. "For the last time, we didn't steal this info. What's so hard to believe?"

The plasma grid flickered, the first sign the gateway was starting to degrade. Wayne checked the timer and spoke into his headset. "One minute left, Mitch."

"Only seven people knew about the QEP, and only one of them is in this room," she pointed to her chest. "This Bische person definitely wasn't involved, and we didn't advertise. If he knew about it—"

"Whoohoo!" At that moment, Mitch leapt back into the room. The grid sputtered, then winked out entirely. Mitch laughed and handed Dean his green pastry. "Made it with time to spare. So, what do you think?" he asked Tamblyn.

"She thinks we're idiots and that Bische is a thief," said Wayne coldly.

"Huh. The old guy at Cheyenne Mountain had the same reaction."

"Wait a minute," said Tamblyn. "Do you mean in Colorado Springs?"

"Yeah. That's all part of the story Wayne said you should know about but we haven't gotten to yet."

"This 'old guy' wouldn't happen to have been Scott Travers, would he?"

"That's right," said Mitch. He and Wayne exchanged glances. "You know him?"

"Uh, oh," said Sam.

Dean frowned and shrugged at them. "What?"

Tamblyn headed back to the door, "I am definitely out. No way am I getting involved again with my ex's questionable science."

"Your ex?" said Dean. And then the light bulb went off inside his head. "Oh, *now* I remember your voice! You're the fail-safe!"

"I'm the what?"

"The safety vortex for the QEP," Dean said. "We heard your voice when the gateway glitched and yanked Mitch out of a light hole and sent him to this observation room in Colorado Springs. That's where we met the old guy. He even called the voice 'CC.' Makes perfect sense."

She looked at Dean like he was a crazy person.

"Wow, Chambers. You only *just* now figuring that out?" asked Wayne.

"Oh, like you knew already," said Dean.

"About two seconds after she spoke. It's so obvious."

"Oh, dude," Mitch said to Wayne, looking relieved. "I'm so glad you noticed too. I thought I was having a PTSD flashback and kinda freaked. She even looked like that agent lady for a second."

"Well, she just said she's the old guy's ex."

"Oh. You mean Marion's their...? Wow."

Dean squinted at Tamblyn and nodded. "Yeah, I immediately saw the resemblance to Giganta. Great job you and the old guy did with her, by the way," he said sarcastically. "She's a real peach." *Ouch.* He cringed inwardly. That sounded bad even to his own ears. As soon as the words left his mouth, he knew he'd crossed the line.

"He used *my* voice?!" She didn't sound thrilled. "*And* involved our daughter in his madness?!" Now she looked outraged. *Yep, line crossed. She's pissed. Real smart, goofball,* Dean chastised himself. Things were taking a turn for the worst.

Mitch tried to salvage the situation. "First, ignore Dean. Second, we aren't, like, friends with the old guy. In fact, it's kind of a funny story. See—"

"Just... stop." Tamblyn held up a hand and took a deep breath. "I don't have time for this. Your interview is over. Pack your gear and get out."

Sam stepped in front of Mitch. "Cecilia, I'm so sorry about all of this. I had no idea," she said, shooting a quick glare at Dean. "But despite the origin of their work, you've got to admit the final product is incredible. Maybe you should hear their side of the story? There might be *some* part of their tech we can use."

Tamblyn said nothing, just stared at all of them for longer than Dean felt was comfortable or necessary. Finally, she said, "Alright, but I still want their equipment out of here." She paused and pointed at the router. "Except that. I want another look at it. Have security escort them and the router to my office after they've cleared out their pit. I'll get started with the next team." The conference room door slammed shut as she left.

Dean let go of the breath he'd been holding. "Thanks, Sam."

She whirled around, eyes flashing. "You should have told me," she said, her voice tight and quiet, the way it got whenever she was super angry. "I could have prepped her if I'd known. You always think I'm working against you, but I'm your *sister*. I try to *help* you. Always."

Dean felt the color creeping up his face but had no good retort for Sam's complaint. She was right. Embarrassed, he looked away.

She called security and arranged their escort. "They'll be here in ten minutes," she said as she put away her phone. She still sounded peeved, though not as much as before.

"We're sorry, Sam," said Mitch, trying to be the peacekeeper.

"Yes," added Wayne. "Our apologies. We definitely should have let you know."

"Love you both, but you aren't my brother. *You* aren't obligated to tell me anything."

Dean gathered his courage and looked up from the floor. "I'm sorry, Sam."

"That's better," she said. "You're forgiven. Next time try trusting me a little."

"Okay, but... Can you cut me some slack? Old habits die hard."

She gave him a playful punch in the arm. "For what it's worth, I think your presentation was excellent, both the Power demo and the magic doorway to San Fran. Mitch, when you opened that blue screen and then leapt into it, I thought I was having an aneurysm. My brain literally exploded. It was awesome."

Mitch smiled. "Thanks. We felt that way the first time too."

"Under different circumstances, CC would have accepted your team on the spot, but she got bad news this morning about funding cuts. Half the teams here will be rejected. Knowing you're somehow mixed up with Scott doesn't help your case."

"We aren't, really," said Mitch. "He's got nothing to do with what we've built. It's a fluke we know him and Marion at all."

"I'll buy that. But"—she stabbed her finger at each of them for emphasis—"when you get to her office, don't hold back. Spill all. Of. The. Beans. She's giving you a second chance, so tell her everything." With a reassuring nod, she left.

Wayne cocked an eyebrow at Dean and said, "'She's a peach?'"

"Yeah, I know. That was a bit much."

*****

They met up with Tamblyn and Sam again at the CEO's office during the lunch break and told their story as efficiently as possible. How Mitch had first trapped light in the clunky Canopy, how they'd shifted their work to Sam's garage to miniaturize the device for individual sales, how Hubert Wilkins had sold the original Canopy to North Korean spies, and finally, how Dear Leader's bodyguard and her brother had helped them thwart Dear Leader's plan to send a bomb through the Canopy to destroy Seoul.

Tamblyn asked a bevy of technical questions, giving Dean the impression that she was still searching for a flaw in their story. But they answered each question as directly and accurately as they could. The longer they talked, Tamblyn became less angry and more intrigued.

"So, Dear Leader's bodyguard, Jin Ae, destroyed your original Canopy and the resulting explosion brought down North Korea's spy headquarters?"

"Right," said Mitch. He'd become quiet and morose as more of the story came out. Now, he looked flat-out miserable. "When the satellite footage showed the building falling in on itself, I thought... " He stopped and swallowed.

Dean picked up the story. "We thought Jin and her brother Chung and their friend Kyung were all dead."

"And I felt responsible," Mitch blurted out. "Jin and Chung had become our friends and the Canopy nearly killed them. The explosion probably killed some of *their* friends too." He paused again, tears in his eyes.

Wayne put his hand on Mitch's shoulder and continued for him. "But the high-res satellite found them in the crowd near the base of the rubble. The guy working the satellite compared the number of people outside the building with an earlier count of the people inside, and the final tally was only off by ten or so. But who knows? Maybe some people left work early or called in sick that day."

"There was no way to know for sure, though," said Mitch, wiping his eyes with the back of his hand. "I'll never know."

"That's when Scott convinced you to shut the QEP down?" said Tamblyn.

Mitch nodded.

"And you're absolutely sure that it's *still* shut down?"

"It has to be." Mitch held up his Jump!GO. "Until we made our own, our fobs didn't work. They were exactly what you said—just glorified batteries."

"So, what made them work today?"

"You're looking at it," said Wayne, indicating the router in the middle of Tamblyn's desk.

"Young man, I'd like to believe you, but there's nothing special about this device. It looks no different from any other router."

"Open it up and you'll see the difference." Wayne handed her a screwdriver from his backpack.

She removed the shell of the router and stared quizzically at the conjoined Jump!GO circuit boards inside, nestled around the router's normal innards. "What am I looking at here?"

"Symmetry, mostly," said Wayne. "I like the things I build to be balanced. I often find that adding two of the same things to pre-existing equipment produces interesting results. In this instance, I combined two Jump!GO boards with the router's own board. I read an article about Rydberg atoms and on a whim included a quartz bridge. Nothing interesting happened until Mitch added the integral equation to the locator routine—"

"Ah, the 'Particle in a 3D Box'—"

"Right. That seemed to join the two field lattices into a kind of giant receptor capable of processing photonic quanta."

Tamblyn got a faraway look in her eye. "That's brilliant."

"Toldja he was good," said Dean.

"What made you realize the connection between those concepts?" she asked Mitch.

"Not sure, actually," said Mitch. He looked embarrassed. "I just kind of... thought it might work. My brain does that sometimes."

"It's true," said Dean. "We call it Mitch's 'Flash Face.' You can totally tell when it happens. He does this." Dean conjured a picture of the event in his mind and molded his own face into what he thought was a fairly good approximation.

"He turns into an idiot?" said Tamblyn. Wayne and Sam laughed.

Mitch was not amused. "I don't really look like that... do I?" His friends didn't answer.

Tamblyn cleared her throat. "Well, gentlemen. You've told your story and I believe you. But pardon my saying so: Campbell, you seem particularly traumatized by the whole experience. Why dive back into it?"

Mitch bit his lip, then said, "Because when we made the first Jump!GOs, before we knew about spies or the government or fail-safes, it was great. We'd explore light holes together and tweak the software... it all felt right. Like creating the Jump!GO was our destiny, what the three of us were supposed to do. Then, when Dr. Travers shut down the gateway and the Jump!GOs didn't work, it felt wrong, like a bad decision. It seemed as if, despite everything terrible that had happened, I chose the wrong solution. Does that make sense?"

Tamblyn locked eyes with him and nodded. "Perfect sense. If you promise to continue that level of commitment, and if my sources can confirm the major points of your story, I'll accept your team into the intern program."

"Yes!" said Dean. Wayne pumped his fist, and they exchanged high-fives.

Mitch, his eyes still locked with Tamblyn's, said, "Thanks, Dr. Tamblyn, but there also needs to be conditions."

She turned to Sam and said wryly, "These kids are amazing. By turns insulting, demanding, and unimpressed," indicating Dean, Mitch, and Wayne, respectively. "I might keep them around for those qualities alone. Alright, Campbell. What conditions?"

"First, help us put protections in place so that crazy people can't show up and misuse the tech. Second, we kind of told your daughter we wouldn't try to use the tech anymore. Maybe you could tell her we're spinning off your original design, so that she doesn't get mad?"

"She's pretty mean when she's mad," said Dean.

"Drives like a maniac too." added Wayne.

"Oh, lord, you *do* know her," said Tamblyn. "Anything else?"

"Lastly, even though we're interns, we're providing you with tech we developed ourselves. Our prototypes make your and the old guy's concepts commercially viable, so... I think Dean, Wayne, and I deserve to keep a percentage of it." He rushed the last part of the sentence, as if he wanted to say it all before losing his nerve.

Tamblyn inclined her head in approval. "Nicely stated, young man. Your true calling might be technological law."

Mitch blushed, but looked back at her hopefully. "I just want to make sure that my friends get credit for their work and that nobody dies or loses their country or anything."

"Commendable. But you are naïve to think you can create dynamite and not have some moron blow themselves or someone else to hell with it. Anybody can misuse anything. A harmless spoon can be sharpened into a deadly shiv. There's only so much about human behavior that we can control. I can't psycho-proof your tech." Mitch's brief burst of optimism faded.

"Having said that, I'll agree to match you with our legal counsel and one or two use-case specialists. They'll help you figure out safeguards for the tech and build protections into its ultimate release. But I can't promise you solutions that will assuage your guilt, Campbell. I'm an entrepreneur, and if you agree to work for me and share in developing this technology, I will also be your boss. Nothing about those two things is slated to help you sleep better at night. You'll have to figure out how to do that all on your own. Agreed?"

"What about the other two conditions?"

"Sam is your advocate. She'll walk you through the paperwork needed to ensure you get credit and keep as much of a percentage control over your designs as our standard contractor agreements allow. As for Marion... well, let me worry about her." Tamblyn offered Mitch her hand. "Good?"

Mitch returned the handshake. "Good."

"Welcome to the TIM program, gentlemen."

"Whoohoo!" exclaimed Dean. He and Wayne took turns shaking Tamblyn's hand.

*****

Ninety minutes of paperwork later, Dean, Wayne, and Mitch were set free.

"It's a new day for us, guys," said Dean as they left the building. "It's not just about summer jobs anymore. We're creators again!"

"And think of all the equipment and cutting-edge tech we'll have at our disposal while we're here," said Wayne.

"I suppose," said Mitch. "Right now, it feels like we made the right decision to tell her about the router and the Jump!GOs. But what if we get into it and some new crazy person comes along?"

"She already told you, Mitch. We're gonna build in controls, add legal safeguards. It'll be fine," Dean assured him.

Mitch brightened. "You're right. Tamblyn Tech's filled with smart people. They'll help us work something out."

"Exactly," said Dean. "It's a multi-billion-dollar company full of lawyers and geniuses. With all that firepower backing us, we can't help but succeed!"

"I tell ya', it's enough to make you want to go somewhere for ten minutes to celebrate," said Wayne.

"Sunset at the Queen Mary?" suggested Mitch.

"People watching at the Wonder Wheel?" offered Dean.

Then the three of them stopped and said simultaneously, "Footlong dogs at Nathan's!"

"We'll just about make it." Mitch fired up his Jump!GO, dialed in the Coney Island hotdog stand, and jumped on through.

Darn near perfect day for the Three Musketeers, thought Dean.

CHAPTER 8

Outshined

Two weeks later, Mitch, Dean, and Wayne arrived at Tamblyn Tech for orientation. This was their third trip to the Golden, Colorado campus, but their first real view of the whole facility.

Sam had been their escort for the other two trips: the one a couple of weeks ago for the TIM competition and once last semester to pick up the 3D printer and integrated circuits they'd used to build the Jump!GOs. Both times, Sam had driven to the same row of buildings and parked in the same exclusive, executive lot. They had taken an elevator to and from wherever, never saw more than ten employees, and left whatever building the exact the same way. Both trips had left Mitch with the impression that the Tamblyn Tech campus was no bigger than a strip mall.

When Sam dropped them off that morning at the same squat row of buildings, his heart sank. He'd half expected their lab to be next door to a Snappy Nails. Maybe a froyo. *Mmmm. Being near a frozen yogurt shop might actually be a perk.* He carried that happy thought with him into Human Resources.

They spent the next hour getting their badges and filling out even *more* paperwork and listening to the legal team explain interning do's and don'ts. Then a burly guy named Kurt stood up and said, "Okay, people. Make sure you've got your badges on. Time to take the grand tour!"

Yes.

Next came the longest two hours of Mitch's life. Kurt led them on an extensive tour of the main campus that included a veritable onslaught of auditoriums, clean rooms, cubicle farms, gyms, warehouses, and food courts, all populated by what felt like thousands of Tamblyn Tech employees. There was even a campus-wide tramway for the complex that connected the endless buildings in one gigantic loop. By the time they reached the company's private airstrip, Mitch was starting to feel a bit overwhelmed.

"Betcha they show us the doomsday bunker next," whispered Dean.

"It's six miles down and houses half a million employees," Wayne whispered back.

"But below *that* is the newly terraformed Earth-2," added Mitch. "It houses two million employees plus a quarter million temps."

"It's infinitely powered by a geothermal vent," said Dean.

"And next door to the vent? There's a froyo and a Great Clips."

They muffled their laughs with their jackets and hands. "A Great Clips," gasped Wayne. "Okay, Mitch wins."

Thankfully, the airstrip was the last stop on the tour. Kurt ushered the group into several tram cars, and one by one each team was deposited at a building with a designated minder to escort them to either a machine shop, or a lab, or a combination room, called a machlab. "It's like the O-negative of workspaces," said Kurt. "A great, all-purpose room for cross-discipline projects."

Mitch, Dean, and Wayne had been assigned to a machlab at the outside rim of the tramway, near the base of Lookout Mountain. Their minder—a friendly, pretty woman with blue- and gold-tinted hair named Darasimi Cumel—pointed the room out as they approached the tram's final stop before it looped back around.

"Alright, guys, this is us," she said. They followed her to the end of the corridor and into a spacious, tidy white room with power tools on one side, standard lab equipment on the other side, and computer workstations interspersed among the apparatuses.

On a bench lining the back wall sat an Ursula T2, an almost exact replica of their own beloved 3D printer back in Sam's garage. "Excellent," said Wayne, patting the top of the machine. "I already feel at home."

"Good deal," said Darasimi. "The first thing you should do is choose a workstation and login. Your credentials are in your orientation packet. You'll probably get prompted to take some training right away."

"Oh, we already know how to work most of this equipment," said Mitch. He'd gravitated to the machining side of the shop and was examining the metal lathe.

"Sweet," she said, "but it's not that kind of training. These are standard compliance and safety classes. They're no big deal, we all need to take them. Just choose 'C' every other answer and you'll be done in an hour or so."

Mitch smiled. "Great tip."

Wayne had joined him in inspecting the power tools. "Is there a supply room?" he asked. "We need some gear." He took a list from his pocket and handed it to her.

"Wow," she said. "This is some pretty advanced measuring equipment. What's your project about, again?"

Mitch and Wayne exchanged glances. Sam and the legal department had made it clear that to avoid leaks, they shouldn't talk about the router or the Jump!GOs with other employees or interns. Not even their minder should be told exactly what they were doing. Mitch parroted the legal team's canned answer. "A passive energy power cell."

"Ah, gotcha. I guess this stuff makes sense now. In your orientation packet there are instructions on how to submit a work plan. Just create one of those and forward it to Supply. If it's not too heavy, a drone'll come by and drop off whatever you need within two hours. If it is heavy, a stockman will drop it off by the end of the day."

"Can't we go and get gear ourselves?"

"Trust me, you don't want to. The lines are incredible. And besides, the work plan might get rejected and you'd make the trip to the stock rooms for nothing. This way is better."

Mitch didn't think so. In fact, it sounded clunky and inconvenient, but he kept that thought to himself. *Probably shouldn't argue with real employees the first day.*

"Sounds convoluted," said Dean from across the room. Mitch covered his mouth to muffle a snort. So much for tact.

Dean had claimed a bench on the lab side and had already set up his tablet from school. He squinted at it, grim-faced, and shook it every couple of seconds as if it were broken. "Is the network down?"

"Shouldn't be. What site are you trying to get to?" Darasimi asked, crossing the room to look over Dean's shoulder.

"The student site at Mines."

"Hey, my alma mater," she said. She activated the workstation on his bench and typed in the address. The site appeared immediately. "Looks like the network's working for me. Wonder if my student account's still active."

An impish smile crossed her lips as she tried to log in. "Invalid Account" flashed on the screen in big red letters and she snapped her fingers. "Darn, locked out. But you're a current student. There's the page. Have at you."

"So weird. I wonder why my tablet can't connect."

"Kurt already explained that, but I don't blame you for forgetting. The tour was loooong," she said with a laugh. "Corporate blocks personal machines from the network. Only encrypted, trusted workstations have network access. More of that security stuff I mentioned."

"All of our programs and notes for the project are on our tablets. How are we supposed to transfer files from them to the workstations?"

"You could upload them to a CSM folder, log in to your account, and transfer that way."

"But these programs are huge. That'll take forever!" said Dean. Mitch winced. He understood Dean's frustration, but even to his ears, Dean sounded like an entitled complainer.

It was Darasimi's turn to squint. Her attitude up to that point had been good-natured and amused. Now she stepped back and wrinkled her nose. "You're Samantha Chambers' brother, right?"

Dean flushed red and mumbled, "Um, yeah... "

"She's head of R&D... probably why you guys got assigned to a nice, new machlab. You could ask her to pull some strings for you."

"No, I didn't mean—"

"Add a loophole for family. Allow *your* device on the net." She folded her arms across her chest. "For the rest of us, though, there's *rules.* And *we* need to leave our personal machines at home. That's what *I* was told to do, but you know, ask your sister." She looked at her watch. "I gotta get back to my lab and check some things. It's across the hall. Holler if you need me." She left abruptly.

"Guess I stepped in that one, guys," said Dean. "Sorry."

Wayne walked to Dean's side of the room and patted his shoulder sympathetically. "No worries. You get one goof a day and now yours is out of the way."

"Right. It's just the first day," said Mitch. "I bet as the week goes on, we'll get better at being corporate. If Sam can do it, we can too."

*****

They took Darasimi's suggestion and uploaded their files to a common folder on the CSM network. From there, it took less than an hour to transfer the router and Jump!GO apps to their machlab workstations. That wound up being their only victory for the week. Wayne's assessment of the situation turned out to be more accurate than Mitch's. They screwed up one or more times each day as the week wore on.

All of them had held part-time jobs of one sort or the other during high school, especially Mitch, who lived with his retired grandparents and needed the extra cash to make ends meet. But their longest employer had been Bische, and while he ran his lab as strictly as his class—enforcing standard processes and procedures—he also allowed them to make their own schedules, take breaks as they needed, and even play video games when things got slow.

Tamblyn Tech, on the other hand, had corporate rules. The guys couldn't start building until they'd submitted a work plan, could only order supplies as explicitly dictated by the work plan, couldn't exceed their stock room allowance else it would come out of their paychecks, and couldn't access most of the web sites outside of the Tamblyn network.

The network access at the exhibit hall during try-outs had been outside the company's firewall. Not true for the machlab. Try as they might, they couldn't get the router to authorize on the internal network. Their progress toward fixing the router's cycling issue slowed to a crawl. By the end of the week, all three of them were bristling and spent.

"Geez, Bische could be a hard ass, but at least we could come and go when we felt like it," said Dean. They were on one of their two fifteen-minute breaks.

"We also could use whatever we needed from his supply room," said Mitch.

"And he never restricted our use of the internet," added Wayne. He crunched down hard on a pretzel bite.

Mitch sighed. "We're getting nowhere with the cycling issue. Tamblyn Tech was supposed to help us get over our problems, but the only people we're allowed to talk to about them are Sam and CC, and they're terminally busy."

"Darasimi seems sharp," Wayne offered. "I bet if Dean apologizes and we explain it to her, she'd have some good ideas."

"I just said we're only supposed to talk to Sam and CC."

"So? We do it anyway and beg forgiveness later. Besides, I doubt she'd blab."

"Guys," said Dean, "maybe interning was a mistake. I mean, what would happen if we just packed up our tent and went?"

"Can't do it," said Wayne, "as much as I would like to."

'Why?" asked Mitch and Dean simultaneously.

"Didn't you listen in any of the legal meetings during orientation?"

"No," they said together again.

"If we leave before the end of the contract, or convince someone else to bankroll the project, we have to pay Tamblyn Tech back for the money they invested while we were on site. It's only been a week, so it's likely we only owe a few grand, but I'd rather spend my money on tuition. We're gonna have to suck it up and work within the system."

"Crud puppet."

"French biscuits."

Wayne bit into his last pretzel and sighed. "At least the snacks are free."

Break-time ended, and they headed back to the machlab grumbling.

*****

The following Monday, they applied themselves to adjusting.

"We've got local data, guys!" Wayne declared after finally updating the router's authorization routine. "Try opening a light hole."

The plasma grid sprang out of Mitch's fob. "Whoohoo!"

To celebrate, Dean leapt to Sutter's Pub and brought back a round of root beers and nachos for them to share. Morale improved considerably.

Over the weekend, Mitch had written down questions for Darasimi that seemed innocuous enough on the surface, but which when answered might give them clues as to why the router cycle continually crashed. After their nacho break, he handed the list to Dean and pushed him across the hall to her lab.

She glanced up when they walked in but continued to solder. "Oh. Ms. Chambers' brother. What do you want? A gold-plated microscope or something?"

Dean blushed. "Hey, I'm sorry about last week. I'm an idiot and I was out of line. You can kick me out if you like," he said, striking a sincerely conciliatory tone while adding in a dash of his natural charm. "But we're stuck and need your smarts to help us. If you have a minute, that is."

She placed the soldering iron back in its cradle and with a slight smile said, "Humility. Nice. I'll give you five minutes. What's the problem?"

Dean called Mitch over, and together they walked through the questions. As Wayne had predicted, she had good answers. They thanked her profusely and ran back to implement her suggestions. By the end of the day, they'd manage to double the router's connection time. It wasn't perfect, but at least they weren't stuck anymore.

The week progressed. To save time each day, they met the night before to discuss how they would approach the next day's problems and what materials they needed for each approach. After that they would submit the work request to Darasimi. Finally, they were getting the hang of the processes.

On Thursday, Darasimi poked her head through the door. "Heads up, guys. Boss is coming."

Seconds later, CC Tamblyn arrived. "Progress, gentlemen?"

Mitch spoke up. "Yes, ma'am. We've got router stability up to twenty minutes."

"Well, that's something. Listen, the board is curious about your project. Any chance you can do the same demo for them you did for me? Minus the insults?"

"If you want us to," said Mitch, tentatively. "But... it might be better to wait until we get the whole stability issue resolved."

"Just open a quick light hole, let the board members jump in and out, then shut it down. That's all. I'll hustle them away right after and you can get back to work. Good?"

"I guess," said Mitch reluctantly.

The next day, CC showed up with about ten board members in tow.

"Whoa," whispered Dean while they set up chairs to accommodate the crowd. "Have we ever jumped with this many people before?"

"I don't think so," Mitch replied. "It'll take a long time coaxing them all through one hole. Maybe we should use two Jump!GOs?"

"Too risky. We've only tested one fob at a time. What happens if the router freaks and the other fob goes out?"

"That wouldn't look good."

Wayne had joined them. "Not good at all. Let's open a hole to the Embarcadero and take only one or two of these guys along for the ride," he suggested. "It's a wider space and they'll definitely see they're in a different city."

"K. Fingers crossed," said Mitch. He laid his Jump!GO face-up in one hand and covered it with the other. Once CC and the board members were seated, he walked to the center of the room and waited.

The group ignored him. Many continued conversations they'd started before entering the room. A few others checked their phone messages. One guy on the end scowled at him as if he didn't want to be there—or thought Mitch *shouldn't* be there. Mitch felt his meager confidence ebbing.

Then CC caught his eye. Conspiratorially, she glanced toward the group and rolled her eyes. A little of his confidence returned. "Are you ready, Mr. Campbell?" she asked, her voice even, but just loud enough to command everyone's attention. The group quieted down. She winked at him. "We're all ears."

Taking a deep breath, Mitch launched into his spiel. "Hello, everyone. Let's imagine the future. Imagine you could go from New York to Nairobi, from California to Canada, or Denver to Denmark in a matter of seconds. Imagine holding the key to instant travel right in the palm of your hand."

Mitch unfolded his hands dramatically, ensuring the Jump!GO's pulsing blue plasma swirl was visible to all.

"Ladies and gentlemen," he continued, "you don't have to imagine. The future is now. Say hello to the Jump!GO. Welcome to the future of travel!"

He held the device out for each board member to see and they followed his movements with raised eyebrows and appreciative nods. *Nailed it.*

"Oh, isn't that pretty!" one of them commented. "It looks like a giant opal."

"Is that all there is to it?" the scowling man demanded. "It's too small. Looks more like a toy than 'the future of travel.' No one will take it seriously." The man waved his hand dismissively.

"We think of the size as a selling point," said Wayne. "Compact. Convenient. Simple."

"If it's so simple, why isn't it finished yet?"

"Marvin, please," said CC. "It's just a demo. There's still weeks' worth of work. You can grill me about the schedule once we get past prototyping."

"Aren't these kids the ones responsible for that CSM debacle a few months ago? The school almost had a major lawsuit on its hands when you boys couldn't deliver the product people payed for. Do you want a lawsuit of your own, Tamblyn?"

CC's lips thinned. "This is a new formulation. And what happened at CSM is beside the point. If you let the demo proceed, you'll be pleased with the product as well as the current level of progress."

Marvin's frown deepened, but he settled back into his chair. CC gestured for Mitch to continue. Mitch had more prepared remarks, but given this Marvin character's reaction, he opted to replace words with action. *Jump holes* are *more impressive than speeches.*

He triggered the plasma grid, expanded the Embarcadero's light hole, and evoked the gasps and exclamations of surprise he'd come to expect when people first experienced the Jump!GO. The Marvin guy stared at Mitch with cold, dead eyes, but he had stopped complaining.

"Is that a portal?" asked the board member who'd made the opal comment, her voice full of wonder. "Can we enter it? I want to experience it myself."

"I was just about to ask for a volunteer," said Mitch.

He leaped into the hole first, and then held out his hand to help her over. As soon as she landed in front of the Ferry Building, she grabbed his arm in excitement. "This is fantastic!" she said. "I would have never believed it if you had just described it. Emily!" she called back through the hole. "You must come see!"

"No, wait—" said Mitch, but Emily moved too quickly, stepping across the threshold to join her friend as she gazed at the Bay Bridge. The other board members followed eagerly, ignoring Mitch's attempts to keep them on the machlab side of the light hole.

Scowlin' Marvin brought up the at the tail end while he resumed his litany of complaints.

"Why is the hole so small? Shouldn't it accommodate more than one person? It's too rinky-dink. No one will be interested in a device the whole family can't use."

"Mitch," Wayne cautioned, "we're reaching the stability limit. You've got three minutes, tops, to get everybody back."

Yikes. "People, we need to move!" He was done with being polite. Firmly, he shoved board members back into the hole. He managed to get everyone through with 15 seconds to spare. Everyone except the ever-bitchin' Marvin. "Sir, the portal's closing. You need to move right now!"

"This is what I mean, Tamblyn. It's all pasted-together, slipshod work, and I think—" Like a window slamming down, the hole closed in front of him.

CC sighed. "Can we get him back?"

"If you really want to," said Wayne. He refreshed the router. Mitch triggered the plasma grid and the hole reopened.

"—lead to a mess, a complete commercial failure!" They'd been able to cycle the router and re-open the hole quick enough for Marvin to not even notice, but Mitch wondered if that was more a testament to Wayne's skill or an indication of Marvin's cluelessness.

Regardless of their hasty exit, most of the board members seemed satisfied with the Jump!GO, but Mitch could tell that several of them still had doubts. As the group filed out, CC turned to Mitch and said, "Good job, but leaving Marvin behind was too close for comfort. Out of everyone here, he can control your funding. We'll need to step up our game. I'll be around later."

"Crud puppet," said Dean as he closed the door on CC. "I thought we had a handle on it all. Guess there's more to do."

But where to begin again? Mitch wondered. He rubbed his eyes. "Did we take our two breaks already today?"

Dean shrugged. "I think so."

"Screw it," said Wayne. "We need one more. Let's go."

*****

They headed to the break room for chips and coffee. The stock price for every Tamblyn Tech division scrolled by continuously on a digital chyron tacked across the back wall. Above the scroll was the break room monitor, which seemed to be exclusively tuned to the Techline News channel. The "New Tech Central" segment was on, the perfect bit of popcorn to fill their fifteen minutes, so the guys grabbed seats at the table closest to the monitor and sat back to watch. An establishing shot of mountains and the Denver skyline implied that today's tech lord was, surprisingly, someone local. When the camera finally switched from the reporter to the interviewee, Mitch did a double take. "Guys, is that Christian Meadows?"

It was hard to tell, since Hubert Wilkins' ex-lab tech had never made that much of an impression. He was scrawny, quiet, and often appeared to be disheveled, unshaven, and unhappy. His only distinctive characteristic was his voice which was deeper than most and had a rich undertone. Mitch often thought Christian's voice should belong to someone else—someone with more confidence and a better haircut.

Mitch moved closer to the monitor to get a better look. Christian *had* gotten the haircut, a change of clothes, but also... something more. He seemed at ease, suave, kind of glowing, actually. Behind him, Mitch heard Wayne smack his lips and whistle. "Hello, handsome. Somebody's been to the gym."

"Hey, Wayne, what's he doing wearing your old jacket?" asked Dean.

Wayne's mouth crooked up into a half smile. "I might have lent it to him last semester."

"Oh, ho! That sounds like a story."

"Not as much of one as you think."

Mitch tuned them out. It was weird seeing someone he knew giving a national interview. He must have created something really hot.

The scene shifted to show Christian guiding the reporter through a lush office park to a warehouse with the words "Quantum Technologies" stenciled into the door.

"He eschews the moniker 'Wunderkind,' " the reporter was saying in voiceover, "but is not shy about his hopes for his startup."

Christian faced the camera. "Here at Q-Tech, we believe our products will be revolutionary." The camera panned back to show him standing inside of a gray, gleaming, three-sided enclosure with a keypad embedded in its back wall. A sign above box read "Q-Pod." He tapped the keypad and said, "In fact, we expect them to change the world." A portion of the Q-Pod's back wall disappeared, replaced by a nighttime image of the Eiffel Tower in the distance.

Mitch's jaw dropped. *Oh, no!*

Then Christian stepped into the scene, proving it to be much more than a video projection. Dean jumped up from the break room table. "Holy shit!"

"You may think this is some kind of trick photography," the reporter's voiceover continued. "But I assure you it isn't. I've experienced it." She walked into the frame of the camera and joined Christian in Paris, eyes ablaze with excitement. "It's all made possible by a discovery first made at his alma mater, the Colorado School of Mines."

"Some first-years stumbled upon the idea, but they were too inexperienced to develop it completely," Christian explained. "The Q-Tech staff is full of all-stars, however. We've matured the technology and brought it fully to fruition." The camera panned across the warehouse showing white-coated, serious-faced scientists and goggle-wearing engineers in deep, possibly staged conversations. Mitch was surprised to see Larry Knight among them.

Christian went on to explain the Q-Pod. "It can be installed like a subway facility but would require only a small building and no underground digging. No additional infrastructure is required. Each pod is self-contained, with its own power and technological spine, functioning much the same as a utility pole. Civic leaders can use it as clean energy replacement for buses, taxis, light-rail stations, etc."

"There are even plans for personal versions of the Q-Pod," said the reporter.

An animation played out across the screen. Against the backdrop of the downtown Denver skyline, a faceless cartoon figure produced a round disk from their pocket and dropped what looked like a glowing drop of water into a recess at the disk's center. Then the cartoon stepped on the disk and blinked out of existence, only to reappear in a different city, Denver's skyline replaced by London's Tower Bridge.

"It's basically physical movement through dynamic entanglement using the collected components in this disk as a kind of monitoring agent," Christian explained. "The official name on the patent is Bipartite Entanglement Activity Monitor. We're calling it BEAM for short."

The reporter stood alone in front of the camera for the wrap-up. "Quantum Technologies is an emerging company, meaning all of its products are in the prototype stage. But the buzz surrounding Q-Pod and BEAM is strong, and industry insiders say big investors are taking notice. That will certainly be the case when Q-Tech officially debuts its product line at this year's Tech Convergence Conference. While it's true that Q-Tech is the new kid on the block, it seems well positioned to become the wave of the future."

The camera panned away from the reporter to a video playing on a monitor embedded in the wall behind her. A single, white particle bounced onto the screen, emitted a squiggle of light that expanded into a wave, and then swirled into a "Q." Eventually, it spelled out the full name of the company, "Quantum Technologies."

"I'm Chithra Muraleekrishnan for Techline News." The segment ended.

"Sweet logo," said Dean.

Mitch was dumbfounded. Not only had Christian stolen their tech, but he'd made it seem infinitely cooler than they ever had.

"At least he mentioned us as the creators," said Wayne.

"Indirectly, as if we were both stupid *and* incompetent," said Mitch.

"Well, of course he did," said Dean angrily. "It makes his own story better. You can't pretend to be a genius if you stole someone else's work."

Their phones buzzed simultaneously. Mitch looked at his messages. "Did you guys just get a summons from CC Tamblyn?"

Wayne looked at his phone. "Yup. Let the firing commence."

"Damn," said Dean. "I was just getting the hang of working at this place."

Time to face the music. Maybe the reporter was wrong, thought Mitch. Maybe she was in on the scam and it was all photographic trickery. He had no idea what he'd say to Tamblyn. "Why do I keep losing control of the one great thing I've done?" Miserably, they headed toward the tramway.

*****

"Why in hell didn't you tell me someone else besides the North Koreans got a hold of your tech?" They'd barely closed the door to her office before CC laid into them.

"We didn't know," said Mitch, which wasn't exactly a lie. They knew the original Canopy that wound up in Dear Leader's basement had started off in Hubert Wilkin's hands and that Christian worked for Hubert, but it had never occurred to them that with Hubert in jail Christian would strike out on his own with their tech.

"So, who stole from whom?" she asked.

"He stole from us, obviously. We were first. We can prove that."

"It's *not* obvious, Campbell. What this Meadows character showed off today looks a helluva lot like the functionality you told me was your own."

"Because it *is* our own tech. What Christian did is different."

"Yeah, his version's way cooler," Wayne said dryly.

Mitch covered his eyes. "Dude, you aren't helping."

"Hirano isn't wrong," said CC. "Once the board members see that interview and compare Meadows' slick outfit against your raw demo, I'll have some explaining to do. And right now, I don't know how I'll explain that your clearly immature product is superior to the one that Techline News just anointed."

"Immature?" said Mitch. Suddenly his cheeks felt hot. "The only thing immature about our tech is the gateway, and it wouldn't be if you were helping out like you said you would!"

"Campbell—"

"I get it, we have a cycling problem. Our demo wasn't as polished as Christian's.

But our devices work. It's still instant travel. The underlying hardware is sound." he insisted. "On top of that, the Jump!GO is way more convenient. It fits in your pocket and attaches to a phone, something everyone has."

"Exactly," said Dean. "Christian's disk thing looked super bulky."

"And an interview with smug comments and animations isn't proof his tech even works," added Wayne.

"Enough!" said CC. "You each have a point, but the monthly call with the board is coming up. They are going to want an explanation as well as assurances. You've given me neither. I can bluff with the best of them, but I'd prefer something better."

"Maybe you can tell them it's actually a good thing Christian can reproduce our tech," Wayne offered. "It shows that the foundational principles are solid enough to support independent recreation."

CC sighed. "That works for science experiments, Hirano, not business. Commercially, external reproduction is suicide. When Amazon came on the scene, Sears didn't say 'Great. That proves mail-order isn't dead.' Sears struggled immediately. Then, Amazon ate them whole."

Mitch opened his mouth to protest, but realized he had no counterpoint for the argument.

"I am not ready to be eaten," said CC. "You need a solution to this cycling problem by close of business Friday. I'll send you my thoughts for resolution. Also, feel free to run ideas by Darasimi. Don't disappoint me." She shooed them out.

Well, at least they hadn't gotten fired.

CHAPTER 9

Wunderkind

Christian held open the door to Unit 411 of the Violet Street business park and flashed his well-practiced, handsome smile at every one of the corporate types that filed through it. Although his growing business, Quantum Technologies, occupied the whole facility, he'd taken to ending investor tours in 411 and showing off the spot where he had read Campbell's paper and gotten the idea for the company.

Today's group was special, comprised of the remains of Hubert's wealthiest donors as well as angel investors keen on finding the next unicorn. Their high-dollar donations had bought them a private demonstration of Q-Tech's most ambitious and impressive projects. But Christian wanted to build suspense as well as stall long enough for Larry Knight and crew to prep the warehouse for the big reveal. Unit 411 was the perfect place to kill ten minutes and milk his backstory for all it was worth.

He kept up a genial patter about what the facility represented and all that he hoped to accomplish once he secured enough funding. Then he switched on a video of his breakout Techline News interview from earlier in the week and let his brain go on autopilot.

He'd come a long way from the days of just a single bench, a swivel chair, and a tiny coffee pot—all thanks to the dew drops. *Amazing how much you can get done once you know the right buttons to push.* Building contractors and interior designers suddenly had openings in their schedule, offered you top-of-the-line materials, assigned their best workers to your project, all at a reasonable discount. As a result, the Q-Tech facility now possessed the level of panache and polish he'd always envisioned when dreaming of his own business empire.

Hubert had had big ideas, but he'd never seemed able to rise above his innate shabbiness. Working for Hubert had felt dirty, as if a thin coating of grime covered everything he touched. *That's where I'm different*, thought Christian, looking around the refurbished Unit 411. It sparkled. The decorations had a lushness to them that conveyed good taste and a healthy appreciation for wealth. The coffee pot shelf had been expanded into an espresso bar. The unit adjacent to this one had been converted into an employee kitchen, staffed 24-7 by a rotating cadre of student chefs. Even the security cameras had been upgraded, the bulky, intrusive kind replaced with smaller, sleeker versions.

At the back of the facility was a wide-open warehouse stocked with cutting-edge equipment, some of which he'd personally designed. The original bench and swivel chair still sat in a corner, as a reminder of his roots. They were all that remained of the "old days," which, when he'd thought about it, had only been a month ago. His business transformation had started the day he'd walked out of President Hayman's office, determined to be more than just another assistant professor. The investor group on the couches in front of him proved that he'd reached that goal.

The sound of applause pulled him out of his reverie. The Techline News interview had come to an end, and the investors were on their feet, watching him expectantly. The handsome, rakish smile returned to his face. "I take it you all are suitably impressed," he said. This prompted hearty chuckles from the group.

"With puff pieces like that, Meadows, how can we not be?" asked one of the investors. "Love the video, but I bet you didn't invite us here to watch your media team's animations."

"Very astute, Mr. Maxwell. What tipped you off? Is there a leak I need to plug?" This drew more laughter.

"Actually, the NDA I signed was a big clue. Or was I the only one who had to do that?" said Maxwell.

"I signed one."
"Me too."
"Same here."
"And no cameras, remember? He took our phones."
Others in the group chimed in, clamoring at Christian good-naturedly.

"Alright, alright," he said, "you *all* deduced it."

"Then, if you don't mind my saying so, stop beating around the bush. Tell us already!" said Maxwell.

"Tell you?" said Christian. "Why tell when I can show?" He opened the door to the warehouse. "After you, Mr. Maxwell."

More applause. "Now that's more like it." Maxwell walked through the door, and the rest of the group trailed after him. One last man, bringing up the rear, paused before entering.

"Christian! Aren't *you* moving up in the world."

It was Bertrand Pollux, ex-politician, local mine owner, and a Hubert holdover. He had never been a direct investor himself, but Christian had invited him, nonetheless. Bertrand's value lay in who he knew: regulators, appropriations managers, as well as a class of people who could only be referred to as obscenely rich. As long as Hubert had promised a 5% finder's fee, Bertrand reliably provided a steady stream of legitimate, lucrative investors. Christian intended to leverage him in the same way.

"I certainly hope so, Congressman."

Bertrand laughed and tapped his famous lapel pin—an American flag adorned with mining tools. He'd often brandished the pin when he was a congressman, claiming to be a "proud miner," which was laughable. Pollux was as much a miner as Jeff Bezos was a librarian. "I appreciate the honorific, my boy, and at heart I'll be a civil servant until the end, but given I lost the last election, it's just Bertrand."

"Bertrand, then. Thank you for bringing some friends today." Christian knew that was an understatement. Not only had Bertrand brought the Mayor with him for the tour, but he'd also managed to snag four of the biggest tech angels in the Mountain West.

"Glad to help you paper the house, as it were," said Bertrand, acknowledging the understatement with a knowing wink. "At least I can do that much with my meager influence."

Christian bowed slightly. It didn't hurt to recognize Bertrand's hand in bringing in the high rollers. "You and they are the only good thing to come out of my association with Hubert," he said, hoping that statement was enough to stroke the main's ego.

The ex-congressman shook his head. "Yes, yes, sad business, that." He leaned closer to Christian. "A financial disaster as well," he said quietly. "I lost a lot of money when Hubert went to jail. His auto-assay prototype would have been a true boon for my mining company. Strange how it disappeared before he was arrested."

Not really, thought Christian. Hubert had a habit of making deals then backing out of them when a better opportunity presented itself. 'More irons in the fire mean more profit,' he'd been fond of saying. But Christian saw no reason to share that tidbit with the congressman.

"Perhaps today will be the first step toward changing that," he said instead. "*If* I can convince this crowd that I'm not insane." They shared a laugh.

"Whether sane or not, my boy, can't wait to see what you've got in store for us today."

"Guess I better not keep you waiting." Christian ushered Bertrand through the door.

*****

Inside the warehouse, Larry had set up risers for the investor group, separating the seats from the demo space with yellow caution tape. The demo space was divided into two sections. On the left was a gray, oblong pod made of frosted plastic that stood ten feet tall and had a sliding door. To the right of the pod lay four raised disks, each disk wide enough for a person to stand on. Mounted behind the demo space hung a large, inactive viewscreen. Along the wall beside it, Larry was husbanding a cart full of controller tablets and several computer racks.

Christian grabbed a tablet and stood in front of the risers at the center of the demo space. "The man in the white coat to your right is my lead engineer, Larry Knight. Are we ready, Mr. Knight?" Larry grinned and flashed a quick thumbs-up. "Excellent," Christian replied. Positioning his finger dramatically above the tablet, he surveyed the audience and said, "Now, as Larry is fond of saying, 'Prepare to be dazzled.' "

He dropped his finger onto the tablet. The pod buzzed, the gray in its plastic walls transforming into a soft, inviting off-white. Christian reached out with his enhanced senses and found the thread of the group's collective energy. The wavelength for excitement stood out—excitement tinged with fear. He had their full attention.

"We call the enclosure to your left a Q-Pod, but *you* might call it the future of mass transportation. Let's see how it works, shall we? Does anyone have somewhere they'd like to go? Some place exotic perhaps? Just shout it out."

"Monte Carlo!"

"Tahiti!"
"Cabo San Lucas!"

"Monte Carlo sounds fun," said Christian. "Let's try the Sun Casino there." He slid the pod door aside and headed toward the back wall. With a thought and a flick of his wrist, he conjured a dew drop into the palm of his hand, but for the sake of the group he made it look as if the plasma ball had been in his pocket all along. He inserted it into the small control panel embedded near the top of the wall. The dew drop bobbed loosely within the panel's casing but after a few taps on the tablet it went rigid. Slowly, the soft white of the back wall dissolved to reveal a lavish room filled with slot machines. The group behind him gasped.

"It's just a projection," declared Maxwell.

"Oh, I assure you. It's quite real." Christian stepped across the threshold of the pod into the casino proper took a drink off the tray of a passing waitress, then stepped back into the pod, holding the glass high in a kind of salute. Maxwell's jaw dropped. Christian walked over to the man and handed him the drink. "Looks like you have a martini."

Maxwell sniffed the glass then took the tiniest of sips. His eyes grew wide, and in one motion he downed the drink. Turning to his fellow investors, he said, "That hit the spot!" His small joke elicited a nervous round of chuckles from the group.

"Care to experience it for yourself?" asked Christian. He held out a twenty-euro note as enticement.

"Free money, Marvin!"
"Take it and run!"

Several members of the group jeered in a genial way, egging him on.

Riding the wave of their encouragement, Maxwell took the bill from Christian, strode confidently into the pod and right up to the boundary between it and the casino. But he hesitated, foot poised just above the casino floor, as if he suddenly doubted the reality of its existence.

"Go on," Christian coaxed him with a smile. "You won't fall in." This drew more nervous laughter from the group.

As if testing the temperature of the pool, Maxwell dabbed his foot onto the casino's red and gold carpet. He did not disintegrate; the floor seemed to hold his weight. Convinced that no catastrophe would befall him, the investor stepped across the threshold and into the casino proper, craning his neck around in every direction, mouth open in disbelief. Then with a giggle and a mischievous glance back over his shoulder at the onlookers, he walked over to the nearest slot machine and inserted the bill.

Christian couldn't have planned it better. Maxwell had chosen a progressive slot sporting a hefty jackpot. With the thinnest of plasma tendrils, Christian reached across the boundary and into the machine, found the proper payout sequence, and smiled inwardly as the vocal investor was treated to a glorious jackpot. "Wahoo!" Maxwell whooped. Other casino patrons gathered round, congratulating him on his win. Once the slot manager arrived, Christian returned to the center of the demo space to address the investors in the audience, who stared back at him, rapt and expectant, no doubt waiting for their own pots of gold.

"Now, not everyone will be as lucky as our friend here. Your own mileage may vary." The group laughed heartily, their eyes glittering with excitement. They were eating out of the palm of his hand. "But the uses for this technology are obvious." He walked to the other side of the pod and inserted another blue glob. With a few more taps on the tablet, the pod's back wall bifurcated, with the Sun Casino and Maxwell on one side and Union Station in downtown Denver on the other.

"Mass transit will never be the same. If anything, it will be better." Union Station became the Washington Monument. "Icons of our nation will become instantly accessible. Financial institutions available at the touch of a button." The scene cycled through Wall Street, the New York Stock Exchange, Central Cardiff, Hong Kong, the Abu Dhabi Global Market. "Not even the sky is the limit."

Abruptly, the site within the portal shifted from the tall, floodlit buildings of the Al Maryah complex to a craggy, gray landscape illuminated by light of a different sort and dominated not by skyscrapers but a lone, octagonal structure, wrapped in amber foil and suspended off the ground by four spindly metal legs. The stiff, American flag to the left of the structure and the general blackness at the edge of the horizon made it clear just where the portal led.

"My god. That can't be real," gasped Bertrand.

"Believe your eyes, congressman. That *is* the moon, and this doorway I've opened to it demonstrates how Q-Tech's offerings can extend to asteroid mining and other space contracts, both government and commercially sponsored. The potential of our technology is out of this world. With the Q-Pod, planetary bodies and the resources they hold are just a stone's throw away." Christian produced a large pond pebble from his pocket and tossed it through the portal. It landed near the edge of the black horizon, the impact generating a thick plume of dust. His audience watched quietly as the regolith settled, the tenor of their brain waves vacillating between shock and amazement.

Triumphantly, he followed their gaze—and in that moment he stumbled. A wave of vertigo washed over him. As the darkness engulfed the pebble, it seemed to reach out toward Christian, drawing him closer to the portal, narrowing his vision, sucking him into the void—

Too far! the fugue of his internal chorus cried out. With an effort, he pulled himself away from the threshold. The dizziness vanished. No one in the audience had seemed to notice and their eyes still riveted to the moonscape.

Forcing a lightness in his tone he did not feel, Christian said, "But your destination need not be important or exotic. You can just as easily go to downtown Denver for a ball game at Coors Field." The scene switched back to Denver and the ballpark.

"The point is, in less than a second, anywhere is accessible with the right vector and the Q-Pod. No more need for planes, trains, or cars. Just dial in your location and away you go. It's eco-friendly, expedient, and expandable. Everyone will want to use it. Like coffee and breakfast, Q-Pods will be a license to print money."

Maxwell, his winnings in hand, returned to triumphant cheers. "And I thought I'd be giving away money today, not winning it!" he exclaimed.

"See what the rest of you have to look forward to?" said Christian. All was going well and according to plan. He took a deep breath. This next part of the demo required energy and concentration. There was the risk of disturbing the balance he'd created, of awakening the internal chorus of Christians if he extended too far. But to gain the backing of the angel investors, he was willing to take the gamble.

With a sweep of his hand across the tablet, Christian returned the pod to its original frosted gray. "Before continuing, let's all take a moment to welcome our Mountain West lions: Blanch Wagner, Don McCormick, Bill Thompson, and Tracey

Reid." He led the group in a round of applause directed at the angels. "Thank you for being here today. Your potential sponsorship can make all the difference for our little startup. In fact, you are critical to the next part of the demo."

The four high-rollers exchanged surprised expressions and glanced quizzically back at Bertrand. Bertrand, so approving just a moment ago, shot Christian a slightly panicked look and made a low slashing gesture with his hand in warning. Christian ignored him, opting to instead enjoy the air of suspense he'd generated with his cryptic comment. *I'm not Hubert, Pollux. You don't control me.* Everyone else seemed intrigued at least. *Let Bertrand wonder what I'm up to.*

"You've seen what our Q-Pod can do. But I bet you're still wondering about these disks on the floor. That's where our lions come in. May I ask the four of you to please come forward and step on these disks?"

Real fear showed now on Bertrand's face. Christian just grinned all the wider at him, and with a subtle nod he tapped into the ex-congressman's wavelength, adjusted it to his own, and conveyed to it, "Trust me." After a moment of confusion, Bertrand's face relaxed. *Now you know who's really in control.*

The four angels each stood by a disk. "Feel free to pick up your disk and give it a good look," Christian told them.

"No casinos for me," joked McCormick as he examined his disk. "Maxwell used up all the luck." They were all remarkably relaxed. Having Maxwell's experience be so positive had no doubt relieved any nervousness they'd initially had.

Christian motioned to Larry. The view screen came to life, divided into four equal quadrants, each a milky white. He then walked over to the disks and helped each investor strap on a slim headset equipped with a camera, ear pods, and a mouthpiece.

"I'm sure our Mayor would say that Q-Pods are well and good for municipalities," Christian said, giving Larry time to set up and test the investor headsets. "We fully expect lucrative government contracts and licensing to be Q-Tech's bread and butter. But not everyone is comfortable around the masses."

Larry signaled to Christian that his setups were completed, and then he trotted back to the main rack against the wall.

"The answer to that concern is of course the Personal Pod. Just like that hot Maserati or Aston Martin, you can also own your own personal gateway." The group oohed and aahed as they began to guess what was coming next. "Now, see that hole in the middle of your disk? It looks like a drop of water, doesn't it?" The angels nodded or shrugged.

He handed each of them a dew drop, again miming retrieving the globule from his pocket. "Let's fill that slot with a special energy ball that I like to call a drop of dew." One by one, the investors put the globule into the center hole of their disk. Each disk glowed a brighter blue, the light consistent with the color of each dew drop. An excited murmur bubbled up among the seated members of the group.

"Now stand on your disk."

They hesitated. "Don't worry," he said, adopting a soothing tone. "They're perfectly safe. Plus, Mr. Knight here is an EMT. If anything happens—and I assure you nothing will—he'll save you. Right, Larry?"

"I'll do my best," Larry replied modestly.

The investors did as they were told. Christian tapped his tablet yet again, and suddenly each person was encased in a shimmering tower of blue. The excited whispering of the others changed to gasps and surprised exclamations. And under cover of their chatter, Christian invoked four thin tendrils of light and snaked them along the floor to the edge of each disk.

"Ladies and gentlemen, say hello to BEAM, your personal travel assistant. Go ahead and try it. Say very clearly 'Hello, BEAM.' "

Each investor repeated, "Hello, BEAM."

"Hello," a male voice emanated from each tower, ethereal, mechanical, but also strangely human. If anyone had listened carefully, they may have recognized Christian's distorted baritone, but the fact of the BEAM speaking at all was likely distracting enough.

"Switch them to private mode, Larry." Larry flipped a couple of switches on the rack, awakening the investors' headsets and seemingly changing the towers to a deeper blue. To the larger group, Christian said, "Larry just engaged a damper field above that section of the room. That shouldn't be necessary for the final product, but at the moment we're still developing the private channel for each pod. We wanted to leave something for you all to pay for," he said, his eyes twinkling.

He donned a headset and addressed the four angels. "Tap the right side of your headset if you can all hear me." Each angel signaled appropriately. "Now, each of you think of where you want to go. When you've got it, don't say it yet, but raise your hand when you're ready." Everyone raised their hands, so Christian said, "Repeat after me. BEAM... "

Though he couldn't hear their voices, their lips moved in unison to form the word "BEAM."

"Take me to... "

"Take me to... ," they mouthed.

"Now, clearly state the name of the place where you want to go."

Their lips moved again, and suddenly maps appeared on the surface of the blue towers, level to their eyes, obscuring their faces. In the middle of each map sat a pulsing white dot.

"That dot you see represents the place you said you want to go," explained Christian. "Did BEAM get it right?"

The angels nodded, more than one of them staring at the heads-up display in wonder.

"The moment you touch the dot, you will be where you want to go. Are you ready? Give me a thumbs-up." With some trepidation, they each raised their thumb. "Great! On the count of three, tap your dot and get ready for the ride of your lives." Christian braced himself. Conjuring the maps had been easy, and the dew drops would handle the actual transport, but triggering and staying connected to each drop could be taxing.

The angels touched their dots, and with just the quickest of blinks, they, their disks, and the shimmering blue towers of light disappeared. On the view screen the opaque quadrants were immediately replaced with images of the startled investors popping into existence at their chosen locations, still encased in the BEAM's blue tower. A beach appeared in the first quadrant, a diamond store in the second, Sydney

Opera House in the third. McCormick occupied the fourth quadrant, but all that appeared when his BEAM re-materialized was a snow-covered ledge. The hollow voice of BEAM reverberated through the warehouse. "Transport Complete."

Christian's heart was pounding. Earlier, he'd practiced activating the dew drops with his light tendrils to send the four BEAM units to the far corners of the world and hadn't so much as broken a sweat. But now he struggled. The dizziness he'd felt after the moon stunt returned. He'd done too much, extended himself too far. The quadrants on the viewing screen blurred and the room tilted ever so slightly, straining his grip on the BEAMs and causing the portals around them to waver. *Going to have to cut this short.*

"See how simple that was? But all good things must come to an end. Repeat after me, please. 'BEAM, cease!' "

The first three investors obeyed, and soon their BEAMs returned to the warehouse floor, their quadrants on the viewing screen winking out as they arrived. McCormick's quadrant remained active, however, with the image continuing to show a snow-covered mountain vista. Over the speakers, they heard him laughing and whooping in exultation.

Christian, working to stay cheery said, "Mr. McCormick. So glad you've enjoyed the ride. Time to come home now."

"But don't you see where I am? Everest! Mount Everest, man! It's incredible! I'm actually here!"

"Yes, of course the BEAM is amazing. But I'm afraid I must insist." He was panting now. The room also felt significantly warmer. Though he handled the actual portal transports, he did so with the help of Larry's network racks. When Christian overheated, so did they.

He glanced over at the racks and could see the aura around the conduits tied to the BEAM units pulsing in time with his panting. The aura around McCormick's disk wavered, its bluish white signature succumbing to a sickly orange frequency. *Danger.* He had to get McCormick back fast before the rack—or his own internal dew drops— collapsed. "The equipment can only stand so much, Don. Really, it's time to leave."

"Leave? Before I've even set foot on the summit? No way. Let me out. How does this 'BEAM' open?"

Unwittingly, McCormick had said the magic words—"BEAM Open." Before Christian could send a tendril to repress the command, BEAM intoned, "Opening. Enjoy your stay."

The blue cylinder split open and ejected McCormick like a wet seed. A massive blast of wind threw chunks of snow and ice into his path. McCormick teetered one second, then lost his footing, and with a yell and flailing arms, plunged down the summit's side.

Christian dropped the tablet. *No time for pretense.* With a thought, he tuned the Q-Pod to McCormick's BEAM unit, leapt across the threshold, and yanked the dumb investor back from the brink with a tendril lassoed around his waist. Together, they floated back through the portal encased in a plasma bubble. He retracted the field into himself once they landed, but he could tell by the stunned looks on McCormick's and the rest of the groups' faces that the damage had been done. *No easy way to explain* this.

McCormick saved him. "My god, man. That belt is fantastic! You really saved the best for last."

Christian looked down. His belt was glowing. It must have retained some vestigial charge from his personal field. Thinking fast, he said, "It came to me in a dream. Last night, actually. It's called the Enviro-Belt." Warming up to the lie, he continued, "I threw it together this morning, but wasn't sure it would work. You're lucky it did. Thanks for the field test."

McCormick gripped his hand. "Ha, ha, just glad to be alive!"

The audience shook itself out of its stunned silence. As one, they stood and applauded.

"Stupendous!"
"Unbelievable."
"Genius!"

McCormick joined in. "Every word they're saying is true. I'm sold. Take my money. All of it. I'll buy a dozen belts and three dozen disks," he said to much laughter.

"Hey, leave some for the rest of us!" an indignant Maxwell shouted in reply.

Christian smiled. Now that the disks were back and the portals shut down, he was starting to feel steadier. He straightened, smoothed his hair, and re-engaged his inner suave devil.

Motioning for quiet, he said, "I'd love it if you all wrote me checks today." He paused to appreciate the scattered laughter, then continued, "But I understand if you want time to think about all you've seen. In fact, I encourage it. Reread the NDA. Ensure you're willing to pay the price to make the promise of this demo a reality. I guarantee you will receive the best return on your investment. The real treasure awaits."

He escorted the group back through the warehouse and held open the door to the parking lot. "My business manager will be in contact with each of you. Thank you all for coming."

The group exited, many patting him on the back and promising their support as they left the warehouse. Bertrand brought up the rear again and stopped at the door. "Quite a show, my boy, quite a show. You've hit the motherlode, and it's just waiting to be mined. The response of the angel investors was perfect. I expect them to invest fully."

"Thank you, Bertrand. That's good to hear."

"And even better," said Bertrand, leaning in conspiratorially, "with that 'Enviro-Belt,' we might be able to hook a defense contract or two."

Christian's ears perked up. Defense contracts could be very lucrative and long term. That kind of steady, government-backed money would make the strain of the demo and the hollow glad-handing with Bertrand worth it.

"Think you could stabilize the Enviro-Belt enough for another demo with a few DoD friends of mine next week?" Bertrand asked, his eyes glittering.

"I'd be a fool not to try," said Christian smoothly.

"Excellent, excellent." Bertrand's phone buzzed in his pocket. As he looked at the caller ID, the tenor of his brain waves brightened considerably, but he made a good show of seeming perturbed by the interruption. "Sorry, I need to answer this, but believe me I will be in touch. Wonderful doing business with you, my boy. You are on the verge of greatness." He clapped Christian on the back like an old friend and left.

Christian sagged against the door as he closed it. He was desperate to return to his office, and hide from everyone until the fatigue passed, until he regained his control. The voices had stayed quiet all afternoon, but now they'd returned to their murmuring. He'd used too much of himself. He felt fractured, on the verge of splitting open.

"Had a lot riding on that demo, didn't you."

Christian nearly jumped out of his skin. He whirled around. A tall, strong-looking, brownish-blond woman had somehow snuck up behind him. He vaguely recognized her as yet another Hubert holdover, but in his weakened state he couldn't completely summon up her identity. She looked down on him, arms folded across her chest, and regarded him with a kind of smirking bemusement. How did he not notice her standing there? *And damn it, what was her name?*

"I startled you," she said. "Sorry. Needed to use the ladies' room. Demo lasted longer than expected."

She smiled amiably and waited, as if expecting him to respond in some way. *Quit staring like an idiot and answer her*, barked one of the voices growing louder in his head. He took a breath, then flashed what he hoped was a calm, charming smile. Her name came to him. "Ms. Travers, right?"

"Good guess," she said, reaching out to shake his hand. "We've never formally met, although I noticed you in the lab at CSM. I usually dealt with Bertrand or Hubert. But I must admit, you seem to have more on the ball than either of them. In fact, with Hubert gone, you seem like a whole new man."

Christian looked up sharply. What did she mean by that? Something about this woman was unnerving. The way she looked at him: clinical, unblinking. *How much does she know about the accident?* worried one voice. *Don't be a fool*, said another. *How could she know?*

She gestured back toward the warehouse. "Very exciting technology. You're sure to make a name for yourself."

Christian pretended to blush, using the 'aw shucks' moment to hide the fact that he was well and truly flustered by this woman who had appeared out of nowhere. "It's less about becoming famous and more about the mission—clean travel, no limits."

"Noble. Ambitious. But what about safeguards?" Her eyes pierced into him, though her smile remained in place. "New frontiers are inherently exciting, but there can be accidents. And dangers."

She waited; the intensity of her gaze was unrelenting. Christian found it profoundly intimidating. On reflex, he reached out to her mind, hoping to bend her frequency more to meet his own. But for whatever reason, he found nothing to latch onto. The woman might as well have been a rock. *Don't panic. Answer the questions, then send her on her way.*

"Those are valid points," he conceded. "But consider this. The pods will be used by local communities and only by staff specially trained and licensed through Quantum Technologies. Local governments would wind up policing them themselves, relieving our company of the burden."

"And what about the personal travel towers?"

"BEAM Boxes," he corrected her.

"Catchy name. That's marketed toward the super-rich I suspect?"

"The target market for early-adopters. The premium they pay will fuel additional research. As the tech matures, we'll find efficiencies. It's not hard to imagine someone like me or a junior lab tech owning a BEAM Box someday."

"Good to hear you will include the proletariat. But there's always one psycho, and psychopathy does not exclude the rich. Any thoughts on managing that scenario? I'd hate to back a company that caters to some James Bond super-villain."

Christian rubbed his forehead and allowed himself to chuckle. "The great thing about inheriting Dr. Wilkins' business parts is that they came with a top-notch legal staff. I'm sure, with their help, we'll create technical guidelines for safeguards—fail-safes if you will. We'll work it out."

She stared at him intently, then with a short nod said, "I'm sure you will. Keep in touch." And with that, she left.

Christian remained by the door. The voices in his head demanded to know his final plans, when they would be let free. Christian closed his eyes, but of course that did not shut out the light. "Soon," he said to the voices. "We'll be strong enough soon. Then you can be free." The clamor was almost enough to break his grip. But he bit it back. The lights dimmed. Once again, he felt completely in control.

*****

Just outside the facility, Bertrand Pollux in hushed, giddy fashion wrapped up his phone call.

"Next week can't get here soon enough... I must admit, you were right to watch the Meadows boy. After Hubert screwed us, I thought for sure we were lost... Christian's capabilities alone would be enough to retrieve our merchandise, but the technology I saw today will take our venture to the next level... Uh huh... I've got excellent pictures thanks to your micro-cam... Right, then. Meet you tomorrow at Tortas Locas."

Bertrand hung up and practically skipped across the parking lot back to his car. Yes, indeed, he was back in business. With Meadows and Q-Tech, he was about to hit it big.

CHAPTER 10

Not Again

Well this is a mess. Marion Travers slammed the door of her oversized SUV and peeled out of the Quantum Technologies parking lot. The whole business with Campbell *and* his damned jump points *and* her father's gateway *and* deluded North Korean assassins had been shut down. The gateway was off, Hubert in jail, the Jump!GOs dismantled. She'd put a stop to the instant travel madness weeks ago, nice and quiet. Yet here was Hubert's unholy spawn—suddenly handsome as Adonis and smarter than Feynman—starting it up again. *How the hell could this happen? Which genius switched the damned gateway back on?*

She jabbed the phone icon on her steering wheel.

"Ready," answered the car's AI.

"Dial Dad," she growled.

"Dialing Dr. Scott Travers," it replied mildly.

He picked up after two rings "What?" he said. No preamble. Her number was in his caller ID. "Good news or bad news?"

"You tell me."

"Aw, cripes," he muttered. "Bad news. Whadja do?"

"It's never me, Dad."

"That's rich. Who let a psychotic asshole leave the country with questionable tech?"

"Who left his old, defective experiment running for the 'psychotic asshole' to exploit?"

Silence. Then, "So what's wrong now?"

"Same thing, different nutjob."

"What?! That's not possible."

"Saw it with my own eyes. Hubert Wilkins' postdoc built a device to rival Campbell's."

"He couldn't have. The gateway is completely off."

"You sure about that? Somebody didn't bump into it? Turn it back on accidentally?"

"I'm staring right at the QEP, Marion. I can see it from my office. Honest to God, it's inert."

"Then explain to me how Christian Meadows sent five rich guys to five different places today through the ether."

"Aw, god. *He's* tryin' to sell it, too? What's with these kids?"

"The rich guinea pigs were salivating. Two have already agreed to large investments. It hasn't yet, but I can see this whole thing getting out of hand. Again. Check the gateway, Dad."

"I'm tellin' you, it's a door stop. Completely dead. I disconnected the circuit myself. You were here. You saw."

"Please."

"Nuts," he grumbled. "Hang on." She heard a rustling and then his footsteps clomping across the slick floor between his office and the Satellite Monitoring Operations Room. The badge reader buzzed, and he said, "It's still off. The kid must've faked the demo."

Marion pondered this possibility, then shook her head. "Looked pretty damn real."

"Then he made his own QEP," said her father impatiently.

"Thought of that. But he showed us every room in the complex, and then his warehouse, which was wide open. I even went snooping around after the demo and saw nothing that looked close to a QEP. You can't just hide equipment like that."

"You sure you'd recognize one if you saw it?"

It was only a slight dig, but it annoyed Marion all the same. Her father never missed an opportunity to nag her about changing her degree. "I didn't flunk physics, Dad. I just switched to something more fun."

"Pfft. Either way, I can't help ya'. I'm... kinda in the middle of somethin' else right now anyways."

"Sending you a video." She connected her micro-camera to the secure uplink port in the SUV's dash.

"I said I'm *busy*, Marion," he snapped. "I might be tied up for... a few days. Maybe more."

"It's not a long video. If he's faking, you might catch it right away. There are pictures of the facility too. Check those, please, just in case I'm stupid like you think and can't tell a QEP from my own a—"

"I didn't mean it that way, Marion, and you know that."

She took a deep breath. "Sorry. Frustrated. Just want to prevent another Dear Leader. A little help, please?"

"Pete's sake, Marion," he said. More silence. She imagined him scratching his balding scalp, desperately sifting through his vocabulary for more ways to say *No*. After a long pause and a heavy sigh, he said, "Alright. But leave the director out of it. If Francine gets wind there's some new whacko with a travel hole, she'll rip my head clean off for sure."

"Deal." She initiated the file transfer from the micro-camera to his phone, and within seconds the uplink chirped "Complete."

"Let me know what you think."

"I'll be in touch. Cripes... " He hung up.

Great, just great. If Baby Hubert wasn't using the gateway, then what the hell else could it be? And why did he look so good? From what she remembered about Christian on the few occasions they'd met, the kid had been nerdy at best, tragic at worst. Not completely cowed by Hubert, but very pallid and low on the dynamic scale. He was certainly not the suave, charismatic, burgeoning tech leader she had seen at the demo. Today's Christian was charming, self-assured, and healthy. Too healthy. Glowing, even. It was creepy—creepy as hell.

From beginning to end, everything about the demo had felt a little off. With Campbell, his tech was extraordinary, yet straightforward. Nothing hidden going on with him or the jump points. There was a "Gee whiz, look what I did! Oh my gosh, this actually works!" quality to him. Never mind the eventual trouble his technology had caused. There was still an innocence to its inception.

Not so with Christian's Q-Pod and the semi-sentient BEAM Box. Where Campbell had innocence, Christian had slickness, coated with a sheen of slime. As Marion replayed the demo in her mind, she realized just how little it resembled Campbell's work, particularly the blue globules that seemed to power the BEAM Boxes. The transport wall and the blue towers were a lot like Christian—sleek, shiny, and new, with no rough edges. Clean wasn't exactly the word for it. Seamless was more like it. Nearly organic.

Something else entirely was going on. Something subtle, just outside the framework of her experience. Not much usually escaped her. Whether it was science, puzzles, or human nature, she could usually figure the situation out, but this one... she couldn't put her finger on it. And that bothered her. Deeply. Maybe if she hadn't dropped science for criminal justice, she'd have a fighting chance of working this out. Instead, she had gone into criminal justice. And all she had left of her previous scientific life was instinct. Her instinct alarm was firing like mad.

I need answers. Gotta get out of my head... Where the hell am I?

She'd been on autopilot since leaving the warehouse, barreling down 6th Avenue, lane jockeying, careening around corners, barely stopping for lights. She looked out the window and was surprised to see the CSM campus dead ahead. *Ha. At least my subconscious knows who to ask.*

She parked in the lot behind the CASE building and slid past other students coming out through a side door. It was late afternoon, the time when most classes wrapped up for the day, and the perfect time to chat up Dr. Gabriel Bische. If she were lucky, Campbell and crew would be there as well—annoying as hell, but sharp as tacks. She needed sharp minds right now. Something in Christian's video might click with them and give her a clue why it felt so wrong.

The door to Bische's lab was propped open, but no students were about, which was odd. During her surveillance of his lab the previous semester, she'd always seen one kid or another hanging around. His office, visible from the door, was also empty. *Damn.* So much for trusting her subconscious. She turned to leave, but a thump from the supply room next to his office brought her back around. Stealthily, she walked across the lab to the supply room and leaned against the door jamb.

Bische's back was to the door. His lab coat was off, a further clue that he was at the end of his teaching day. He was a tall man, about an inch taller than her, with a strong back reminiscent of a swimmer or a fencer. He moved with a precision and intensity that was quite frankly intimidating. Even simple gestures like reaching for an item on one of the storage shelves telegraphed a kind of benign lethality, which she doubted he'd picked up in grad school. Aside from his obvious intelligence and the lab coat, there was nothing remotely professorial about the man. That her father already seemed to know him only deepened her suspicions that the whole professor gig was a dodge. But the mystery of Bische was a rabbit hole for another day.

A large backpack sat on a step stool to his right, the flap opened as if he'd been packing it. The item he'd pulled from the shelf was a small, black box that Marion thought looked kind of like a receiver. He was studying it, turning it over in his hands several times before fixing his dark, intense gaze on a small screen near the box's bottom. He furrowed his brow and his eyes drifted up to an empty spot on the back wall. *Good time to interrupt.*

"Got a minute?" she said.

Unlike Christian, Bische took her sudden appearance in stride. His eyes left the empty spot on the wall, and he smiled his sly little smile. "Marion," he said. It wasn't a question or a greeting. "Not sure if I should be happy for the visit or worried about why you're here." He put the black box into the backpack and closed the flap.

"Maybe a little of both?" she said, returning the smile. "You wouldn't believe where I've just been."

She launched into a quick summary of Christian's demo, her discussion with her father, and her overall bafflement at how Hubert's lackey suddenly had the smarts to build an alternate version of Campbell's device without the benefit of a pre-existing QEP gateway.

Bische listened patiently, but when she ended the recap, he remained silent. "So... what's your take?" Marion prompted.

He shrugged. "Quantum entanglement isn't a new concept. Somebody else was bound to independently create a way to harness and safely commercialize it sooner or later. Of course, Mitch, Dean, and Wayne will be disappointed if Christian has beat them to it."

"The question is what to do about it."

"Seems to me you have the capacity to do whatever you please. Just call your stormtroopers and wave your badge, and Christian's warehouse gets cleared out by midnight. Problem solved."

She chuckled. "I'm flattered, but I'm not as powerful as you think. Besides, the situation hasn't escalated to the point of needing an all-out attack. At least not yet."

"Then what's the issue? If you think it hasn't risen to the level of breaking the law or public safety, why are you worried?"

"Can't quite put my finger on it. The demo was... unsettling. His employees looked too happy. Meadows seemed too slick, almost messianic. Except near the end. He got the shakes and looked like he was about to pass out. Then when his transport tower talked, that just made my skin crawl."

"Come again?"

"Yes, you heard me right. The tower talked. I've got footage."

He glanced down, the intense, far-off gaze returning. It only lasted a moment, then his attention snapped back, and he looked at his watch. "As intriguing as that sounds, I'm afraid I need to leave." He picked up the backpack and headed to his office.

"You're kidding me. I just told you Christian Meadows is up to some Lex Luthor-level super villainy and you say 'Sorry, gotta go'? "

"Bad timing, yes, but I'm kind of in the middle of something. Might take a few days to sort out. Perhaps more." He pocketed his car keys and shouldered into his jacket.

"Curious. My father said the same thing to me right before I showed up here." For the second time, Bische was uncharacteristically quiet. "Not like him to just pick up and go. Are you two working on a project together?"

Bische didn't look at her, busying himself instead with shutting down his workstation and taping up a box filled with more pieces of obscure equipment. "It's likely a coincidence," he said finally. "Anyway, good luck with your thing."

"Kind of a blasé attitude. Baby Hubert wants to take his magic travel portal worldwide. You saw what almost happened with Dear Leader and Campbell's version. Can you imagine the chaos if Meadows succeeds and the tech spreads?"

"I'm sure you and your Agency pals will figure out a proper response." He slung the backpack onto a shoulder, tucked the box under his arm, and started to head out the office door.

Marion blocked his way. "Maybe. But what I can't figure out is why you don't seem to care."

Bische's eyes flashed, giving Marion a brief glimpse of the menace buried deep within. She wasn't fazed. "*There* you are," she said. "The real you, I'm guessing. The person you are outside this professor shit." She squared her shoulders and planted herself firmly in front of him. "Here's the real me. I don't scare easy, bub, something you should already know, and I'm not moving until you give me an explanation."

They were locked into each other, eye to eye, toe to toe. His jaw muscles twitched. *A prelude to violence?* she wondered. Marion braced herself.

A small laugh escaped past his lips. "Bub?"

She relaxed. "Dad's line. Works for him."

"He *has* used that on me once or twice." He smiled, but then turned serious. "Tell me... is there a ticking time bomb?"

"No, but—"

"Are assassins or super spies targeting my students?"

"Not this time, but how's that a requirement for you to help out?"

"Are millions of lives—right now or in the next few hours, days, or weeks—in jeopardy?"

It was her turn to be quiet, but after some seconds she opted to admit it. "No."

"Then seriously, Marion, step aside. This is not a crisis and you don't need me."

She sighed. "Alright, I'll grant you that." She shifted to let him pass and followed him out of the lab. "What about your boy band? As much as I hate to say it, they're the real experts on this kind of thing. Got any idea where they might be."

"On assignment. Everyone in the Innovation Program gets placed with a local company to garner real-world experience. They'll be there through the summer and present whatever they build at the upcoming Tech Convergence Conference in Denver." They'd reached the parking lot and his car. He put the box into his trunk, but stowed the backpack in the passenger's seat. She was itching to know what he was up to, what the equipment was for, and was certain that her father was somehow involved, though she fought the urge to ask about it.

"Sounds useful," she said instead. "Who's the lucky company?"

"You aren't going to like it." He smiled wryly. He got into the driver's seat, started the car, and rolled down the window.

"If you say Quantum Technologies, my head will explode."

"Ha! Not quite. Think closer to home."

"Oh... no... Not Tamblyn Tech?"

" 'Fraid so."

"This day just keeps getting better."

"So, if you need to consult with Mitch and crew, that involves a couple of things that you don't want to do. One, you'll have to make nice with Dean Chambers. And two—"

"I'm going to have to talk to my mom." *Crap.*

Her phone buzzed, and when "Dad" flashed on the caller ID, a feeling of relief swept over her. "Or maybe I won't."

"Gotta go, Marion. Good luck." Bische sped out of the parking lot and toward the highway.

Marion tapped her dad's picture. "What've you got?"

"Not much, but the Meadows kid is definitely not using the QEP. I had Charlie point the chroma bird at the Violet Street complex while Francine was on break. If Meadows were switching the QEP on and off, there'd be E4 emission lines all over the block. Charlie couldn't find a single one."

"What about the video?"

"Definitely weird. When he chucked a rock at the moon flag, I nearly broke out in hives."

"Can you scan it to find out how he's opening the portals?"

"It's a flippin' video, Marion. From a micro-cam, no less. No special detectors or nothin'. What you see is what you get. And like I *said*, I ain't got all night for this. I gotta leave in—"

"About an hour and a half. That's when your buddy Bische will be there, right? It takes about that long to drive from Golden to the Springs and he just left."

Again, silence. *Dad sure is delivering the awkward pause today. Uncharacteristic as hell.* She waited nearly half a minute for him to speak. "Don't know what you're talkin' about," he finally said.

"Oh come on, Dad. Your New York accent is thicker than pea soup and that only happens when you're upset or you're hiding something. I'll find out eventually, so you might as well fess up now."

"My business, Marion," he said, his tone grim. "Let it alone." The silence returned.

Now she was really worried. Normally he'd argue, holler, and carry on, especially after she'd caught him covering up some issue. Blustering Dad was annoying, but Silent Dad was unnerving. "Sounds serious. Fill me in. Maybe I can help."

"I'll have Charlie send you the logs from his scan. He probably added a couple of other detectors to the readout. The extra data might help you figure out what's up. Anyways, the Meadows kid looks harmless to me." He paused, then said, "And, uh, don't worry, 'kay? I'll be back in a few days." The line went dead.

Great. Marion drove out of the lot, feeling more uncertain than she had when she'd arrived. Both Bische and her father had agreed that though unusual, Christian's demo wasn't cause for alarm, but their assurances had only made her internal warning bells clang louder. *Why?*

The data light on her dashboard blinked and the comm unit intoned, "Incoming transmission from Charlie Wilson." The satellite logs, no doubt.

"Let's hope you're right, Dad. It better be nothing. And you and Bische better not be driving into another mess."

CHAPTER 11

Aspirin

Cecilia Tamblyn muted her phone and dropped her head into her hands. She was stressed out, overworked, sleep-deprived, and battling a raging headache. The pressure of her cool fingertips against her sandpaper-raw eyes offered a brief respite from the strain. They also blotted out the press release on her desk fawning over Quantum Technologies and its "fantastic travel breakthrough."

She longed for a second pair of hands, or a noise-canceling headset or sudden onset deafness to plug her ears. Anything to blot out the asshat stockholder verbally assaulting her on the phone right now. Marvin Maxwell's thin voice was grating in the best of times. The current moment was not one of them.

She was deep into the second hour of what was supposed to have been a thirty-minute touch-base with the board, the press, and Tamblyn Tech's top stockholders. Her carefully prepared statuses and profit projections lay discarded beside the phone, forgotten five minutes into the call as reporters and board members had begun to pound her with questions about Quantum Technologies and Christian Meadows. The upstart founder's bombshell interview with Techline News had stunned them all, particularly Cecilia. She knew the company had been caught with its pants down, but had expected at most one or two questions regarding its response.

Instead, the board and stockholders had launched into a complete onslaught of second guessing, with the subject of Meadows and Quantum Technologies dominating the discussion. As the minutes ticked by, she fielded question after question from one paranoid bigwig after another. Then Marvin started in with his nasal-based whining, and it was all she could do to keep from shouting "Shut up! Just shut up!" at the phone. *Thank god for mute.*

"You see, the problem is," said Marvin, slowly, as if talking to a child, "we still don't know your plan to address this threat. I've invested a *lot* of money in your company. You can't ask me to sit still while it all flies away because a new kid's come to town with superior tech. We need assurances, Tamblyn. I'm not hearing any."

She sighed and disabled mute. "As I explained an hour ago, Marvin, Meadows' systems are similar to tech we've recently brought in-house. This internal version of the tech was developed independent of Meadows and on a much more sustainable framework. "

"You *say* that, but you don't *know* that," he whined.

"Actually, Marvin, I do. You, like everyone else on this call, should remember my DARPA background. Twenty years ago, my team was at the forefront of light-based tech. I know the fundamentals; I co-developed them. And I assure you our version not only works but is superior to Meadows' implementation."

"A lot has changed in twenty years. Younger minds are modernizing the systems that you and Uncle Sam abandoned. My sources say this Meadows character has the brains, the funds, and the *will* to pull it off. Your crew, on the other hand, is still wet behind the ears. We're getting smoked but good because they can't keep up."

Grrr! Back on mute. It was oh-so-tempting to verbally rip Marvin a new orifice. Unleashing a thick stream of well-deserved vitriol and profanity would be cathartic and might even relieve the painful pounding behind her eyes. But Marvin wasn't the only frightened stockholder, and she needed them all to keep the company's funding. *Better to err on the side of reason.*

She took a calming breath went off mute. "Fair point, Marvin. I totally hear you. You've articulated perfectly valid concerns. But rest assured, I understand the baseline concepts in play. I also know the pitfalls—ones which I doubt Mr. Meadows has yet to consider. That's why speeding up development is not in our best interest. Let the Christian Meadowses of the world rush in and fail hard. Meanwhile, my team will carry on with better tech and more stability, and *we* will survive the long haul. "

"But you can't guarantee that. Now, *I* think—"

"You've already made it clear what you think, Marvin," Suriya Nuri, a long-time shareholder, interrupted him. "And Cecilia has explained her strategy to combat it. Let's move on."

"Thank you, Suriya," Cecilia said, then sighed in relief. "The space division is doing well. Satellite contracts are up 5% this quarter, and we expect to double that by the end of the year."

"But you're behind on developing a reusable vehicle," said Marvin.

Cecilia gritted her teeth. "Not entirely true. The prototype passed its wind tunnel test but afterward displayed minor damage to the engine casing. We need an additional week to resolve it, but the impact to the schedule is minimal."

"Pfft," Marvin grunted, the extent of his rebuttal. Small mercies.

"The sales division is exceeding expectations," she continued. "That's mostly due to our 3D printer, the Ursula T2. Sales to schools and hobbyists are higher than projected, meaning we'll show a profit by the end of third quarter, sooner than expected." Profit always perked up the shareholders. This bit of good news prompted congratulations and a smattering of applause. The call was turning around.

"That takes us to R&D status. Our transparent nano tablets are in pre-production testing. There's a battery usage issue, but one of the CSM intern projects may help resolve it. Regardless, we're still on target to be in stores by Black Friday."

"With fewer units, I'm told," Marvin complained.

"Purely to breed consumer interest and to limit corporate espionage, which you would realize if you or your spies were in *any* way competent." *Oh, that was wrong to say, but it felt good.*

"My sources are quite competent, I'll have you know," said Marvin, taking her irritation as license to voice his own indignation. "It is our business as the board to know what's happening inside the company. Founder or no, if you can't handle the oversight, we will downgrade your position and find someone who can."

"As the founder and majority stockholder of the company, I can buy you out and revoke your seat on the board."

"Now, now, people." Suriya stepped in again. "Let's put our spoons away and wrap up the hasty pudding." Chuckles trickled out of the conference phone speakers, alleviating some of the tension caused by Marvin. "Cecilia is managing these challenges effectively. She is the face of the company, and her vision drives it.

Everyone on this call knows and respects that."

"Thank you, Suriya," said Cecilia. *Finally, someone else has the balls to shut Marvin down.*

"Still, as much as we have faith in you and your vision, Cecilia, Marvin has a point of sorts—"

"Damn right I do!"

"—in that you're putting positive spin on, let's say, 'less than flattering' disclosures."

"Hmmph." Cecilia wasn't about to confirm the idea that her division assessments amounted to 'spin.' From her perspective, she merely espoused the eternal optimism of invention. Issues were expected but would be overcome. She did not expect anyone on the call to understand that.

"We're happy with the latest progress and projections and will take this month's presentation at face value. But we expect more transparency at our next meeting. Until then, everyone." The call ended.

Cecilia's face found her hands again. *The world needs more of Suriya's diplomacy,* she thought, *and less of Marvin's idiot parade.* She wasn't sorry for calling Marvin on his threat to oust her from the company, yet the whole exchange had drained her, and she welcomed the darkness of her hand mask. It was comforting. *I wonder if I can sneak out of here. Just go home and take a nap.*

Her office manager chose that exact moment to knock. He poked his head around the door and said, "You've got a visitor."

Gawd. "Not now, Ted."

The door closed, but the whisper of soft breathing suggested Ted had remained. "Look, tell whoever it is to go away. Then come back with coffee and aspirin."

"That'll tear up your stomach. At least that's what you used to tell me."

Marion? Cecilia looked up and there was her daughter—tall, athletic, and severe, though sporting an impish half-smile. People often remarked to her how much she and Marion resembled each other, but what stood out most to Cecilia was a wisecracking, pugnacious streak in Marion that could only have come from her ex-husband Scott. "Good lord, girl, you really picked the wrong time to try to reconcile."

"Nice to see you too, Mom," said Marion with a quiet little laugh.

Cecilia stood up and gave her a hug. "Really, dear, you didn't have to stay away so long. I'm not as mad as you think."

"I suppose I knew that, but honestly it wasn't intentional. You wouldn't believe the amount of work there is ferreting out corruption and keeping the country together."

"That's my girl, saving the world. But I'm guessing you aren't here to justify your move to criminal justice from biophysics. Oh, *thank you*, Ted."

Her office manager had returned. Wordlessly, he handed her a large mocha and a bottle of Bayer, then left. Cecilia waved Marion toward a seat while she popped two aspirin from the bottle and gratefully washed them down with a large swallow of the creamy, sweet drink. *Small mercies indeed.*

"Actually, I'm looking for three of your interns. I need their input on a situation I'm working on."

"You mean Campbell, Chambers, and Hirano?"

"Yes, those three. How did you know I—?"

"Tell me this isn't more of that mess with your father and North Korea."

"Not directly, and FYI, that's supposed to be classified. They've been talking to you?"

"Of course they have. I demanded it. You don't think I'd take them in and have them working on their Jump!GO technology without getting the lowdown first. Is there another problem with that Jin person and her brother? Your father had no business leaving the QEP on. I told him it still needed work before I left, but he wouldn't listen to reason."

Marion's jaw dropped. "Slow down a minute, Mom. How do *you* know about the QEP?"

Cecilia covered her eyes. "Throughout the whole of that business, did your father ever once mention me?"

"We were kind of busy. Why would he?"

"Because the QEP was *my* idea—a DARPA side project that *I* proposed. We worked on it together until... well, until something happened, and the brass shut the project down. So don't give me that 'classified' garbage. No offense, dear, but my clearance is way above yours. That's the one thing I got to keep in the breakup."

Marion shook her head. "Obviously I had no idea."

"I suppose your father liked it that way. It wasn't his best hour."

"Then maybe you should see this." She pulled out her phone and played a video.

"Who are all of these people?"

"Potential investors."

"Wait." Cecilia paused the video with an angry tap. "There's that bastard Marvin Maxwell. He's on Tamblyn Tech's board. What's he doing there? And is that—?" Exasperated, she pointed to another spot on the video. "That's Christian Meadows."

"What, you know about *him* too?" asked Marion. "Please don't tell me he's my long-lost brother."

"Of course not. Your secret brother's taller and lives in Florida."

Marion reared back and studied her mother, her eyebrows knit into a frown. "You're joking," she decided. "Aspirin must be working."

Cecilia patted her hand reassuringly. "To be perfectly honest, dear, I learned about Meadows the same way everyone else did: from Techline News. They must have played that interview ten times this week. And I just spent a painful couple of hours on the phone trying to convince Marvin and the board that Quantum Technologies isn't a threat."

"Do you really believe that?"

"I wasn't impressed, frankly. The interview showed a lot of pretty pictures and animations. A standard media package, really, all flash and no substance. If your video is more of the same footage, then I can tell you now, Christian Meadows is all talk."

"Well, just watch. You... might want to sit down."

Marion restarted the video, and soon enough, Cecilia saw reason for her daughter's concern. Either Meadows was a master magician, or she had drastically underestimated the sophistication of his tech. "The blue towers weren't on Techline News. What'd he call that feature again?"

"BEAM: Bipartite Entanglement—"

"—Activity Monitor. I remember now. Interesting that BEAM talks."

"More like creepy."

"You say potato... " Cecilia sighed. "When did this demo happen?"

"Right after the Techline News piece."

"Why'd you wait so long before contacting me? Did your father try to talk you out of it?"

Marion blushed. "Actually, *I* talked myself out of showing you. Dad sent me a satellite scan of Meadows' facility. I thought our analysts might come up with something after reviewing it, but frankly, they're as baffled as I am. What do you think?"

"I don't believe any of it. A transport wall, conveyance tubes, plasma balls... none of that is consistent with what your father and I created. Must be a sham. The energy required alone would be massive. The QEP needed its own electrical substation. Where's his facility?"

"In the warehouse district on Violet Street, the other side of town."

"That's nowhere near a substation."

"Exactly. He did mention an energy issue and that he needed investor funding to fix it. The energy usage was the only aspect of his demo that seemed inferior to Campbell's work. I could smell the ozone out in the parking lot. Campbell's Jump!GOs, on the other hand, have no scent, even in proximity. Granted, his original version of the device relied on the QEP, but—what's the matter?"

Cecilia caught herself chewing her lip. "You mentioned Campbell, which reminded me that he and his buddies *also* bypassed the QEP. Their work-around seemed like a one-of-a-kind deal, but if Meadows has come up with something similar... damn it. That makes Q-Tech look more legit."

"You know," said Marion, "when I first met Campbell, I had my doubts about his abilities, but he proved to be the real deal. The first version of his machine was huge and unwieldy, held together with chewing gum and duct tape, but by god it worked so well we had to shut it down. Chambers and Hirano are no slouches either. Might not hurt to have them look at the video, get their opinion. They might even think of a way to replicate or counter Meadows' tech."

Cecilia nodded, but she felt tired and had the sudden urge to cover her face again and blot out the world for a minute to help her think. Instead, she rubbed her chin and said, "Maybe. Let's go. They'll be happy to see you."

"Ha. Highly doubtful."

"Oh, come on. Chambers himself told me he thought you were a real peach."

"Uh huh. And *I* told them if I caught them working on the Jump!GO again, I had every right to put them in jail."

"Hmmm. Then I suppose this will be an interesting reunion."

They headed out of the office in search of the wunderkinds. Her headache was completely gone.

CHAPTER 12

Babble

"Hello. If you're hearing this message, I'm unavailable. Leave a message of your own and I'll call you back. *Beep!*"

"No you won't," muttered Mitch at Bische's recording. He hung up. It was the third time he'd called the professor in as many days, but Bische had neither answered nor called back. He'd disappeared for short periods before, when they were in high school, so Mitch wasn't worried—just annoyed. If ever he needed his mentor's advice, it was right now. *Bad timing, Doc.*

They'd been in the machlab almost every waking hour since Christian's interview had debuted on Techline News, scrambling to resolve the gateway router's cycling issue. After applying Darasimi's suggestions, a solution had seemed imminent, but as the hours—then days—slipped by with no significant improvement, their hopes of meeting CC's deadline slowly evaporated.

Mitch, dreading the thought of CC blaming him for the failure, worked frantically: changing a connection here or shifting a jumper there, hoping the constant fiddling would unconsciously trigger an unexpected insight. But his brain felt as sodden and flaccid as a soapy dishrag. Try as he might, no flashes would come.

Wayne and Dean fared no better. They'd both decided the problem was too hopeless to resolve. Dean had flopped to the floor and summarily passed out. He'd awakened thirty minutes ago and gone in search of coffee.

In a tepid show of solidarity, Wayne had stayed awake with Mitch. But instead of helping with the cycling problem, he'd devoted his time to cracking Tamblyn Tech's personal machine restriction. His test case attempted to send a holographic projection through the plasma grid to PicsterGram, his theory being Tamblyn's network couldn't block data sent through packets of light.

He'd propped up his phone on the center worktable, focused it on Mitch's back, and had finally gotten Mitch's disembodied torso to appear floating above his workstation. But the tunneling routine crashed before the video stream reached PicsterGram. He hummed absently as he stepped through the code, stopping and starting the projection over and over as he wrapped the feed in different packets and tried to trick the proxy ports.

"Making progress?" asked Mitch.

Wayne nodded "Yes" in time with his humming. "Pretty tedious, though."

Mitch would've traded places with Wayne in a heartbeat. *At least you're getting somewhere.*

They'd all contributed to the tunneling project, but Wayne had accomplished the most with it, likely because he'd taken the most breaks from the cycling issue. Any other day, Mitch wouldn't have minded. Bische had taught them that taking breaks from a problem was sometimes the best way to subconsciously solve it. But Wayne's humming and the constant, peripheral flickering of an enormous 3D version of his own head was starting to grate on Mitch's nerves. Even more irritating was the idea bubbling just beneath the surface that his friends had abandoned him.

He immediately rejected the idea. Like him, Wayne and Dean were tired and discouraged. Unlike him, though, they had accepted their fate. Mitch couldn't—he hated to lose. The problem was solvable; he could feel it in his gut. He just had to think about it some more.

Maybe a calculation is wrong. Mitch opened the gateway config file, but the numbers and words blurred together. He squeezed his eyes shut then opened them again, but still, nothing in the file made any sense. The massive image of his head appeared again on the edges of his vision, hovering like a parade balloon. He gritted his teeth.

"Hey, Wayne, can you help me with this? You're the real math whiz. We should switch places."

"I *am* the Math Whiz, but *you* are the Flash Face. Your lightbulb comes on and you save the day. I'm just waiting for the magic to happen."

"I'm all out, dude. Can't see straight. Want to poke it for a while?"

"Nope. Already told you, have been telling you for days now, and will continue to tell you until you believe me: the cycling is unfixable."

Dean returned just then carrying a coffee tumbler so big it might well have been a popcorn bucket with a sippy lid. "Gotta agree, Mitch. I say we embrace the cycling and embed a timer. What's so wrong with doing that?"

Mitch shook his head. On this point he'd remained adamant. "What's wrong is that's not what CC told us to do. A timer means a crappy user experience. It's like we're throwing in the towel. Only lame-o's throw in the towel. Hell, we'd be no different from the guys who made Warrior Ops XV, for crying out loud!"

"That's a low blow, Mitch. Uncalled-for burn. It's not like we're hiding pre-ordered jump holes behind a pay wall or blocking jumps until you play tic-tac-toe or something."

"But aren't we though? If people constantly have to cycle their plasma grid every ten minutes, we might as well be adding microtransactions or loot boxes."

"But banging our heads against the wall trying to fix the unfixable is ridiculous," said Wayne. "We need to start over with a different approach instead of continually running down this same rabbit hole with no end."

"But we already did the calculations," Mitch argued. "The current approach is more efficient, you know that. If we start over with something else, we'll need to generate at least twice as much energy. No matter how efficient we make the fob's innards, we'll hit a threshold that is unsustainable. The fobs will burn out after two or three jumps. We sell something that fries people's phones, it'll be *worse* than loot boxes."

Wayne rolled his eyes. "Well, if you won't agree to change the base motherboard in the fob, then we'll have to build in some kind of hop system that auto-cycles the grid instead of forcing users to cycle it themselves. They'd have to wait on the cycles, like waiting for a bus."

"Oh, that'll go over *real* well," said Dean. "Can you imagine the ad campaign? 'Ride a beam of light, but only slightly faster than a city bus.' Or maybe 'Jump!GO—at least it's not the Greyhound.' So very lame. Christian Meadows would have a field day."

"Exactly," said Mitch. He stood up and paced. "I mean... I can almost feel it. I think we're close to figuring it out—"

"You said that three hours ago," Wayne replied wearily. "Hasn't happened yet."

"We just have to keep trying different things," Mitch said with a sigh. He walked back over to the diagnostic workstation, determined to find something in the config file to rearrange.

"That's the one thing I really, really hate doing, Mitch," said Wayne. "Trial and error is for the birds. If you can't predict what to do with math, then the thing you are trying to do is. Not. Possible. You have to trash what you've got and start. All. Over." He smacked the table and tossed his controller to the side. Mitch ignored the rare outburst and turned his attention back to scrolling through the config file.

Dean took the bait. "Okay, Wayne. Let's say you're right—"

"I'm right."

"I'm serious."

"So am I."

"Okay, whatever!" said Dean in disgust. "My point is, we *should* describe the cycling mathematically, but we don't *have* to. Mitch didn't for the original Canopy. He just magicked it up and voila! It existed. Where was your math then?"

Wayne swiveled around to face him. "Granted, Mitch built the Canopy before writing an equation. But once we sat and thought it through, we saw that the functionality adhered to certain principles. We didn't just pull it out of thin air."

Mitch straightened up. "Thin air... " he said, his eyes losing focus again, but this time not from lack of sleep. "Could it be that simple? Does the router just need more air?" His gaze disappeared into the machlab wall.

He flung open the toolbox and set to disassembling the spare router; his thoughts still not quite congealed, but coming more and more into focus as he rearranged the contents within the shell. Slowly, a smile spread across his face as the rightness of the solution manifested itself as it always did—through the sure movement of his hands.

"This is going to work," he said to no one, with the certainty of the old Mitch having just made an intuitive leap.

"Congratulations," said Dean, clapping Wayne on the back. "You triggered the Flash Face. He'll be in Flash Land for at least half an hour. Hungry?" He looked at the clock on the wall. "The Donut Farm's still open. What can I get you?"

"A wheat bagel."

"Dude, seriously, it's a donut store. You *always* get the bagel."

"They sell them. I like them. It's not like I asked for baked salmon or a can of hash."

"How about an old fashioned or a chocolate glazed?"

"I want a wheat bagel... and a can of hash."

Dean laughed. "Alright, but next time it's your turn to get snacks." Dean dialed in the jump point for the Ferry Building at the Embarcadero and was just about to jump when the door opened. He looked over his shoulder and skidded to a stop. "Yikes!"

He'd yelped loud enough to snap Mitch out of Flash Land. Wayne rushed over to turn off his tunneling grid. The three of them stared disbelievingly, if not guiltily, as Marion strode through the door behind her mother.

"At ease, gentlemen," said Marion. She nodded curtly at Dean. "You too Lothar."

"Giganta. Surprised you didn't melt in the sun."

"And I'm surprised they let you out of your cage."

Mitch hurried to CC's side. "It's not the deadline yet. We've got another day."

"Relax," she reassured him. "We're not here for that. Although, if you *have* solved the cycling problem, I'm all ears."

"Mitch was flashing before you two walked in," said Wayne, "so, maybe?" He glanced expectantly at Mitch.

"Um, well, sorta," Mitch stammered. Self-consciously, he rubbed the back of his neck and looked over his shoulder at the disassembled router. "It's the air flow in the router, I think, but... I don't know. We need to do some tests." He lapsed into silence and seemed to shrink in on himself.

"Tests, Campbell?" said Marion with a smirk. "That's a switch. A couple of months ago, you'd have already been filing the patent."

Mitch winced. "A lot's happened since then, I guess."

Her expression softened. "I like your new sense of responsibility, but the lack of confidence isn't healthy," she said. "We'll circle around to that later. Right now, I need some expert advice and you three are the closest thing to experts I've got."

"You're here about Christian' s interview, aren't you?" asked Wayne.

Marion graced him with a genuine smile. "Still the smart one, I see, Mr. Hirano."

Wayne shrugged. "What else could it be?"

"You're right, of course. The functionality displayed in the interview was stunning, to say the least. Given our recent adventure in the Springs, it grabbed the Agency's attention. The brass' first reaction was to arrest him and the three of you, but nothing subtle about that. I convinced them otherwise."

"We were worried that he discovered something new, too," said Dean, "but we watched the interview again and realized it's mostly animations and hand waving. I'd be surprised if he actually had anything that works."

"I got invited to his investor showcase a few days ago and still can't tell if what he's doing is real or if it's some kind of sleight-of-hand. I've also verified that the QEP is disabled. So, just like your team, he's found an end-around." She held up her phone. "Real or not, I recorded his tech in action. Think you can figure out what he's doing?"

"Sure. Probably. Well... geez. I don't know." Mitch mumbled himself into silence.

"How long has he been like this?" Marion asked Wayne.

"Off and on for a few weeks. He'll get better. Show us what you got."

CC tapped a lock code into the door, then Marion propped her phone up near one of the workstations and played the video.

"The screen's so small," said Dean. "Too bad we can't bring it up on one of the monitors."

"Who says we can't?" said Marion, reaching for a workstation connector.

"I do," said CC. "For security reasons. I trust my employees, but corporate espionage is alive and well. Your phone's gonna have to do for now."

"Doesn't need to," said Wayne. He used the workstation connector to join his phone to Marion's and with a few more taps, the blank plasma grid engaged, rendering a holographic projection of Christian's Q-Tech warehouse right above Wayne's Jump!GO.

Marion let loose a low whistle. "You boys don't disappoint."

CC nodded in agreement. "Truly stunning, Hirano."

"I couldn't have done it without Mitch's light-trapping matrix. We find more uses for it every day," said Wayne. "I'm calling this new feature a HoloStage. The images are bigger, and the 3D rendering helps us view a picture or recording from all angles."

"It's a lot like the Tamblyn 3D projector," added Dean. "Except without all the mounts and reflective mirrors. All you need is a Jump!GO fob and Wayne's add-on app. Combined with the plasma grid, the rest is fancy math, but Wayne's the math whiz."

"So I'm told," replied Wayne dryly.

CC shook her head in amazement. "All I can say is 'Wow.' If you'd shown this to the board earlier in the week, they would have had a better response to your demo. But let's focus on the video."

"Starting it up." Wayne hit play and Christian's smooth baritone filled the room.

Christian's image and devices rendered in three dimensions made his antics in the video seem all too real, one product after the other upping the ante, each one more badass than the last.

"Did he actually just toss a rock onto the moon?" asked Dean.

Mitch felt he'd never pick his jaw up off the ground. The way Christian had expanded on their tech was beyond amazing. If the demo were real, they'd have a hard time competing with Christian's company. *Just when I'd figure things out. Man...*

He cast a sidelong glance at Marion and wasn't surprised to find her studying him. "Well, Campbell, what do you think?" she asked.

He closed his eyes. *So tired.* But closing his eyes stopped the flood of astonishment and gave him time to think. When he opened them again, he had an idea based upon the two most striking parts of Christian's video: the moon portal and the speech-enabled BEAM. Both events would require a lot of computing power and energy, but nothing in the video indicated how Christian might have generated each. He simply pulled lightbulbs out of his pocket like a magician, crammed them into the battery slots on his devices, and miracles happened. It didn't make sense.

Turning to Marion, he said, "Without the QEP, it takes a lot more energy to generate the light-trapping gateway. We're only barely compensating for it, but Christian's acting like it's not a big deal. Is his office next to a power station or something?"

"Not at all. And now that you mention it, the place did seem to heat up the longer the demo lasted. After the moon trick, I noticed a sharp smell in the room. Like wires melting."

Mitch closed his eyes again. The moon and BEAM parts really bothered him. *But what was it?* "Guys, when he tossed the rock on the moon, did you hear anything?"

"You mean besides him prattling on about the sky not being the limit and flying off to other worlds?" asked Dean. "Now that you mention it, yeah. Kind of a screeching sound."

"Like feedback," said Wayne, but he looked uneasy.

Mitch shook his head. "To me it sounded like something else."

"I know what you mean, Campbell," said Marion. "But Hirano could be right. It might've just been white noise."

Marion rewound the video to BEAM's introduction, and they listened again as the hollow voice floated out of the speakers. Wayne blanched; CC's eyes widened; and Mitch felt a cold tingling in his lower back like a ghost had reached out and pinched his spine.

"When you focus on it," said Marion slowly, "the sound makes your skin crawl. It's almost like—"

"Voices screaming," said Wayne and CC simultaneously.

"Screaming and on fire," said Mitch. He shuddered.

Only Dean seemed unaffected. "I was going to say it sounded like a pterodactyl, but if the consensus is folks getting tortured, then alright."

"The point is, we agree that some kind of vocal expression is involved, but what could that mean?" asked CC. "Could voice waves power his version of the gateway?"

"Kind of a stretch," said Marion.

"No more than the existence of a light-based gateway," CC countered.

"I don't think it's sound waves," said Mitch. "Everything he did required a light ball from his pocket."

"He called them 'dew drops,' " said Marion.

Mitch sighed wearily. "Whatever. Something's happening. I just don't know what." A wave of apathy swept over him. He slumped against his lab bench and swiped both hands through his curls. *Man, Marion, can't we do this later?* His eyes rested on the nearly reassembled spare router. *I'm so close to fixing it. And after I do, I just wanna go home and go to bed. Christian's stuff can wait.* He opened his mouth to sigh again, but a yawn came out instead.

Marion started to speak, but CC held up a hand to stop her.

"Campbell, how close are you to fixing the cycling issue? How much more time do you need? No hedging your bets, now."

"I'd say about… ten seconds."

"Great. Do it."

CC's command revived Mitch like a splash of cold water to his face. With a few quick snaps, he'd reattached the router's shell and swapped it into the diagnostic rack. "Open a hole now, Dean."

Dean tapped his phone, the coordinates for the Donut Farm already primed in the Jump!GO app. As his fob re-engaged, everyone gathered around the diagnostic monitor.

"What should we look for?" asked Marion.

"The Stability Time marker on the lower right," said CC.

Mitch crossed his fingers, hoping for at least 90 minutes, but he braced himself and was ready to settle for half. The final value appeared in the corner, large, black, and bold: 2.1 million hours.

"Whoohoo!" Mitch exclaimed.

Wayne elbowed him. "Thought you said it was impossible?"

Mitch grinned. "I was just tired."

"Fantastic," breathed CC. "That's a load off my mind. Well done, Campbell. Now I can tell Marvin Maxwell to go pound sand."

Marion held up her phone and said, "I'm happy for all of you, truly, but what about Christian?"

"Can you transfer your video to Hirano's phone?" asked CC.

Marion swiped and tapped her screen a couple of times. "Done."

"Perfect. Hirano, I'll clear your device and account for the full network if you promise to stop trying to tunnel your way through to the internet." said CC.

Wayne wrinkled his brow. "I'm not trying to—"

"Please." CC nailed him with a piercing glare.

Wayne raised an eyebrow. "How did you know?"

She rolled her eyes and said to Marion, "It amazes me how every intern thinks I won't notice a security breach in my own company."

Shifting her attention back to the boys, she said, "That's enough weirdness. I declare the workday over. Go home, all of you. We'll regroup tomorrow morning."

"We've got a mandatory intern meeting at school in the morning," said Mitch. "Is the afternoon okay?"

Marion started to object, but CC squeezed her arm. "That'll be fine, boys. See you tomorrow." She steered Marion out the door.

"Break time," declared Wayne.

"Let's get you that bagel," said Mitch. "And coffee."

Dean called over his shoulder from the edge of the light hole, "And a can of hash!"

CHAPTER 13

Illumination

Bische's Practical Design students waved goodbye to Larry as they filed out of the lab. Larry, who'd had to cover for the absent Bische, puttered around behind them, cleaning up their work benches and resetting the demonstrations for the next group of students set to arrive at the bottom of the hour. He hummed as he laid out modeling kits, straightened stools, and replaced the completed equations on the smart board with the raw diagrams and hints the students needed to spawn them.

The hints hadn't been part of Bische's notes about the lab. Larry included them to add an element of fun for the students as they struggled to solve Bische's gnarly design puzzle. He taped index cards containing additional cryptic clues to the walls, bench tops, and toolboxes with the same care and glee of a doting parent hiding jelly beans and chocolate eggs on Easter morning.

And though he enjoyed the secret setups, Larry knew the real fun would begin when the next class arrived and started working through the lab. If the new students were anything like the previous ones, it'd be a hoot watching their expressions change from perplexed to determined to downright joyful as they solved the final problem and figured it all out.

That was the best part, that "Aha!" moment. It always happened, and when it did he felt such satisfaction knowing that he had caused it, if indirectly. 'The wheels turn and then you learn,' Dr. Forbus often said. Larry laughed. *True dat, Dr. F.*

Forbus' stock phrase summed up Larry's recent experiences. He'd felt daunted by the prospect of covering for the brilliant Dr. Bische while the prof was out on leave, but once he'd gotten into the swing of things, he'd found that he quite enjoyed it. Unlike Forbus' lessons, Bische's material was firmly ensconced in the modern day, leaning heavily on practical applications and relying on class participation. This made covering for Bische a challenge, as Larry had to learn the material first himself, but he didn't mind. He found it invigorating. *This is how teaching should be!*

Everything seemed to be rolling his way lately, what with his promotion, Forbus' return, subbing for Bische, and living on the bleeding edge over at Q-Tech. Christian's product line was off the hook. Every day, he showed Larry some new implementation or needed Larry's help with a brand-new schematic. The man's ideas were crazy-fresh—or maybe just crazy. Larry still wasn't sure, but for the first time since Campbell's light-trapping revolution, he didn't feel left out.

Christian's plasma globs—"dew drops" he'd called them—were the real-deal disruptor, and unlike the Campbell kid, Christian had real investors, a state-of-the-art facility, and the need for scientific talent. Larry felt lucky to count himself among that talent and was more than ready to contribute. The stack of issues Christian had handed him that morning meant the boss considered him ready too.

They had another demo tomorrow, this one for the Department of Defense. If all went well, they'd get more funding, more time for innovation, and infinitely more amounts of amazing, world-changing projects. *I may have missed the appetizer, but at least I'm here for the main course. Can't beat that!* Yeah, this new phase of his life was good.

But first things first. He had to begin the lab. Students had begun to trickle in. Most folks he knew already from Dr. F's classes, but many were surprised to see him instead of Bische. He just waved and waited for them to arrange themselves around the workbenches. A few students cast curious glances toward him while they donned their protective gear. He kept his face neutral, mysterious as the Sphinx. *You'll find out soon enough.*

Once they were ready, he slipped into his lab coat and felt so happy he could no longer hide his smile. Q-Tech was his promise for the future, but the classroom would always be his place of comfort. *I do love this,* he thought. *Maybe when I postdoc, Dr. Hayman will let me stick around.*

He strode to the center of the room, the heart of his domain. "Alright class, are we ready to play?"

*****

As in all of Bische's classes, the students listened earnestly while Larry laid out the parameters for the lab. When he was done, they wasted no time in attacking the problem. With the game set in motion, all Larry needed to do was sit back and wait for each design team's results—as well as revel in the ineffable sounds of "Aha."

The previous class took the full fifty minutes, but he had a feeling this new crew would move faster. *Bet they cinch it in thirty-five.* That gave him enough time to analyze at least one of Christian's problems and get him a few steps ahead of schedule before he returned to work. He donned his headphones, fired up his concentration playlist, and dived in.

The Enviro-Belt's permeability issue sat at the top of the stack, but he was confident it had already been resolved. The great Maggie Heinz—one of Bische's super-stars and Q-Tech's best intern—had been introduced to the problem the night before. He'd gotten maybe three sentences into describing the issue before she'd nodded and assured him, "I'm on it." Case closed. Bische's geniuses sure made life easy.

The next issue was more gnarly. The BEAMs sucked up too much energy. They overwhelmed the monitoring systems and tended to short themselves out. Why they did this, no one knew, but the rack had nearly melted during the investor demo and the amount of ozone in the room afterward would've alarmed the EPA. Plus, they used up dew drops faster than ants ate sugar. The already over-taxed dew drop generator couldn't keep up.

"Find the hot component," Christian had ordered, but for the life of him Larry couldn't. He ran test after test but came up empty each time. Desperate for any kind of result, he made random changes to all of the components on the off chance that one of his tweaks would stop the energy build-up dead in its tracks. But that approach was time-consuming—and worse, hacky. He hated it.

During the drive into Mines for class today, he'd had his own "Aha!" moment. He'd analyzed everything about the BEAM Box except the most obvious thing: the dew drop. He'd ignored the dew drops for a stupid, fan-boy reason—he liked them. *How could the new hotness be defective? Dew drops are awesome! No way they're the problem!*

But as Larry parked his car, he'd realized only a hack would think that. *Yech. That's Dr. Wilkins-level incompetence, son. You're better than that.*

Now with the data in front of him, he manually masked the values for the dew drop cavity and *Bingo!* The energy signatures stabilized. He'd found the bad component. But how to fix it? He turned on his tablet and applied the same elimination mask to a spectral analysis of the BEAM he'd completed the previous morning. The wavelengths leveled out but spiked below the graph at the point of photon transfer, signifying a charge imbalance. If the dew drop's plasma shell detected the imbalance, it might rev up and run hot.

With that insight, Larry sliced through the Gordian Knot. All he needed was a virtual siphon to stabilize the imbalance and prevent over-compensation by the plasma shell. If he also added a collector, he could redirect the excess energy into the battery to increase the functional life of the device.

Yeah, this'll work. Man, I love the bleeding edge! The ideas flowed out of him. Furiously, he typed calculations into his tablet, then sketched a new configuration for the controller board, keeping the dew drop cavity at its center, but balancing the other components around it more logically.

The playlist reached "A Flat," an old school jam and funky favorite. He cranked the volume and put it on repeat, bobbing his head in 4/4 time. The improved BEAM Box took shape, and as the final design materialized before his eyes he felt the euphoria of a mad scientist breathing life into his creation. He held the tablet up to admire his handiwork and couldn't help but let loose a maniacal laugh. "Bwahahahaha!"

The students at the bench in front of him looked back nervously. "It's alive! Alive, I tell you!" he said, thrusting his tablet at them, wild-eyed.

"Watch out, it's Larry Frankenstein," one of the students said with a giggle.

"That's *Doctor* Larry Frankenstein, thank you!" The rest of the class laughed along with him. "Alright, back to work," he said, re-taking his seat. "Sorry for the interruption. You've still got plenty of time."

He chuckled as he plugged his calculations into Christian's validator. *Hehe, Frankenstein's BEAM Box.* Not a bad analogy, really. The spectral graph of a dew drop aligned surprisingly closely to that of a biomolecular network. He'd analyzed plenty such networks back when he'd entertained the idea of pursuing a biophysics doctorate instead of a pure physics PhD. The pattern was so familiar to him that when he'd run the initial spectral analyses on the dew drops as part of the Q-Pod development, he'd noticed the similarities immediately.

What would happen if you could treat your body like a BEAM Box and attach a dew drop to it? he wondered. *Would it integrate as tightly to a person's physiology as his new design for the BEAM's controller board integrated the plasma shell with the unit's other components?*

He shook his head. *Naw. Crazy thought.* The only way to integrate a dew drop into your body would be to swallow it or absorb it or shove it up your—well, into another cavity besides your mouth. He knew enough about human physiology to surmise most bodies wouldn't respond well to flaming suppositories.

Still, if you managed to survive "integrating" with a dew drop, that'd be something. You could tune yourself like a photon, access your quantum properties, customize your own quantum state. You could instantly make yourself faster or smarter, stronger or more handsome. You might even be able to influence other people, reach out with your quantum field and fine tune *their* state—if you got close enough to them, that is.

But you'd have to be careful to internally maintain a balance of states, otherwise your whole system would become unstable and whatever you were tweaking—body or mind—would fall apart. You could short out like a battery or melt down like a nuclear core. A person might even ex—

"Hey, Larry, here's our results." One of the teams had arrived at his desk. He checked his watch. *Bingo!* He'd called it exactly: thirty-five minutes. Soon the other teams were lined up behind the first. A quick scan of the results and the contents of the workbenches showed that everyone had figured out the clues and completed the design challenge successfully.

"Excellent. You guys are on fire today. Dr. Bische would be pleased."

The lab was effectively over, so he dismissed them and gradually everyone drifted out of the room. As the door closed on the last student, Larry's stomach growled.

He'd skipped lunch, taking the time instead to create the helpful hints for Bische's students. Now that his classes were over and he was coming down from the excitement of it all, his empty stomach demanded attention. *Wonder if Murli's Curry is still around?* But the lab needed tidying. His stomach would have to wait.

He'd just started removing the index cards when his phone rang. "Hello?"

"Larry, it's Maggie." She sounded breathless and shaky. "You gotta come back."

"What's up?"

"It's Christian. He freaked out and locked himself in his office."

"What?! Why?"

"It's a long story. I'll tell you when you get here."

Whoa. "Class is done. I'll be there soon."

"Hurry, please. There's a weird sound coming from his door."

Maggie's voice was calm and polite, but her breathlessness left no doubt: she was scared. He jotted a quick note of apology to Bische for leaving the room a mess, locked the lab, and ran to his car.

Christian freaked out? That must be some story, he thought as he peeled out of the parking lot. Maybe the bleeding edge wasn't all it was cracked up to be.

CHAPTER 14

Trouble

"Why won't this work?"

Christian had spoken aloud, but no one was close enough to hear him. He'd sequestered himself near the back of the warehouse, at his original bench. The space served more as a museum exhibit than a functioning work area these days. "A reminder of my humble beginnings," he'd tell visitors while giving them the standard tour. It was too far away from the supply room and other benches to be considered a convenient workspace, and even Christian hadn't done any real work there for weeks. But the DoD demo was tomorrow with the so-called Enviro-Belt as its focus. To hide the fact the belt never actually existed, Christian announced he would "improve" it and returned to his bench to quietly make it.

Two versions of the belt lay on the counter in front of him—an actual version with real hardware along with the "prototype" he pretended to have worn during the investor demo. Neither version worked. Christian stared at both in despair.

He'd made a lot of progress over the past week. The real belt had internal circuitry, a controller board, a wireless communicator, and the all-important dew drop slot serving as its power source. He'd gotten the belt to generate at least a square foot of protective field directly above the dew drop slot. But even triggering that proved to be problematic, with the switch working erratically if at all.

He'd tried every trick he knew to create a larger energy field, but nothing resolved the issue. There were too many parameters to juggle, too many holes to plug, before the device could function on its own, and to Christian's horror he felt his grasp on the problem—on himself—slipping away.

The confidence and self-possession that had settled into his core after 'the accident' and after he had rejected the chaotic self-image he'd glimpsed of himself in the mirror weeks ago, seemed to have been dislodged by the unexpected strain of the investor demo. In the days since he'd felt... fractured. As if only the thinnest of energy tendrils was keeping the shards of his mind and body together. The confident internal voice had grown weaker, drowned out more and more by a mocking, nattering chorus spouting derision and doubt. He couldn't concentrate; every waking moment was a struggle. He feared that another strain could completely shatter him into an infinite number of pieces with no hope of ever reconnecting or becoming whole. He was a wreck.

Larry had somehow sensed that Christian was stuck and had offered to help. Because of the deadline, Christian almost allowed it, but then changed his mind. Larry was too curious and asked too many questions. He'd see through Christian's deception right away and demand answers.

"Thanks for the offer, but I've got a handle on it," Christian had told him instead. "I might ask an intern to help out with some minor wiring," he added to sell the idea that the project was actually easy. "I could use your help with these other problems, though." He'd handed Larry a stack of outstanding issues as a further distraction and sent him on his way.

What I really need is peace and quiet. When he'd created the dew drops, he'd been alone. Before hiring all these Tamblyn intern rejects, he'd built the Q-Pod and basic BEAM disk—alone. *I can make this damned Enviro-Belt too, as long as everybody leaves me alone.*

So, he'd retreated to his corner. The quiet served to quell the Others' negative murmuring. The fractured feeling had begun to subside, and possible solutions to the problem had begun to manifest at the edge of his mind. *Maybe boosting the oscillation on the magnetic resonator will—*

"Hey, Christian, can you sign for this delivery?"

Damn it.

He tasted anger and contemplated conjuring a fireball the size of a boulder to lob at the idiot behind him who thought interrupting him to sign for something as trivial as mail was a good idea. He repressed his rage, only just. The wrench in his hand glowed.

"Kind of busy now, Ms. Heinz."

A different voice spoke. "Need a payment authorization before I can leave this box. The kid here says you're the money guy."

"Hmmph," he grunted impatiently, but turned around long enough to scribble his signature on the mail carrier's tablet before returning to glowering at the belt.

"Thanks." The mail carrier handed the box to the Heinz girl and left.

"Where should I put this?"

Why is she still standing here? "Give it to Larry. He'll put it away." Then, casually, as if it were an after-thought, he added, "And ask him to stop by here. When he has a minute."

"Larry's gone."

"What?!" He whirled around. "Where'd he go?" Panic knifed through him. *Oh, god. Did Larry quit?*

"He's at Mines covering a lab for Dr. Bische. Said he'd be back by three."

The panic receded but was quickly replaced by his own self-loathing. *Why do I need him? Why can't I do this myself?* He tossed the wrench aside in disgust.

"Anything I can do?" she asked.

"No!" he shouted. The other workers—who'd had the sense to stay away from him—surreptitiously looked over at the scene in his isolated corner. He lowered his voice and continued, "It's complicated. If I can't fix it, neither can you."

Heinz set aside the box and scanned the parts on the table. "Seems simple enough. Besides, Larry said I could help. Let's try—"

"How else can I say it, *girl?* This isn't some trivial, freshman lab. This is a real-world problem. You won't understand."

The intern's eyes blazed. "The name's Maggie, and I understand well enough, *Christian.* What you need is a projected resonance field, but you don't know how to make one and you're too proud to admit it. Just because you were my TA once doesn't give you the right to treat me like I'm stupid. I'm not. You hired me to help you, so let me do it."

She pushed past him to get closer to the table. "My mom's a nuclear researcher. I've worked in her lab every summer for the last three years. They make smaller variant fields like this all the time. Is that real-world enough for you? We can fix this with—"

"Stop. I don't need you. Just go away and leave me a—"

"Christian, my boy!" Bertrand Pollux's voice cut through his and Maggie's argument.

Now what? He turned around to find Bertrand standing near the Q-Pod mockup beside a tall, angular, clean-shaven man dressed in military greens, his uniform hat tucked under an arm. *First the mail carrier and now these two.* He really needed to chat with the front desk greeter about who to allow into the warehouse.

"Christian, come over," Bertrand called again. "I've got someone you should meet."

"Don't touch anything," he said to Maggie. Then, plastering a smile to his face, he crossed the warehouse to the Q-Pod.

Bertrand greeted him with a hearty handshake. "Hope you don't mind the intrusion."

I do, he thought, but said out loud, "Of course not. Always a pleasure to see you, Bertrand. But you're a day early."

"With good reason," Bertrand said, grinning. He leaned into the handshake and said into Christian's ear, "A very lucrative reason." He tapped his lapel pin, then gestured toward the service man. "This is Major Bart Hallett, DoD research division."

Hallett nodded, wrapped an enormous, sinewy hand around Christian's, and pumped once. "Mr. Meadows." He did not smile. His gaze lingered on Christian, eyes full of judgement, sizing him up. He said nothing more, but Christian got the impression that Hallett had found him wanting.

"I've described your product line to the major," said Bertrand. "He was quite impressed but wanted to come down to see for himself."

Christian gritted his teeth and forced himself to remain cordial. "Isn't that what tomorrow's demo is for?" he said, turning toward the major. "We're still setting up for it today, but when you return tomorrow, I promise you won't be disappointed."

"Dog and pony shows are just that: shows," said Hallett, his voice crisp and direct. "If what you created is real, my arrival today shouldn't change that. I'm here for what's real. Not the show."

"But is that fair to the other DoD reps? You'll have them at a disadvantage."

"There are no other reps. Higher-ups saw no reason to waste their time, so I was elected to come in their stead. You could say I drew the short straw."

"Which is better in the long run," said Bertrand, patting Christian's shoulder. "Too many cooks and all that. Major Hallett is very influential in the R&D division. His recommendation will take you far, my boy. If your products do indeed work."

"Why wouldn't they? You were here for the demo. You saw what the tech can do."

"Well, yes." Bertrand cast an uneasy glance back at Hallett. "The investor showcase was quite impressive. The four angels continue to rave about their BEAM excursions, and Marvin Maxwell can certainly attest to the reality of his stack of casino cash. But as to whether any of them were actually transported somewhere or just experienced a kind of enhanced virtual reality... Well, let's just say that since the demo there have been some doubts. Especially given—"

"—the amount the congressman here is asking for our investment," said Hallett. Some silent communication occurred between Bertrand and Hallett, setting off warning klaxons in Christian's mind. *What are the two of them hiding?*

"All the major needs," Bertrand continued, "is a more concrete demonstration. Something definite and provable."

"Like that wearable... what's it called?" Hallett added.

"The Enviro-Belt," said Bertrand. "It was the main thing on the agenda for tomorrow. Demoing that should be enough to prove the worth of Mr. Meadows' quantum-based tech. How about it, my boy?"

Christian had known the suggestion was coming, but he cringed regardless. There was no way to wriggle out of it. The moment he'd decided to save McDonald from Everest's chasm was the moment he'd painted himself into a corner. Now, the one unplanned aspect of the investor demo was the only thing they wanted to see.

Don't panic, he told himself, keeping a benign smile on his face. *Just recreate the visuals, if not the effect. They'll eat it up, agree to the contract, and leave.*

"Alright. We can do that. I was just adding the finishing touches to it when you arrived. Come this way."

He led them back to the corner but stopped short and stared at the bench-top in shock.

Maggie hadn't left. Worse, she'd ignored his command to not touch anything. Most of the pieces he and Larry had added to the belt lay disassembled and strewn to the far side of the table. The only parts that remained attached to the belt were the dew drop slot and the controller board. She'd attached a thin strip of mylar to the length of the belt, and in her hand she held a cage full of other parts that Christian didn't recognize. He couldn't believe his good luck.

"What did you do?!" he yelled at Maggie. "It's in pieces! You've ruined it!" That assertion might have been true, but Christian was too relieved to care. Although he'd been annoyed by her meddling earlier, he could have kissed her now. *Thank god for stubborn interns.*

"Chill, boss," Maggie replied, flashing him an impish grin. "I think I've just made it work." She picked up the belt to demonstrate, but Christian, keeping his back to Bertrand and Hallett, silently mimed for her to stop with a low, frantic wave of his hands. Maggie's brows knitted together, but she didn't protest.

He continued the ruse of shouting at her. "How could you? Who let you over here? You've wired it completely wrong." He turned around and addressed Hallett. "I'm sorry, Major. She's just an intern and should be working on a different project. I can try to fix this by tomorrow, but no demo today."

Bertrand pointed at the counter. "You could use the version you shared with the investors. Isn't that it against the wall?"

Damn it. Damn Bertrand. Damn Bertrand Pollux to hell. Back to Plan A.

"Oh, yes. Didn't see it there. I suppose so." Reluctantly he retrieved the mockup and strapped it on. He put his hand in the pocket of his lab coat to hide the generation of the plasma ball. He pulled it out as if he always kept an extra dew drop on hand, then wedged the ball into the makeshift dew drop slot. Closing his eyes to gather what little concentration he could, he pushed the light of the dew drop out into a gentle glow that enveloped him like a cloak from head to toe.

"Ah, perfect, Christian," said Bertrand, rubbing his hands together.

"Interesting effect," said Hallett. "I suppose that glowing light is supposed to be a kind of protective armor, like a tortoise shell, right?"

"That's the idea," Christian replied.

"Nothing can penetrate it?"

The fractured feeling was returning. Christian took deep breaths to suppress it before attempting to answer Hallett's question. "Of course not," he said through gritted teeth. "That's the whole point."

"Can it stop a bullet?" asked Hallett.

"I, uh, we haven't tested that yet," said Christian. He was gasping now and felt his control over the field beginning to slip.

Hallett gazed at him intently, then said, "Let's find out." He unholstered his pistol and leveled it at Christian.

"Wait!" Maggie yelled.

Christian sensed her springing to his side, but then Hallett fired and... time slowed. Christian saw the bullet rotating toward him, headed for the space between his eyes. *I could burn the bullet,* he thought, *but can I burn it in time? I don't have the time!*

He closed his eyes and waited for the impact, hoped that whatever heat he could generate from his own internal suns would vaporize the metal before it destroyed too much of his brain. He heard two more shots, but... nothing happened. *Am I dead? Am I in shock?* He opened his eyes.

Standing in front of him was Maggie, a perfect blue bubble of oscillating light wrapped completely around her.

"Like I said, it's a resonance," said Maggie, picking up their conversation from earlier. She was about as breathless as Christian but kept her tone matter of fact. "You need a stimulating frequency. Sort of like a seed crystal in chemistry. Once you have that, the frequency strengthens your field and you can vary it—make it contract or expand or oscillate—to make it more permeable or hard as a rock. Pretty simple once you grasp that."

Hallett looked Maggie up and down, appraising her in much the same way as he'd earlier surveyed Christian. The result of this judgment was much more favorable.

"Congratulations, Mr. Meadows. Looks like we have a deal." He holstered his gun. Turning to Bertrand he said, "You'll be sure to drop off the paperwork tomorrow?"

Bertrand stared disbelievingly at Hallett, but eventually shook himself and reapplied his politician's smile. "Of course, Major. My pleasure."

With one last glance at Maggie, Hallett said, "Good work, young lady." Then he and Bertrand walked out.

Maggie waited for them to exit the warehouse completely before switching off the belt.

"Wow, what a whack job, right?" she said over her shoulder as she unsnapped the belt. Her hands shook as she straightened it out on the bench and shoved her tools aside to make room.

It was Christian's turn to be confused. "Did... did you know the belt would work?"

"Against this hammer, yeah, but a bullet? Hell no. Nice of Major Asshole to clear that up for us."

Christian's jaw dropped. "If you weren't sure, then why did you... " He couldn't say it. She'd almost taken a bullet for him. Maggie had saved his life.

"I just reacted, to be honest. His aim was off a little. Worst case, he would have grazed me." She pushed stray lock of hair behind her ear. Her hand till shook.

In his mind, Christian replayed the scene. The major had glanced at Maggie, momentarily distracted by her swift movement. He may have hesitated before pulling the trigger, but as the scene unfolded in slow motion, Christian still saw the bullet travel in a straight line toward his head. Hallett's aim *wasn't* off. Maggie was being kind. If the belt had failed... He swallowed hard. "Thank you," he managed to say.

"No worries, boss," she said with a slight smile. "Kind of selfish on my part, though. You can't pay me if you're dead."

A light burned at the back of his eyes, the voices in his head rose up, and a fiery pain shot through his brain, sharp enough to cause his knees to buckle. It took a great effort to stay standing.

"Are you alright?" asked Maggie.

Christian detected real concern. *She's still shaking; I should be the one comforting her. I was a bastard to her. Why did she jump in front of me? Why does she care?*

He opened his mouth to say, "I'm sorry," but instead of words a tone like a dissonant chord came out. He clamped his hand over his mouth and stumbled toward his office.

"Christian, wait—" Maggie called after him.

He locked the door and a wave of vertigo overtook him. He just about made it to the trashcan before the pressure in his stomach got too much to contain. His mouth opened wide, but instead of vomit, a cone of light shot out, accompanied by that same dissonant chord. It erupted like a fountain from his mouth, his eyes, and every pore in his skin until his office disappeared, and he was surrounded by the light.

A figure coalesced in front of him and then more figures around that one, like spokes on a wheel. The tone reverberating through the white space changed cadence all at once, still discordant, but less musical—more human.

["*You idiot,*"] the voices said as one. ["*Get a grip! You're blowing it!*"]

*****

Hallett whistled idly to himself as he and Pollux left the Q-Tech facility. He figured Pollux would call him on his stunt as soon as they cleared the bystanders. He didn't care. *The little weasel damn near peed his pants when I pulled my gun. Probably did when I squeezed off a couple rounds.* "Heh-heh," he chuckled, amused at having finally found a way to wipe that smug look off Pollux's face. *Yeah, that was worth it.*

And the power of Meadows' dew drops was hugely impressive. Hallett wondered if maybe *they* were the true treasure. He might need to acquire a few just to see.

They arrived at the parking lot, no one around but them, and Pollux turned on him as expected. "Are you crazy?!" he hissed.

"Like a fox. I forced his hand," said Hallett, unlocking his jeep.

"You could have killed him! And the girl!"

"I aimed for his shoulder."

"Bullshit. I've spent enough time on the gun range to know a kill shot when I see one. You targeted his head. Without the girl, he'd be dead."

"That wouldn't have happened. Didn't you see his eyes? How they flashed? Or the fireball that sprouted on his forehead as soon as I drew my gun? He was activated. All those dew drops he absorbed got switch on. My bullet would have burned to ash before it hit him."

"You don't know that. And what if the girl's Enviro-Belt hadn't worked? It would have been a mess, that's what, and we'd be no closer to retrieving our merchandise."

"I saw the video. I know what he can do. You worry too much."

"I'm *prudent*. As for the video, you'll need to put an access block on it. If *you* found a way to view his security cam footage that means someone else can as well. The Agency's got to be watching him too. What happens if this stunt of yours goes live?"

"Nobody cares about this piss ant."

"Last month that was true, but not anymore. Now he's all over the media."

"Just another flash-in-the-pan techy with a far-out idea. Hell, you said it yourself—even his investors are losing interest."

"You want to bet on that and risk losing trillions?"

That's cute. He thinks I'll let him keep his cut. Might as well play along. "Alright, I'll put a clearance lock on the security servers. Happy?"

"For the time being. You've got to remember, we need him. He is integral to our plans. Without that belt and his abilities, we can kiss our merchandise goodbye."

"You sure about that? The girl might do. She's smarter than Meadows. Made of sterner stuff too."

"I'm positive. The one thing I've learned about Christian from Hubert is to not underestimate him."

"Pollux, you might say the same about me." He stared down at the little man long and hard to make sure he got the point.

The ex-congressman swallowed and said no more. Hallett laughed outright. He climbed into his sport car, stomped on the gas, and sped away, leaving Pollux behind in a cloud of dust. *Eat gravel, weasel. I play to win.* He whistled and contemplated the best way to cut Pollux out of "their" plans.

CHAPTER 15

Real Trouble

Larry arrived back at the warehouse and made a beeline for Christian's office. He pushed through the crowd of onlookers to where Maggie stood with her ear pressed against the door. "What happened?" he quietly asked her.

"Congressman Pollux showed up with some army asshole who called off tomorrow's demo and demanded to see the belt today," she whispered back. "I fixed it like we talked about before you left and it worked, but then the military guy shot up the place."

"What?! Why?"

"I don't know. To make a point? He said it was a test, but... I think it was something else and Christian knew it."

"But now the door's locked and he won't come out?"

"Right. At first it sounded like he was hurling, but now there's just a hum like he turned on an exhaust fan."

"Wouldn't you? If you're right and he *was* hurling, probably smells like puke in there."

"Ugh." Maggie grimaced. "Hadn't thought of that." She shook her head. "Now I can't unthink it. Thanks for spoiling my dinner."

"Sorry. Could you tell if he was hurt?"

"He wasn't bleeding. The bullets never penetrated the shield. The belt works." She flashed a tight smile.

"Knew you could crack it," he said, looking her in the eye. "Whoever turned you down for an internship missed out."

Maggie beamed. "Seems like I'm having a more interesting adventure here."

"There is that. Won't last long, though, if the guy running the company is out of commission."

Just as he raised a fist to pound on the door, someone tapped his shoulder. "Hey, Larry. What's goin' on? Folks are weirded out back here."

He turned around and was greeted by the anxious faces of his coworkers. For a second, he wondered if he should comfort them with a lie—tell everyone Christian was simply taking a nap—but he discarded the idea immediately. It was a legitimate question; Larry knew that had he asked it himself and been lied to in response, he would be angry. *Best to be truthful.*

"Still figuring it out, Paul." Then, switching to his teaching voice, he said loud enough for the everyone else to hear him, "It's close enough to quitting time. I suggest you all go home. Q-Tech will be here tomorrow, and if not, we'll think of something."

Paul hesitated for a moment, but then shrugged and turned away. Eventually, the rest of the workers followed suit.

"Should I leave too?" asked Maggie.

"If you want to. Wouldn't blame you. But frankly, I'm as weirded out as Paul, and I could use the company."

"I'll stay, then."

They waited until everyone had left the warehouse before turning their attention back to the door.

"Christian!" Larry pounded on the door, then put his ear against it, praying for any kind of response. All he heard was the same odd hum. And strangely, the surface of the door was starting to feel a little warm. He pounded again, but this time the sound seemed to echo, and a brightness appeared around the outer edges of the doorframe, orangish-white and seemingly growing in intensity. Alarm bells went off in Larry's head.

"Did he take a BEAM unit in with him?" he asked Maggie.

"No, but... " She scrunched up her face and didn't continue.

"But what? Seriously, anything you can tell me will help. Even if it sounds weird."

Maggie hesitated, then seemed to come to some sort of conclusion. "I could have been imagining it, but just before he freaked out and ran into his office, we were talking and... " She lapsed into silence again.

"Not a lot of time, Maggie."

"Alright. He kind of seemed to break down, and when he opened his mouth, something that sounded like the BEAM voice came out instead. He clapped his hand over his mouth as soon as it happened and then ran off. Does that sound crazy to you? Maybe I was hearing things."

Immediately, Larry thought back to his own imaginings less than an hour ago while sitting in Dr. Bische's lab, contemplating how a dew drop could transform you if you could integrate with it. An image of Christian from three months ago popped into his head. Thin, scrawny, awkwardly shuffling between classes in ill-fitting clothes, obviously bright, but not a hint of swagger or charisma. He compared that image against his memory of Christian from that morning: trim, polished, buff, and brilliant, oozing suaveness out of every pore. *Oh no.*

He renewed his banging on the door in earnest. "Christian! Open up! Come on!"

"What? What is it?" asked Maggie. Alarm registered on her face, mirroring his own.

"The damn fool. He ate a dew drop. Probably more than one."

"You can do that?" she said, aghast.

"Can, yes. Should? Probably not. In the body, the encapsulation matrix could become unstable. Just like the BEAM units, you could short out. Or worse." He stepped back from the door and threw a kick at it, just above the lock. It barely moved. He tried again and again, but it wouldn't budge. "Damn it, Christian!" he shouted through the crack at the edge of the door. "Open up, buddy. You're about to blow!"

"Use the fire ax!" Maggie pointed at the emergency break-glass cabinet on the wall.

More orange-tinged light seeped from the cracks around the doorframe. The hum from the room was now loud enough to be heard without either of them putting an ear to the door.

Larry stepped back, considering the suggestion, then shook his head. "It's metal. The ax would take too long." Larry looked around the room desperately, his eyes landing on a battery-powered circular saw. He picked it up. "Stand back."

He put his mouth close to the door, then said in his booming voice, "Christian, we're coming in!" He raised the saw and...

*****

The light streamed out of Christian, out of every orifice and every pore. Around him, his office transformed into a space without form or function, a limbo of fuzzy white. He was on his knees still, arms gripped around his stomach. And trailing out from him like spokes on a wheel unspooled a reflection of himself, repeated over and over again as images embedded in a series of transparent shells.

Each image was a perfect reflection of Christian and mimicked his current physical state—on his knees, bent over, and holding his stomach. Every image, but one. A lone reflection stood in front of Christian glaring at him with a white, hot rage.

["*You're absolutely blowing it!*"] the aggressive image shouted from within its shell.

"Calm... down," Christian gasped. "I can... control it. Just rattled. Give me... a minute." He swallowed hard. The nausea was returning. He felt the room spinning beneath his knees. He gripped his stomach tighter.

["*Just rattled?*"] the Aggressor yelled. ["*You almost got us killed!*"]

Christian shook his head. "No. I would have burned the bullet before it reached our head."

["*Who do you think you're talking to?*"] The Aggressor pointed at himself and the others. ["*Everything you do or think, feel or see, we experience it too. If not for the Heinz girl, our brains would be splattered on the warehouse floor.*"]

"I can handle it."

["*No, you can't. Your plan isn't working!* "]

["*He's right,*"] said a reflection in a far-away shell. ["*We've done the calculations. Your dimension's probability is no longer favored.*"]

"That can't be true. I'm Prime," said Christian, wanting to shout at the reflection, but also feeling a complete lack of conviction. The reflection merely gave voice to what he'd been feeling earlier: that his need for help meant he no longer controlled his thread. The nausea in his gut turned to pain. He closed his eyes, no longer able to bear the blinding white fuzz nor the disappointed stares of his repeated selves.

The Aggressor, his image flickering, struggled to his feet. ["*Time to replace your thread with mine.* "]

["*Idiot!*"] the second reflection called out. ["*Why did you have to say 'Time'?*"]

At that moment, between Christian and the Aggressor, another shell appeared containing a boy. ["**It is not just a matter of time,** "] said the boy. ["**It is also a question of probability.**"]

Christian looked on, stunned. As with all the reflections, this boy was himself, but obviously a version of himself from the past. While he gawked, the boy aged into a man, becoming the idealized projection he'd taken to showing to the rest of the world, but even that self-image faded as the seconds ticked by:c finally between him and the Aggressor stood a wizened old man.

Time Christian faced the Aggressor. ["**Prime's probability remains strong.**"]

["*You're wrong, old man! His blunders weaken him. My thread is more probable.*"]

[**Only momentarily. "**] Time Christian was once again a child, but he spoke with an authority Christian Prime never remembered having. [**What matters is the long term—time coupled with probability.**"] And again, Time Christian morphed into his perfect self. [**Eventually, Prime's thread will succeed.**"]

["*Our threads are nearly identical. My path is quicker,*"] the Aggressor insisted.

"[**Is it smarter?**]"

["*Of course it is. Faster is better.*"]

[**But at what cost? "**] Time Christian asked. [**Your thread is friendless, sterile, and hopeless in the end. "**]

["*Who cares? I will win!*"] The Aggressor twisted around and pressed his hands against the shell separating him from Prime. The palms of his hands ignited with dew-drop fire. His image solidified, while the shell around him trembled under the blue-white blaze.

["*Hurry!*"] screeched the far-off reflection. ["*When Time cycles again, the probability window will close.*]"

"[**You are choosing the path to destruction, not success.**]" Time Christian had morphed back into the old man.

["*Who are you to choose, old man?*"] The Aggressor's shell began to vibrate violently, and Christian Prime looked on in horror as the barrier protecting him from his reflection's burning palms slowly dissolved.

"[**I am the one who has seen it all.**]" And with a smile, Time Christian morphed again into his boy self.

["*He cycled! You're too late!*"] shouted the far-off reflection.

The blue-white fire died in the Aggressor's palms. The shell around him re-formed, his solidity faded, and he fell back to his knees.

["*Noooooooooooo!*"] he cried, the other reflections mirroring his pain and frustration. ["*You fool!*"] he howled at Time. ["*Prime accomplishes nothing! His thread leads nowhere! We never win!*"]

Young Time Christian regarded the Aggressor, his eyes filled with pity. [**"You are the true fool. Your thread dies in loneliness and despair, while Prime's way leads further. He is not alone."**]

Time Christian touched his bubble, and from his finger leapt a beam of light which landed where Christian Prime's office door had been. A window formed, and through it, Christian saw Larry and Maggie begging him to open the door, clearly worried about him.

[**"Not alone."**]

The beam of light shifted from the door to a spot just in front of Christian, and showed him Larry, always eager and full of ideas, ready to help with anything. Then it showed him Maggie jumping in front of a bullet to save his life. *Can't let them down. I won't let them down.*

Time's light landed in his chest and blossomed into a spark of hope. Christian fashioned it into a tendril and like it was a barbed whip, flung it around the Aggressor's shell and dragged it toward him.

[*"No! No! I won't go!"*] the Aggressor protested.

Christian ignored the wails. He clenched the tendril tighter, buoyed by Time Christian's spark, and soon more tendrils flowed from his fingertips and pores, latching onto the other reflections and pulling them in. The images collapsed within their shells, back to the size of dew drops.

A multitude of lights streamed into his body, and with the reintegration of each thread Christian grew stronger, more confident. The nausea and lightheadedness disappeared, as did his uncertainty. He could do anything, be anybody, accomplish any goal. Hallett could shoot a million bullets at him—they'd all fall to ash. The light coursed through him and he felt invincible.

I am invincible. I. Am. Prime!

Thread after thread entered him until only Time Christian's shell remained. The tendril drawing him in had been the longest. As he floated closer to Christian, the Boy Time looked at him solemnly. [**"Your thread is most probable,"**] Time said. [**"But it is not inevitable. Remember the path that you chose."**] The bubble was close enough for Christian to absorb. The boy morphed into the more perfect man. ["**Make it count**,"] he said as he disappeared into Christian. The white fuzz dissolved with him and suddenly Christian was back in his office.

Larry's voice boomed on the other side of the door. "Christian? We're coming in!" The distinct sound of a circular saw starting up drifted through the cracks.

"Stop!" Christian shouted, then he opened the door.

Maggie looked in at him from behind Larry. "Christian, what the hell?!"

Larry powered down the circular saw. He cast a concerned eye over Christian's shoulder into the office, and then examined Christian closely. "Had us worried, Chief. You okay?"

"Yeah, sorry," Christian said sheepishly. "I... kind of lost it for minute. I'm alright now. It won't happen again."

Larry and Maggie exchanged glances. "What was going on in there?" asked Maggie. "The door got hot. Lights flashed. Larry thought y—"

"—that the joint was on fire," Larry interrupted quickly. He and Maggie exchanged another covert glance. The three of them stood silently in front of Christian's office, shuffling their feet and avoiding eye contact.

Christian couldn't tell if he was detecting Larry and Maggie's discomfort or projecting his own onto them. They continued to wait, but he had no idea what to say. Time Christian seemed to think they were important to his thread. After they'd showed such concern for his welfare, he knew he owed them *something*—but what? An explanation? An apology?

"I'm hungry," he blurted out.

The admission startled them into looking at him. Maggie nodded. "I'll bet. Heard you barfing earlier. Stomach's pretty empty, huh?"

Larry finally put down the saw. "Want us to get you a snack? The espresso bar is still open."

He was botching it. He felt his old awkwardness returning, but then Time Christian's voice echoed in his mind. [**Make it count**].

Calm descended on him, and for the first time in weeks, his lips curled into a genuine smile. Not the smile of his practiced, perfect image, but an expression of pleasure as close to his real self as he could muster. "Sorry," he said. "What I meant to say, er, to ask, was whether either of you were hungry."

Larry looked at his watch. "The day's shot, so yeah, I could do dinner."

"I skipped lunch working on the belt. Food would be nice," Maggie chimed in.

"Great. How about we go find some... together."

"Okay," Larry said slowly. "If you feel up to it."

"Yes. There's a Thai place not far from here," Christian said. "Their Tom Kha Gai is good. Want to try it out? My treat."

Maggie brightened. "I'll take free food."

Larry regarded Christian quizzically. "Alright. You can fill me in on Pollux and whatnot. Let me put this away." He picked up the circular saw and headed toward the supply room, pausing to sniff to air. "I might shut down the rack too. Smells kinda hot."

"I'll get my backpack." said Maggie.

Christian entered his office to get his jacket. *When was the last time I went to dinner with anyone?* He couldn't remember. Suddenly a lump formed in his throat and hot tears stinged his cheeks. He'd been so lonely, the thought of that changing made him tremble. He closed the door, but instead of turning around, he rested his forehead on the frame and fought for control.

"Chief, you okay?" asked Larry.

Hastily, he rubbed the tears from his eyes and turned around. "I'm fine," he said. "And please, call me Christian."

CHAPTER 16

Blocked

A jump hole whined open in the dark alcove in front of the machlab's break room. Mitch, Dean, and Wayne jumped out and settled down to eat a late lunch at their favorite table, which was close to the coffee pot and within clear sight of the always-on news screens. They ate quickly, eager to analyze Marion's video, not because they shared her urgency to understand Christian's shenanigans, but just to get it done.

"Marion's alright I guess, but this secret spy stuff sucks," said Mitch. 'The sooner we analyze her video, the sooner she'll be gone."

"At least she asked this time," said Wayne, taking a big bite out of his sandwich. "She was even a little nice about it."

"Only a little," added Mitch. "Still felt like a command."

"Exactly," said Dean. "She pops up out of nowhere without so much as a 'Howdy Do', then railroads us into helping her all cuz she's paranoid about light tech." He drained his coffee cup and headed over to the pot for a refill. "We told her we've got a handle on the jump points. Heck, even her mom told her everything's fine and she, like, *invented* the idea. But Christian goes and does a deep fake and now Marion's all freaked out."

"Oh, so you're back to thinking his demo's not real?" asked Wayne. He held his coffee cup out for Dean to refill.

"I replayed the video in my head last night while I was in the shower and that's the only thing that makes sense. Christian's smart, but come on; some of that's *got* to be fake. Rock on the moon? Please."

"Doesn't explain the screaming we heard," said Mitch.

"I've got a theory about that too," said Dean. "Maybe it wasn't screaming. Maybe it was just some feedback from Christian's machines. Marion shows up in crisis mode and gets us spooked enough to hear anything."

Wayne pondered the idea. "I *really* don't think it was feedback."

"Fine. Then it was steam escaping or kids playing outside."

"Kids playing? In the warehouse district?"

"Look, all I'm sayin' is, cats making out sound like babies crying."

"Ugh! Glad I'm done with breakfast."

"Do we actually have to monitor Marion's video?" asked Mitch, turning to Wayne. "Can't you just automate the Holo Mode analysis and record the results? That way we can work on our Tech Convergence demo instead. Spend as little time on Marion as possible."

" 'Just automate it,' " said Wayne. "Simple as that?" He shook his head. "You must think I'm a wizard."

Mitch shrugged. "Because you are."

"Fair enough. Might take half an hour, though."

"That long?"

"Maybe a full hour if we run an audio augmenter on the 'screaming.' "

"Wow, a whole sixty minutes," said Mitch. "I guess that'll have to do."

They cleaned up their trash and headed back to the machlab. People from other labs greeted them along the way.

"Yo, guys."
"How's the project?"
"Ready for the weekend?"

Even Darasimi waved at them from her perch across the hall, "Looking good, interns."

Mitch felt a surge of optimism. They were starting to fit in. So much of his time from middle school until now had been tied up with Bische's projects and making good grades. But working at Tamblyn Tech was giving him a glimpse of what could come next, clearing away the fog of failure he'd felt since the Springs with Chung and Jin. *I like it here. This could be my life.*

He looked at his friends and they were grinning too. "Guys," said Dean. "I predict today will be awesome. Wayne will work a miracle and set the Holo Mode on autopilot. Then we'll ship the results to Giganta and that'll be that. Goodbye, Marion. Back to interning."

Mitch clapped him on the back. "You said it, buddy." He pushed open the door to the machlab and immediately wished he hadn't.

"Boys. You're late."

Crud puppet.

Marion had been leaning against the central table reading her phone. She straightened as soon they entered and said with a terse nod, "Let's get started."

There goes our awesome day. Mitch glanced behind him. His friends' smiles had disappeared. Wayne had slipped into his poker face, a kind of overstated blankness that always reminded Mitch of a grown dog tolerating an annoying puppy. It was the closest Wayne ever got to displaying irritation in front of an adult.

Dean, on the other hand, openly glowered. He strode over to his bench and slammed his backpack down, hard. "Not even a 'Howdy do,' " he mumbled.

Marion regarded him with a half-smile. "Not happy to see me? After all we've been through together?"

"Unwillingly," Dean retorted. Then, stabbing the air, he said, "And if you ask me, you can take your video and sh—"

"Actually," Mitch stepped between them, "we were talking about the video on our way here." Dean clamped his mouth shut, but continued standing behind Mitch, huffing like a wolf. Mitch raised his hands placatingly at him, then said to Marion, "Wayne thinks he can automate the Holo Mode scan so we don't have to watch it like last night. We'll set it off and send you the logs. You don't have to stick around."

Marion smirked at Dean over Mitch's shoulder, then said, "Nice try, Campbell, but logs won't do. It'd take time to digest them, time I don't have. And no one else at the Agency would understand them. You three are the experts. As much as it pains Lothar to be in the same room with me, I think I'll 'stick around' for real-time analysis."

Dean threw up his hands and sulked back to his bench.

Wayne, still blank-faced, turned to Marion and said flatly, "Even so, we'll still be looking at a low-quality video recorded on your phone."

"Meaning?"

"The source is poor. I'll slap on more detectors and augmenters, but they might not tell us anything more than we already know."

"Right," said Dean. "Holo Mode is good, but your video is crap. If you want different answers, you need a higher-quality file."

"Or we could jump over to Q-Tech with all of our equipment and measure their systems directly," Mitch offered, rolling his eyes.

Dean snorted. "Oh, that'd go over *real* well."

"You think?" said Wayne. "We could ask nicely. 'Oh... hi, Chris. We're the competition. Care to show us your industry secrets?' "

Mitch expected Marion to interject with some cutting remark, but she just listened to them grouse, her expression thoughtful. "What if I can get you a near real-time video feed?"

"How?" asked Wayne.

"My mother mentioned giving you access to the internet. Did that happen?"

Wayne logged on to his workstation and navigated to the Warrior Ops XX feed on PicsterGram. "I'd say yes."

"Perfect." Marion slid in beside him and typed a numeric address into the browser. A non-descript login page appeared with a barcode on it. She held her phone up to the screen and scanned the code. Immediately, the page filled with a list of building addresses. She scrolled a quarter of the way down the page before stopping. "Great. It's still there," she said, and then clicked the link that read "Violet St. Warehouse, Suite 411". A new page of serial numbers displayed. "There you go."

"What are we looking at?" Wayne asked.

"CCTV security cams for Mr. Meadows' place of business."

Mitch's jaw dropped. "Is that even legal?"

"All security cams for the area are processed through the Lakewood Federal Center. As an Agency employee, I've got purview. Think you can cast video from one of those links through your Holo Mode?"

"Let's see." Wayne connected his modified Jump!GO to the workstation and set his phone screen as a secondary display device. A plasma grid appeared above the phone, blue and ethereal as always, but empty of jump points and lying flat on its back. When he clicked the first link and cast it to his phone screen, the main lobby of Quantum Technologies blossomed in full 3D splendor upon the plasma stage.

"It worked!" Mitch exclaimed, forgetting for the moment to be mad at Marion. "Great job, Wayne. See, you *can* do anything."

"Within reason," said Wayne, his poker face replaced by the slightest hint of a grin. "The display looks crisper too. Real-time video definitely rules."

"Find the warehouse," said Marion. "It should be about four links down."

Wayne clicked the link, and a 3D rendering of the inside of Christian's warehouse appeared on the stage, with many of the same elements in view as they'd seen in Marion's video: the Q-Pod near the center, a table piled with BEAM disks, the row of controller racks along the walls. Q-Tech employees milled around the warehouse floor, and over in a far corner of the room, Mitch caught sight of a familiar face.

"Hey, there's Maggie," he said excitedly. "And over there's Cassandra. And Billy Hoag and Paul are by that rack. Looks like Christian picked up everyone CC didn't."

"All of these guys are sharp. Especially Maggie," said Dean.

"I'm not saying they're rejects or anything. It's just interesting seeing all these people we know working on the same kind of stuff as we are. It's like we're all on the cutting edge."

"Whoa, she's really laying into Christian. Wonder what he said to set her off?"

"He probably got all high and mighty about something she knows better than him. She hates that."

"Yeah, and Christian's the kind to assume you're stupid before he actually talks to you," said Dean. "You go, Maggie. Give him what for."

"Hmmph," said Marion, frowning at the stage. "That's unexpected."

"What's the matter?" asked Mitch.

"Trouble just walked in."

At the left side of the stage, Christian's receptionist opened the warehouse door and led two men into the room, one in uniform. Mitch only recognized one of them. "You mean Congressman Pollux?"

"No, the soldier. His name is Hallett. He was a field officer a few months back, but now he's a desk jockey in the research division. He shouldn't be there."

"Why not?"

"First, he represents the wrong department. If Pollux is offering Meadows a DoD contract, he should have brought an energy rep. Hallett's with the Geological Survey. Investing in quantum research companies isn't something the USGS does. Second, rumors say Hallett's a loose cannon. Field officers don't just lose their units. They either get promoted under a senior commander or are discharged, usually via court martial. He didn't get either. I don't know all the details, but he's riding a desk for a reason."

"You said this guy was in the research division," said Dean. "Maybe Q-Tech has a product related to his research."

"Unlikely. I'm not aware of any quantum projects run by the USGS. And from what I know about Hallett, he has a mechanical engineering degree that he's never used. He enlisted in the Marines right out of college, spent twenty years in the field, and now this. That Pollux even knows him makes no sense. "

Wayne interrupted. "I've added the extra energy and audio detectors. Wanna see what we pick up?"

Marion nodded. "Go for it."

The plasma stage flickered briefly as Wayne brought each detector online, then it settled into an even sharper view of the warehouse equipment.

The Q-Pod's wall panel lit up as expected, as did the dew drop cavity of the BEAM disks, all of them glowing white in the center and outlined in a bright, light-blue.

"These emission signatures seem closer to the Jump!GO's plasma grid than they do to any one jump point," Wayne observed.

"It's like each dew drop is a cluster of trajectories instead of one discrete vector," added Mitch. He glanced at the logs on Wayne's workstation. "The detector can't even tell what holds a dew drop together. Weird."

Marion squinted at the 3D display. "Can you pinpoint anything in the room that might generate the dew drops?"

Wayne rotated the stage, first examining the controller racks, then the hodge-podge of other equipment spread out among the workbenches. He shook his head. "No likely candidates."

"Check Christian's pocket," suggested Dean. "In Giganta's trash-tier video, he pulled dew drops from his lab coat pocket like rabbits out of a hat."

"Good point, Lothar," said Marion. "I'd assumed he'd added a bunch to his pocket before the demo. Didn't think he had a device to create them on the fly."

"It's possible," said Mitch, stroking his chin. "Despite all the dew drops he pulled out, the shape of his pocket never changed. Maybe he's got a device like the Jump!GO, except instead of displaying a plasma grid, it folds the grid in on itself until it becomes a ball. Target his pocket, Wayne."

Wayne grimaced. "K. I might be able to do that. But please understand, I excluded humans from detection on purpose. Our normal electromagnetic signature looks a lot like static. I didn't have time to assign it a unique color, so it might clog up the display."

"If he's got a machine in his pocket, though, won't that give off a mechanical signature, like a controller or a hand tool?"

"If the static from his body doesn't hide it." Wayne sighed. "I'll see what I can do. Give me a few minutes." He sat down at his workstation, pulled up the diagnostics code, and set to work.

Maggie stood just behind Christian, brow furrowed, looking decidedly perturbed and holding a strip of mylar with various electronics attached to it. Christian reached passed her and picked up what looked like a fake utility belt from the bench top.

"Ah, the Enviro-Belt," said Marion.

"Enviro what?" asked Dean.

"Enviro-*Belt*."

He wrinkled his nose. "What a horrible name."

"True," Marion agreed. "Wonder what Pollux and Hallett want with it?"

Christian snapped the belt in place, and after a furtive glance around the room, his body lit up like a flare.

"Wow, you weren't kidding about the body static," said Mitch. "Christian's as bright as a Christmas tree. Nobody else is lit up, though. How'd you isolate the detector on just on him?"

"Huh?" said Wayne, still focused on the workstation screen. "I'm still entering the equations. What're you talking about?"

"So... you haven't changed the detector to include humans in the scan?"

"I *said* it would take a few minutes. I know you think I'm fabulous, Mitch, but seriously, I'm not a miracle worker. Unlike you, the rest of us actually have to *think* before we build things."

"Shit," Marion whispered.

"Marion, I'm going as fast as I can," came Wayne's flat, poker-faced reply.

"Wayne, she's not complaining at you," said Mitch. "Turn around."

Impatiently, he spun his workstation chair around, but whatever sarcastic thing he had planned to say died on his lips. Christian floated above the stage, and though his body was outlined in a kind of off-white shield, the rest of him, head to toe, was crammed with what looked like hundreds of dew drops, pulsing in time with the beating of his heart. And every dew drop around him—lodged in the Q-Pod, the BEAM units, and the strip of mylar clutched angrily in Maggie's hand—pulsed in unison with them. "That's... unexpected," said Wayne.

"*He's* doing it. *He's* the Jump!GO," said Mitch, awed by what he was seeing.

"The 'tech' is Christian," said Marion. "It's been him all along."

Hallett's voice, crisp as a martinet, rose above all of theirs. "Nothing can penetrate it?"

"Of course not," said Christian. "That's the whole point." His words were more confident than his tone.

"Can it stop a bullet?"

"I, uh, we haven't tested that yet."

"Mm hmm." Hallett nodded. "Let's find out." The soldier unholstered his pistol and aimed it at Christian's head.

"Holy crap!" said Dean.

"Guys, move!" shouted Mitch at the holo. Reflexively, he swatted at Maggie and Christian to brush them out of harm's way.

"He's not really gonna shoot him, is he?" asked Wayne.

As if he'd heard Wayne, Hallett's face broke into an ugly grin and he squeezed the trigger.

Before they knew it, Maggie was between Christian and Hallett, wearing the mylar strip around her waist and surrounded by a semi-opaque blue blob. Sparks—Hallett's bullets?—bounced off the blob's surface, but neither Maggie nor Christian fell. The blue blob seemed to protect them both.

"What did she just do?" asked Wayne.

"Like I said, it's a resonance," Maggie explained breathlessly on the feed. "You need a stimulating frequency. Sort of like a seed crystal in chemistry. Once you have that, the frequency strengthens your field and you can vary it—make it contract or expand or oscillate—to make it more permeable or hard as a rock. Pretty simple once you grasp that."

Hallett nodded, seemingly satisfied. "Congratulations, Mr. Meadows. Looks like we have a deal." He holstered his gun and walked out of the warehouse, a stunned Pollux trotting after him. Maggie maintained her stance in front of Christian until they left, then tugged at the mylar strip. The blue blob disappeared.

Mitch realized he'd been holding his breath. With Hallett out the door, he allowed himself to exhale.

Dean sagged against his bench. "That was tense."

"Your friend's got the heart of a lion," said Marion. "She's wasted working for Christian."

"They all are if there's no real technology," said Mitch. "If Christian's producing the dew drops from his own body, how can he build upon that? He can't lay dew drop eggs indefinitely. It's unsustainable."

"We don't know that," said Marion. "We don't know how he got that way. We also don't know what he can or can't do."

"I'm with Mitch," said Wayne. "There's no way he can keep all those dew drops under control."

Dean pointed at the stage. "Look at him shaking. He's freaking out as much as we are. See his insides pulsing? I'd say he's about to blow."

Christian's face had gone pale.

"Are you alright?" Maggie asked him.

Christian opened his mouth to speak, but instead of his voice, a tone like a dissonant chord came out. The indicator on Wayne's audio detector went off the scale. The sound that emanated from the speaker on the workstation was nearly the same the sound they'd heard the night before, except crisper—a multitude of voices, all Christian's, all screaming.

"Not good, not good," said Dean.

Christian fled to his office and slammed the door. But soon white light, with flashes of orange, bled through the cracks around the door. They all recognized it.

"He's gone into the jump space," said Mitch.

Marion gripped the back of Wayne's chair. "Get a lock on him, Hirano."

"Now *that* I can do quickly. Routine's still embedded in the diagnostics." He pulled up the module he'd used all those months ago when he'd tracked the jump space bogey who'd turned out to be the North Korean leader's bodyguard.

With just a couple of clicks he'd tied the module into the HoloStage code, then triggered the old monitoring service for tracking jump space activity. A chaotic series of graphs sprouted and cascaded across his workstation screen.

"Whoa," said Mitch.

"What's happening, Hirano? What's all this interference?" asked Marion.

Wayne didn't answer. He just stared at his workstation. Mitch had expected him to rattle off a data-heavy explanation, full of jargon and high-level mathematical analysis. In other words, a typical Wayne answer. But instead, his friend frowned at the screen, tight-lipped and immobile. *He looks scared*, thought Mitch. Dean's words echoed in his mind. 'Not good.' *Not good at all.*

On the HoloStage, Maggie pounded on Christian's door. "Christian, open up." *Pound, pound, pound.* "Are you alright?" *Pound, pound, pound.* "Boss, please answer!" No response.

"Hirano, some information would be pretty good right now," pressed Marion.

Wayne shook his head, his expression growing more perplexed. "I... don't know," he said finally. "It should be just one graph. One ordered collection of inverted vectors. But... I've never seen these patterns before. It's not like the Jump!GO. Not like anything. It's just... chaos."

"What is?" CC Tamblyn asked as she arrived for her usual end-of-day check-in. Crossing to Wayne's workstation, she peered over his shoulder to study the screen. "Huh. Looks like a collection of Rabi oscillations. Is this a composite overlay of some kind?"

"No," answered Marion. "It's energetic emissions from Christian Meadows' office."

"Gawd. What new machine has he built now?"

"Actually, we think he's been experimenting on himself," said Wayne.

"Nonsense. The human body doesn't emit those types of waves. And if it did, that's still too many for any one person. There are dimensions upon dimensions depicted in this first graph alone. There would have to be millions of Christians to create a pattern like that. The energy required would be massive."

Her gaze landed on the scene playing out on the plasma stage. Mitch noticed their TA Larry Knight standing beside Maggie in front of Christian's door. "Strange. I don't remember this being part of the video," said CC.

"It's not," Mitch explained. "This is a live feed."

"From his warehouse? Right now? We can't be doing this, people. We can't be spying on the competition. You are putting me in violation of any number of corporate laws right now."

Marion turned to her mother contritely. "Sorry, Mom, my fault not theirs. But if what you said is true, we've got bigger problems than corporate espionage. Those waves *are* coming from Christian Meadows. Somehow his body's become cavitated by his photon 'dew drops.' He's likely on the verge of quantum overlap."

"Ah," said Wayne, a look of understanding replacing his earlier confusion.

Mitch was shocked. "How'd you know that?"

Marion waved dismissively. "Previous life. The real question is, how severe is the overlap?"

"Excuse me, Hirano." CC slid in front of Wayne at the workstation and expanded the diagnostic window. The data had trended higher in the last minute alone, spawning more erratic spikes on the latest graph. CC frowned. "I'd say very severe. And at the trending rate, we might see something ugly in the next ten minutes or so."

Mitch didn't like the sound of that. "Ugly like how? Like difficult data, or like buildings exploding?"

"Closer to the last one, but it's not entirely certain."

Oh, no. A wave of panic washed over Mitch. "We better warn Maggie. Tell her and everybody to get out." Instinctively, he reached for his Jump!GO and dialed in the coordinates for the Q-Tech warehouse.

"Hold on, Campbell," said CC. "You can't go rushing in there like it's some kind of emergency."

"Why the hell not?!" He hadn't meant to get angry, but the thought of the building exploding was too much like the Bureau's destruction. Unbidden, images of black smoke, people fleeing, and Jin and Chung covered in ashes flashed through his mind. "You said explosion. That sounds like an emergency to me."

"I said it's not certain. You popping in there half-cocked and unannounced is sure to throw everyone into a panic. Calm down and give me a minute to think this through."

But he couldn't calm down. "It's North Korea all over again," he blurted out. "I can't just watch while people die. Not again."

"But the plasma grid might amplify the quantum overlap. You won't be helping."

"Look!" Dean pointed at the HoloStage. "Larry's got a buzzsaw!"

Everyone's attention shifted back to the holo display. Larry—huge, imposing, and in full commando mode—raced toward Christian's office door swinging a circular saw one-handed like it was Thor's hammer. The light bleeding out from around Christian's doorway had grown brighter while the cacophony of voices in distress had risen in volume.

"I think the quantum whatsit's about to happen," said Dean.

Now Mitch was truly alarmed. "I'm going in!"

"Campbell! Stop! You'll make it worse!"

"You don't know that!" He triggered the plasma grid.

"Yes, I do!" Moving faster than Mitch expected for a person her age, CC dashed to the router and reached for the plug.

"Mom, don't," said Marion. "We'll lose the f—"

Just as she said it, the HoloStage and Buzzsaw Larry winked out.

"What?!"
"Gah!"
"Crap!"

They all stared aghast at the empty space where the HoloStage had been.

"Damn it, Mom."

"It wasn't me, Marion." She stood aside for them all to see. The router was still plugged in.

"Then what's going on?"

Wayne examined his workstation, brows furrowed as he sifted through the many cascaded windows. "The bubble's gone."

"We *know*, Hirano," snapped Marion.

"Not the holo. The jump space bubble. We don't need the feed to detect jump space. But there's no trace of it anymore. The bubble just collapsed. "

"Then that must mean the quantum overlap has stopped as well," said CC. She returned to Wayne's workstation. "Seems to be the case. Looks like it stopped just after the feed cut out. Crisis averted... probably."

"But what stopped the feed?" asked Marion. "Like Hirano said, it was separate from the jump space." She joined her mother in looking over Wayne's shoulder.

Wayne tabbed to the browser window for the CCTV site Marion had accessed. The list of security cam links had been replaced with a message written in large, red font.

ACCESS DENIED

"Your account's been locked out."

"That can't be right. It must have just timed out." Marion closed the browser window, opened a new one, and navigated back to the site. A new message displayed.

ACCESS DENIED
Gamma-Level clearance required.

Marion gritted her teeth. "Dagnabbit."

"What's 'Gamma-Level clearance?' " asked Wayne.

"A DoD phallic symbol. Excuse me." She whipped out her phone and angrily punched in a number. "It's Travers. Put me through to Ramona, please."

Mitch had tried to be patient, but he couldn't wait anymore. He targeted his fob at Q-Tech's coordinates and this time the plasma grid displayed. Turning to CC defiantly, he said, "I'm going to Q-Tech to check on Maggie."

"Campbell—" CC began.

"I'll jump to the parking lot and peek in a window. No one will see me. I just need to know she's okay." Before CC could protest any further, Mitch hopped through the jump hole.

"Don't worry. I'll keep an eye on him," he heard Dean say from the other side. He left the hole open, and soon Dean joined him near the dumpster in Q-Tech's parking lot.

Barely a minute had passed before the warehouse door opened, disgorging Maggie, Larry, and Christian from the building. Mitch dragged Dean behind the dumpster and the two of them peered around its side as the trio walked toward the few remaining cars.

"You think Christian's holding Maggie and Larry hostage?" whispered Dean.

"Can't tell," Mitch whispered back. "They aren't happy, but they don't look scared either. I'll bet they're just leaving for the day."

Maggie veered off toward the lone center car, then called over her shoulder, "I'll meet you guys there. It's just off Ulysses Street, right?"

"Right," Christian replied, his voice deep, sonorous, and completely devoid of the agonized chorus Mitch and Dean had heard earlier. "Thai Won E.Z. You can't miss it."

Maggie waved and flashed a hint of her trademarked smile. "See you soon." She jumped in her car and drove off.

"Well, answers that question," whispered Dean.

Larry and Christian stood awkwardly together staring after Maggie's car. Finally, Larry asked, "Where are you parked?"

Christian looked embarrassed. "I, um... don't have a car."

"Really? How do you get here every morning? I didn't think the bus came out this way."

Larry's tone sounded light, but Mitch detected a probing undercurrent. Leaning close to Dean's ear, he said, "I bet Larry suspects something."

"You're tellin' me," said Dean quietly. "He's got that look on his face like he gets in class when he asks you a question he already knows the answer to."

Christian raked a hand through his hair. "It's... complicated," he said.

"No duh," whispered Dean.

Larry studied Christian then said, "You know, it might not hurt to confide in someone. It's obvious you're not being straight with us. And, well... I saw some things in the data you gave me this morning. It'd help if you, you know, leveled with me."

"Maybe. While we eat."

Larry sighed, but didn't press it. "Sounds like a plan. My car's over there. I'll give you a lift."

As Larry and Christian walked away, Dean leaned into Mitch's ear. "Maggie's fine. They're getting dinner. Let's go back."

Mitch sighed. He knew Dean was right, yet he still felt unsettled. Christian had become an unstable human Jump!GO; some military hard-ass wanted Christian's "tech" for unknown reasons; Maggie and Larry had almost been sucked into a quantum catastrophe. It was a lot to process.

But the sun was going down and there was nothing more to see. "Okay," he said reluctantly, then re-engaged the light hole.

Behind them, the sound of metal on metal echoed across the parking lot. Dean crossed the light hole's threshold, but Mitch, his nerves on edge and senses heightened, dropped back into a crouch and craned his head cautiously around the dumpster just in time to see the warehouse door slowly close shut.

"Dude, come on," said Dean from the other side of the hole.

"Somebody went back into the warehouse."

"So? Maybe they forgot something."

"What if it's a burglar?"

"The alarm would have gone off. He's got a security system, remember?"

"Oh, yeah. Okay." He scanned the parking lot and the front of the building once more to ensure that no one else was around, then in one swift move jumped through the hole to the machlab and shut the plasma grid down.

Marion was still on the phone with her office. "But what's this 'Gamma-Level' garbage? I'm within my jurisdiction. We've got an active investigation in progress." She paced in front of the workstation while Ramona presumably investigated the source of the Gamma-Level lock. "On whose authority?" Marion listened, then scrunched her face as though she'd stepped through goose turds. "Look for options. Thanks." She pocketed her phone. Turning to her mother, she said dryly, "I've confirmed it wasn't your fault."

"Indeed. Whose was it?"

"That jackass Hallett." She noticed Mitch and Dean's arrival. "How's your friend?"

"Seems to be okay."

"Good." She stared angrily at the floor, then said, "Gotta go."

"Seriously? You can't just leave," said Dean.

"Thought you couldn't wait to get rid of me, Chambers. What was it you said in the hallway? 'Goodbye, Marion. Back to interning.' "

"That was before all the pistol-poppin', buzzsaw-wielding, dew-drop-slinging madness. Christian just about admitted to Larry that he's got a secret. Shouldn't we try to find out what it is?"

"Didn't we? He's full of plasma bees. Secret's out. Normally, I'd handle something like this with a discreet Agency raid. But things just got messy. Hallett's put Q-Tech surveillance on lockdown. He's not just a loose cannon anymore. He's crossed a line into actively blocking an investigation, presumably for his own interests. Campbell wasn't far off. This *could* escalate into another North Korea. Better for you—and Tamblyn Tech, by association—to back out now."

"But we could still help without Hallett knowing," said Wayne. "If we jump to Sam's, I could re-establish the feed. I've got more code in her garage, Tamblyn Tech won't be implicated, and we'd have better luck outside Tamblyn's network anyway."

"I appreciate the offer, Hirano, but until I get a handle on what he's planning, you guys are done. I'll be in touch." Marion headed toward the door. "Gamma-Level clearance, my ass" she grumbled under her breath and then was gone.

"Aren't you the least bit curious about what Christian did to turn himself into a Jump!GO?" Dean said to CC. "You said it yourself, quantum overlap is unstable in a human matrix. He could be a ticking time bomb."

"He seems in control at the moment. We have other concerns, namely prepping for Tech Convergence. Marion can handle it."

"But she's just a cop!"

CC turned steely cold eyes on Dean. "I'll have you know she's got more schooling, experience, and sense than the three of you combined. The Agency hired her *for* her science background, not in spite of it. So, get off your high horse and shut up about my daughter. Clear?"

Dean gulped. "Perfectly."

"You are all on thin ice. I'd be well within my rights to fire all three of you. You were told to help with the static video, not open real-time surveillance on a competitor. The only reason you aren't having exit interviews in HR right now is because I'm on the hook with the board to have a counter for Meadows at Tech Convergence, and for better or worse, your Jump!GO router is it. You'd better hope I can scrub whatever sloppy tracks you've left of Meadows' network from ours, otherwise there'll be more to answer to than your irate boss."

"Yes, ma'am."
"Sorry, ma'am."
"Completely understood."

"Good. Now, for Tech Convergence, here's what I think we should do to have the best showing." She walked over the smart board and started scribbling out her ideas.

Mitch attempted to listen, but try as he might, he couldn't focus. CC's words faded into Maggie's panicked pleas for Christian to "Open up!" and the sound of Larry's circular saw. The sight of Larry ready to attack Christian's door with the saw flashed before his eyes. 'Another North Korea,' Marion had said. *Please don't let her be right.*

CHAPTER 17

Revelations

Marion slammed on the brakes at the third stoplight she'd encountered in as many minutes, immediately regretting not confiscating one of Campbell's Jump!GOs in the name of national security and expediency. Why in hell her mother had built Tamblyn Tech fifteen minutes from the highway, she couldn't fathom.

She was tempted to blow through the light and just flash her badge at any cop who tried to stop her. *It'd be just my luck to get pulled over by some frustrated commando, spend fifteen minutes chewing him out, and be no closer to finding out what Hallett's up to.* She sighed and resigned herself to waiting, but only just. Once the light hit green, she lane-jockeyed the rest of the way to US 6, and then lead-footed it back to the Agency's Lakewood offices.

She scanned into Building 42, passed the duty guard, and headed straight for Ramona's desk. "Ramona, what—"

"Travers!"

Damn it. Ralph Peters, surveillance supervisor and Marion's boss, stomped out of his office, wrestling a sheath of papers and nursing a grimace. He situated himself deliberately in the middle of her path to Ramona. The look on his face dared Marion to sidestep him.

Marion accepted the challenge and sidestepped. "In a minute, Ralph. Working a development in the Meadows case."

"Not anymore you aren't."

That stopped her. "What's that supposed to mean?" She shot a glance at Ramona, who just rolled her eyes and shrugged.

"You know damn well what it means. Gamma-Level lock, by the DoD no less. You're blown. Case is closed."

"That's bullshit, Ralph, and you know it," she said impatiently. "The DOD's got no jurisdiction over us. We're an independent agency. Just log a bypass with the Inspector General. Case re-opened." She cut over to the side aisle and continued toward Ramona's desk.

Ralph turned so red she could practically see steam coming out his ears. Head down like a bull, he charged into the aisle and blocked her way again. "My office, Marion."

I don't have time for this. "Ralph, listen—"

"Now!"

Marion felt her eyes flash and the words of reason poised on her lips transformed into a stream of glorious invective that only Ramona's frantic throat-slashing motion convinced her to contain. Clamping her mouth shut, Marion marched into Ralph's office and waited. *Womp!* Ralph slammed the door shut and tromped to his chair, then slapped the sheath of papers down in front of him on the desk.

"The veins really bulge in your neck when you shout like that," she said.

"So that's your strategy? Give me a stroke?"

"Just kidding."

"Nothing funny about it, Marion. Your cases keep blowing up. It's a bad pattern. The Agency's independent, but loud cases make us vulnerable. Especially to jokers like Hallett with influential friends."

"You mean Pollux."

"Exactly. Mr. Appropriations Committee. He may be out of office, but he's still damn influential. Major Hallett talks to Pollux, Pollux whispers in the right committee member's ear, and our funding goes straight into the toilet."

"We're scaredy-cats now? Afraid to tell a joker to buzz off because he's got a uniform and congressional ties?"

"What we are—what we're *supposed* to be—is *covert*. We *surveil*. We don't draw attention to ourselves. All you had to do with Meadows was observe. Watch his demo, take some pictures. Simple, quiet, neat. Now there's a Gamma lock on a case no other agency should know about. So, my question is, what did you do?"

"Nothing, Ralph."

"Garbage! The DOD's spooked. You must have tipped your hand."

"The DoD could care less. And I'll bet you a week's salary nobody above Hallett is even aware he ordered a Gamma. He and Pollux are up to something. They need Meadows' help and don't want anyone else to find out for what. If you log the bypass with the Inspector General, we might smoke them out."

"It's not that simple, Marion."

He drummed his fingers absently on his desktop, a tan folder beneath his hand muffling the sound. He still seemed angry, but in a distracted way. *What is going on with him?*

"We have to tread carefully here," he continued. "The higher-ups will ask me the same question I just asked you: what did we do? How did they know we were watching Meadows? I've got no answer. They will also wonder why I'm bucking the brass, especially a guy with decorations pinned on by the honorable Bertrand Pollux himself, I might add. The guy saved a whole village. He's a flippin' war hero. He wants to protect a few files, so why do we care? Hallett's beyond reproach."

"He lost his commission!"

"He got transferred to a new assignment. That's how Pollux will spin it anyway."

"He shot at civilians this afternoon in Meadows' warehouse, unprovoked!"

Ralph winced. "That's your interpretation. What you saw might not be what you think you saw."

"Come on, Ralph, I know you don't believe that!" She leaned on his desk and said, "All I need is a few minutes with Ramona. I guarantee you we'll get proof enough to justify keeping the case open."

"For the last time, Marion, I can't let you violate a Gamma-Level lock. We mess with the DOD, they find a way to cover us with a ton of bricks. We're better off leaving this in their court. If either Hallett or Meadows' goes ballistic, it's Defense's problem."

"Or we wind up with another North Korea—in which case, it's back to our problem."

"Or you'll foul it up some more and get us slammed with an Omega-Level Lock. Then the whole Department will be muzzled, not just you and your academic miscreants."

"It's more than that."

"Damn right it is! More than Meadows and Hallett and Pollux combined! It's—"

He stopped short as if he'd said too much. The guilty look on his face told Marion that he had.

"You've got to be kidding me," she said. "Have you been using Meadows' surveillance as a blind for spying on someone else?"

His continued silence was all the answer she needed. "Don't tell me it's P—"

"Keep your voice down," he said.

"We're the Agency! Who else could be listening?"

"Before the Gamma-Level lock, no one. Now? Who's to say."

"Does this have anything to do with his busted deal with Hubert?"

"Let's just say there's reason to believe more multinationals are involved and that there's a chance they can still get whatever Hubert and his associate were trying to sell."

"But I bet you're going to tell me you've got no proof."

"Exactly. And if we draw too much attention our way, we likely won't find any. The mark's got the power to shut it all down."

"Shouldn't Hubert have provided whatever proof you needed?"

"You'd think, but he's an idiot and knows nothing beyond what we already knew, so now we're back to the original target. Or at least we were. Who knows after today."

"That's why you need to let Ramona find a workaround and pull Meadows' surveillance files. There must be something they don't want us to see, and that thing could just be the smoking gun you need. You know I'm right."

Ralph wouldn't meet her gaze. Instead, he stared hard at the scattered papers and files on his desk, his hands clenching and unclenching. After about a minute, he seemed to come to a decision.

He gathered up the papers into a binder clip and stuffed them into the back of the tan folder. "You're on the Cardiff-Grant Factory case. Take this out to Ramona, and tell her I need the factory's video logs. She'll fill you in on other particulars of the case to get you started."

Marion sighed. "So, you need me to shift gears right this minute, then."

He pondered. "Not immediately. We've got a two-week surveillance window. You can get started Monday. But first, I need you to help Ramona get me the log list within the next"—he glanced at the clock on the wall—"fifteen minutes. Got that? Exactly fifteen minutes. Now get the hell out of my office."

He was making a concession of some kind, but Marion wasn't sure exactly what.

As soon as Marion stepped out of Ralph's office, Ramona caught her eye and beckoned her over to her desk. "You survived."

"Barely," said Marion dejectedly. "He yanked me off the Meadows' case. Says I have to work Cardiff-Grant instead."

"You sure about that? The CG factory surveillance won't start until next week." Ramona eyed the file folder in her hand. "For me?"

"Yeah." She handed Ramona the folder. "He says he needs the video log list in fifteen minutes, whatever that means."

Ramona paged through the packet, then laughed as she reached the clipped papers at the back. She pulled the topmost paper out of the clip and waved it triumphantly at Marion.

"What?"

"Ralph just handed you a virtual server surveillance mask."

"For the Cardiff-Grant video logs, right? "

"Yes, but guess which servers house those logs?"

A slow smile spread across Marion's face. "You're kidding me?"

"Nope. Secure Metrics. Same as Q-Tech's."

"That sly dog. So, we can launch an anonymous Citrix workspace to log on to the server and—"

"—spoof a local service account like the scheduler or the virus scanner to bypass the clearance lock."

"And since we're doing it for a different case, we aren't in violation. Fabulous, Ramona!"

"Only partially. We can't retrieve the Q-Tech live feed, just any saved video from the past thirty days."

"Good enough. A month's worth of evidence is bound to turn up at least one clue. But you better hurry. Ralph said fifteen minutes and we're down to ten."

Ramona started a virtual session, logged on to the server, then triggered a virus scan of the CCTV folders. "The scan will make our file accesses look legit. We should be free now to look around."

She navigated to the Cardiff-Grant factory folder first and saved off the video logs. Then she opened the Violet Street warehouse folder. The status bar noted sixty-one files.

Marion raised her eyebrows. "I thought you said there'd be only thirty days of videos."

"That's what's supposed to be there. For some reason, the purge job's been skipping this folder for... a bit over a month?" She sorted the file list by date.

"Oh, good lord," said Marion.

"What?"

"The date stamp on the first file. It's the same date we carted Hubert Wilkins off to Supermax."

"I'd say that's a clue."

"Of some kind, anyway."

"The folder dropped off the purge list two days later."

"Who removed it?"

"Nobody. It was archived. The purge job ignores archived folders."

"Why was it archived?"

"I've got a theory"—Ramona clicked away from the workspace and searched the Agency's database—"and I appear to be right. Meadows finalized the lease on the warehouse the same day but didn't renew the security contract. Secure Metrics archives existing folders while they pressure new tenants to re-up. He's still in the grace period, so the folder stayed archived."

"Lucky for us. We're down to six minutes. See anything else interesting?"

Ramona clicked back to the virtual window. "Maybe. Get a load of this." Ramona pointed at the 'Accessed' column. "Not only does the first file have Wilkin's arrest date, it's also been accessed at least twenty times. So has this other file further down the list."

"Hmmm. The second file was created the same day Meadows held his investor demos."

"Another clue? We're getting close to a bingo."

"Only if you can prove that Hallett was the one doing the accessing."

"Simple enough." Ramona expanded the file history event log. "First we do an IP trace... then filter out the local server's IP... then compare the remaining ones to the IP blocks allocated for our complex and... there it is. Building 51, military workstation for one Major—"

"—Bart Hallett. There's your bingo."

Ramon laughed. "I'll need you to stamp my card."

"Ramona!" Ralph leaned out of his office door. "Bring me that log list. Now!"

Marion checked her watch. Ralph had timed it down to the exact minute.

"His lordship bellows," said Ramona. "Need anything else from me?"

"Can you copy those two videos to my workstation without anybody noticing? "

"Done."

"You're fantastic. I can take it from here."

"Ramona!" Ralph hollered, his impatience echoing across the room.

"On it, Chief!" Ramona called over her shoulder. With an apologetic shrug, she shut down the surveillance mask and replaced it with a case search window. "King Ralph awaits."

"Precisely why I switched to field work. Good luck."

"Wait." Ramona closed the Cardiff-Grant packet and handed it back to Marion. "You're gonna need this."

"Ralph said I could start next week. I'll come get it then."

"No, really. Look at the clip of papers in the back. Interesting reading."

*****

Marion took the packet back to her office, closed the door, and slumped into her chair. *Hoo boy, what a day.* She'd accumulated a lot of answers, but where it all led was hard to tell. Hallett had been spying on Meadows at the same time as the Agency. That coincidence might be suspicious enough for Ralph to ping Hallett's superiors.

But the defense department had its own intelligence division. Maybe they *had* ordered the surveillance. If so, Ralph's approach might be smarter: let DoD handle Meadows, then any trouble he'd cause would be up to them to contain. Or they'd find a way to make Pollux tip his hand.

Her stomach growled. She glanced at her watch: 6:30. *Sheesh, dinner time already.* Her eyes drifted to the window and landed across the highway on the brightly lit Rubio's Mexicali sign. Its parking lot overflowed with cars and the patio was crammed full of Happy Hour revelers enjoying a relatively temperate evening.

Questions and answers might be easier to decipher after a lime shrimp burrito bowl and a couple of margaritas. But there was the matter of crossing the highway, no minor feat during rush hour. Given the patio crowd, there'd likely be no seat at the bar when she finally arrived. And the take-out line would snake to forever.

Maybe I'll just watch the first video, she thought. *Fast-forward through it to see if something obvious leaps out.*

If nothing presented itself, she could head out, grab a cheeseburger at a drive-thru, and wash it down at home with a beer—maybe two—then start over again tomorrow. Because seriously, short timeline or not, it had been a *weird* day.

She'd seen a lot of disturbing stuff, not least of which was the sight of Meadows packed head-to-toe with his own dew drops. She imagined there being a logical explanation for that. He could have made himself a body suit and embedded it with thousands of his fun-sized portals. Meadows was just the type of neurotic scientist to create something squirrely like that.

And the videos Hallett targeted might simply show Meadows sewing the pieces of the suit together. Or reading technical journals. Or sewing and reading while eating a peanut butter sandwich. Hallett watching and rewatching them like the Zapruder film didn't *have* to mean anything, did it?

Marion rubbed her eyes and admitted to wishful thinking. No matter how tired she was, she'd have to suck it up, especially if there was a chance to find Ralph's smoking gun.

She sat up to log in to her workstation, but the tan folder in her lap slid off, spilling its contents to the floor. The thick stack of papers Ralph had shoved into the back flopped out away from the others. On top of the stack was a news clipping from the Gunnison Daily Post with a photo and headline that gave her pause.

Bart Hallett stared up at her as Bertrand Pollux pinned a medal to his chest. *Is this what Ralph wanted me to see?*

The headline for the article declared "From Miner to Hero: Local Man Receives the Bronze Star." She picked up the stack of papers and read:

WASHINGTON, DC Outgoing third district representative Bertrand Pollux was on hand at Walter Reed Hospital today to present the Bronze Star to Gunnison-native Captain Bartle Hallett, son of Mark Hallett, the late owner of Gunnison's Placer Valley Mining and Construction company (PVMC).

Captain Hallett was awarded the medal in recognition of his bravery in leading the liberation of the village of Kohinarange outside of the Washir district of the Helmand province in Afghanistan.

The village was the site of a joint Afghan-American mission to improve road access between the district and Delaram by building a tunnel through a local mountain. PVMC representatives, participating in the mission on a humanitarian consultation contract, were taken hostage with villagers when local insurgents launched their attack.

Hallett led troops in eliminating the insurgent threat, pushing them out of the village while simultaneously thwarting an attempt on his life. Unfortunately, two soldiers under his command lost their lives and the tunnel sustained severe damage as a result of the hostilities. Several tons of equipment were buried in the cave-in. Construction is on hold pending the assignment of a new construction team once the threat lessens. PVMC's spokesman, Gilbert Gottlieb, said that, "Because of the obvious danger, plans to retrieve our equipment will need to proceed at a later date."

Congressman Pollux, Mark Hallett's business partner prior to his election to office, commented during the ceremony that he was "proud to bestow such an honor on the son of his late friend." He also stated that the younger Hallett had "prevented excessive bloodshed and saved the lives of his fellow Coloradans."

Hallett is currently recuperating at Walter Reed from injuries sustained in the attack. Along with the medal, he was also granted a promotion to Major and will begin a stateside assignment upon his release from the hospital.

Huh. So Pollux had been business partners with Hallett's late father; that explained how they knew each other. But it didn't quite explain how his ex-partner's employees got roped into a construction project "for humanitarian reasons." It also seemed strange that insurgents would attack while said employees just *happened* to be in the country along with their dead boss' son.

If she were the suspicious type, the whole episode would sound like a covert deal gone wrong, with Hallett's tale of bravery an obfuscation of events and his promotion to stateside a bribe. Some aspect of the deal had definitely gone sideways, likely due to Hubert or Pollux's greed. Then the tunnel was destroyed, burying whatever secret thing they'd been trying to extract and sell.

The big question mark in all of this was Meadows. What role exactly did Pollux and Hallett expect him to play? None of Q-Tech's toys were geared toward mining or construction. What did the Enviro-Belt have to do with a collapsed tunnel half-way around the world?

Her stomach rumbled again. *Hang on, baby, cheeseburger's coming.* With any luck, the video would tell her everything she needed to know.

She shifted her focus back to her workstation, where a message from Ramona blinked for attention. She opened it and clicked the link to the internal share containing Meadows' security cam videos. She clicked the first one, and to save time set the viewer to run at twice the normal speed. What she saw next was enough to rival the weirdness of Hirano's image of Meadows stuffed full of plasma bees.

A hail of dew drops exploded out of Campbell's Canopy and rained down on Meadows like fiery bullets. But instead of his body burning to ash under the plasma onslaught, it glowed almost as bright as the sun as he absorbed the dew drops one by one. Then the explosion's concussion shook everything around him, burying Meadows under a ton of tools, racks, and equipment.

He should be dead, thought Marion. *His body should be crushed in the rubble. Did Hallett see the explosion and send someone over to dig him out?*

She was wrong, of course. No one came to Meadows' aid. But as abruptly as the wreckage had overwhelmed him, the twisted pile of metal shifted and shot up into the air. The pieces were ejected to all sides of the warehouse, followed by a hard blast of light that hit the back wall, gouging out a great chunk of rock.

Meadows rose up from the scorched floor, encapsulated in a bubble, and floated through the hole in the wall toward the rising sun. *Wow. Now I understand the repeat viewings.*

Clearly, Hallett had concluded that Meadows was capable of levitation and telekinesis. He must have shown the footage to Pollux and together they'd concocted today's ruse. Their visit to the warehouse had nothing to do with Q-Tech's products, and Hallett's shot wasn't meant to test the Enviro-Belt. They wanted to force Meadows to reveal his abilities, and then exploit those abilities for their own gain. Whatever was buried in that mountain must be worth a lot for them to risk enlisting Hubert's unstable sidekick in a scheme to retrieve it. But what on Earth could it be?

She was certain Ralph wanted her to find out and to do it as quickly as possible before anyone else got wise to their investigation.

She reached for her phone and dialed her mother's number.

"Mom? Think I can borrow one of Campbell's Jump!GOs? There's something I need to check out in a hurry on the other side of the world."

CHAPTER 18

Confession

Christian leaned over his bowl of tom kha gai and gratefully inhaled the steam. The rich scent of spicy curry tingled his sinuses and made his mouth water. He eagerly dipped a spoonful of brown rice into the concoction, then crammed it into his mouth, truly hungry after his ordeal, but secretly hoping his eating would dissuade Larry and Maggie from asking any more questions.

"You actually got Campbell's Canopy to appear?" asked Maggie. "Get outta town!"

He nodded. "Mmm, hmm." He fished a particularly large piece of chicken thigh out of the soup and packed it into his mouth with the rice.

"So what went wrong?" asked Larry.

He shrugged and kept chewing, expecting one of them to say something else for him to respond to mutely. But Larry just kept staring at him, patiently waiting for a reply. The longer the silence dragged on, the more uncomfortable Christian felt. Finally, he swallowed and said, "Well, nothing at first. Everything went right. The Canopy popped out just as described in Campbell's paper. But..."

The accident had dominated his memories of the night he'd recreated Campbell's Canopy for so long he hadn't really thought about the steps leading up to it. Now, forced to by Larry, he couldn't help but smile remembering his accomplishment with pride. Just before it all went to hell. "I could see a way to extend it that Campbell missed. The calculations showed room for slack in the plasma lattice. As soon as I adjusted the matrix, the shells around the portals appeared."

"Wow, I would never have thought of that," said Maggie.

"Must have been something to see," said Larry.

"It was." The memory of the dew drops condensing along the roof and walls of the Canopy filled his mind's eye. "I remember them looking like... a thousand jewels. Like bulbs on a huge chandelier. Or bright, ripe fruit dangling from an enchanted tree." His spoon slowly sunk down into the tom kha gai, forgotten.

"And that's when it exploded," coaxed Larry.

Christian nodded. "Still don't know why. But it was like a gigantic fist hammered down on top of the Canopy. The whole thing shook and then..." His memories had come full circle, and once again the trauma and shame of the accident stymied him.

"Then what?" asked Maggie.

"What happened to you?" Larry leaned forward, invading his space just like in the parking lot, his tone insistent and probing.

"I—" Inside his head a war of voices collided.

[**Tell them**], Time Christian urged him.

[*No!*] screeched the others, fainter, but no less demanding. [*They won't believe you. They'll think you're crazy. They'll tell everyone that the technology is fake, then quit.*]

[**Not true,**] said Time.

But the idea planted by the screechers—that Larry and Maggie would quit—resonated. The backlash from revealing a reasonable truth might be overcome. But expecting them to believe he'd survived being pummeled by thousands of plasma packets was a stretch. Even if they did believe him, telling them further that the plasma portals imbued him with interdimensional, photon-warping abilities was asking too much.

Worse, they'd know his business was built on a house of cards, made all the more precarious by his tenuous hold on what made the business possible: the dew drop portals he'd absorbed. If even the crazed Christians trapped in those portals considered his predicament insane, how could Larry and Maggie, two of the most level-headed people he'd met, not think otherwise?

The screechers were right—Larry and Maggie would bolt. He'd be alone again. And for the first time in his life, he couldn't make himself feel good about loneliness.

"I ran," he said finally. The lie quieted the cacophony, but a wave of sadness washed over him, and he knew the sadness wasn't entirely his own.

[**Lying only delays the inevitable,**] said Time. [**And makes your final path harder.**]

Christian closed his eyes. *I don't care,* he answered. *I don't want to lose them.*

[**You lose more with every lie.**]

"That's all?" said Larry.

Christian opened his eyes. Now that he'd made his choice, he knew he could riff on it. "The energy build up was too much. I knew Campbell's setup wouldn't handle it. I only barely made it to the parking lot before the whole thing exploded." The embellishment came easier than the truth.

"So, nothing hit you? No plasma balls touched your skin?" asked Larry, his eyes boring into Christian's yet again.

"No." *Coward.*

"Hmmph. Lucky break. But that doesn't explain the dew drops. Did any survive the explosion?"

"I waited a few minutes before going back in, and when I did they were all over the floor. Thousands of them. I put some into a beaker to study and swept the rest up into a box that I keep at my apartment. "

"How'd you make the dew drop generator? It looks nothing like Campbell's Canopy. From what I can tell, it doesn't function like it either."

Christian was really feeling the act now. He hung his head and said, "I'm sorry. I haven't been completely truthful with you."

Larry nodded knowingly. "Yeah, buddy, come clean. We'll try not to judge."

"I—I lied about the generator. It can barely produce one dew drop. Every morning, I bring in more from my stash at the apartment and just pretend with you all that the generator works. But it's like the belt. It only half works. I'm ashamed." He added the shame business hoping that would solidify his sincerity in their minds.

Maggie looked appropriately sympathetic. She patted Christian's arm and seemed on the verge of saying something soothing, but Larry, whose expression had shifted from smug to puzzled, held up a hand to stop her.

"Alright, then, what about the lights we saw coming from your office? What was that all about?"

Christian was taken aback. He hadn't even known that the white space he'd been transported to had leaked out enough for anyone else to perceive. *What should I say?* None of the internal voices came to his rescue. He looked down and caught sight of his belt, and an excuse came to him.

"It was the Enviro-Belt prototype. Before Maggie fixed the actual belt, I'd been tweaking the prototype, trying different settings on the protective field. Guess I tweaked one thing too many."

Understanding dawned on Maggie's face. "Of course," she said. "I bet the gain was turned up too high, and that amplified the dew drop until the whole thing shorted. Makes perfect sense."

Larry seemed unconvinced. Brow furrowed, he sat back, applying the same intense scrutiny he reserved for students who avoided showing their work. *Come on, Larry, let it go*, Christian begged silently. But what if he didn't? His palm itched and the screechers returned.

[*Influence him! Change his mind!*]

Christian winced. He didn't want to manipulate Larry and Maggie. What good were fake friends?

[*But you've already lied to them. You're manipulating them with your words. This is no different. He keeps pressing. Just do it!*]

He dropped his left hand beneath the table and let a tendril grow in its palm—a thin one, for only the slightest nudge to Larry's psyche. He hoped it would be enough.

But before the filament reached him, Larry started laughing. Christian halted the tendril and added a carefully confused smile to his own face. "What is it?"

Larry and Maggie exchanged glances until she burst out laughing as well. "Seriously, what are you two laughing about?" asked Christian.

"Sorry, man," said Larry. "It's crazy."

"What's crazy?"

Squashing another fit of giggles, Maggie turned to him and said, "Larry had me convinced you were 'enhanced.' "

"Enhanced?"

"That *you* produced the dew drops."

"But I did," said Christian cautiously. "From the Canopy. Just like I told you."

"Right, but Larry thought—" Maggie began, then was overcome with laughter again. "Oh, I can't say it. It's too stupid." Larry's shoulders bounced up and down even harder and he covered his face with his hands.

"What's stupid?"

"Larry thought you could 'manifest' the dew drops. From out of one of your... cavities."

Uh, oh. Christian's blood ran cold. "That's insane!"

Maggie spread her hands. "I know, right?"

Why did they have to be so smart? Filled with self-loathing, he slipped his other hand under the table, sprouted a tendril for Maggie as well, and mourned internally. He'd never be able to trust them when they agreed with him or complimented him or laughed at his jokes, if he ever learned to tell any. He snaked out the tendrils slowly, wanting to prolong the genuine feeling of being cared about for just a few minutes longer. The restraint made the nerve endings in his hands burn.

Larry had been leaning weakly against the table, laughing and gasping, but he glanced up at Christian's solemn face, pushed himself away, and worked to pull himself together. "Christian, I completely misread the situation. I thought for sure you had eaten one of those dew drops. Maybe lots of 'em."

"Just tossing them into your mouth like popcorn," giggled Maggie.

"Eaten one? You *can't* eat them. If that had happened, I'd have exploded along with Campbell's Canopy," Christian said.

Maggie opened her hands wide and said, "Kaboom!" She and Larry collapsed into peals of laughter yet again until finally Larry said, "Sorry, Chief. We're just relieved."

They meant it. He could feel it. They weren't angry or scared. Neither of them looked ready to run. But he had to be sure.

"Now that I've told you the truth, I suppose you'll tell everyone else. And quit."

"Oh, hell no," said Maggie, chuckling as she bit into a spring roll.

"Certainly not," seconded Larry. "Could you pass the hot mustard?"

Christian was confused. He could still feel they were serious—excited even. "But... why?"

Maggie scoffed. "Are you kidding? I blocked a *bullet* today. Wild horses couldn't drag me away."

"Honestly, Christian," said Larry, "there's no way we can leave now. Not when you have such a big problem to figure out. We can help you. It's a challenge!"

Maggie nodded. "I swear, this job is the most interesting I've had, like, ever. That MRI thing with my mom was important and all, but you said it yourself: we can transform the *world* with your tech. Why would I skip out on that just because you don't know how to ask for help? That'd be stupid. Plus, Mitch and those guys would never let me live it down."

He gulped involuntarily, then took in a massive breath. The flood of air traveled from the depths of his lungs out to the tips of his fingers, cooling his nerves. *They believe me. And they're staying. I don't have to go through with this.* He unclenched his fists and extinguished the tendrils.

"Glad to see you finally chillin'," said Maggie.

"She's right, you know," added Larry. "No offense, but you've been looking ragged for days."

"It's obvious you're over-extending yourself," Maggie added.

"Try delegating more. You hired a lot of smart people. Don't just suffer in silence. Let us help."

Maggie nodded. "Even Dr. Bische asks Dr. Rebar for help once in a while, and he's a freaking genius."

"Exactly."

Christian didn't know what to say, didn't trust himself to speak at all, he was so choked up. But he felt he had to say something.

"I... I'm glad you two came to dinner with me," he said finally.

"Sure, any time," said Larry. They fell into an awkward silence.

"You're still going to pay for it, right?" asked Maggie. Larry snorted.

Christian laughed. He couldn't remember the last time he'd genuinely felt like laughing. It was a wonderful *feeling.* "I will," he said. "And I'll give delegation a try."

"Great!" said Maggie, her eyes glittering. "Because I've already got some ideas about the generator. We can start over with a bigger frame like this." She took out a pen and started sketching on a napkin.

Christian started to object, but Larry beat him to it. "Whoa there, scholar. It's been an intense few hours. How about we call it a week?"

"Aww! Just let me show this last thing. See, we line the box with mylar, just like I did for the Enviro-Belt, which is a horrible name by the way, and—"

Christian put his hand on hers. "That sounds great, Maggie, but I kind of agree with Larry. It's been a long day. Let's regroup on Monday, first thing."

Maggie sighed. "Oh, alright. The weekend will give me more time to design it anyway. Hey! I'll write it up in the network docu-share and send you guys the link."

"Wonderful. Can't wait." He waved the waitress over to pay the check.

"So, what's wrong with the name 'Enviro-Belt'?" asked Larry.

"It blows, that's what," answered Maggie. "One word would be better. Like 'Armor,' for example. It's efficient and descriptive."

"Can't copyright 'Armor,' though," said Larry. "Good or bad, 'Enviro-Belt' is not being used."

The waitress arrived and handed Christian a pay fob.

"For good reason," Maggie continued. "It sucks. You can copyright 'Armor' if you spell it weird. Like 'R-M-O-R' or something."

Christian finished paying and they got up to leave.

"But what does 'R-M-O-R' stand for?" pressed Larry. "You can't just jam letters together. They have to mean something. It's not like the 'S' in Harry Truman."

"Uh, what?" said Maggie.

"You know. His middle initial. It didn't stand for anything."

"How do you even know that?"

"We might be getting off the subject a little," said Christian. They'd reached the parking lot and were walking with Maggie to her car.

She snapped her fingers. "Got it! The letters mean exactly what it is—a 'Resonating Mylar Optical Relay.' RMOR!" She leaned against the driver's door, pleased with herself.

"Wow, you pulled that one straight out your backside," said Larry.

Maggie punched his shoulder playfully. "Backside, armpit, doesn't matter. I'm all brain." She flashed a final smile, then drove off.

Larry chuckled, then said to Christian, "I'll drop you off at your apartment, if you like."

Christian shook his head. As much as he was enjoying having company, he was also tired. If Larry started asking more questions during the drive, he didn't know how he'd react. He couldn't trust himself. *Better to be safe.* "Actually, it's a nice night. I think I'd like to walk."

"Suit yourself. Oh, and one other thing."

Christian tensed. *What now?*

"I know you're friends or whatever with Congressman Pollux, but people shouldn't be able to waltz into your business, shoot up the joint, then order you to take a contract as if that kind of behavior is normal. You might want to rethink that relationship."

Christian considered it. The same thought had already crossed his mind. He didn't need DoD money. The angels and other investors had assured him of a steady income stream for the foreseeable future. "You're right. I'll call Bertrand in the morning. We can do better."

Larry smiled. "Good deal. Catch you later." He started across the parking lot.

"Larry!" Christian called.

He turned around. "Change your mind about a ride?"

"No. But... thanks again."

"Any time, Chief. See you Monday."

It'll be interesting having friends, thought Christian. He watched Larry drive away, then stepped behind the Thai Won E.Z and opened a portal for home. The gray, spare interior of his apartment appeared within the portal and a feeling of deep claustrophobia gripped him.

He was tired and jumpy all at once and just couldn't bear the thought of sitting with those feelings at home with nothing to drown out his vocal, secondary selves. So, he switched the trajectory of the portal to land him at the warehouse, just inside the front door.

The soft glow from the dew drop hopper illuminated the path from the door to his workbench. But the intensity was off. *Has it gotten dimmer?* That would only happen if the box were less than full. He consciously kept tabs on the fullness of the hopper so that he could surreptitiously replenish it before it got too low. When they'd left for dinner, he distinctly remembered noting that the box was about three quarters full.

Looking at it now, he could tell that the quantity had dropped significantly. For a panicked moment, he wondered if the dew drops had dissolved. But if they had, they'd have left behind some kind of depleted plasma residue. He examined the hopper and found none.

Someone had dipped into the till. That was the only other explanation. He reached out with his mind and searched for a different residue: brain waves. The stronger waves would be the most recent. He easily picked up Larry and Maggie's waves and ignored them both. They'd left together and neither could have returned to the warehouse as quickly as he had. Other brain signatures were there, but weren't quite as strong except—

He'd almost skipped over it, its duration was so short, but a third strong wave lingered just above the hopper. He spread his mental field wider, and there it was, sharp as a spike and not matching any of his employees. Some stranger had robbed him. But who?

*****

Major Bart Hallett hid in the alcove across from the maintenance elevators and waited for the night janitor Julian to complete his rounds. He hid an additional five minutes after Julian departed then emerged and crept into his office.

Keeping the lights off, he locked his door and hefted the sack of goodies he'd stolen from Q-Tech's hopper. He guessed the bag contained a hundred capsules, maybe more, though it was just a drop in the bucket compared to the thousands he'd left behind. Nobody would miss them. Meadows would just replenish the hopper Monday morning, if the security videos were to be believed. It was the perfect crime.

Hallett closed the shades, deepening the darkness in the room. He pulled back the drawstrings of the sack and stared at the dew drops, fascinated by the pulsing photons within. "A bag full of gateways," he whispered, the plasma shells bathing his face with their soft, blue-white light. "Golden tickets to anywhere."

At least that was what Pollux had called them, but that weasel's vision was too limited too focused on retrieving their "merchandise." He was too caught up in recouping their losses from Hubert Wilkins' interrupted Chechen deal. Pollux only saw the dew drops as a fast way to make a buck. But as Hallett admired his ill-gotten bounty, he thought for the hundredth time, *Why settle for money?*

They'd watched the security footage of Meadows' accident together. Then Hallett had re-watched the video alone, over and over more than a dozen times. It baffled him how Pollux could watch the Meadows kid get hit with plasma, *survive* the experience—and gain powers for crissakes—but only think 'Let's use that to make money.' The small-minded fool.

The dew drops were the real treasure, not some buried lumps of metal in an Afghan cave. And Hallett was convinced that whoever controlled the dew drops could become more than rich. They'd have god-like power. If Pollux couldn't see that, the sooner Hallett got rid of him the better.

But there was still some work to do before he could put the politician in his place, like figuring out how to generate his own little "accident." He'd watched the video enough to devise a simple experiment: he would eat a dew drop. The Meadows kid, squealing like a pig, had appeared to suck down hundreds of the capsules and *lived*. No burst stomach. No burned-out throat. Just the ability to fly, lift rocks, project a force field, and teleport. Dandy!

"I'm at least ten times as strong as that egghead," he told the bag. "I bet I could eat half this sack. Just pop 'em one at a time like breath mints. Then *I'd* have the powers. That'd be a kick. Hehe. I'll show that kid how it's done."

Of course, it could all go wrong. The kid might be a freak, possess some quality Hallett lacked, some natural ability not captured in the video that had helped ensure his survival. Eating the dew drops was a gamble for sure. But somehow, he knew it would work.

And if it didn't, he wasn't afraid to die. Dying was no worse than being cooped up in his office, taking orders from a toad while barred from soldiering in the field. He'd rather risk it all than wither in an office, caged like his father. The old man had owned Pollux and half of the other politicians in the state—until he'd lost his fortune from bad mining deals. Stricter government scrutiny caused the politicians to abandon him, with the exception of Pollux. The congressman had forced him into even shadier international deals, until the old man died, licking Pollux's boots.

"I won't go like that," he said to the glittering capsules in the bag. "You all are my tickets out."

He pulled a dew drop out of the sack, the first time he'd actually touched one with his bare skin. For all the fire at its center, the bluish-white jewel felt surprisingly cool against his fingertips. Taking his coffee cup to the water tank in the corner, he filled it, then with one big swallow of water, he downed the dew drop and waited.

The tingling started deep inside his gut, not an unpleasant sensation. It felt kind of warm, in fact, spreading out and up into his chest and neck, almost the same warmth he might feel after a gulp of bourbon.

Then a supernova exploded in his gut. Molten fire burned his insides. Power surged through him. He felt he could crush his file cabinet or burst through his office wall. The burning filled him with euphoria and fear. Next, the fire crept up from his stomach, spreading from his chest and neck up toward his eyes. He knew it was escaping.

Try as he might, he couldn't prevent it. It spiraled out into a hollow core, erupting from his eyes and his mouth, his fingertips and ears. "Aaaaaaargh!"

His shouting ended. Eventually. He didn't know how long it had been. Could have been seconds, likely was minutes. But when he came back to himself, he was on his knees, the room shrouded once again in darkness, his insides wrung out and his mind empty and cold. He looked at his hands and tried to conjure the light, but nothing came. *What's wrong? Meadows shot lasers out of his hands right after his accident. Why can't I?*

Maybe one dew drop wasn't enough. He plunged his hands back into the sack filling both fists full of dew drops. He popped as many as would fit into his mouth, then clamped it shut, tightened his fists, and closed his eyes. *No escaping this time.*

Heat and light flooded his body again. Power pounded through his veins again. *Yes! This is it! This is what Meadows must have felt like!* As the heat and power rose into his brain, the bubble of light exploded and then... the whole world went white.

He dared to open his eyes. The light had spread out, engulfing his office in a fuzzy white cloud. Around him, translucent panels sprang from the "ground." His reflection stared out at him from within each panel, either dressed in his formal blue uniform or decked out in full combat gear. All of them wore the same disaffected smirk and waved at him from their glasslike cells.

"Hey, fellas. What is this place?"

A new panel appeared in front of him, but instead of his own face staring back at him, a pugnacious boy looked out. [**"Hiya, asshole,"**] said the kid, flipping him the bird.

Wait a minute, he realized. *That kid is me. Hehe. I always did have a lot of cheek.* "Back atcha', you bastard. Where am I?"

[**"In your office, doofus. Congrats on your desk job. Is it fun being Pollux's slave?"**]

"Watch your mouth." Himself or not, he wasn't going to let some snot-nosed kid give him hell. "You don't know shit."

[**"I know a mistake when I see it. And you just made it."**]

"Pfft. I can shoot lightning, boy. That's not a mistake. That's a win." He laughed at the kid. His reflections jeered and joined in.

[**"Stop laughing! You think you're tough? Shooting fireballs, breathing fire? You're burning up inside!"**]

It was true. His insides boiled, his lungs burned, and he could feel his blood circulating hot as lava. But that's all it was—heat, no pain. "That's just power. I feel fine."

[**"Now who's full of shit, dumbass?"**]

[*"Don't listen to him!"*]

"He's scared!"
"You're doing great!"
"The kid can fuck off!"]

His reflections encouraged him, and as he surveyed the lot he felt more in tune with them than with this surly boy. He was about to tell the kid to scram when the reflection morphed into his current self. *That's better*, he thought, but unlike the other reflections, Current Bart scowled at him in disgust.

["**Getting power this way is wrong**"] he said. ["**These other assholes are wrong.**"]

"Maybe *you're* wrong. They say you're scared of my power. I'm starting to agree."

["**It's a trap!**"]

"I can break out of it. Do anything. Get revenge for Afghanistan. Drag Pollux to hell. I can bring the entire world to order."

["**What you'll bring is destruction, mostly to yourself. Your 'power' will fade. Let it. If you try to keep it, you'll be destroyed.** "]

["*He's weak!*"
"Ignore him!"
"Eat more dew drops!"
"Then we'll all be free!"]

His reflections rallied again and the twist in Hallett's gut loosened. Turning back to Current Bart, he said, "I believe these guys. They seem to know me better than—gah!"

He stared in horror as Current Bart morphed again only to be was replaced by a shrunken, hairless ghoul in a hospital gown. Instinctively, he knew the ghoul had to be his older self, but in whatever moment this represented, his older self resembled his father far too much: the perfect portrait of his dying, cancer-riddled old man.

["**You think you know better, but I'm telling you. Take their path and this is what you'll become. A shell of a man, broken and empty. But stop this madness...**"] said the old man, morphing again into a hale, vital, though older version of himself, ["**...and you can be me instead. No superpowers, mind you. No patron of order. But unbroken and alive.**"]

As much as the ghoul had shaken him, this complacent reflection filled him with anger. "So, you want me to shut up, let go of these powers, and just 'survive,' huh?"

["**Right. Do it!**"]

The command slapped him in the face like one of his father's backhands. He'd had enough. *This ever-changing me can go straight to hell.*

He met the older man's hard eyes and said, "I'm sick of people telling me what to do."

The hardness turned to fear. ["**Wait—**"]

He didn't. Rearing back, Hallett punched the old man's panel, shattering it into hundreds of translucent pieces. The shards dissolved into slivers of light that incinerated the reflection, then enveloped Hallett the energy it released.

The white room disappeared, and he was suddenly back in his office, the glow of energy in his skin dissipated, but the feeling of power was still very much within. Current Bart had been right. The power coursing through him would eventually fade. But what had the other reflections said?

[Just eat more!]

He'd have to get a new bag of dew drops. Maybe find a way to get *all* of the dew drops.

But for the moment, he felt so good. *This is terrific!* He laughed and it reverberated through the walls of his office, the laughter of a multitude. The clock may have been ticking, but he was sure that would change. He just needed more dew drops, then *everything* would change.

"I have the power now. Let's see what I can do."

He curled his fingers into claws and thrust his hands out in front of him. Thin bolts of lightning sprang out of each finger, opening ten portals on the opposite side of the room. Inside each portal stood another version of himself, laughing and pulsing with just as much power.

He addressed the throng as he would a platoon. "Soldiers! Are you ready for some fun?"

["*Yep!*"] they answered. ["*Been ready for years!*"]

He dragged the bolts on a collision course, pulling them together until they overlapped each other and became one giant portal. He leapt through and the portal collapsed.

The sack of dew drops lay abandoned on Hallett's desk and quivered with echoes of sinister laughter.

CHAPTER 19

Competition

Maggie showed up bright and early Monday morning, but Larry had arrived even earlier and was already neck deep into prototyping her dew drop generator design. "Almost done," he told her. "Beautiful work. I only made a couple of changes. Give me a few more minutes and I'll bring it around."

"Whoohoo!" She danced to her workbench. On her monitor flashed a note from the production team asking her to confirm the Enviro-Belt fabrication request. She changed the product name on the request to 'RMOR' first, clicked 'Send,' then filled a sack with enough dew drops to satisfy Congressman Pollux's order.

As she headed over to Christian's corner to retrieve the belt, the eyes of her fellow workmates followed her, some curious, others skittish. Friday's shootout must have left an impression.

"You know, everybody's calling this the 'Kill Corner' now." Billy Hoag poked his head around Christian's partition, the unofficial dividing line between R&D and the production team.

Maggie snorted and held up the belt. "Good thing I've got protection. You still on production-line duty?"

"Crud, yeah. Through Wednesday. All we do is press buttons and pack boxes. It's *so* dull. Please tell me the belt job has a custom build. My brain cells are dying. I'd kill to get on the 3D printer."

"You're in luck. I trimmed the dew drop slot." She scooped a dew drop out of the sack and plopped it into the smaller compartment to demonstrate. "That means we need a new mold. The 3D printer is yours."

"Score! You need anything else?"

"You could be my stand-in while I gather baselines. Or will that violate the production team's quality assurance standards?"

Billy waived dismissively. "Eh. Those standard's are overrated. I did notice you renamed it."

"Yeah, we're calling it 'RMOR' now."

"Fire name. 'Enviro-Belt' slagged big time."

"No kidding. About as bad as 'Zune.' 'Enviro-Belt' sounds like the knockoff gift Grandma buys when the Infinity Gauntlet is sold out. 'Because Billy loves the superheroes, don't'cha know.' "

"It's got great accessories, though. Like 'Radar-sock'!"

" 'Molecule-tie'!"

" 'Glitter-pants'!"

Maggie giggled. "I'd actually buy a pair of those." She handed him the belt. "You sure you wanna be the guinea pig? I mean, it's working and all, but I haven't run through every scenario."

"Mags, you built it. I'm not worried." Maggie regarded him, eyebrows raised. Billy had never complimented her before. With him, everything was a joke. Billy coughed and looked away, a line of red creeping up his neck. "In fact," he continued, still avoiding her gaze, "I'd be over at the fabricator right now cranking out your order if 'Production Cop' Paul hadn't beefed about us 'Bische kids' skipping protocol."

"Which you Bische kids always do." They both jumped. Somehow Paul had snuck up on them from the production side. "The protocols are there to ensure quality, not to be ignored."

Billy turned to face him. "Come on, Paul. It frickin' stopped a bullet last week. That quality enough for ya'?"

"No exceptions," Paul huffed, then stepped back to his own workstation.

"See?" said Billy, lowering his voice. "The guy *totally* hates us."

Maggie smiled ruefully. "Sure it's 'us' and not 'you'?"

"Thanks a lot." He pasted an impact sensor onto the belt, wrapped it around his waist, and snapped the clasps in place. "Ready?"

Maggie picked up her test projectiles and took several steps back. "Ready. Turn it on."

Billy flipped the switch, and soon his body was encased in the same whitish-blue oval that had enveloped Maggie days earlier. He flexed his biceps. "Lob stuff at me, I dare ya'."

"Remember, you asked for it," said Maggie. She started small, shooting a rubber band at him, then worked her way up to a brick, recording the impact sensor output for each item. The projectiles bounced off RMOR's force field and landed harmlessly at Billy's feet.

"Is that all you got?" Billy taunted. "Huck a chair at me. Or a soldering iron. That'd sting if it got through."

"How about a sledgehammer?" said Larry. As promised, he'd arrived at Christian's bench with the new generator prototype on a cart. Aside from the temporary plastic door on the hopper, the device looked about done.

"Yay!" squealed Maggie. "It looks just like I drew it!"

"Certainly," said Larry with a smile. "Can't beat good design."

Paul popped up from his workstation. "What's that?"

"New dew drop generator," said Billy. He switched off the RMOR belt and walked over to the cart to look at the device. Maggie noticed other workers stopping to stare.

She and Larry exchanged glances. They were supposed to be discreet about the new version of the device. Larry shrugged. "Just trying to ramp up capacity. The current box has limitations and is more of a proof of concept. Now that we've got real customers, the boss wants to make it more robust."

"Just in time too," said Paul. "The old one's almost out. When I pushed the 'Regen' button, it hardly made any dew drops at all."

"Almost out?" Larry looked across the warehouse to the rack containing Christian's fake device. Low enough for only Maggie to hear, he said, "That's strange. The box was nearly full when we left on Friday."

"Paul's right, though," said Maggie quietly. "The hopper looked low when I came in this morning, but I just assumed it was from normal use."

Larry frowned. "Interesting." Adjusting his volume to include Billy and Paul he said, "Well, I guess we ought to get moving on this new one."

"Say, you wouldn't need some help with that wouldja?" asked Paul. "Billy here can have my slot on the production line if you guys need an extra set of hands."

Billy, standing behind Paul, gestured silently at Larry, pleading and mouthing "no".

Larry chuckled. "That's alright, Paul. It's really Maggie's project. She's got a handle on it. I'm just here to supervise."

"Geez." Paul threw up his hands in disgust. He turned to head back to production, but whirled around and said, "Look, don't take this the wrong way, but the rest of us are pretty tired of the Bische kids being handed all of the best stuff. We get it, they're Innovation Program whizzes, but the rest of us interns have to post reports too. They aren't the only ones who need work credits. Geez! Cut us a break!"

Maggie was taken aback. She glanced around the warehouse at the rest of their workmates. Some were avoiding looking in their direction, but those who did either smirked or nodded in agreement with Paul. Had Larry and Christian been showing a preference with assignments? *I just thought I was killing it.*

Larry didn't skip a beat. Looking Paul in the eye he said simply, "They do good work and have good ideas. I know you do too." He paused, considering, then said, "The BEAM map's voice modulation issue could use your attention. You're taking Dr. Quiver's accessibility elective, right?"

"Damn straight. Pulling an 'A,' too, thank you very much."

"Perfect. You're just the guy to troubleshoot the issue. Take it apart if you have to. I know you'll find the problem. Also, great suggestion to have Billy cover your rotation as Production Cop. It'll help him learn the protocols." Larry grinned at Billy over Paul's shoulder.

Billy sagged, but kept quiet. He'd seen the rest of the team's reactions. Now was not the time to complain.

Paul straightened up and shook Larry's hand. "That's what I'm talkin' about. Thanks for listening. I'll keep you posted on my progress." He smirked at Billy, then made his way to the BEAM side of the warehouse.

"Guess I'll get started on the RMOR order," said Billy. "Later, Mags." He picked up her sack of dew drops and headed toward the fabricator.

As Larry returned his attention to the generator, Maggie said quietly, "You and I both know that the 'problem' with the voice modulator is that the gain's too low on the mic."

"You've figured that out, but Paul hasn't," said Larry. "Now he's got the chance to prove himself. He'll take the system apart looking for the issue and, in the process, learn about voice recognition and the accessibility software. Dr. Quiver's final is coming up, so the experience will reinforce the material for him."

Maggie shook her head, marveling at Larry. "You're always teaching."

Larry smiled. "It's what I do."

Near Christian's office came the soft chime of a BEAM unit returning followed by the familiar voice of BEAM intoning "Transport Complete." The blue tube surrounding Christian collapsed into a disk beneath his feet. All around him, employees shouted out greetings.

"Morning, boss."
"Hi, Christian."
"Need some coffee?"

He silently acknowledged everyone, picked up the disk, and let out the sigh of a man who'd just completed an onerous task. He stared morosely at nothing as he squished the disk down to its storage size and dropped it into the pocket of his pants.

"Hmm, he's not happy," said Larry. "Guess his talk with Pollux didn't go as planned."

"I wouldn't be surprised, especially if Major Asshole was there. But our baby here should cheer him up." She grinned and waved at Christian enthusiastically while patting the top of the box. "Boss! Come over!"

A look of relief spread across Christian's face. He smiled, though it looked a bit wan, and made his way to the Kill Corner. Larry glanced at Maggie sideways. "You're always cheering people up."

Maggie shrugged. "It's what I do."

*****

The cool track lighting and cement walls of the Q-Tech facility came into focus around Christian just as Bertrand Pollux's unctuous, disingenuous face faded away.

Glad that's over, he thought, gratefully inhaling the warehouse's air, rich with the fragrance of toasted bagels and freshly brewed coffee. The pleasant aromas were powerful enough to knock the odor of Pollux's office, heavy with the congressman's musky cologne, from his nostrils. *Gods, what an odious man.*

And what a strange meeting. Christian had been ready to tweak Bertrand's mindset if he objected to Q-Tech backing out of the DoD contract. But the expected protests never happened. Instead, Bertrand greeted him to a display of disappointment as studied and well-acted as his customary avuncularity. "Frankly, my boy, I don't blame you after the stunt Hallett pulled. Lucky for you the belt worked."

"Thank you for seeing my perspective."

"Mind you, I am losing out on a solid commission. But Hallett isn't my only defense contact. We might sell your belt yet. And with the luxury market for BEAM as well as the mayor's interest in deploying the Q-Pod for Tech Convergence, any money lost from the DoD is a wash."

Just like that, Christian had gotten what he'd wanted. Or had he? He couldn't shake the feeling of there being hidden subtext to Pollux's comments. He'd folded far too easily, and had bid Christian farewell far too heartily. "Don't worry, Quantum Technologies is still the flavor of the month," he'd said, giving Christian a fatherly pat on the back. "Surely nothing will happen to compromise your existing agreements. As long as you keep pumping out dew drops and devices, Q-Tech will thrive. Take care, young man!"

What did he mean? Why am I still worried? All had gone as he'd planned, yet why did it seem like he'd lost?

Maggie's excited waving interrupted his ruminations. Like the kitchen smells and the friendly greetings from his employees, her and Larry's enthusiasm wafted over him like a breath of fresh air. And the sight of Maggie's new vision for the generator successfully converted from her napkin into a full-fledged prototype sent a thrill up his spine. Shoving Pollux to the back of his mind, he joined the two of them at his workbench to admire their creation.

It had looked crude from across the room, like a doorless mini fridge jammed on top of a hot plate, but up close he could see the functional purpose for the design. The "hot plate" contained the device's engine which was the Canopy's dish and magnets laid flat. The box above the engine contained the trapping lattice and storage cavity for housing any dew drops it generated. Both were big improvements over his original construct of breadboards and a coffee can taped to a packing crate.

Larry and Maggie regarded him anxiously, no doubt waiting for his assessment. "You two have been busy," he said simply. "Does it work?"

"Don't know yet—" began Larry.

"—but we're *dying* to try it out," interrupted Maggie, bouncing up and down. "Can we test it now? Please?"

"Whoa there, Heinz," said Larry. "I was about to explain that the plasma emitter still needs to be hooked up."

"I can do that in flash!" She rummaged around on the desktop for a tool pack, then thrust her head into the box, edging Larry out of the way.

Larry laughed and backed off. "Kids, huh? Always in a rush. How'd the talk with Mr. Pollux go?"

The dark cloud threatened to descend on Christian again, but keeping his tone light, he answered, "Gave me exactly what I wanted."

"That's good, right? Cuz you didn't look too happy stepping out of the BEAM. We were kinda worried."

"It's never fun talking to politicians. But he understood my perspective and agreed to call off the contract with Hallett."

"Good! We'll survive without the revenue, right?"

Christian forced half a smile. "With Pollux's finder's fee, it wouldn't have been that much anyway."

"Haha! I heard *that*."

Maggie popped her head up. "K, I think I'm done."

"I'll setup the blast shields for the test," said Christian, relieved to have an excuse to break away from Larry's inquiries.

Larry swapped places with Maggie at the box and inspected her work. "Pretty good, Heinz," he said. "This new emitter's bigger though. Might have to edge the detector back a scooch to reduce interference. Give me a hand."

"A 'scooch'? That's a new one," she said. She looked back at Christian and winked.

"It's like a smidge," said Larry, his voice muffled from within the box.

"Of course it is. What's a 'smidge'?"

Larry looked up, exasperated. "Come on, Heinz. A skosh, then."

" 'Skosh.' Seriously? Are you having a stroke?"

"You gotta be kidding me. You don't know 'skosh' either?"

"These aren't words!" She tried to look indignant but snorted as she said it.

"Aw, I get it. You're messing with me."

Maggie giggled. "Busted. But you talk like my grandma." Her head and hands re-entered the box. "K, 'Nana,' the smidge is in."

"Thanks, 'dearie,' " said Larry, popping the door into place.

Christian wheeled three thick, protective plexiglass walls into place around his workbench, enjoying listening to Larry and Maggie's easy banter. He handed them each a pair of goggles, slipped on his own, and said, "Let's give it a try."

Larry grabbed the device's controller tablet and remote and they trotted out of the danger area. Once they were all safe behind the blast shields, he pointed the remote and asked, "Ready?"

"Fingers crossed," said Maggie.

"Alrighty, then. 1... 2... 3!"

The machine's interior color shifted from dark gray to azure blue. Then a multitude of white spots appeared within the blue matrix, like crystals of ice falling into the night sky. Slowly, a web coalesced around each particle, condensing loosely into the familiar dew drop shape with a glowing bit of light pulsing in the center.

"Hooray! We did it!" shouted Maggie. She turned to Larry ready with a high-five but stopped short. Neither he nor Christian were celebrating. "Didn't we?"

Christian frowned at the chaos unfolding across the controller tablet screen. The wave patterns should have been smoother, leveling out as soon as the lattice formed, but instead they wavered wildly. "The system's not stable yet, Maggie," he said.

"Looks good to me. There's dew drops in there. It worked!"

Larry shook his head. "Not completely. The shells aren't solidifying. I guess the deflector's still out of whack."

Christian didn't have to guess. Given his heightened senses, the frequency misalignment was as obvious to him as a clanging bell.

Maggie leaned over Larry's shoulder, studying the data, and said absently, "Maybe it needed a jot instead of a scooch."

It was Larry's turn to snort. "Now who's the grandma?"

Christian debated. He could realign the deflector from behind the blast shield, but the movement of the detector would be clearly visible through the transparent door and hard to explain away. *Maybe I could blame spooky action at a distance?* He dismissed the silly thought. "I'll try to adjust it," he said, stepping out from behind the shields.

"Wait," said Larry. "Let me turn it off."

"Don't bother. This shouldn't take long."

"The box has a pretty heavy magnetic field, Chief."

"I'll be fine. It's a small adjustment. Won't take more than a minute." Christian grabbed Maggie's tool pack, then blocked the front of the device from Larry and Maggie's view. Forming a tendril in his palm, he undid the connections around the deflector and gave it a push in what felt like the right direction to bring it into alignment. The plasma shells within the lattice glowed brighter, but to his surprise they still refused to solidify. *So close.* He nudged it again.

"I'm picking up major instability," called Larry. Christian could see it. The more he pushed the deflector, the more the device's waveforms rippled like riptides through the azure matrix. "We better shut it down," Larry insisted.

"It's almost there. I can feel—I mean, I can see the plasma shells tightening."

"A little, but—Whoa! What just happened?!"

Damn! Distracted by Larry, Christian had lost his concentration and overcorrected the deflector's position, sending a power surge through the system. The plasma shells dripped away from the trapped photons like hot wax, and the surrounding blue matrix oozed up the sides of the generator like lava, pinning Christian's arm in place and forcing his tendril back into his body. The pain seared his palm and it was all he could do to keep from shouting out. Through clenched teeth he called over his shoulder, "Alright, you win. Shut it down. Now!"

"The button's not responding."

"Try it again!"

"I am! It's not working! Get back here, Christian, it's gonna blow!"

If only he could, but his arm was solidly stuck. He tried reaching out, tried wrapping his bubble around the runaway energy of the generator box, but it was no good. Over-correcting the deflector had created a field that somehow negated his own. No bubble would form.

"I've got it!" Behind him, Maggie snapped her fingers. He heard her rummaging through a drawer at a nearby bench, and then she was by his side. "Look out!" She tossed a white cylinder into the center of the generator. The object stopped short, hovering half an inch from the bottom of the box. After a tentative wobble, it began to spin.

As it spun, the pressure around Christian's arm lessened until, like a spring-loaded piston, it shot out of the box. The blue exudate receded, the trapping lattice dimmed, and the plasma shells re-formed around the lights in the cavity. One by one, solid dew drops appeared in the trapping lattice, multiplying by the hundreds. They'd done it.

"Yippee!" exclaimed Maggie.

Christian couldn't believe it. Massaging his arm, he asked her, "What did you do?"

"I tossed in a stir bar," she said, seeming incredibly pleased with herself. "It runs counter to the field generated by the dish and magna coil housed beneath the box. In a beaker, the bar moves everything around until the solution is uniform. I figured the same thing would happen with the particles in the box and low and behold it did. Look at that lattice. It's beautiful!"

"Good job, Heinz." Larry had emerged from behind the blast shields. "That's the second save you've made at Christian's bench. The crew's gonna have to come up with a new name for this corner. 'Kill' doesn't quite fit it anymore."

Christian turned to him, looking quizzical. "They call it *what*, now?"

"Uh..."

Brurp, brurp. Larry got a reprieve as Christian's phone rang. "Excuse me," Christian fished the phone out of his pocket and had to work to keep a scowl from his face.

"What is it?" asked Maggie.

"A text from Pollux. 'Turn on Techline News,' it says."

Larry raised an eyebrow. "Huh. Okay."

They headed to the break room.

The monitor was already turned to the Techline News channel and Chithra Muraleekrishnan appeared to be doing a remote. What could Chithra be talking about to make Bertrand take notice? Then he heard the low, confident voice of CC Tamblyn and his stomach sank.

"… but with my company's acquisition of the original developers of the light-based technology, we are on pace to deliver on the promise of the tech at the same time as, if not sooner than, Quantum Technologies."

"And by original developers, you mean the students from the Colorado School of Mines who created the prototype?" asked Chithra.

"Correct."

"Oh! I bet they're talking about Mitch, Dean, and Wayne," said Maggie.

"Yup," Larry agreed. "Sounds like Campbell's Canopy alright. But he and Chambers told me it was flawed. Why would she want their defective tech?"

Maggie shrugged. "Guess one of them found a fix. I used it once and survived. Maybe the problems were minor."

"Quiet, please," said Christian. He got closer to the monitor. *I should have known this could happen,* he thought. *But why would Pollux text me? Must be something more to it.*

"We recruited the original student team for a different program," CC continued, "and only found out about their light-based work after the fact. Although they arrived at their implementation independently, I led a project with DARPA several years ago that laid the foundation for the framework they eventually devised. The combination of the two workstreams has led to innovations neither group originally imagined."

"Our camera crew was only given a quick glimpse of these additional applications for the light-harnessing technology, but what we did see was extraordinary." A pre-recorded clip rolled of Chithra and the camera crew entering one of Tamblyn Tech's labs. Right away, Christian spotted Campbell tapping his phone and opening a portal that showed the Space Needle against the Seattle skyline in the background of the opening.

The camera panned to a back wall of the lab, where Wayne Hirano seemed to be connecting a circuit box to a blue plasma grid and checking the power output on a diagnostic tablet. The camera panned once more to a station across the lab and showed Dean Chambers interacting with a 3D projection of the wildly popular Warrior Ops XX streaming game.

CC Tamblyn narrated. "As you can see, over there is our core instant travel functionality, which we've managed to build into a compact component that that you can attach to your phone and control with an app. In the back corner, we're testing out a renewable energy option, derived from the light-capturing component of the travel device. And we've also uncovered a 3D rendering capability within the light-capture matrix that enhances any streaming feed. We can see this being extrapolated to real-time collaboration and social media interactions. The technology really has proven to be versatile, and it is so much more than moving people back and forth from one place to the next."

The montage ended and the camera view shifted back to Chithra. "All of this looks and sounds really impressive. Who's the target market?"

"Because of the versatility of the technology, there's no need to limit it to certain groups. We are fully committed to developing the right products for personal, business, and government use, for as wide of a distribution as possible, to include *all* who could benefit, rather than just the lucky few."

"And when should we have more specifics about official launch dates and the overall product roadmap?"

"We'll have a presence at Tech Convergence and plan to showcase several aspects of the technology in our booth, including live, hands-on demonstrations. I'm sure you and the rest of the tech world will like what you see. Now, if you'll excuse me, I have a meeting. See you at Tech Convergence."

Tamblyn produced her phone from her pocket, tapped it in the same way Campbell had, and stepped through a portal into a conference room filled with awed executives.

Chithra looked on, wide-eyed as the portal collapsed and disappeared. "Simply amazing. Having experienced both Quantum Technologies' and now Tamblyn Tech's light-based applications up close, I must say the seamless nature of the Tamblyn devices gives it a solid advantage over the former. Now that a tech behemoth has stepped onto the playing field, Quantum Technologies may be in for some stiff competition. Back to you, Todd."

The piece ended. Todd introduced the Space Technology segment, which was some story about strange pings coming from several near-Earth orbit asteroids. The break room had become unusually quiet. Christian hit the power button on the remote and the monitor went black.

"Huh," said Larry. "Well, what do you know?"

Maggie turned to Christian, a worried expression on her face. "So, is Tamblyn Tech having Mitch's Canopy, like, a problem?"

Before Christian could answer, his phone buzzed with a message.

"Pollux?" asked Larry.

"No. Actually, it's Marvin Maxwell. He wants me to give him a call."

"Uh, oh."

Christian waved it off. "It's probably unrelated. And if he did see the interview, he probably just wants some reassurance. I'll handle it."

His phone buzzed again. And again. Soon a cascade of messages flowed into his mailbox, all of them from different investors expressing varying levels of skittishness over CC Tamblyn's not so subtle reassertion of her company's dominance. More than one threatened to pull their funding, convinced Q-Tech wouldn't survive a head-to-head battle with the behemoth.

Pollux wasn't among them—conspicuous by his absence—but Christian did notice that seven of the objectors were investors suggested by the ex-congressman. A tired laugh escaped his lips. "Well played, Bertrand."

"What? You think—"

"Yes. Every one of these messages is from an investor he brought in, including the four big angels. He wants me to know that what he giveth he can taketh away."

"Wow. No wonder he lost the election," said Maggie. "What a bastard."

"*Influential* bastard," Larry corrected her. "Christian, you need to do damage control. Put out a rebuttal or something. Say that there's room in the market for two approaches."

Christian pursed his lips. "Maybe. I've found face-to-face conversations to be more... persuasive." He unfolded his BEAM box and headed toward his office. "Do the two of you mind finishing up with the generator? I need to step out for a bit."

"Not at all, Chief. Anything we can do to help?"

"Thanks, but I need to handle this."

He closed the door to his office. "BEAM, pre-set Pollux," he directed the unit.

The blue sheath transported him to the ex-congressman's office, but the man was nowhere in sight. Where the hell *was* he? Christian pulled out his phone and dialed Bertrand's office number.

"Pollux and Associates," said Pollux's administrative assistant on the other side of the door.

"Melody, it's Christian. I'm looking for Bertrand."

"You just missed him. He's traveling and won't be back for a few days."

"Oh, really. Where'd he go?"

"Just taking some vacation time."

He put a smile into his voice. "Any place fun?" His tone implied the question of where.

Melody wasn't to be tricked by a bit of social engineering. "Can I leave a message?"

Damn. "No, that's all right. I'll check back later."

He hung up and took tally of the messages on his phone. Marvin Maxwell had sent the most messages, every one of them filled with vitriol. He was vile and emotional and exceedingly vocal, qualities that made him the next best place to start in Bertrand's absence. If Christian influenced Marvin, Marvin would share his opinions with the other investors and start a chain reaction. They'd fall into step behind Maxwell, especially if Christian visited each of them to provide a nudge of his own.

But it wasn't enough to be charming while he invaded each of their minds. Charm opened the door to coercion, but sensory attacks made the coercion stick beyond the period of contact. It wouldn't be permanent but would buy him enough time to come up with a contingency plan. Damn Bertrand for forcing him into this.

He combed his hair, applied a fresh layer of deodorant, and summoned the visage of his most perfect self until he virtually glowed with health. Then, projecting charisma, desirability, and virility to the point of dominance, he stepped into the BEAM Box and called Marvin.

"Mr. Maxwell," he said, the tone of his voice modulated to its most suave setting. "Got your message. Mind if I drop by?" With a wave of his hand, he activated the BEAM and sent it directly to the executive suite of Maxwell Industries. Marvin stared open mouthed as BEAM materialized in front of his desk. Christian stepped out, an energy tendril growing in the palm of his hand. "Let's talk."

CHAPTER 20

Soldier's Story

The sun drifted down behind North Table Mountain, casting shadows across the machlab monitors while throwing the Holo mode stage into sharp relief. Three soldiers crept across the desolate Warrior Ops XX landscape, ready to ambush a renegade band of mutant War Talons run by an online team out of Metro State. They'd zeroed in on a set of loot crates stacked at the edge of the mine-riddled field. All Mitch, Dean, and Wayne had to do to stop them was to trigger the mines, then saunter in, and grab the loot. Easy-peasy if they worked together, but Mitch didn't want to wait.

"I'll draw their fire. You guys shoot the mines."

"What? That's nuts," said Dean.

"I agree," said Wayne. "They'll laserize you in two seconds flat. We won't have time."

"Sure, you will. Piece of cake."

"No, dude, wait—"

Ignoring Dean, Mitch launched a half-hearted attack on the War Talons' flank. He lasted ten seconds instead of two, enough time for Dean and Wayne to dispatch most of the mines. His health bar blinked away to zero under the laser blitzkrieg, then drained to gray. *Finally.*

"Welp, I'm dead. See ya'." He dropped his headset and controller and practically ran back to his bench.

Out the corner of his eye, he spied Dean's soldier avatar leveling his bazooka from behind a shack. "Revenge!" Dean yelled, then he leapt out and laid waste to the rest of the mutant band. The frustrated shouts of the Metro State team poured out of Mitch's abandoned headset. "Take that, roadrunners! Hey, there's health casks in these loot crates. Come back, Mitch, I'll regenerate you."

"In a sec. Checking something." He'd logged in to his workstation and was studying the output of a packet tracker he'd been running against Christian Meadows' freaky bioelectric signature the past few days. Ever since Christian's quantum overlap episode, Mitch had been scanning every frequency of the jump space, looking for evidence of another explosion or any hint that Christian was building up to one.

So far, the tracker had picked up zilch, which should have been a relief. But the longer he waited for another surge, the more anxious he felt. It seemed every day without an incident just brought Christian's next blow up terrifyingly closer.

Click.

He refreshed the tracker. Still nothing. Larry and Maggie had gotten lucky once, but what about the next time? *There must be a way to stop a next time. But how?*

Click.

"You doom trackin' again?" Dean called over his shoulder.

His friends knew him too well. "Somebody's got to. I don't get Marion. Christian's a ticking time bomb, yet she's more worried about some old-fart politician and a crazy army guy."

Wayne pulled aside his headset. "Thing is, Mitch, if the tracker detects a surge from Christian, what exactly can we do?"

"I don't know! That's what's making me crazy. I feel like we should be able to do something, but... Gah! I just can't figure it out."

"So stop thinking about it, buddy," said Dean. "Shoot some mutants, crack some crates, then *boom.* The Flash Face'll happen, and you'll have it."

Mitch sighed. "In a minute." *Click.* "Just checking once more."

The door opened and like an answer to a prayer, Marion walked in. "Glad to see you boys are being productive."

Dean waved without looking up. "Howdy do. Just testing out the HoloStage for Tech Convergence. Wanna help?"

"Pfft. If I want roid rage, I'll drive. Campbell, you got a minute?"

He trotted across the room. "Hey, you here about Christian? Need our help? I've been keeping tabs. He hasn't exploded yet, but he's been portaling everywhere. The guy just never drives anymore. And he's left the state like three times, but usually to talk to some rich dude. Don't know what that was about, but it's cool. No blow ups, though. Yeah, thanks for coming."

She nodded and listened patiently. When he finished, she said, "So, you're stalking Meadows, then?"

Mitch's neck felt hot. "No, I'm not. I'm just... watching him."

Dean snorted. "That's kinda the definition of 'stalking,' dude."

"You're siding with Giganta?!"

"It's okay, Mitch. You're embarrassed," said Wayne. "Doesn't mean Big G is wrong."

Marion continued, "Christian's on the backburner for the now. Pollux's partner, Major Hallett, might be the bigger problem. Those two are dragging Meadows into a mess that could send him over the edge if I don't nip it first."

Mitch frowned. "I thought you didn't want us messing with Hallett."

"Yeah, well, I still stand by that. But the truth is... I need to go somewhere. Quickly, and without drawing too much attention to myself."

"Where to?"

"Afghanistan. A little village in the Helmand province."

Wayne's ears perked up. "The Middle East? We haven't been there before. If we record your trip, we can update the Jump!GO's virtual map."

"Now hold on, this isn't a joy ride. I'll be working, and when I work, it's classified."

"Then I guess you'll just have to charter a flight," said Dean. "You want our gear, we need some data. There's gotta be some give and take."

"Campbell, you see my position, right?"

He didn't want to piss her off and lose out on a chance to thwart Christian. "You think jumping to this village will help you stop Hallett from pushing Christian over the edge?"

"Absolutely."

"Then I promise to delete anything that's classified. But if you want to use the Jump!GO, we need to record location data at the very minimum."

Marion ground her teeth. "You damn, stubborn kids. Alright, you can record, but don't fight me about what to delete. I can still shut all this down, my mom's business or no."

"Fine." Mitch stuck out his hand and they shook on it. "Let's get you geared up."

*****

Campbell led her back to his workstation and waved his hand at the pile of equipment on a nearby bench. "Pick out your gear while I configure the monitoring." He plopped into the swivel chair at Hirano's bench, flipped on the display, and started opening the standard diagnostic apps.

Marion inspected the haphazard stack of Jump!GOs, vests, headsets, and miniature cameras on the bench behind Campbell and drew a blank. "Where do I start?"

"Seriously?" Campbell spun around to face her, frowning. "All this time watching us, and you *still* don't know how a Jump!GO works?"

"To be fair, each time I was a little distracted by assassins with bombs and people filled with plasma bees."

"Yeah, but I mean come on. It's, like, super simple."

"Just show me, Campbell."

"Alright," he said, sighing heavily. "I'll tell you what to do, but you'll have to actually do the steps. It's the only way you'll learn."

Marion couldn't help but smile. "Sure thing, Doc."

Campbell looked up at her, startled. "Did I sound like Bische?"

"A little bit."

"Good. That means you'll listen." He handed her a vest and a camera. "Put the vest on. Then attach the camera to the clip on the right chest pocket."

"Why the vest?"

"It contains sensors that track your vital signs when you jump. That's the database stuff Wayne was talking about."

"Gotcha. What about the headset? It's awfully bulky."

"Oh, that's for me." He took it from her and put it on. "Your earbuds should be in the chest pocket."

Marion found two small pods in the pocket, inserted one, and tapped it to turn it on. Backing away a few paces, she said softly, "Can you hear me?"

His voice crackled in her ear. "Loud and clear. We've got video too." He waved and the image appeared in one of the ubiquitous windows open on his monitor. "Last piece now." He handed her one of the actual Jump!GO fobs.

"It's so light," she said, realizing that this was the first time she'd actually held one for any significant amount of time.

"Yeah, that's new too. My idea," Campbell said proudly. "Back at Sam's, we only had hard plastic polymer for the 3D printer, so it used to be heavier. Here, we've got access to carbon fiber, which is *way* lighter. The heaviest part is the controller board and that's only an ounce or so. You barely notice it on your phone now."

"Nice. So I just attach it to my phone's power port?"

"Right. Listen for the click and voila!"

She snapped it into place. Immediately, the fob's color shifted from a solid azure to a swirling light blue, its innards a maelstrom of slow-moving plasma.

"Pretty mesmerizing, isn't it?" said Campbell in her ear.

Marion caught herself. She'd been staring dumbly at the device. "Right. Um, what else?"

"You should see the app install request on your screen. Accept it, and after it installs, it'll ask you where you want to go."

"K, I see that."

"Type in the location and you should be good to go. Like, literally."

Marion typed in "Washir Bazaar, Helmand Province Afghanistan." The plasma grid sprang out of the fob and displayed the pulsing light hole for the Washir district, outlined in blue.

"How do I activate it?"

"Just lean in and walk through. Piece of cake."

With two steps, she was suddenly at the edge of the market area in Washir, just on the other side of the high hills leading to Kohinarange Village, the site of Hallett's last command.

"That was easy," she said.

"Toldja," Campbell crowed triumphantly.

"Don't get cocky. Me liking it doesn't make your scary tech a good idea."

"It's a start."

"Alright where do I go now?"

"Where do you wanna go?"

"There should be an Marine office nearby. Engineer Corps."

"Got it. Just walk through the market to the end. It'll be on the right. Wouldn't it be smarter to talk to the locals, though? What if Hallett's still got friends there?"

"I'll be discreet. First rule of spy school."

"Maybe you need backup or something? Want me to jump to the Springs and get Briggs?"

"Only if you want to freak out Francine. Pop into the SMOR unannounced and she'd shut you guys down in a heartbeat."

"But what if something happens to you?" The kid was starting to sound really worried.

"For god's sake, Campbell. One minute you're cocky, and the next you're a mother hen. Get your mood swings in check, please. The whiplash is killing me. "

"Okay, okay, sorry. But if you need to leave right away, just get to an open space and hit the 'Recall' button in the app. It'll auto-open to the machlab tut suite."

"Thanks for the tip. Now pipe down. Mama's gotta work."

Marion had reached the end of the market area. Some of the locals watched her curiously but didn't seem too surprised to see her. That she was clearly on her way to the Marine office likely helped. *Just another jarhead, that's me.*

She knocked before opening the door. Campbell may have been paranoid, but he had the right idea. If any trigger-happy soldiers were on the other side, it was best to give fair warning before barging in.

"Anyone home?" she said, peering cautiously around the door.

"Hello, there." A stocky, freckled, sandy-haired Marine sat behind a beat-up wooden desk, rifle in his lap, tablet in hand. The name on his breast pocket read "William Platter." He stared at her incredulously. "We're not expecting any visitors today, least wise any American civilians." He kept his left hand on the tablet but dropped his right down to his lap and the gun.

Marion smiled and kept her arms relaxed at her sides. "I'm a little surprised to be here myself. But couldn't be helped. I need some information."

"You got some creds?"

"Sure do. I'm going to have to take them out of my pocket." She looked pointedly at the rifle. "That okay with you?"

The soldier returned her gaze with his own, steady and solemn. "I'll wait."

From the other side of the doorway behind the soldier, Marion caught a glimpse of laser light and heard the unmistakable sound of the safety disengaging on an assault rifle. A red dot flitted across her torso, then settled on the left breast pocket of her monitoring vest.

"Yikes!" Campbell's voice cracked over the headset.

"Quiet," Marion whispered.

Moving slowly, she retrieved her passport and Agency ID from a side pocket and handed them to the Marine. His eyebrows went up. "Didn't expect Agency creds."

"No one ever does. Are we friends now?"

He snorted. "I wouldn't go that far, but at least now I know not to shoot you." He handed back her IDs and called over his shoulder, "Stand down, Gord."

"K, Sarge." There was an audible *Click*, then the red dot disappeared.

Propping his rifle against the desk, the sergeant asked, "What can I do for you, Agent Travers?"

"Well, Sergeant Platter—"

"Bill's fine."

"Bill, then. I'm here about the tunnel incident. We've been asked to evaluate the situation and see whether we can get the project back on track." It was as good of a story as any, and well within Agency purview to do.

"They're thinking of sending the engineers back in?"

"Possibly. Do you see an issue with that?"

"Not at all. Honestly, it's about time. My squad is restless. Since the shutdown, all we do is patrol and chase rats. When the engineers were here, we had more to do. Transportation, construction, community liaison. All that's more interesting than checking the perimeter and defusing IEDs."

"Certainly."

"And the folks here in the village deserve it. They helped us get rid of the hostiles terrorizing this area. Least we can do is return the favor and build them a proper road."

"Noted." Marion started to feel a little guilty for showing up under false pretenses. *No matter how things turn out, I better convince Ralph to send a real rep out here to help these people.* In the meantime, she'd still have to play the part. "To build the case, I'll need to inspect the site. Maybe talk to some locals."

"Not much to see anymore, but I can take you there." He grabbed his rifle, stood up, and called over his shoulder again. "Hey, Gord?"

"Yo." The hidden soldier—brown, tall, and maybe five years younger than Bill—stepped out from behind the dividing wall and into the doorway between the two rooms, rifle slung over his shoulder and tablet in hand.

"Hold down the fort, will ya'? I'm taking our visitor tunnel side."

"Sure, Sarge." He sat down in the chair Bill had vacated, pausing to study the sergeant's tablet. "You still on *Abaddon's Gate*? I'm already four chapters into *Cibola Burn*. So's Jeff."

"It ain't a race, Gordan." His tone, so even since Marion had arrived, edged over into irritation and a little red crept up his neck to his cheeks. Gord seemed unfazed. A knowing smile brushed his lips.

"Oh, so now it's my full name, huh? Look, all's I'm sayin' is, you know Jeff. He's gonna want to talk about it. You might hear some spoilers."

"Fine," the sergeant grumbled. "But don't be like last time. Just wait 'til I'm out on patrol. Please." He took a deep breath, turned back to Marion, and—even-toned once more—said, "Let's go."

They walked along the edge of the market through a mostly residential area. "So… you guys do a lot of reading?" asked Marion trying to break the awkward silence.

"It helps pass the time. Guys in the main unit at Delaram send us book series every now and then. Detective novels, science fiction. They've all done a rotation out here and know it can get a little dull. Anyways, let me show you around." Marion could see he wanted to change the subject, so she didn't press.

Bill proceeded to identify the dwellings of many villagers, waving at those that were home. They followed the old dirt road down an artery that dumped out into a large abandoned area separated from the rest of the village by a gate. A young, blond soldier, red-faced in a pre-sunburned way, sat in a booth behind the gate.

"Jeff."

"Hey, Sarge. I thought shift change wasn't for another hour?"

"It is, but this person is an Agency inspector and needs to see the tunnel site."

"Yes, sir." The young man opened the gate. "By the way, sir, I'm eating up *Cibola Burn*. Amos is killing me. You're gonna love the part where he—"

"Save it, Jeffrey," he said, cutting off the young man, eyes ablaze.

"Sorry, sir. Gord mentioned you read kinda slow, but this part with Amos is hilarious and I know you'll—"

"Later! Please."

"Yes, sir. Ma'am." Jeff escorted them through the gate and returned to his seat. Marion thought she caught a hint of a grin as he turned back to scanning the perimeter.

"Slow, my ass," Bill mumbled under his breath. "For the record, I like to savor the books instead of barreling through them."

"Sure."

"We've got zero entertainment out here. I like to make them last."

"Completely understandable."

He took a deep breath and let it out slowly. "Anyway... So, that was the school," he said, pointing to one of the sturdier buildings in the clearing. "We built that. Kids loved it." One wall was singed. Next to it was something that looked like a memorial. The flowers were fresh.

"And that over there was our official squad post." He pointed to a similar building across from the school. It was smaller, but obviously followed the same architectural scheme. "The commander's office was in the front. That's where they found Campo and Yohannes."

Marion's ears perked up. "Those are the two soldiers who were killed, right?"

"Yeah. Big shock to everybody, especially the villagers. Everybody loved those guys." They turned a corner, and there in front of them was the mountain, blocked by construction equipment and piles of rubble.

"Obviously that's the tunnel site. Or at least what's left of it."

"What a mess."

"You got that right. Near the front there is where the opening used to be. And off to the side there, those rocks were the malick's admin building. Malicks are like mayors. He and the village's mullah ran in there just before the commander went ballistic."

"Interesting choice of words."

"Yeah. But that's kind of what happened."

"Tell me what you know about it."

"Not a whole lot. I'd only rotated in the week just before it all went south. And then the only part I saw was the commander—"

"Hallett."

"Right. I heard shots from his office, and the malick and mullah ran out and he's chasing them, but his left side is all bloody. Then he runs over to a Jeep and gets a missile launcher. The malick and mullah freak out and run to the admin building. Then the commander shouts, 'You hit the king, you better kill the king!' Before anybody could stop him, he shoots a missile and blows the admin building to rubble, and then another missile goes off and the whole tunnel got buried."

"Any workers in the tunnel?"

"No, the team was at lunch, so lucky break. Otherwise about a dozen people besides the malick and mullah would've been crushed."

"How'd the rest of the village react?"

"Well, the commander crumpling a building on top of their top two leaders didn't sit well with some folks, so it got pretty tense. We thought we'd have to evac completely back to Delaram. But it kind of helped that the malick and mullah weren't the best of people, to put it mildly. The four or five guys waving guns at us got overrun by everyone else who was glad to be rid of them. Once the company commander in Delaram agreed to ship Hallett out, things calmed down pretty quick."

Fascinating. The sergeant's description of Hallett's actions didn't line up with the newspaper article at all, but it did lend credence to her theory of corruption and a blown deal.

"Bill, do you know what it looked like inside of the tunnel? Was there anything that seemed out of place about it?"

"No, just rocks and dirt as far as I could tell."

"What about with Hallett? Anything strange you noticed about him? Either right before or immediately after he went 'ballistic.' "

Platter considered the question, then shrugged. "He flipped out, but you know, they'd just killed two of our guys and had tried to kill him. He was in a state. Still... " He paused and chewed his lip.

"Go on. It might come out anyway as I do more investigating. If you know anything, you're better off telling me now."

"There was a lot going on all right, but I do remember after the tunnel collapsed, the commander ran over and started frantically pulling rocks away, which was weird. Like I said, it was lunch time. The crew were on break, so there was nobody in the tunnel who needed saving. Plus, the malick and mullah were buried under the admin building. Why wasn't he scrambling there? It made no sense, almost like he was searching for something in the tunnel."

There it was: independent corroboration of her gut feeling. Hallett had screwed up and buried something in the tunnel that he needed, something valuable. And there was only one way to confirm her suspicions. She'd have to find a way to look inside the tunnel.

Marion help up her phone. "I'll need to take pictures and make some measurements. Might be a while."

The sergeant checked his watch. "K, I need to go manage the shift change. Just drop by the office when you're done so's I know you're out."

"Sure thing."

She busied herself sizing up the admin building's rubble while Platter went back up the alley to the guard gate and Spoiler King Jeff. When he was out of sight, she tapped an earbud. "Campbell, you still there?"

"Yeah. Geez Louise that Hallett guy's a psycho."

"Or an opportunist. Either way, I need to know what's in the remains of this tunnel. Can you get me a trajectory inside of it?"

"You want to jump inside of solid rock?"

"If that's all there is under the rubble, then no. But I'm guessing there's still a cavity inside. Hallett thought so. And I'll just bet he and Pollux want Christian to get whatever they left in it."

"Alright, you can use the same trick Chung and I used to escape the conference room back at Cheyenne Mountain. I've added a method to the Jump!GO app to invoke it. Point your phone at wherever the entrance used to be."

Marion squeezed past a bulldozer and got as close to the front of the tunnel as she could. "I'm in position."

"In the app, choose 'Short Range' from the menu and wait for a grid to display."

She tapped the option, and immediately a plasma grid appeared on the wall of rocks, filled with light holes, some brighter than others. "Okay, the grid's here. Now what?"

"Poke the brightest holes until you find the one that's not solid rock, then jump."

It took three tries, but eventually Marion's hand passed into an air pocket, and a quick wave of her phone flashlight into the cavity revealed the high ceiling and dirt sides of the tunnel. She stepped through the hole, wrinkling her nose at the musty smell within. "Ugh."

"What's the matter?" asked Mitch.

"Smells like something died in here. Can you detect an exit point beyond my location?"

"Behind you it's wide open, of course, but jump trajectories seem to die about half a mile on."

She panned the flashlight along the walls on either side of her and down at her feet as she walked. "I'm a little disappointed," she said. "I half expected to see a big gold boulder or diamonds sticking out of the walls. Some kind of smoking gun."

"Hmmm," said Mitch, his voice taking on that far-off quality she'd heard so often back at Cheyenne Mountain.

"You've noticed something."

"Huh? Oh. It's probably nothing."

"Damn it, Campbell, what is it?"

"Well, your fob's kinda twitching. Whenever you turn it toward the walls, it's like it flat lines or skips or something. Like the magna coils get canceled out."

"Theories?"

"Don't know. Wayne's better at this stuff than I am. Curve's coming up, by the way."

She'd noticed. Her eyes had adjusted to the dim light, and she could see the slight turn in the grooves of the dirt walls. Even so, she still yelped when she rounded the curve and found the source of the sour smell.

On the floor with his back to the wall sat the mummified remains of a soldier. To his right was a metal cart full of rocks. To his left, was an open duffel bag filled with money. Holding down the money was a gleaming piece of equipment Marion didn't recognize, but the soldier's hand laid upon it as if he had used it before he'd died.

"Holy shit!" said Mitch.

"This is surprising." She bent to examine the soldier's body.

The cut of his uniform looked Chechen, but the weapon across his lap was definitely Russian in origin, and instead of the rough shoes of a separatist, his feet were clad in shiny, new, Armani-labeled boots. On his wrist was a diamond-studded Bolivar watch. This was no common soldier. Whoever he'd been, he'd been running a con.

"Yuck. Do you have to get so close to him?"

"Be squeamish on your own time, Campbell. I'm investigating here." The body had no visible wounds. She undid the man's uniform jacket and didn't find any blotches on his torso, so he hadn't been beat up. "I'm going to guess he died of starvation after getting trapped in here. And that Hallett and Pollux are likely after whatever this tool is in the bag. The rocks are curious, though." She walked over to the cart and picked one up. "They look like they came out of the wall, but there's nothing interesting about them otherwise."

"Whoa, your fob started twitching again."

"Curiouser still. What kind of rock would make a magnet flatline?"

"If we had a laser, we could find out."

She fished her keychain out of her pocket and held up a small tube attached to it to the vest cam. "Will this work?"

"Perfect. Point it at a rock and wave your fob in front of it while I run a wavelength scan." She did what Mitch asked and waited while he typed and clicked on the other side of the headset. After a minute, he paused and in typical Mitch fashion said, "Whoa."

"What do see?"

"Lanthanides. The cart's full of them."

"Rare earth metals. Of course." Marion looked at the duffel back and the strange piece of equipment. "I wonder..." She picked up the device, probing it gently with her fingertips in search of a button or switch. She found a switch above what felt like a screen, flicked it on, and pointed the device at the cart. The readout lit up and displayed, in English, a table of elements, their percentages, and the going rate for each in USD. The numbers changed as she pointed the device at different sections of the cart. In one swipe the device told her what was worthless and what was not.

"So, there's all of these rare earth metals. What does that mean?" asked Mitch.

"It's the equivalent of the village having struck oil. But the fact that no one has said anything also tells me that whoever our dead friend here was dealing with did not tell them. Or maybe the malick and mullah knew, and Hallett was trying to stop them from blabbing. Either way, it's an indictment. Somebody might have to pay. Save the output from this vest cam, Campbell."

She turned off the device and debated whether or not to take it and the duffel bag back with her. But how would she explain having duffel bag with her when she returned to the sergeant's office? "Campbell, can I open a point back to your location from where I'm standing right now?"

"You'll have to manually enter the coordinates, but it should work. Won't the sergeant guy wonder what happened to you?"

"I'll leave the way I came, but I think it would be smart to pass this bag off to you."

Mitch fed her the coordinates, and she handed him the duffel bag, the device, and a rock from the cart.

"Thanks. Now, how do I get out of here?"

"The recall button is kind of like a backspace key. Just tap that to get to the front of the tunnel again. Then hit it again to get back here, or you can just use the manual coordinates."

She tapped the button and inhaled the hot air. It had felt oppressive before, but after the musty scents in the tunnel, the outside air smelled as sweet as a fruit orchard.

She walked back to the guard station. Shift change must have completed, as Gord had now replaced Jeff. He turned to face her once she got close to the gate, rifle low, but in ready position. "Permission to pass, soldier?"

"Certainly, ma'am. Enjoy the rest of your day."

Back at the security office, the sergeant sat grimly at his desk, desperately attempting to ignore Jeff as he and Gord traded stories over the walkie talkie about the plot of *Cibola Burn*. When Marion walked in he jumped up and said loudly, "Get what you needed, Agent?"

"More or less."

"Need me to take you anywhere?"

"Thanks, but I have a car on the other side of the bazaar. I can drive out from there. Thanks again for your help."

He frowned. "Sure thing." Jeff continued describing in detail what Marion assumed was a juicy spoiler. Bill gritted his teeth and said, "Try to make a good case for starting up again. We could use some actual entertainment."

"Will do." She walked back through the market to the edge of town and a few steps beyond to ensure she was completely out of sight before hitting the Recall button.

At the machlab, Mitch was examining the assay device. "Maybe you and your friends should have built a similar tool," she said. "It would be a lot less trouble than the Jump!GO."

"You're not going to believe what's on here, though." He handed her the device. "Turn it over."

Marion had felt the steel plate on the back of the device as she searched for a way to turn it on, but the light had been too dim to read the words engraved on it. Now under the bright lights of the machlab, the engraving could be clearly seen: CSM Lab 422.

She groaned. "Don't tell me..."

"Yep. Wayne tacked the same label onto his magna coils. That assaying gizmo was made in Dr. Rebar's lab at Mines."

Marion laughed. "Ah, Hubert. You're the gift that keeps on giving."

Mitch looked shocked. "You mean he stole somebody else's project?"

"It was his hobby. At any rate, I think I've found my smoking gun."

CHAPTER 21

Cornered

Christian worked well into the night hunting down every Bertrand investor to "convince" them to continue their Q-tech funding. He knew it was temporary, buying him no more than a few days. He'd have to go on the hunt again at the end of the week to apply a fresh set of persuasion tendrils and ensure the shift in their mindsets was retained.

The whole process was more exhausting than it had to be. If Bertrand would just stay in his office, Christian could tackle him and 'persuade' him to call off the investor defections. It would be much easier to manipulate one person rather than seven.

But Bertrand remained elusive, and with adept precision, the ex-congressman managed to destroy all the good will Christian had wrangled from the funders. Within days, a new barrage of messages arrived, all from the same group of Bertrand investors, their assessments more decisive and final.

"There's no way you'll fight Tamblyn."
"Tamblyn's take is far more stable."
"I'm not in business to throw good money at a lost cause."

One by one, they pulled their funding. In the end, only the mayor remained and not by choice. He'd already committed to Q-Tech providing seamless transportation between venues for the Tech Convergence Conference, and his social media campaign touting Denver's support of the local tech scene was already underway. Dropping Q-tech so close to the conference would just make Denver look bad and him look foolish.

The contract with the city was lucrative, but as Christian assessed his budget he knew it wouldn't sustain the company through the end of the year. It took a *lot* of resources and energy to maintain the company's production system. He needed more funding before circumstances pushed him to either hand out pink slips or cut people's pay.

Christian spent the next week taking his charm and special 'persuasions' on the road in search of new investors, ones that had neither heard of Bertrand Pollux nor paid him any mind. The task was easier said than done. The congressman had his own tendrils of influence, born out of privilege and long political ties. Pollux had poisoned the well and primed Christian's targets to ignore his overtures. "I'm sorry, young man, but CC Tamblyn has the staff and resources to dwarf whatever it is you think you're doing," one prospect told him. "You'd be better off cutting your losses. Or hope she buys you out."

He returned to the office, disconsolate and empty handed. A quick glance at the financials dropped him down a well of despair. The numbers didn't lie. He'd be broke by the end of the month.

[*Still think yours is the better path?*]

He staggered. The Aggressor's taunt ripped through his reverie like a serrated blade. the Others had been quiet for so long he'd almost forgotten them. Pressure built in his stomach and the sting of hot plasma beat beneath his skin. *Can't lose control now.* No matter how bad the situation, getting forced into a limbo dimension would be worse. *Keep it together. Don't let them win.*

He needed both air and a distraction. He opened the door and thankfully caught sight of Maggie. She waved him over. "We've got it, boss! We scaled the generator! Come see!"

"Wonderful." He pasted on a smile.

[*Perfect. Just in time for you to shut the company down,*] the Aggressor said with a sarcastic sneer.

Be quiet.

He headed to the Kill Corner, still smiling. Maggie bubbled in her endearing way, much to Larry's amusement. Christian tried to listen, nodding at all the right times as she breathlessly described the hurdles they'd overcome. Brilliant work from them both, as always, but wasted effort without a permanent solution to Bertrand's meddling.

[*Oh, there's a solution,*] the Aggressor persisted. the Others muttered their assent. The heat beneath his skin pounded and white lightning pressed against the back of his eyes.

Stop. You just want to get out.

[*Because you don't have the guts to do what must be done!*]

Please...

[*Just a handshake, a simple shock, and "Bye-bye, Pollux."*]

Shut up!

[*Then I'd parade Marvin in front of the investors and make him sing our praises until his voice gave out. I'd have Q-Tech on top again. I'd—"*]

"Christian, are you listening?"

He felt a shake and looked up. Maggie's concerned expression dragged him out of the Aggressor's sinister pit of schemes. *No more!* he told the Others, then to Maggie he said, "Heard every word. Great work, guys."

"No, really. Are you okay?"

He sighed. They'd find out soon enough once the paychecks stopped. *Time to come clean.* "It's just that... Well, Pollux is—"

"Christian, my boy!"

Speak of the devil. Bertrand, the back-stabbing bastard, breezed into the warehouse, chest puffed out, cheese-eating grin on his face. As he crossed the demo space toward them, it was all Christian could do to keep from blasting a hole right through the man. *You've ruined me. You know it and still you come in here smiling.*

Maggie whispered, "Ugh."

"Think we'll take five, if you don't mind," said Larry.

"Sure. Wish I could join you."

The two of them headed to the break room.

Bertrand grabbed his hand in a hearty handshake. Christian's palm itched. "I was at the mayor's office just as he finalized your contract. He was going to drop it in the mail, but I volunteered to bring it over. Save Henry a stamp, ha ha."

"Kind of you."

Turning serious, he said, "Truth be told, I wanted to check up on you. In light of the recent investor desertions."

"Which you orchestrated." *To hell with pretense.*

"Oh," he chuckled, "you give me far too much credit. If anyone's to blame, it's CC Tamblyn. Tamblyn Tech is gargantuan, with limitless resources, and CC's always on the hunt for the next new thing. I knew she'd subsume this light technology eventually. It was only a matter of time. Be thankful the mayor is still on your side."

"Yes, quite fortunate. Too bad you aren't."

"Pshah, my boy. Of course I am. It's just investors these days need more song and dance. I tried to convince them to stay with you, believe me. But with so much money on the line and Tamblyn Tech in the wings, well... Trust was hard to come by. So." He paused and looked around the warehouse. "Any thoughts on how you'll compensate?"

"Working on it," said Christian.

"Hmm." Bertrand stroked his chin. "Well, I know someone who wouldn't mind working with you. Someone who has faith in your 'abilities.' "

Christian started. Bertrand had emphasized "abilities" in an odd way. He didn't like it. Bertrand continued to smile at him innocently enough, but the undertone of the comment worried him.

"If you're talking about Major Hallett, I'm not interested. He shot at me. Some show of faith."

"Yes, yes, that was unexpected. My apologies. As I've said, his test wasn't my idea. Still..." He tapped his lapel pin thoughtfully. "Let's go to your office. I've got a proposal, and I'm sure you'll appreciate what I have to say."

Christian ushered him in and closed the door. "I'm listening."

Bertrand spread his hands wide. "Consider this. Military contracts tend to be stable contracts. The defense department knows exactly what it wants and doesn't change requirements at the drop of a hat. Plus, they pay well. Believe me, in the long run, a contract with Hallett could work in your favor."

"Perhaps I should reach out to the DoD directly and gauge their interest for myself. I'm sure they'd love to hear about how their representative endangered me and my employees. I could ask why they thought Q-Tech was useless and why Hallett seems to be courting me all on his own."

"Or you could forget your anger and let the major foot the bill for *all* of your products. Not just the Enviro-Belt, but the Q-Pod and BEAM as well."

"Enviro-Belt is called RMOR now."

"A better name for sure. But you're sidestepping my proposal."

"What's the catch?"

Bertrand laughed. "You wound me, young man, but your instincts are good. Hubert always said so. I shouldn't be surprised."

Christian braced himself. Of course there was a catch. Bertrand wouldn't have maneuvered him into this position without one. *But can I overlook it for the sake of the company?*

"There's a small operation we'd like your help with," Bertrand continued. "No defense interests. It's something more of a, shall we say, *personal* nature for Hallett and me. Because it's personal, it can't be part of the contract, but you'll be compensated handsomely all the same. If you do well, we can offer similar small jobs. Along with the larger defense contract, of course."

"What operation?"

"There's some merchandise we need retrieved."

Christian shrugged. "So go get it."

"Alas, it's not that simple. The merchandise is in Afghanistan. A spoil of war, as it were. Hallett claimed it off-hours during his tour of duty, but there were... complications bringing it home. We've spent months fighting to retrieve our property, but to no avail. Then you and your wonderful company came along. With a BEAM Box and an RMOR belt, I dare say you could accomplish in a day what we've failed to do in a year."

Bertrand locked eyes with Christian and pulled him closer. "What we've found is worth billions, if not trillions, my boy. Hubert betrayed us for it. But bring it to us and you can sign your own check."

Christian stepped back from Bertrand. "The Chechen deal?" Hubert had met with the Chechens before the feds carted him away. Christian hadn't realized the depths of Pollux's involvement in that meeting. His regard for the ex-congressman reached a new level of disgust.

"More like Russian deal, but why quibble over borders? Besides, the Russians are richer. Had Chechnya submitted a bid, they might have paid with pails of dirt."

the Others returned.

[*Free money!*]
[*Take it!*]
[*It's illegal! Blackmail him!*]

And to his surprise, he found himself seriously considering their urgings. Illegal money was indeed more lucrative, and he had no doubt he could blackmail Bertrand, bleed him dry in exchange for silence. He'd be able to keep the company and simultaneously reap his revenge on this contemptible excuse of a man.

[*Do it!*]
[*He deserves it!*]

But at the edge of the murmuring came the calm voice of Time.

[**Revenge is hollow. Refuse.**]

He knew Time was right, but Bertrand's smirk and punchable face made it oh so tempting to give in to the Others.

With an effort, he willed himself to composure and said, "Thank you, Bertrand, but that's a bigger bite than I can chew. The mayor's contract is good for now, and I suspect if I keep looking I'll find a new angel or two not poisoned by you." He opened his office door and gestured for the ex-congressman to leave.

Bertrand didn't move. His lips settled into a thin, hard line. "I understand your position. But I have something else that might convince you." He unpocketed his phone, tapped the video app, then held it up for Christian to see.

Timestamped security cam footage of the warehouse unspooled before Christian's eyes. There he was, prostrate under the disintegrating Canopy. Dew drops bombarded his body; a tendril ripped a chunk out of the warehouse wall; his body glowed as he levitated through the hole.

Bertrand tapped ahead to different timestamps. One showed Christian shooting dew drops into the hopper from the palms of his hands. Another showed him snaking tendrils into Larry's racks as they tested a BEAM unit.   In yet another, he conjured a dew drop for the RMOR belt while Maggie had her back turned.

The video went on and on, each scene depicting a different aspect of Christian's powers. He watched it all, appalled. Bertrand's eyes gleamed.

"You really should look into the security camera firm for this building. In fact, it would have been smart for you to verify their retention policies, especially after you purchased the rest of the complex." Bertrand feigned sadness. "Sloppy. So very sloppy, young man. How long do you think Q-Tech would survive if this video got out? What will your remaining customers think of you and the company when they learn there is no real technology? That your 'hardware' is all a fraud?"

Christian eventually found his voice. "It's not fraudulent. We've built out the tech. It doesn't need me anymore. At least not completely."

"Your customers don't know that. I'm respected and established. I think I've proven these past weeks who they will believe, and it's certainly not you."

The video stopped. "Let me show you something else." Bertrand opened a slideshow with pictures of people Christian didn't know. Some pictures showed a woman who vaguely resembled Maggie. Others showed a little boy riding a bike, who looked suspiciously like Larry.

"What are you playing at, Bertrand? Who are these people?"

"Oh, it's just some minor surveillance of your employees' families. If you aren't up to helping us, perhaps we can persuade the industrious girl, Ms. Heinz, to lend a hand. I'm sure she'd want to keep her mother safe. Or maybe your Tech Lead Mr. Knight would do. Hopefully he loves his nephew enough to ensure nothing happens to him as well."

"Bastard."

"You don't have to let any of that happen. What we're asking, you can easily do. It's just one job. Take the money. Save your company."

" 'Just one job.' We both know you won't leave me alone after that. You'll come back asking for more and more."

"Better to serve us and gain financial stability than to fade away into obscurity. Surely you don't want to die penniless and disgraced. Given what you did to Hubert— oh, yes, we know about that too—you owe us, young man, whether you want to or not."

Christian looked away. On the other side of his office door he could hear Larry and Maggie joking with each other as they tested the new generator. He enjoyed working with them. He liked having his own company. And he firmly believed in the promise of his tech. He was certain he could hold his own against CC Tamblyn. People would see Q-Tech's value. He would prevail—but only if he had the chance to keep things going.

[**You will,**] the calm voice of Time reassured him. [**There is another way.**] And suddenly, his path forward was clear.

"I accept your offer," he said.

Bertrand clasped his hands together and smiled. "There you go, using your good instincts. I told Hallett you'd make the right decision."

"What exactly is it that you need me to retrieve?"

Bertrand pulled up a new picture, this time of a dark, hollow passage. Workers were loading chunks of smooth, rust-colored stones into a large mining bin. Aside from the color, nothing else presented itself as being the source of Pollux' fascination. "So, you want the rocks?"

"Oh my, yes. That reddish orange rubble is almost completely bastnäsite, the rarest of the rare earth metals. So valuable, yet so hard to find. Extract it for the right buyer and we'll make a mint."

"I'll need a few days to prepare."

"Of course, my boy." Bertrand got up to leave. "Just call me when you're ready and I'll set up a rendezvous." He paused at the door and said, "I'm glad you reconsidered, Christian. You won't regret it." He winked and left.

Christian waited for Bertrand to clear out of the parking lot, then closed the door to his office and portaled to his apartment. He opened the bottom drawer of his bureau and felt around until he found the Agency business card he'd taped to the side months ago. Beside it was a false compartment containing a disposable phone, an audio filter, and the phone's battery, wrapped in a sock.

For an added layer of security, he opened a new portal and stepped through it into the train station in downtown Flagstaff, Arizona.

I won't regret it, Bertrand, he thought as he inserted the battery and punched in the number on the card. *But you will.*

CHAPTER 22

Conquered

The back porch of the Tortas Locas sandwich shop was hot, hotter than the hottest day Hallett had ever spent in the Afghan desert while decked out in full battle gear and patrolling rat holes in Washir. His chair propped against the wall, chili smoke and foreign cuss words wafting over him, he could close his eyes and almost imagine he was back in that little village, itching for action and bored out of his mind.

The English speakers butchering sandwich names at the order window around front told him otherwise. He also had to admit he wasn't bored. Far from it. Not with lightning in his veins and fire in his breath. He plucked the plumper of the two jalapenos that came with his torta from his paper plate, bit it in half, then for kicks blew a kiss, vaporizing the rest. *Hehe. Dragon Bart.*

Yes indeed, Meadows' dew drops had spiced up his life: the lightning bolts, eye lasers, levitation, the whole instant travel thing. Hell, he'd even acquired his own personal set of soldiers when he destroyed that preachy old man's shell. All he had to do was rip open a few portals, and *Bam!* Instant army—with built-in weapons of their own, no less. Booyah.

But it didn't take long to figure out two key components were missing from his arsenal: Meadows' protective bubble and, worse, the kids' ability to retain his powers. Try as he might, Hallett could manage neither. He couldn't stop lint, much less a bullet. And at unpredictable times each day, his boiling blood returned to ice like someone blew out his pilot light, and a crash worse than any hangover he'd ever experienced descended on him. Dragon breath? Hell no. He'd barely manage a smoke ring.

How'd the Meadows' kid keep his energy from dribbling out? Hallett searched the security cam footage but saw no evidence the kid ever lost his powers. There had to be a trick to it, but what?

After trial and error, popping dew drops every morning like Tic Tacs, he'd extended his powers out to two, sometimes three days max. Ten dew drops seemed to be the limit. Any more than that made his insides twist, his head pound, and—he was ashamed to say—got his soldiers screeching out in agony like whiny women. Whooee, that'd been a rough day.

For now, he was stable, but the sack was getting low. He'd need more—soon. *Better conserve.* He held up the burnt pepper stem in his hand. No more dragon breath.

This last bit of business with Pollux, though, just might change that. He patted the manila envelope next to his paper plate. The report inside could be just enough leverage to turn the tide his way and give him all the dew drops he'd ever need. It all depended on what the weasel actually told the kid. You never knew with him.

As if he'd conjured the politician with that thought, Pollux rounded the corner of the shop and came up the back way as usual to their meeting spot, a tactic they'd agreed to long ago. The heat and loud music kept people away from the porch. They remained undisturbed. Unobserved. It was the perfect spot for a quiet chat.

The weasel plopped down into the only other chair. "Good god, it's hot back here. You look like shit. Is that a sunburn?"

Hallett took a bite of his carnitas. "Maybe. Got any news?"

Pollux laughed and tapped his lapel pin in satisfaction. "Meadows never knew what hit him." He launched into an overly congratulatory description of their encounter, playing up how he'd maneuvered the kid into a corner, smirking all the while. Nothing made him happier than getting the upper hand on someone.

"After he turned down the contract, I thought getting our ore and the auto-assayer back was a lost cause. Never thought I'd ever say this, but thank god for CC Tamblyn. Her announcement provided just the pressure I needed to turn the angels and other investors against him. He had no choice but to side with us to keep his business alive. And now we can move the ore out of that backwater village and into my Gunnison mine with the snap of his fingers. No one will be the wiser. But we, my friend, will be all the richer!"

"Uh huh." Pollux was far too pleased with himself. Hallett ate another jalapeño, savoring the smoky, roasted flesh, and the pleasant buzz it left at the back of his throat before it disintegrated in his plasma furnace. He belched and allowed a little flame to escape past his lips. It got the desired effect. Pollux shuddered and blinked, and for once in the ten minutes since he'd arrived, he stopped talking. *What do you know? Finally got him to shut the hell up.* Too bad it didn't last long.

Pollux cleared his throat and continued, "Splendid idea, by the way, insisting we spy on the boy through his own cameras. He never suspected. Once I showed him the video, he was suitably shocked."

"I'll bet." He took a sip of cinnamon tea to help wash down a particularly spicy torta bite. "What about the pictures? My operatives put in a lot of work to get them." Killed a day of practice for him and his soldiers. Better have been worth it.

"Oh, ho," Pollux chuckled. "I don't want to downplay the video—it was pivotal—but the pictures of his employees' families were *truly* persuasive. Showed him we weren't playing around. He folded like a camp chair."

"Interesting. I expected a more ruthless response."

"Not when it comes to his two pets. Out of everyone we've monitored in his lab, Knight and Heinz have the most brain power. He can't afford to alienate them. He *certainly* can't afford anything happening to them. He had no choice but to comply with our plan."

"I suppose. But considering what he did to Wilkins, it's surprising."

"Speculation. Although I used that accusation as a bluff to great effect. Honestly, we don't know for sure who turned Hubert in. Meadows wasn't his only postdoc, and lord knows they all hated him."

It seemed too easy an answer. The kid had an obstinate streak that should have presented itself. Hallett hated relying on Pollux's interpretations of things, which tended toward emphasizing successes and glossing over other details. Typical politician. But there was no help for it. The kid might have bolted had he gone with the weasel. Then where would he be? Out of options *and* powers.

Pollux rubbed his hands together greedily. "As soon as our young friend deposits the ore down the shaft of my gold mine, we can get to processing it and sit back and watch while the profits roll in."

Here's my opening. Time to start modifying the terms of "our" plan.

"Been thinking about that, Pollux. Might be smarter to dump the rocks in a neutral location first. Sort out the crap from the quality. Might be more lucrative in the long run."

"Why Hallett, are you starting to smell the profits finally? I knew you'd come around once I'd turned the boy to our side. So, where do you suggest we sort out the 'crap'?"

"The old munitions storage vaults beneath my building at work. They were never dismantled, so there's still a fully functioning lab down there. Been on ice since the new facility moved to the Springs. I'd be surprised if anyone even remembers those vaults are down there. The only reason I know is from reading old USGS assay reports."

Pollux stroked his chin. "I like not having to build our own facilities. It wouldn't be cheap transporting the necessary equipment over Cumberland Pass."

"My point exactly."

"But if the lower levels are cut off from normal traffic, how do we get a team into them to do the work? And how do we avoid someone noticing we're there?"

"The area is soundproofed and has its own generators. We're talking Cold War paranoia here. The government needed some place that could be self-sufficient and still be able to pump out weapons when the shit hit the fan. It's meant to be snoop-proof. As for access, we get the kid to set up one of them Q-Pods between it and the PVMC mine. Then we can test and dump rocks, and nobody'd ever know." *And I'd have control over who—and what—comes and goes, including the weasel. Easier to cut him out once I make my move.*

Pollux stared at him skeptically. "That all sounds good, but frankly I'm still not convinced. The assayer tool should be more than enough to separate the wheat from the chaff. And I've already scoped the land for a processing facility in Gunnison. Outfitting it will cost some money, but with my connections it might not be any worse than updating your subterranean lair."

Time to play the trump card. He nodded as if he agreed, then asked casually, "When can the kid get started?"

"In a few days. He said he needs time to prepare."

"For what? All he has to do is open a portal, slice out the rock, and we're done."

"I thought it wise to throw him a bone. Prove to him that we can be reasonable under the right circumstances. We've already waited a year. A few more days won't matter."

"We might have to speed things up." He slid the report out from under his plate and handed it to Pollux. "That's this month's server audit. Someone else accessed Q-Tech's security cam folder."

Pollux shrugged. "A hacker?" He extracted the report from the envelope and thumbed through it with disinterest.

"Nope. I wouldn't even mention it if that were the case. Hackers are easy to deal with. What you're looking at right there is your normal, everyday, garden-variety spy activity."

"What?!" That got the weasel's attention.

"They tried to cover their tracks with a masking program. That's why I didn't notice it right away. Just looked like normal access from the anti-virus scanner. But they screwed up. The scanner software version they chose for the mask wasn't the same as the one on the security firm's server."

"But which spies? Ours or theirs? Don't tell me the Russians are back."

"Ours. Agency offices are in the same building. An access mask request was made around the same time as the so-called 'software scan.' "

"Well do you have a name? We need to discredit this person at once."

"I don't know, Pollux," said Hallett. He was starting get exasperated with the politician. "Calm down. No need to get your panties in a twist."

"But it's the Agency," Pollux bleated. "That's not standard surveillance. They mean business."

"They could be just like us. Just keeping tabs on Hubert's old assets."

"But what if they find out about us? Where would we be then?"

Us. We. Pollux only used those pronouns when he needed help or wanted to spread the blame. Hallett would be amused if it weren't so annoying.

"Pollux, it's unlikely. We've done nothing to make them suspect anything. Unless of cours *you've* been talking about our operation to someone?"

"No, of course not." Bertrand wrung his hands. "But you've got to figure this out. If the Agency finds out about the plan, I'll be ruined." So much for *us* and *we.*

Hallett hid his irritation behind another bite of his sandwich. "You still think the only thing we're trying to do is recover precious minerals?"

Pollux looked confused. "What do *you* think we're doing? Because of your bungling in Washir, you left the product behind in the worst possible condition. Luckily, Meadows can extract it and we'll still be rich. What could be better than that?"

There are a host of things better than that, Hallett wanted to say, but he kept it to himself. "You're right Bertrand. Sorry for losing sight of what's really important here. But I think this just proves the need for a more secure location for our merchandise, don't you?"

"Yes, yes, of course. I see your point now. Thank you for thinking ahead."

"Good." He wiped salsa from his hands and picked up his hat to leave. "I'll be in touch."

The congressman seemed to rally. He mopped the sweat from his face with a handkerchief and stood up as well. "Our time *is* coming, isn't it?"

"Uh huh."

"At last. Well, see you in a few days."

Pollux slunk away. Hallett thought about opening a portal to his office, but then wondered why. What was the hurry? Did he really need to rush back and catalog the latest USGS maps? No one cared, least of all him. *It's a beautiful day. Might as well walk.*

And as he walked, he planned: how to find the Agency spy who'd targeted them; how to get Christian to give up his secrets; how to cut Pollux out of everything completely. He'd use the kid to get Pollux's pile of rocks, but after that he would take what was his, and neither Meadows nor Pollux would stand in his way.

The path back to building 57 was littered with dandelions. On impulse, Hallett singed one with a tiny blast from his hand. Then he imagined Pollux's face in the middle of another and incinerated that one too. It didn't take much energy and he got a kick out of practicing a new skill. He walked on, whistling tunelessly and leaving a mass of shriveled weeds in his wake.

CHAPTER 23

Tricked

Christian stood in his office reviewing the equipment list for Q-Tech's booth at the convention center. The team had spent most of the day shuttling gear back and forth between the convention center and the warehouse doing final setups for Tech Convergence. Only a few items remained undone on the list. He peered out the door at the team, scurrying about, popping in and out of existence, working to complete the remaining items. He had no doubt they'd finish all the tasks. He could taste the team's excitement without even trying, every one of them was so psyched.

They'd made an impressive showing already, arriving to the main hall that morning via BEAM units much to the amazement of other companies busy adorning their booths. Then Christian unveiled the venue Q-Pod to considerable fanfare and a large dose of hyperbole—thanks to the mayor and celebs from a local morning news show. Before he knew it, videos of BEAM's appearing and disappearing and the mayor surprising commuters with free trips through the Q-Pod began trending on social media. Even Chithra Muraleekrishnan did her part to amp up interest in Q-Tech, interviewing exhibition hall workers on their first impressions of the company's products. The hype-train had left the station with Q-Tech comfortably situated in the first car.

Tamblyn Tech's arrival was only slightly less dramatic than Q-Tech's—the Jump!GO's mute, square grids a marked contrast to BEAM's sleek and verbal travel tubes. But the unveiling of their set piece, holographic social media, garnered as much if not more hype than the Q-Pod. And when CC Tamblyn materialized for an interview like a rock star from a bedazzled, azure void, the networks exploded with comparisons and speculation.

"Which tech is hotter?"
"Which company will win?"

BEAM and Jump!GO videos battled for the top of the trending charts. The conference hadn't even started yet, but Q-Tech held its own against the Tamblyn behemoth. Christian was so proud of his people. Seeing them and the products shine made him determined to keep Bertrand or anyone else from derailing their progress and success.

He checked the clock on the wall. It was almost quitting time, but still no word from the ex-congressman on where they were supposed to meet. Pollux and Hallett had grown weary of his stalling and had declared today the day that he would help them, mostly out of spite. He had no leverage to refuse—Pollux threatened to play his accident video at the conference if he dared to. So, he'd agreed, but like children they were making him wait for the meeting location. "There are prying eyes everywhere," said Bertrand. "Be patient."

Pollux had made that promise yesterday. Why was he still silent today? He couldn't have found out about the Agency, could he?

Burrup, burrup, his phone vibrated, alerting him to a text. He fished it out of his pocket, expecting to see an address. The text contained coordinates instead. He did a quick calculation in his head and his heart sank. The location appeared to be underground. Maybe Pollux had gotten it wrong.

He closed his office door and opened a small window to the location. *Crap.* The place was legit. It looked like a storage room, and as far as he could tell felt cool and deep—very deep. At least the portal hadn't opened into solid rock. The Agency contact still wouldn't like it, not one bit. But Christian had no other options. He'd have to call it in.

Retrieving the burner phone, he portaled to Flagstaff to make the call. The contact answered after one ring. "This happening today? I was about to send the crew home."

Christian engaged the audio mask. "Texting you the location now." He typed in the coordinates and waited.

"Coordinates? What the—hang on. Harry, get over here." The dead air told Christian he'd been put on mute. A few seconds later the agent returned, clearly peeved. "This location's bogus. My guy says it's dirt."

"It's a room underground. Check again." More silence.

"That location's not possible. My source says it shouldn't exist."

"Harry's wrong. See you there."

"Wait! We'll need some time to move our people into place and make sure we can cover all escape points. Isn't there some topside location you could lead them to instead?"

"If I could control what they do, I wouldn't need your help." *Idiots.*

His contact cursed on the other end, then treated him to another dose of dead air. Christian considered setting up a Q-Pod for the agents. but doing that would tip The Agency off that he was the whistle blower. He'd taken pains to hide his identity. Handing them a Q-Pod would be a dead giveaway.

The agent returned. "K, we think we can make it, but it'll tough."

"Look. I'll do what I can to leave you some breadcrumbs. You've got a lot of smart people at the Agency. Figure it out."

He hung up and portaled back to his office. If they didn't show up, his plan would fail and he'd be forced back into a life of humiliating servitude.

[*Fool!*]

"Gah!" He doubled over. The resurgence of the Aggressor wracked him like a punch to the gut.

[*You* haven't *done better! We're back where we started! It's the same damn thing as Hubert!*]

The plan will work! The Agency will find the location, wherever it is.

[*What if they're late?*]
[*What if Pollux gets away?*]
[*What happens to* us *then?*], the Others whined.

He had no answers. There was no Plan B. All of his eggs were in the Agency's basket. If they didn't come through... he wasn't sure what he'd do.

[*Yes, you are. You'll have to act. Handle it yourself!*] The Aggressor had spoken, the sneer in his tone telling Christian all he needed to know about how his worst self thought he should "handle" it.

I can't do that.

[*Weak!*] the Others screeched.

Hate these guys. He closed his eyes and concentrated on willing the chorus back into silence. In his mind's eye, Time Christian appeared.

[**You know they're wrong.**]

What choice do I have?

His own face stared back at him. [**The one you already made that night in the restaurant. I tried to warn you. Now this is your path.**]

If I'm wrong, Pollux will own me. Maybe I should just disappear.

[*Coward!*] yelled the Others.

[**Running is worse than cowardly,**] said Old Time. [**Remember Pollux's pictures. You'd be endangering your friends.**]

[*Forget them! They're employees. Start fresh in a new place. Hire more 'friends.'*]

The thought was alluring. He didn't need much, just his backpack, a tablet, and his workstation drive. Anything else he could get through a tendril of influence until he'd amassed enough to begin his business anew, in a new country, with a new identity. He'd done it before; he could do it again. Running looked better and better. Larry and Maggie would be fine.

The old man shook his head sadly. [**You know they won't be.**]

A knock sounded from the door. He reached out with his mind to touch the wavelength on the other side of his office door. Maggie. *Damn it.* "Come in."

She bounced through the door all smiles. "Heya, Christian, we're done! Larry's taking us to Chennai Oven for dinner. Wanna come?"

The image of Maggie's mother, serious, focused, and completely unaware of being watched passed before his mind's eye. He sighed. "Sorry. Got some paperwork to do."

"More of the congressman's shenanigans, huh?"

"Sort of."

"Man, I used to like that guy. My mom voted for him *twice*. What a jerk."

Larry appeared over her shoulder, his face open and happy, so much like his younger brother's. "Chief, you comin'?"

Maggie answered for him. "He's still cleaning up after Pollux."

"Too bad. Anything we can do to help?"

How could he have ever thought these two weren't his friends? He managed a weak smile. "Wish you could, but I need to deal with this myself."

Larry watched him with concern but accepted the answer. "K. If you need a naan burrito or anything, call me. Be happy to drop back by."

"Me too," Maggie chimed in.

"Thanks. Both of you. Means a lot," said Christian, deeply feeling every word.

"Anytime, Chief. See ya'."

Once he was sure they'd left, he retrieved a Q-Pod kit from production and dropped the burner phone into his pocket. Then, tuning himself to Pollux's coordinates, he opened a portal.

"Christian, my boy! Right on time."

The portal opened into a large, high-ceilinged, dimly lit room with thick, unadorned, concrete walls. The room was empty except for a table and five large plastic hampers, the kind janitors used to haul trash. Pollux and Hallett stood near a set of steel double doors, nearly as tall as the ceiling and as thick as the walls. They had to be in a storage vault of some kind.

"There's nothing here," he said, turning to Bertrand. "What happened to your cavern of rocks?"

"Perceptive as usual," Pollux replied. "That's what your Q-Pod's for."

"Did you bring it?" Hallett smirked at Christian like an arrogant prick.

"I did," said Christian, pointing to the box under his arm. He held Hallett's gaze, throwing in some contempt of his own, and allowing the itch in the palm of his free hand to transform into a blob energy bright enough for Hallett to see. *You won't get the drop on me again, you sonuvabitch.*

Hallett chuckled. "Guess you grew some balls since last time we met. But guaranteed, son, you flex on me, you won't win." He grinned without humor and Christian swore he saw a flash of light behind the man's eyes. The pea of energy in his palm grew into a ball.

Pollux stepped away from Hallett's side, visibly alarmed. *Had he seen the flash as well?* thought Christian, but then he noticed the congressman staring at the light in his palm. Christian shook his head. *I must have been seeing things.*

Pollux raised his hands placatingly. "Now, now, you two. No time for fighting. Not when we're all so close to our goal."

Christian squelched his fireball and asked, "So where's the cavern?"

"You'll find it here." Pollux handed him a Post-it with new coordinates.

"Guess I'll get started." He looped a tendril around the leg of the table and dragged it to the far wall to unpack the Q-Pod. Surreptitiously, he used his other hand to hit the recall button on the burner phone, leaving the line open for the Agency contact.

Behind him, he heard Pollux whispering angrily at Hallett. He sensed Hallett tuning Pollux out and could feel the man's eyes boring into him, watching his every move. The tenor of Hallett's brain waves felt familiar somehow, but Christian couldn't put a finger on why.

He squeezed out a dew drop and deposited it into the Q-Pod's processor cavity. Hallett's interest intensified. The man's emanations felt strange and unsettling, not unlike… hunger. Christian pushed the thought away. It was as ridiculous as thinking Hallett's eyes had flashed. He attached the generator to the base of the Q-Pod, activating it and suffusing the far side of the room in a soft, white light.

"Alright, it's ready," Pollux hissed at Hallett. "Now keep it together, or so help me I'll cut you out of this deal."

Christian turned around and found both men staring at him. Pollux's eyes were full of anticipation and avarice while Hallett's were dark, angry, and cold.

"Open it, my boy," breathed Pollux. "Time's a wasting."

Indeed. He searched his brain for a reason to stall, but he couldn't think of anything aside from typing the new coordinates slowly into the Q-Pod's keypad. *Where was the Agency?*

The Q-Pod's wall dissolved and revealed the cavern from Pollux's picture. The atmosphere in the cavern was musty, dank, and rich with the smell of decay. Christian had stumbled upon enough dead things in his life to recognize that smell. Wherever this cavern was, something had died in it.

Hallett and Pollux appeared by his side, Hallett with a flashlight. Christian noted that the cavern had a pattern of grooved walls. About ten paces away from the Q-Pod's entrance lay a shriveled husk inside a soldier suit. To the left of the husk sat a cart full of ore, and on its right was an open duffel bag brimming with money.

"It's still here!" cried Pollux ecstatically. He rushed into the cavern and grabbed up the sack of cash.

Hallett stared at him in disgust. "Real broke up about your buddy Berezhnoy, I see."

"Don't lay that on me. *You're* the one who trapped him there. He knew the risks. Besides, the moment he made a side deal with Hubert was the moment we ceased to be pals." Pollux rummaged through the bag and frowned. "Where is it? It should be here," he mumbled.

"A bag full of money?" asked Christian. "Is that it? I thought you wanted the rocks?" He checked his watch. No matter how deep underground this room was, the Agency should have locked on his phone signal and shown up by now.

Then he felt a shift in Hallett, an emanation of malicious glee. "We'll get to the rocks and more, thanks, but right now, I need to grab something else."

He sidestepped Christian and tapped new coordinates into the Q-Pod's keypad. The cavern disappeared, replaced by the inside of the Q-Tech warehouse near the dew drop hopper to the side of the front door.

That got Pollux's attention. He abruptly stopped searching through the money bag. "Hallett, man, what are you doing? This isn't the plan."

"Not *your* plan, but it fits my plan perfectly. I'll be taking these." He reached across the Q-Pod's threshold and proceeded to scoop dew drops out of the hopper into a bag.

Suddenly, Christian realized why Hallett's brain waves seemed familiar. "You're the thief!" He whipped a tendril around Hallett's arm, intending to fling him out of the portal, but Hallett stiffened, his feet seemingly fused to the floor. Christian tugged a second time, but the man remained unmoved.

Hallett grinned. "You're full of neat tricks, boy, but I've learned a few of my own." He opened his mouth and breathed a stream of fire into Christian's tendril, snapping it in two.

Christian gaped at Hallett. "How did you do that?"

"Surprised?" he said. "You shouldn't be. If you can have a dew drop accident, I can too. Except mine wasn't an accident."

"But... but... "

"Yeah, I figured you thought you were special. News flash: you aren't. It's the dew drops. Like my gun, they're just a tool. Anyone can learn to use them and well, I sure did."

He made a move toward the warehouse. Christian lunged to stop him, but Hallett blocked his path with a wall of flame. "Keep back, boy. See, that's the difference between you and me. I *know* how to use *my* tools."

Hallett went back to looting the dew drop bin, but as he grabbed another handful out of the hopper, his knees buckled and all of the color drained from his face. The hunger Christian had sensed from him earlier had returned, stronger and more intense than before. The major stumbled back into the storage room and leaned heavily against the table as if he were about to faint. A hot wave of radiant energy billowed out of him and in that moment, Christian realized the true difference between the major and himself. *Hallett's dew drops leak. He can't retain their energy. Why not?*

Suddenly, there came a banging on the door. "Attention! You are trespassing on government property! Open up or we will blow the door!"

The Agency. Finally!

Hallett crushed the dew drops in his fist and their effect on him was immediate. He stood up straight—his strength renewed—and pointed a fist full of fire at the door.

Christian seized the opportunity in his own way. With two tendril strikes he disconnected the Q-Pod, folded it up, and tucked it back under his arm.

"You stupid bastard!" Pollux shouted at Hallett. "I told you, I told you! The mine was safer. Now they've found us. You idiot!"

"Back to 'us' now, is it?" said Hallett. "I think they'll be finding *you*, not me. I can jump outta here."

"Damn it, man!"

"I'm gone," said Christian. He took another second to short the burner phone in his pocket, then opened a portal.

"Wait!" called Bertrand. "Take me with you. I'll pay you. I can't be found here. I'll be ruined."

"You *are* ruined. You did this to yourself."

"No!"

Pollux lunged at him, but Christian engaged his bubble and blocked the man. "Say hi to Hubert for me."

The warehouse materialized around him, though he didn't feel any safer. Hallett had integrated with the dew drops! But even worse, he couldn't contain them, and seemed to actively *hunger* for them. If the Agency didn't stop the major, it'd only be a matter of time before he returned wo the warehouse looking for an unlimited supply. *I can't allow that.* But how to stop him?

A copy of the Tech Convergence setup list lay on the floor at his feet and the last item caught his eye: "RMOR" demo. He picked up the sheet of paper and soon had an idea.

*****

The bangers at the door—Agency agents, Hallett guessed—had stopped their pounding and sounded like they were cutting into the steel instead.

The Meadows kid disappeared. Hallett thought about stopping him, but he was rather enjoying watching Pollux's breakdown. Besides, he needed what little energy he had left to escape. *I'll get out of here, and when I do I'll catch the little shit. Take what's mine and make him pay for today.*

Pollux grabbed his lapels. "Open a portal! Get us out of here! *Do* something!"

Hallett looked down on him. "Time for you to go." He wrapped his flaming hands around Pollux's and listened with delight as he screamed. Then Hallett shot white heat into the little man's arms, torso, and finally up into the politician's neck. Fiery, red light glowed beneath the man's skin.

"Help! Help! Aargh! Aaaarrrrrgh!" Pollux and the duffel bag burst into flames as Hallett's inner light burned him until his body was as much a husk as the long-dead Berezhnoy.

Hallett shook the husk and the pieces collapsed into a heap of dust at his feet. "Hehe. Take that, weasel."

The metal around the latch on the door began to buckle. With a final middle-finger to the pile that had been Pollux, Hallett grabbed the sack of dew drops, opened a portal, and leapt through.

*****

The lock on the door melted off. "We're coming in!" yelled the lead agent, Chuck. He pushed through the door, Marion and the rest of the agents behind him, just as a swirl of light winked out.

The room reeked of burnt hair, rotting rat, and Pollux's cologne. "Yuck, what's that smell?" asked another agent.

"Eau de death," said Marion.

"But where'd everybody go?" asked Chuck. "Where's the whistleblower?"

She'd seen enough portals lately to recognize the source of that swirl of light. The whistleblower had to have been Meadows, and given his recent transformation, he must have portaled away. "I'm gone," they'd heard him say over the phone link. That must have been when he'd left.

He could have taken Pollux and Hallett with him. But they'd clearly heard Pollux shouting and then screaming after the phone link died. Now the room was empty. No Hallett. No Pollux. And in the middle of the floor lay an odd pile of ash.

Something glinted up at her in the midst of the dust pile. "Welp, I think we found Pollux. "

"Seriously?" said Chuck.

She fished the lapel pin from the heap. "Pretty distinctive jewelry."

The agent gulped. "Wow. Is Hallett in there too?"

"Maybe." Marion retrieved a pen from her pocket and stirred the dust. "Don't see any brass buttons, though, so I doubt it. But you never know."

"Geez, what happened?"

Marion had an idea but didn't voice it. These guys knew nothing about Meadows' enhancement. But if Campbell had been right all along about Meadows, and Meadows had lost control and disintegrated Pollux, he needed to be brought in, pronto. If Hallett had survived and was working with him, the need to find them both increased tenfold. A bomb lost in the ether was one thing. A man willing to use it was another. *Great. Just great.*

"Scrape this pile into a bag and dust the room for prints. We need to identify the whistleblower and whoever else was here with Pollux."

"Come on. You know it had to be Meadows and Major Hallett."

"Knowing's not proof."

The agents got to work. Marion scanned the room for the money bag. They'd heard Pollux retrieve it, but just like Hallett and Meadows, it was gone. Before returning it to the cavern, Marion had asked Ramona to drop a tracking beacon into it. She fired up the app on her phone and hit the "Locate" button. A light flashed in the pile of ash. *Wonderful. Now what?* It took a minute, but she thought of an alternative.

Marion turned to the lead agent. "Chuck, the rest of your group can stay here, but I need you and one other agent to come with me."

"Sure thing, Marion. Hey, Harry, get over here."

She led them into the corridor, out of sight of the other agents in the room, and pulled out Campbell's Jump!GO.

"Hey, that looks like one of those travel grids."

"That's because it is." She dialed Mitch.

"Hullo?"

"Campbell, I need to know where Christian is. Now."

"Right! Let me go to the machlab and check the tracker." The connection cut out while he portaled, but he returned in less than a minute.

"He's at the warehouse. Sending the points to your grid."

"Thanks. I owe you nachos."

"What's happ—?"

"Sorry, no time to explain." She dropped the call and invoked the grid. Q-Tech's coordinates blinked in the corner. "Alright, gentlemen, draw your weapons and be prepared to shoot."

She expanded the light hole and they leapt.

Christian whirled around from his bench; surprise was etched on his face, but then he recognized Marion.

"I knew you weren't a venture capitalist," he said.

"Hands where we can see them."

He raised his hands and asked, "What's this about?"

Marion pulled out her phone and played the whistleblower's audio. Christian flinched when the playback started, but as it ended, he stared at her, the picture of nonchalance, and said, "Pretty distorted. Sounds like somebody prank called you."

"Now with the distortion off." She applied a de-masking filter, restarted the playback, and suddenly, Christian's voice could be heard, loud and clear. "You were at the meet tonight. You arranged it."

"That makes me a good citizen, then. Why the guns?"

"Because when we got there you were gone, and Pollux was burned into a pile of ash."

"What?!" He seemed genuinely surprised, but Marion wasn't buying it.

"You heard me. At least you left his lapel pin behind to help with the ID. We might have overlooked the dust pile if not for that."

"He was alive when I left. You heard the recording. I said, 'I'm gone.' That's when I came back here."

"I was almost convinced you were still a stooge, serving Pollux like you did his old buddy Hubert. But the smell of his greasy burnt hair changed my mind. Hallett's missing too, and I'll bet we'll find his ashes in the Pollux Pile." She nodded at Chuck, who took a pair of handcuffs from his pocket. "You're under arrest for murder. And I promise you, if you try to run or even think about conjuring a fireball, I'll unload my clip into your head faster than you can burn the bullets."

Chuck advanced on Meadows but didn't get far. Christian threw up an energy shield around himself, then knocked the cuffs from Chuck's hand with a thin energy beam. His fists glowed inside the shield.

"He's about to fry us!" shouted Harry and he squeezed off a shot. The bullet bounced off Meadows' shield. "Shit!"

Marion yanked Chuck back and jumped between him and Christian. "Stand down! Everybody, just stand down!"

"I didn't kill Pollux," said Christian. "I won't hurt anybody. I swear."

"Prove it," said Marion. "Get rid of the shield."

Meadows powered down and the light left his hands. "I'm telling the truth. I portaled here right after you knocked. Both of them were alive when I hit the road."

"We've got no evidence of that. I've seen you in action; I watched the security cam footage of your transformation. You destroyed the back wall of this warehouse with a bolt of lightning from your hand."

"But Hallett can shoot lightning too."

"Bullshit. He was nowhere near the Canopy that night. I'm going to cuff you, and if you so much as blink, my team will put you down."

He let her put the cuffs on him but continued to plead his case. "You have to listen. It must have been Hallett. He stole dew drops from my hopper. He found a way to integrate with them."

"Nice try, but I'm not falling for it." She marched him toward the warehouse door.

"Didn't you listen to the whole call? Didn't you listen up until the end? He said he had tricks of his own. Didn't that sound odd to you? That's when he showed it. Even Pollux didn't know. You have to believe me!"

Marion stopped. She *had* wondered what Hallett meant by that. "What exactly did he do?"

"I'd brought a Q-Pod. He commandeered it and opened a portal to the warehouse so he could steal dew drops from the hopper over there. I shot a tendril at him—"

"A what?"

"Like a lightning whip. But he breathed a fireball and snuffed the whip out."

"Excuse me? He breathed fire?"

"Yes! He hated Pollux. I could feel it in his brainwaves."

"Goodness. Now you read minds."

"Not completely. But believe me, Hallett probably breathed fire on Pollux and snuffed him out."

Oh, no. Damn this psycho-breeding technology. "And he can portal to places too?"

"You heard him on the link. 'I can jump outta here.' "

"This just gets worse."

"There's one difference between Hallett and me, aside from the fire breath. I can't do that."

"I guess we should be thankful for small favors."

"As far as I can tell, what happened to me is permanent. But Hallett seemed… hungry. Like his powers were low. I could tell that he felt better after he ate some dew drops from my hopper. But the fact that he keeps stealing dew drops tells me his powers run out eventually."

"If that's true, then you know what that makes you and your warehouse?"

Christian furrowed his brow. "The help you need?"

"No," said Marion. "Bait."

Christian sighed. "That's fair."

"If I uncuff you, how do I know you won't try to save your own skin and run?"

"I won't. My employees—" He stopped and shook his head. "No, my... friends would be in danger if I ran. I want to protect them. And I've got a plan."

Marion stepped back and regarded Christian. The first time she'd met the boy he'd been a self-centered, neurotic, virtually nihilistic mess. He still seemed neurotic, but whether through maturity, or experience, or his dew drop transformation, something deep inside of him had changed.

She motioned for Chuck to take off the cuffs. "Alright, Meadows. Let's hear this plan."

CHAPTER 24

Convergence

Tamblyn's booth crew assembled at the company's main loading dock early the next morning, the official opening day for Tech Convergence. Sam and Darasimi walked up and down the rows of booth workers handing out convention hall credentials and cards with each team's booth display number along with directions for getting there.

Mitch squinted at his card. "Directions? I know where to go. We were just there yesterday."

Sam paused and explained, "You only saw the staging area. You'll thank us once you see the full booth."

"Gee whiz, how big is it?"

She and Darasimi exchanged glances and laughed. "You'll see," said Sam. "Be sure to put your badges on. The guards will think you're in grade school otherwise." They continued to the next team.

"What's our number?" asked Dean. He had just walked up dragging a pallet full of their gear. Wayne followed close behind carrying a box of modified fobs for the HoloNet demo.

"Forty-two," said Mitch.

"Hmmm. Pretty high number. We're probably somewhere near the back."

"Not surprising," said Wayne. "We're CC's side project. I'll bet Tamblyn's got bigger things to show off than the Jump!GOs."

Mitch put the directions card in his back pocket and handed the guys their lanyards. "Fine by me. The fewer people we have to talk to, the more time we can spend holo-streaming Warrior Ops."

"Or in your case doom-tracking Christian," said Wayne.

Mitch accepted the dig with a smile. "Not anymore. Marion called me last night to get his location, and this morning the tracker's not even showing a blip. I bet she found a way to shut him down and arrested him." He exhaled. Since Marion's call last night, he'd felt like a great weight had been lifted off his chest. "I wonder if he and Dr. Wilkins are sharing a cell?"

"Bad news for Wilkins if that's true. He used to insult Christian quite a bit. Now that my man's ripped, he'll snap 'ol Hubert in half at the first dis."

"Ow."

"Nothing but the truth." Wayne set down the box and started testing the fobs with his phone. The holographic back of Mitch's head floated above the screen again and again. "HoloFobs work."

"Great, then we're all set," said Dean, gesturing toward the pallet. "I've got headsets, music, the gaming console, Power Pills, and check this out."

He balanced a tablet, face-up, on top of the pile of equipment, attached a HoloFob to one of its free ports, and invoked a HoloStage. Not only did Warrior Ops display above the tablet, but in mid-air, spaced around the 3D-rendered battlefield, holographic game controllers appeared.

Mitch went bug-eyed. "No way!"

"Yes, way! Virtual controllers, dude. Took all night, but they are *fire*. Just hold your hand over one to activate it."

Mitch reached a hand tentatively toward one of the floating controllers and waved. The hologram changed from a dull gray to a bright purple. "Yikes!"

"I know, right?" Dean laughed. "Kind of freaked me out when they appeared, to be honest."

"How do I work the buttons?"

Wayne cupped his hands around the neon-green controller closest to him. "The same as on a real one from the look of things." He'd "pressed" a button labeled "Menu" and activated his avatar's weapon inventory.

Mitch did the same, then sent his avatar jogging toward a treasure box. "Amazing. Pretending to hit buttons feels almost like actually hitting buttons."

An evil grin appeared on Wayne's face. "But can you find your weapon? Defend yourself!" *Pew! Pew!* He sent a couple of phaser blasts over Mitch's head.

"Hey, no fair! I'm still figuring it out!" He'd only just managed to stumble out of the way of the blasts, but muscle memory found the key combination to duck. He hid behind a rock while Wayne headed for the treasure box, then squeezed off a couple of shots of his own. Black char bloomed on Wayne's armor. "Ha, gotcha!"

Dean activated the third controller and jumped into the fracas. To Mitch, it felt like being back in Sam's garage. The trash-talk and laughter flowed easily, just like old times—the thrill of the hunt enhanced by the HoloStage's 3D interface. They chased each other around the pallet, forcing their avatars to drive Jeeps, jump off cliffs, blast through buildings, and carpet bomb each other under a constant barrage of blaster fire. They didn't notice the heads swiveled toward them, the jaws dropping, or the conversations petering out.

"Ahem." CC had somehow snuck up behind them. With a start, Mitch dropped his hands from the purple controller and turned around only to be confronted by a sea of stunned faces.

"Oops." He straightened to attention.

"That's an understatement," she said with a raised eyebrow. Then corners of CC's mouth quirked up and Mitch relaxed. "Very entertaining, but let's save it for the booth, shall we?"

Dean shut down the console and the guys scurried off to the side while CC found her way to the elevated dais at the front of the room. She didn't say a word, just waited for the assembled to notice her, which didn't take long. Even silent, CC commanded attention. Within seconds the group had quieted, and all eyes had turned her way.

"Thank you," she said, the smile in her voice carrying easily through the high-ceilinged dock. Gesturing toward Mitch, Dean, and Wayne, she added, "How about our interns? Pretty amazing, wouldn't you say?"

The room broke out in applause. Everyone turned toward the guys, many of them nodding their heads and murmuring approvingly. Mitch's cheeks suddenly felt warm under all the scrutiny. Dean poked him in the shoulder and whispered, "We must not have screwed up too bad." From across the room, Sam caught his eye and flashed him a quick thumbs up.

Wayne, standing on the other side of Mitch, whispered, "Sam approves. I'll take that."

The murmuring died down and CC continued. "The interns' impromptu show is just one reason why I'm so excited for this year's Tech Convergence. They, and all of you, have contributed so much to the innovative products we're showcasing to the world this week. You are all simply fantastic."

This prompted more applause and several shouts of "Whoot!" from the back. CC knew how to play a room.

"We've already generated great excitement within the tech community with yesterday's unplanned yet *very* successful display of our Jump!GO portals versus Quantum Technology's BEAMs. Yesterday was just the beginning. As I told Techline News, we're at the forefront of a revolution, one that will lay a new foundation for transportation and communication. Tamblyn Tech isn't just riding the innovation wave. We're making it. This is our moment. Are we ready to seize it?"

The applause swelled anew and a lone voice from the back of the room shouted, "Let's do it!" The rest of the room took up the chant. "Do it! Do it! Do it!"

CC stepped down from the dais and turned to Mitch, Dean, and Wayne. "Gentlemen?"

Mitch held up his Jump!GO. "Show time, fellas." They opened three portals and the group surged through.

*****

Sam had been right. The Tamblyn Tech booth was massive, covering about the middle third of the floor in Exhibit Hall D. It didn't take long for Mitch, Dean, and Wayne to get completely lost within it.

The directions were *zero* help. "Look for a partition with your number on it," Mitch read, but with all the people milling about, the partitions were nearly impossible to see. After ten minutes, they wound their way back to the edge of the booth, hoping somebody wiser would eventually take pity on them and point out where they needed to be.

"Hey! How'd you kids get in here?"

One of the convention center door minders hurried up to them. "This area is for exhibitors only. What are you doing in here?"

"Uh, we're exhibitors too," said Mitch.

"Where are your badges?"

Doh! Mitch's hands were full, and his badge was in his backpack. He glanced over at Dean and Wayne who just shrugged. They didn't have their badges on either.   "Uh, give us a sec, will ya'. Just gotta put our stuff down." He dropped his box and began rummaging through his backpack.

"No you don't. I'm tired of you kids sneaking in here trying to sell your crap."

"Better than flinging it," said Wayne.

Mitch elbowed him and asked the guard, "What do you mean?"

"You heard me. Your fake Butterfingers and dollar store popcorn and lord knows what else. I oughta confiscate it all right now." He kicked at Mitch's box to loosen the flap and peered inside.

"Is there a problem here, Cyril?"

The minder about jumped a foot at the sound of Sam behind him. Luckily for the guys, she'd chosen that moment to walk by carrying a box of her own. Mitch couldn't tell if she actually knew the man or had just read his name tag. Either way, she smiled pleasantly, employing her considerable people skills.

"No problem at all, Ms. Chambers. Just clearing out the buskers." He pointed at Mitch. "Pick up that box. Go on, get!" He waved the guys toward the entrance like he was fanning out a bad smell.

Sam nodded sympathetically. "Mmm hmm, I'm sure that's a problem. These guys here are alright though."

"Excuse me?"

"Oh, yes. They're three of Ms. Tamblyn's interns. In fact, they're responsible for the light show you saw earlier."

"You mean those big blue ovals that appeared out of nowhere? That was these *kids*?"

Sam nodded again. "The one on the end is even my brother."

The door guard blanched. "Sorry, Ms. Chambers. I mean, they look so... young."

"Not a problem, Cyril. Thanks for looking out."

The man hustled off, but Sam continued to smile after him until he'd retreated back to the door. Then she turned around and said sternly, "I *told* you to put your badges on. Good god, you look like infants. Do it *now*."

"Eh, old Cyril's just a crab," said Dean, digging his badge out of a box and draping the lanyard around his neck. "I betcha we coulda bribed him with a couple of Butterfingers if we'd had some."

"That's probably what he was hoping for," said Wayne. "We just ruined his mid-morning snack."

"What are you doing here at the edge of the booth anyway?" asked Sam. "I saw you shut the light holes down 20 minutes ago. Why aren't you setting up?"

The guys looked away sheepishly. Eventually Mitch said, "Well, we, uh... couldn't find our display space."

Sam laughed and turned to Mitch. " 'Directions?' " she said, scratching her head and mimicking what he'd said to her earlier. For a long as Mitch had known Sam, she'd always done a perfect impression of him. He *hated* it.

"You were right, okay? Happy? Just point us to wherever we're supposed to be at the back of the booth, please, and we'll go."

"The back?"

"Yeah, we're number forty-two. That's like one of the last spaces in the booth, right?"

"What gave you that idea?"

Dean scoffed. "Cuz we're just interns, Sis."

"Didn't you hear CC? Light-based tech is the New Wonderful. It's this year's Tamblyn Showcase. And like it or not, you three are the New Wonderful's ambassadors."

"So maybe near the side, then?" said Mitch pointing to a far corner.

"Look at your card, goofball. What does it say?"

" 'Forty-two. Innovation Showcase.' "

"Now look around. See the numbers?"

Miraculously, the people who'd been cluttering up the booth dispersed, many heading for the concessions. A couple of marketing guys busied themselves around the pamphlet stand. Beneath the Tamblyn Tech logo, Mitch caught site of a large triangle, each side of the triangle embedded with one word from the company slogan: *Smart, Efficient Innovation.*

The marketing team had already erected the displays for Tamblyn's Energy and Tools divisions under the Smart and Efficient sides of the triangle. The area under *Innovation* was mostly empty, save for the banner "The Future is Light." Directly beneath the banner hung blown-up images of the Jump!GO, Power Pill, and a 3D still from the HoloNet. The number forty-two was stamped into the partition and the carpet. The guys gaped. They were the main show. Dean stared at his sister in disbelief.

"That's right, boys. Center stage. *That's* how much CC believes in light-based tech. Here's your scripts and pamphlets. When people walk up—and they *will*—give them that spiel and show off your wares. Welcome to the big time."

Another intern team stumbled into the booth and stared in confusion at their directions. Sam slapped on her professional face and read their card. "One seventy-six? That's in our Development block. I'll show you the way." She tossed a wave over her shoulder at the guys as she led the newcomers to the back of the booth.

"See?" said Dean. "It's not just us."

They dropped their gear and Wayne picked up one of the scripts. He skimmed the first two pages, then tossed the packet aside. "I'm not reading that."

"Ah, come on, it can't be that bad," said Dean. He picked up the discarded packet and thumbed through it.

Mitch read over his shoulder, " 'At Tamblyn Tech, we live for innovation.' "

"Okay, so it might be that bad," said Dean.

The marketing guys laughed loudly at the front of the partition. Both had abandoned the pamphlet stand once Sam left and were gathered instead around one guy's phone. Dean's eyes gleamed. "I've got an idea."

Grabbing a technical spec sheet for the Power Pill and plastering on his best "Aw shucks" grin, Dean walked over to the Marketing Pals, waved the script, and said, "Hey, guys. Great copy for the Jump!GO. Really spot on."

"Sure," said Pal #1, deep in his phone and disinterested.

Pal #2 on the other hand fell for the flattery. He smiled a smarmy smile, shook Dean's hand, and said, "Thanks, kid," before returning to Pal #1's phone.

Dean persisted. "We're real excited about reading it to prospects but thought it could use some more technical details. Mind if I run them past you?"

Pal #1 rolled his eyes and didn't bother to reply. Pal #2, having already committed to playing the nice guy, continued smiling, but shifted his attention back to Dean reluctantly enough to convey annoyance. "What do you suggest?"

"Somebody really interested in the devices would want to hear how we added the microcircuits to the controller board. Like right here." He held up the spec sheet and wove a thread of technobabble worthy of Gene Roddenberry. Pal #2 nodded politely for the first ten seconds or so, but as Dean expounded on the metallurgical properties of the miniature magna coils, his eye-roll rivaled Pal #1's.

He pressed a hand against Dean's chest. "Kid, thanks, but no one cares, k? Just flip the switch on whatever and let us do the talking. Got it?"

Dean transformed his hayseed earnestness into a hangdog droop. "If you say so. Sorry to have bothered you."

He shuffled away, his lips curling upward the closer he got to Mitch and Wayne. "And that, dudes, is how we avoid the lame."

Mitch high-fived him. "Nicely done, Chambers," said Wayne.

They set to arranging their stations. Dean connected the game console and HoloStage to the showcase area's main monitor and sound system to project the 3D setup to everyone in the exhibit hall. Wayne tethered HoloNet fobs, Jump!GOs, and Power Pills to the hands-on station to give prospects a chance to try out and randomly win one of each after a marketing pitch. Mitch prepped the Jump!GO station, priming two plasma grids to send people wherever they wanted to go or to a pre-selected location for ten minutes a pop.

Dean noticed him laying out monitor harnesses and said, "I'll betcha ten bucks most people ask to go to Disneyland."

Mitch chuckled. "I'll bet most people go home to drop off luggage."

"You're both wrong," said Wayne. "I'm gonna bet most people duck home to use the toilet," said Wayne.

"Ha! Good one," said Mitch.

Dean tossed a bill on the station counter. "You're on."

Faintly behind him, Mitch heard someone call his name. He scanned the crowd for the source.

"Over here! Mitch! What's soup, Campbell?"

It was Maggie. The Q-Tech booth was catty-corner to Tamblyn's but seemed farther away due to the Tamblyn booth's massive size. She waved at him. He waved back and called, "Playing ketchup, Heinz!" his standard response to her playful greeting.

"Oh man," said Dean. "I wonder if she knows about Christian?"

"Doesn't look like it," said Wayne. "She's too happy."

"But that's just Maggie, right?" said Mitch. "She was usually happy." Aside from her dressing down Christian the day they eavesdropped on the warehouse, he couldn't recall the last time he'd seen her in a bad mood.

Wayne nodded. "True. But *everybody* over there is jolly." He was right. Larry and the rest of the team joked at each other through their final setups. Billy said something too quiet for him to hear, but the Q-Tech crew burst out laughing. "See? They even think Billy is funny."

"We know better," said Dean.

"If CC had been arrested, I'd at least *try* to look worried or sad or scared. Mitch, are you sure Marion picked up Christian last night?"

He *wasn't* sure. Christian was nowhere in sight, but he realized now that that didn't prove anything. CC, off giving an interview, wasn't in their booth either. The relief he'd felt since Marion's phone call began to dissipate, slowly replaced by worry.

Maggie waved again. "Come over!" she called. Mitch checked the hall clock. "We've got fifteen minutes before the place opens up. Let's go say hi." They trotted to the Q-Tech booth.

"Guys!" She gestured around her excitedly. "Can you believe it? We're all demoing our tech at a major conference! Is this great or what?!"

Mitch couldn't help but smile; Maggie's enthusiasm was contagious. "Not too shabby, Heinz," he said, and then added cagily, "too bad about Christian, though."

She scrunched her nose. "What?"

Mitch traded glances with Dean and Wayne. "I... heard he couldn't come to the conference today."

"Who told you that? Billy? You know how he is. Besides, Christian's here."

Crud puppet. I must have misread the tracker. "Oh yeah? Where is he?"

"Off prepping for—"

"Shh!" Larry said from a nearby station. He held up a finger and said, "Careful, Heinz."

"Oops." She covered her mouth as if to take back the words. "Almost spilled the beans. But it's *so* cool!"

"Now we're intrigued, Maggie," said Wayne.

"Yeah," said Dean, "you're kinda obligated to tell us now."

She regarded them coyly. "If you really want to know, come by later and spin the prize wheel." She led them over to a twelve-slot, upright, spinning wheel at the booth's front station. Eleven slots contained the name of a landmark or a destination. The last slot contained a question mark.

"It looks kind of like our Jump!GO reservation sheet," said Mitch.

"Except for Denali and Mauna Kea," said Dean. "We shoulda included those."

"Our system's still better," said Wayne. "We let people choose where they want to go. We don't taunt them with a game of chance."

Maggie waved dismissively. "Says the king of Warrior Ops. Games are better and a lot more fun. Folks will eat it up."

"So, what's the game?" asked Mitch.

"You spin the wheel, and wherever it lands, we'll BEAM you there for ten minutes."

"Ten whole minutes?" said Dean. "Aren't you guys generous."

"It's not the length of time, Chambers, but how you use it. Since the news blast yesterday, people are *dying* to use a BEAM. I'll bet we could limit it to five minutes and they'd still be happy."

"What's with the question mark?" asked Mitch.

"*That* is a mystery," said Larry, adopting his theatrical classroom persona. "To find out, you must spin to win."

Billy jumped in front of him. "It's a party."

"Shut up, Billy!" Maggie swatted his arm.

"So what if I tell them? They'd keep snoopin' and find out anyway. You know these guys. Am I right?" He turned to the guys and they nodded.

"Yeah."
"Pretty much."
"Figured it out already, frankly."

"It'll start around Happy Hour," Billy continued. "We're giving the people who hit the mystery slot single-use BEAMs. At quittin' time, we'll activate the BEAMs simultaneously and send them all to some swanky joint."

"Where?" asked Mitch.

"No idea. Christian wouldn't tell me."

Maggie rolled her eyes. "I wonder why?"

"I don't have to know. I've got my ticket." He produced a single-use BEAM from his pocket. "And I guarantee you the party's gonna be live as f—"

"Thanks, Billy." Larry handed him an RMOR belt. "How about you suit up and man your station."

Billy grinned. "You guys get the idea." Larry pointed him toward the Personal Security station and pushed him forward.

Had Maggie mentioned the party to him last night, Mitch would have felt confident about finding its location. His tracker app, tuned to Christian's unique signature, would have told him. But Christian's blip had disappeared when he'd checked the tracker that morning. They were going to have to use other means to find the party, or somehow get Maggie to tell them. Asking Maggie would be faster.

"So, guess we'll meet you at the Hilton around Happy Hour," said Dean slyly. "Which ballroom did you say again?"

"Nice try, Chambers, but I didn't."

"Come on, Maggie," said Mitch. "We're buds."

"Not today. You work for our rich and powerful rival. Can't have you show up, flaunting your Rolexes, shining your monocles, and drinking all the champagne." Dean and Wayne took the joke in stride, but Mitch couldn't quite hide his disappointment. Maggie noticed. She patted his shoulder sympathetically. "Sorry, just kidding. I know you guys are alright."

"Are you sorry enough to tell me the address?" he asked with a crooked smile.

"Oh, you!" She punched his arm.

"That's a trade secret," Christian said as he appeared suddenly behind the group.

Wayne stepped aside, casting Christian an appraising eye. "Hello, stranger."

"Oh. Hirano," he said with a small smile.

Dean leaned into Mitch's ear. "He never *did* tell us that story."

Mitch nodded, but worry overshadowed his curiosity. His phone was linked to the tracker program running on his machlab workstation and should have at least sent a ping alerting him to Christian's proximity. It hadn't. Why had it stopped working?

Wayne held on to Christian's attention. "So... I hear you're throwing a party. Need a date?"

Christian laughed. Before he could answer, Cyril the door minder announced, "One minute 'til open!" over the PA.

Christian turned back to Wayne. "I should go."

"That's my line."

Dean pulled Wayne's arm. "We'd better head to our booth too. See you, Maggie."

"Good luck today," said Mitch.

"You too, guys! So excited!"

They hustled back to the booth just as people began streaming into the exhibit hall. "He would have told me where the party was," said Wayne as they manned their stations. "Would've taken just one more minute."

"Cyril, the master of bad timing," said Dean.

"No dollar popcorn for him." said Wayne.

The Marketing Pals were already fielding prospects eager to try out Tamblyn's light-based products. Sam's pitch script would take a few minutes to get through. Mitch figured he'd have just enough time to check the tracker to see what could be causing it to be on the fritz. He'd barley opened the app before Dean accosted him. "Mitch, focus. Don't start doom-tracking again."

"Just need a minute."

"To do what? At least call Marion before you get yourself worked up. I'll cover if marketing sends someone over. 'Now go on. Git!' " he said, affecting Cyril's old-codger accent.

Mitch ducked outside the booth and made the call. Marion answered after two rings. "Not a good time, Campbell."

"Hi, Marion. Did you try to arrest Christian last night?"

"Change of plans. I might need your tracker."

"But Christian's here, right in front of me. Come get him."

"He's not the target. Wait... can your tracker pick up any dew drop energy?"

"It's keyed to Christian's frequencies. I'd have to adjust it."

Marion cursed.

"Want me to jump him?"

"No! For the last time, he's not the threat."

"Okay, but seriously—"

"Gotta go." She hung up.

No sooner had the line gone dead than did his phone began to buzz loudly. *The tracker. Finally!* He opened the app and looked on in horror as the tracker showed a plume of energy spreading out across the map. Oh, no! He rushed to the edge of the Tamblyn booth, to get the catty-corner view of Q-Tech, expecting to see Christian raging and incandescent. He was wrong. Instead, Christian stood near Billy, calmly explaining the RMOR belt to a prospect. Then he handed the prospect a bag full of items to toss at Billy's white-blue shell.

Mitch checked the tracker again and realized that the energy cloud was nowhere near the convention center. The source seemed to be near the Q-Tech warehouse, but on second glance seemed to be dissipating quickly. Dean caught his eye and beckoned him back to their station impatiently. Mitch sighed. *Damn it.* The tracker had to be malfunctioning. And so was his brain. He felt foolish. Everyone from Marion to Wayne said Christian wasn't a threat. Maybe it was time he started believing them.

He pocketed his phone and took his spot at the Jump!GO station just as the Marketing Pals sent him hist first customer. "Hello, ma'am," he said. "Where would you like to go?"

"The Liberty Bell museum in Philadelphia. My brother works in the gift shop, and I want to surprise him."

"Sounds like fun." He invoked the plasma grid and the woman took two steps back.

"That looks freaky. Will it hurt?"

"Not at all. The Jump!GO's so easy to use, you'll hardly notice it at all." He expanded the light hole and the woman, eyes wide with wonder, stepped through.

"Charlie!" she shouted at a man working the cash register.

"Gah!" The man jump away from the counter and clutched his chest.

Mitch laughed. The tracker app buzzed again in his pocket, but he ignored it. As the morning wore on and more people arrived, he hardly noticed it at all.

CHAPTER 25

Trap

Two hours earlier, Marion paced the aisle behind Christian Meadows' workbench at the warehouse while Meadows continued building out the trap central to his plan to capture or, as he put it, neutralize Major Hallett.

He'd worked through the night and had only stepped away via the Q-Pod a couple of hours after sunrise for a brief visit to the convention center to check on his team. Marion had followed him as insurance, and though she promised to stay out of sight, she also made it clear that she could take him out at any time should he try to run.

"I have as much invested in putting a lid on Hallett as you do," he'd said. "Maybe more. I'm not running anywhere."

True to his word, he talked to his tech lead, Larry, and the Heinz girl, then returned to where Marion hid beside the Q-Pod to go back to the warehouse. "Is anybody else from your team coming to work today?" she asked

"No. I gave anyone not working the conference the day off. We've got the place to ourselves. Until Hallett arrives at least."

"I wonder what's taking him so long? I half expected to find him here with you when we arrived last night. And now that we know he's enhanced like you, he should be on the offensive. Yet not a peep out of him."

"He's avoiding me, conserving his power I suspect. Fighting takes energy, and he knows I'll fight before I let him steal from me again."

"So you think he's waiting until he's sure you're not around?"

"Precisely. Both he and Bertrand knew I'd be at the conference today. Bertrand even scheduled an investor meeting for me in about ninety minutes. Once Hallett thinks I'm at that meeting, he'll strike here."

Marion checked her watch. "How much more do you have to do?"

"A couple more adjustments. We'll have to test it. Then I'll need to leave for that meeting as well as do some setup for the after-party this evening."

He'd returned to his workbench. Marion prowled the aisles, wary of the slightest shadow passing in front of the warehouse windows as the sun rose higher in the morning sky. Chuck and Harry fanned out on either side of her, just as watchful, until daybreak, when Harry let loose a mighty yawn. Chuck paused at the edge of the break room, eyeing the adjacent kitchen wistfully.

"Mind if we go find coffee?" he asked. "Been a long night."

"Knock yourself out," said Marion.

He and Harry headed toward the break room. Harry turned on the big screen while Chuck drew water at the coffee bar. Soon the smell of fresh-brewed coffee and toasted bread wafted across the room, and the rowdy chants of Eintracht Frankfurt fans broke the tense silence. Chuck handed her a mug before joining Harry on a pub stool in front of the game.

Before long, Meadows looked up and said, "It's ready."

He held up a box no bigger than his hand. It resembled the same type of dew drop chamber used for all of Q-Tech's devices, with the exception of a white bar lodged in the central cavity in place of the dew drop. Marion checked her watch. One hour to go before the official start of Tech Convergence. If Hallett planned on visiting, he'd better do it soon.

She held out her hand to take the device. "Show me how to use it."

"You don't." He walked over to the dew drop hopper by the door, fastened the box to it just out of sight, and flipped a switch on the box's side. The light within the dew drops pulsed brighter briefly, then gradually dimmed until all but a few of them flickered out.

"Impressive," said Marion. "Are you affected?"

Meadows held up his hand and opened a portal to the convention center. "It appears not."

"Good god. You spent all this time on something that won't even work!"

"Calm down. It should work on Hallett, just not for me. My dew drops are different... embedded. The Canopy explosion fused them into my body."

Marion threw up her hands, exasperated. "What's that got to do with Hallett?"

"It points to the biggest difference between him and me, a difference I'm going to exploit. For whatever reason, Hallett gets hungry. His power drains over time. That means his integration with the dew drops is superficial and thus accessible. As soon as he touches the hopper, his power will dim, just like all these dew drops. Then you'll have him. At least, that's the theory."

"What about when we take him away from the warehouse and this draining gizmo?"

Meadows switched off the box and removed it from the hopper. The dew drops inside remained dim. "It's permanent."

Marion frowned. "I wish I could believe you."

Meadows made a fist, exhaled, then opened his hand. A single dew drop lay in his palm. "You could become like Hallett. Test it on yourself."

Though she was years removed from her original course of study, a part of Marion was still scientific enough to see the validity in Meadows' suggestion. They needed to test the device on a Hallett analog, and of everyone present she was as good a choice as any. But still...

What have I gotten myself into? After all of this time fighting to keep a lid on light tech, here I am in this position.

Months ago, when Campbell had first invented his damn crazy Canopy, she'd been dead set against the technology, seeing it as an agent of chaos if not a harbinger of doom. Today she had a miniature Canopy in her pocket; her mother's company had embraced the goofball who created it; a loose cannon was using the technology to burn people alive; and a human Canopy stood in front of her now, offering her a portal to eat like a hard candy. *And* she was actually considering doing it. Unending slippery slopes with this technology, all of them leaving her dangling over a precipice.

"Chuck! Harry! Get out here!" she called. The big screen went quiet and Chuck and Harry ran out of the break room, Harry still munching a bagel.

"Is Hallett here?" asked Harry.

"Not yet, but he might be on his way. I need to test the trap before he gets here. Draw your weapons and point them at me."

"Say what?" Chuck asked, incredulous. Harry merely shrugged; he put down his bagel and unholstered his gun.

"Do as I say. If at any time I go berserk and become a threat, plug me."

"That's crazy," said Chuck. "We can't—"

"You will! Don't argue!"

"Yes, ma'am."

Reluctantly, Chuck reluctantly drew his gun, then he and Harry stepped to either side of Marion, raised their weapons, and waited.

Marion took the dew drop from Meadows hand, marveling at how cool it felt in her fingers. "Seems harmless."

"Hell, you aren't gonna eat it, are you?" Chuck's incredulity changed to real alarm.

Marion ignored him. The clock was ticking. "Do I need a cup of water or something?"

"Probably not. Hallett swallowed one easily. Despite the plasma casing, it's still just a photon. Perhaps it will melt in your mouth like a sugar cube."

Not very encouraging. But she couldn't back out. She had to be sure Christian's energy-draining box would work and if eating a lump of fire was the best way to test it, then down the hatch. She opened her mouth wide and forced the dew drop in as far as it would go.

Meadows was right. It wasn't hard to swallow the photon. In truth, it felt no worse than taking an aspirin. She barely felt it pass through her throat. But once it landed a warmth spread through her torso, from her stomach to her back, a gentle, pleasing sensation—until a bolt of lightning shot up her spine, filling every capillary, very cell with light.

She wanted to roar, but fought against it, some instinct or inner voice—no, voices—telling her to clamp down, hold it in. She closed her eyes and her mouth and waited for the jolt from the lightning to pass, but it didn't. Whatever fatigue she'd felt from being up all night disappeared. She felt as if she could touch everyone and everything, as if she were not just herself, but a every Marion that had ever existed. She knew without a doubt that if she concentrated, she could build up enough energy in her fist to punch a hole through the roof and lift herself into the sky.

[**Control it,**] the manifestation of her multitude demanded. Behind her closed eyes, she could see the image, ever morphing—old self, young self, current self, all selves—fierce, encouraging, and ready to explode, but smart enough to not let go. [**Control!**]

With an effort, she repressed the impulse to throw all her energy against the ceiling and take flight. Once she felt under control, she opened her eyes. Chuck and Harry just about jumped out of their skin. *What must I look like?* She didn't really want to find out.

"Alright, I've survived," she said, turning to Meadows, her voice a multitude of Marions. "What now?"

Christian flipped the switch on his energy-draining box and stepped back. "Try to touch the hopper."

She walked—no, floated—toward the dew drop container. The desire to zoom returned, but she tamped it down. *Stay in control. You only need a small burst of light.* She held up her hand and it blossomed with energy, but she reduced it by sheer strength of will into simple light, a single beam around her index finger. She heard a gun cock behind her.

"Don't shoot," said Meadows. "She's in control. I can feel it."

She'd reached the hopper. *Now or never.* She picked up a lifeless dew drop, and as soon as she touched it her feet dropped to the ground, her hand felt heavy as lead, and all the light that had spread into her stomach and up to her brain flowed out in a steady stream from her index finger, sucked into the spinning center of Meadows' trap until she cried out for the draining to stop, but it didn't stop until all of it was gone. She fell to the floor breathless, and when next she spoke, the multitude had left her, and her voice sounded dry, raspy, and brittle to her ears. "I guess that worked," she said.

Meadows helped her stand. Chuck and Harry stowed their guns. Harry picked up his bagel.

"That took guts," said Chuck. "I'm impressed."

"Don't be. It was stupid." Marion gasped. She took several deep breaths and finally started to feel steady again. "I'm lucky to be alive."

Meadows studied her for a moment then said, "At least you proved it will work on Hallett. I still have work to do at the hotel and need to leave. Besides, Hallett won't show up until I'm gone."

"Right. Take this." She retrieved a small earpiece from a pocket of her flak jacket. Meadows put it in his ear. "Can you hear me?" she asked.

"Loud and clear."

"Good. We'll stay in touch this way. You'll hear what we hear and vice versa. Tap to mute and unmute."

"Got it." Meadows opened a portal to what looked like the back of a ballroom. "Good luck," he said before stepping through.

Marion checked her watch. Thirty minutes until Hallett's expected arrival. Chuck and Harry alternated between glancing in her direction and sheepishly avoiding her gaze.

"Who wants to tell me what I looked like hopped up on dew drops?"

That broke the tension. Chuck pointed at his partner. "Harry volunteers."

"Hey!" Harry protested, his mouth full of cream cheese from an exceptionally big bite of his bagel.

"You can *both* regale me while we get more coffee," said Marion. "But make it quick. Hallett's due in a few minutes."

*****

Chuck and Harry took turns providing Marion with unflattering details of her energy drain until she cut the conversation short and had them build a box and cart barrier to hide behind while they waited for the major.

The clock ticked to the top of the hour. Tech Convergence had officially opened to the public, but still no Hallett. Marion tapped her earpiece. "No sign of him, Meadows."

"He'll be there. He's low on power and needs a fix."

"Maybe not as much of one as you think."

"No, I felt it. He practically panicked when I blocked him from taking more dew drops last night. He'll be there. Hold on, I have to talk to a customer." He muted his earpiece and was gone.

Crap. Marion sighed, more frustrated with herself than with Meadows. She knew Hallett was a loose cannon, the instigator of this latest mess. She should have had someone tailing him the minute he'd squeezed off rounds at Meadows and the Heinz girl.

Burrup, burrup. Marion looked at her phone. Campbell's number. *Goodness, what now?* "Not a good time, Campbell."

"Hi, Marion. Did you try to arrest Christian last night?"

"Change of plans. I might need your tracker."

"But Christian's here, right in front of me. Come get him."

"He's not the target. Wait... can your tracker pick up any type of dew drop energy?" Maybe Campbell's Christian stalking app could be used to find Hallett.

"It's keyed to Christian's frequencies. I'd have to adjust it."

"Damn it," she muttered.

"Want me to jump him?"

"No! For the last time, he's not the threat."

"Okay, but seriously—"

A sharp whine pierced the quiet of the warehouse, followed by an oval burst of blue-white light near the hopper. Hallett appeared at the face of the oval carrying a bag. He stumbled forward as if he'd been pushed and came to a stop near the dew drop hopper.

"Gotta go." She hung up and crouched down with Chuck and Harry behind the barrier, their firearms at the ready, and waited for him to make his move.

"Place is empty," he said. He turned his head from side-to-side, searching the warehouse, a confused look on his face. "What am I looking for?" he said.

Strange question, thought Marion.

"Who's he talking to?" asked Chuck, his mouth close to her ear.

"How should I know?" whispered Marion.

"It's behind you, dumbass," someone said.

A shiver went up Marion's spine. Hallett had spoken again, seemingly answering his own question. But why did it sound like the voice came out of the portal?

Chuck was back near her ear. "He's talking to himself?"

"Quiet," she hissed.

Hallett spotted the hopper and laughed. "Heh-heh. There they are, ripe for the picking."

"Scoop 'em up already. Be sure to take 'em all."

Marion's skin crawled. *Why was the portal speaking? Were they hearing an echo?* "Damn, that's creepy," whispered Chuck.

"On second thought, just grab the whole thing," said the portal.

Hallett dropped the bag and grabbed either side of the hopper. Immediately, his body went stiff. "Yow!"

"What is it?" asked Hallett's echo.

"I... I don't know," said Hallett. "It's got a hold of me. I can't move!"

"Drop it. Get back here."

"I can't! Aarrgh! Aaaaarrrrrgh!" Hallett's body had begun to glow, his skin taking on an incandescent hue.

Marion gripped the top of the cart. "Did I glow like that?"

"Not at all," whispered Chuck, eyes wide. Harry gulped beside him.

"Shit!" said the portal. "We're outta here." The oval began to flicker.

"No! Don't leave me!" Hallett cried. His body started to vibrate and—*good god, is he flickering too?*

Like a thunderclap, the portal snapped shut. Hallett's vibrations increased, his body shaking so fast it became a blur and then—*Crack!* Hallett shattered into pieces. Bits of him shot across the room while the rest fell to the floor and crumpled in front of the hopper like brittle sugar glass.

Marion, Chuck, and Harry left their hiding place. Harry edged close to the Hallett pile, nudging the shards with his shoe. Thankfully, none of the shards nudged back. He looked up at Marion. "This *definitely* didn't happen to you."

"Great. Just great," said Marion, holstering her gun. "Two sure-fire corruption suspects and both of them reduced to desiccant."

"You think this was Meadows' plan all along?"

Marion thought about it, then shook her head. "No. If his magic box were lethal, I'd have shattered along with Hallett. Something tells me that this, whatever it is, wasn't supposed to happen." She tapped her earpiece. "Meadows, you there? Meadows!"

She heard rustling, the mic on the other end rubbing against fabric. "Sorry," he said. "Had an interview. Traded your earpiece for a headset, but I'm back now. What's up?"

"Hallett exploded."

Silence and then, "That's not possible."

"Come see for yourself."

A few seconds later, Christian stepped through an eye-shaped tear in the middle of the room and joined them at the hopper. He knelt beside the jagged remains of the major, his expression a picture of perplexity and alarm. "He didn't explode. He *shattered.*"

"Your point?" asked Marion.

He raised his hands helplessly. "I... don't have one. I'm just surprised. But why didn't the same thing happen to you?"

"We were hoping you could explain it."

"I can't." He stood up and retrieved the energy-draining box from the side of the hopper, turning it over in his hands.

"Kinda convenient if you ask me," said Chuck. "Both of the guys you ratted on are history. Your old boss is in federal prison. All three of them screwed you. Now here you are sitting pretty, the main attraction at a big tech convention, your company ready to rake in the gold."

Christian looked up at Chuck, frowning. "What are you implying?"

"He's thinking you either killed or betrayed your partners in crime for fame, riches, and revenge," said Marion. "And I must admit, I had been leaning in that direction myself."

" 'Had been'?" said Chuck. "Come on, Marion, back me up on this."

"Chuck, if Meadows were a killer, we'd already be dead, and Hallett and Pollux would have bought the farm weeks ago. You don't need alibis and sting operations when you can vaporize your victims. He could have zapped us *and* them, swept up the leavings, and nobody'd be the wiser." She turned to Christian. "Am I right?"

"I wouldn't," he said.

"But you could."

He nodded slowly. "Yes... but I won't."

"Good. Don't get any ideas. Also, you're not completely off the hook. We'll need a deposition, any records of your and Hubert's dealings with Pollux. The Agency can come up with a cover story, but eventually Pollux and Hallett will have to be explained, and that explanation may include you."

Christian held her stare and said, "I understand. But let me finish the conference first, put Q-Tech on solid footing so that at least my employees and the company can survive any 'explanations.' "

"Fair enough. We'll be here for a while running through our standard field analysis. Keep the earpiece. I'll check in at the end of the day."

"Thank you." He ripped open another hole in the fabric of space and left.

Harry and Chuck exchanged glances. "This'll be one helluva report," said Harry.

Marion sighed and called Ramona. "We need an unmarked field team out at Q-Tech."

"Unmarked? Sounds like a doozy," said Ramona. "At least you're wrapping it up."

If only. The field analysis was just the beginning. Combined with the cover story, she'd be working the rest of the weekend on the report. Then Monday would come, and the brass would want to be briefed, and she'd spend the rest of the week on addendums and further report pages. A crispy-critter congressman would not be easy to explain away, and she didn't even want to *think* about what military intelligence would demand regarding Hallett.

And still, out of those odious tasks, there was one she dreaded above all others. *What the hell am I going to tell Ralph?*

*****

Hallett slammed into the dumpster behind the Tortas Locas as the Q-Tech portal snapped shut. He would have rather landed at his condo or office, but both places were crawling with Agency teams. The sandwich shop wouldn't open for an hour, and no one would think to look for him there, so it made as good a hiding place as any.

That's what he needed right now: a quiet hole and some time to clear his head and get his bearings. Meadows had booby-trapped the hopper and effectively cut off Hallett's power supply. Hallett had to find a way to disarm the death trap. An hour should be long enough to think up something—as long as the Tortas' staff didn't notice him. He stood up, brushed off the trash, and forced himself to think.

He hadn't enjoyed watching his reflection shake itself to pieces. Not because he'd miss the guy; his soldiers were a dime a dozen. What galled him was that the attack had happened at all. It made him look foolish and weak and there was no way he could let that stand. *You made the wrong move, Meadows. Now I'm* seriously *pissed off.* If the kid wanted to play hardball, he'd show him how it was done. But first, he'd have to recharge.

"Yo, vato. Alejarse de allí."

Emilio, the owner, had arrived to open up the place. Hallett climbed out of the dumpster and waved. "No, problemo, primo." *Time's up, gotta go. But to where?* He walked far enough down the alley away from Emilio for the man to lose interest, then ate a dew drop from the bag he'd nabbed last night.

Once again, lightning coursed through his veins. *Oh yeah, that's the stuff.* The ringing in his head stopped. He felt a hundred times better and suddenly knew where he should go. He drew a circle with his finger, then just for kicks, breathed fire at it until the portal opened. "Get ready, kiddo. You're in for a surprise."

CHAPTER 26

Crashed

Mitch cut a path through the convention center crowd back toward the Tamblyn Tech booth carrying a cardboard tray full of free munchies he'd gathered from marketing drones scattered along the way. The conference was winding down to the best part of the day—Happy Hour—and exhibitors were pulling out all the stops. So far, he'd managed to score fries, gelato, kebabs, and cookies, and he was now on the hunt for three cups of fizz. Dean had insisted he find beer, but right now he'd willingly settle for any liquid poured over ice. He'd jumped the gun and bit into one of the spicy kebabs, so now his mouth was on fire and he desperately needed something wet and cold to calm it down.

Thankfully, the Beverage Bot booth lay directly ahead, their robot bartender expertly dispensing shot-size cups of malted lager. *Well, gosh darn it, beer it is,* he thought. Cocking his head to the side in what he hoped was a suitably mature, if obscuring angle, Mitch extended his lanyard at the marketing matron so that she could scan his badge and hand him a drink.

It almost worked. She stopped mid-scan to study him closely, then said. "Uh, uh. Move along."

"Problem with my badge?"

"No, sweetie. Your face."

"Oh, I just look young."

"'Cuz you are. You're one of Tamblyn's whiz kids." She leaned hard on "kids," and pointed to the big screen where CC was currently being interviewed. "She's been flaunting your faces—and ages—all day, so shove off."

Crud puppet. He tried two other prospects and got essentially the same response. At least the last booth had ice and seltzer. He accepted three cups gratefully and returned to the Innovation station with his haul.

"Ooh," said Dean. "Cookies and wine cooler."

"Seltzer, but after you taste a kabab, you'll thank me."

"You had one job, Mitch."

"I know. Blame CC not me. She's been telling everybody how old we are all day. We're 'whiz kids' now, apparently."

Wayne bit into a kabab. "Makes for a more compelling narrative."

"Totally," Dean agreed. "I think she's pushing the Jump!GOs at the youth market. BEAM is pretty sleek, but it seems like a product your dad would buy."

Wayne gulped his seltzer. "Exactly. You ride a BEAM to your corporate meeting. But hitting the gym or the club? Point your fob and go. Kind of genius marketing, really."

Behind them, the horde of spectators around the HoloStage erupted in cheers and groans. The guys turned around just in time to watch Darasimi obliterate a troop of shadow operatives with a lucky team of participants. She traded high-fives with that group but made sure to sympathize with the losing side. She adjusted her mic and addressed the spectators. "How's that for a super-charged gaming experience, folks?" she said.

"Man, she's good," said Mitch.

"Wouldn't expect anything else," said Dean. "Just glad she's on our side now."

She put down her controller and told the crowd, "That wraps it up for today." They booed when she shut down the HoloStage and the interactive holographic chat. "Don't worry," she assured them. "You don't have to leave. There's food and drinks at the front of the booth."

The grumbles stopped immediately. Mitch laughed. It was amazing the amount of goodwill a company could build with chips, luncheon meat, and beer.

"Thank you all so much for attending this demo. Remember, at Tamblyn Tech we live for innovation."

It was the guys' turn to groan. The marketing line sounded only slightly less goofy coming from Darasimi, but only just. As the crowd dispersed, she put the game console into demo mode and hurriedly packed away the headsets and marketing materials.

Dean called to her, "Hey, Darasimi. We're breaking for a snack."

"No problem. The day's pretty much done. Where'd you find kababs?"

"Three booths over. Better hurry. The line was getting pretty long when I was there."

"Gotta shoo the rest of these folks to our own Happy Hour section first. Then I'm gonna jet," she said, her eyes twinkling.

She stepped in front of the cloud and clapped her hands to get their attention. "Hello! This will be the last runs for our Jump!GO and for the HoloFob giveaway. Hors d'oeuvres and drinks are available in the front. Thank you all!" She winked at the guys over her shoulder and headed toward the kebob booth while the Marketing Pals hustled people in the direction of Tamblyn's snack train.

The guys took advantage of one of the tall, now-empty brochure tables to divvy up the snacks between them and lay into the treats Mitch had procured. It felt good to sit down. The table they'd chosen was at the edge of the Tamblyn booth, giving them a good vantage point to people watch while they ate. The hall was still jam-packed. Or rather, their section of it was. Mitch took in the rest of the hall and only then realized that the majority of the people were crammed into the Tamblyn Tech/Q-Tech neck of the woods.

On top of that, an inordinate number of attendees appeared to be in possession of Tamblyn and Q-Tech giveaways. Both booths had had raffles and prize wheels running for most of day, handing out limited-use versions of their tools. Mitch just hadn't noticed the sheer volume of people who'd participated. Scattered throughout the exhibit hall, plasma grids opened and closed, blue BEAM columns expanded and collapsed, and—most surprisingly—HoloFobs projected 3D videos of it all.

He checked the HoloNet feed and realized that it was still populated despite it being the end of the day, with users starting up holo chats of their own and hanging out on the network like it was the most normal thing. They'd created HoloNet largely as a demo for the conference. He'd never expected it to be used so extensively. He glanced over at Wayne and Dean. They'd stopped eating and like him were staring at the mobs of people enjoying Happy Hour at Tamblyn's and Q-Tech's booths. "Been a weird day," he said.

Dean turned to him. "A lot of people using light tech out there."

"Uh, huh."

"Light tech that's available because of us."

"Uh, huh."

"Guys... *we* did this."

"Would seem so," said Wayne. "But what's the problem? Isn't this what you raved about when Mitch first showed us the Canopy? 'We'll be like Richard Branson,' you said. 'We'll be travel gods,' you said. None of that's gonna happen unless people use what we make."

"I mean, yeah, but it's one thing to think about it in theory or mess around with the tech in Sam's garage or the lab. It's another thing to actually see it used by other people. In the wild."

"That's exactly how I felt when I saw Chung's version of the Canopy," said Mitch. "It's... unnerving."

"Get used to it. You guys just normalized the future." Sam had snuck up on them again. She reached into Dean's food pile and filched a fry.

"Maybe we'd feel better about it if CC didn't keep harping on how young we are," said Dean, smacking Sam's hand as she tried to sneak another fry. Mitch offered her a cookie.

"Well, *someone* loves me," she said, accepting it and taking a big bite. Mitch blushed. "And CC's just focusing on your ages for marketing reasons."

"Toldja," said Wayne.

"Everybody wants to buy what the kids think is hot, especially anything having to do with social media. Don't get me wrong, distributors love the Jump!GO and it's set to do solid business, but the HoloFobs? They're on fire."

She was right. Their corner of the convention center crackled with energy and the constant excitement of 3D exhibit hall scenes projected from HoloStages above many phones. Anyone with a HoloFob had acquired an instant entourage, as people gathered around them and waited for some new image to appear. Jump!GO and BEAM winners were more than willing to provide holographic material. They opened plasma grids, projected heads-up displays, and magically disappeared through white ovals and blue columns. The HoloFob followers ate up every minute of it. Wayne's side project was a roaring success.

"CC wants to leave the HoloNet running for as long as possible today. Maybe longer," said Sam. "That's why I came over. We'll need more content. Any ideas?"

Dean logged in and checked the servers. "Looks like we don't need any. People seem to be uploading their own content. Amazing, guys."

"But for how long?" asked Sam. "Once the doors close, what else is there to show? I doubt you'll enjoy playing Warrior Ops all night."

"You have a point. Never thought I'd get tired of collecting mech and busting things up."

"And yet here we are," said Wayne. "Guess I'll raid your player stash tomorrow morning."

"I never said I was tired of busting *you* up."

Sam patted the table for attention. "Stay with me, people. We need something to keep the buzz going. What's trending? What's everyone talking about?"

Mitch turned his gaze to the convention center floor and recognized someone immediately. Miniature Maggies blossomed on several HoloStages as HoloFobs were pointed at the Q-Tech booth. Larry appeared beside her with his tablet, making faces and gesturing grandly. Maggie threw back her head and laughed.

Mitch smacked his forehead. "Of course! Christian's secret party!"

Sam nodded, "K, good, but after the reveal their booth will shut down for the day just like ours."

"But the after-party reveal isn't the only thing people are curious about. What they'll *really* want is actual footage of the party. The people on the HoloNet will go nuts if we find a way to broadcast."

"Brilliant idea, Mitch!"

"Only if we can get in," said Dean. "Larry's the only person besides Christian who knows the location, and he's not sharing. I've already tried to get him to blab."

"There's bound to be a way to figure it out. In the meantime, we can put the reveal up on the main screen." Mitch removed a minicam from one of the Jump!GO monitor vests and hooked it into a HoloFob. Soon, Maggie and Larry appeared on the booth's HoloStage, the image about as crisp as the one projected on the big screen. This was going to be great.

A nearby spectator aimed his HoloFob back and forth between the screen and the HoloStage while moderating a holographic, group-chat session. He caught sight of Mitch and said, "Too bad this is the last spectacle today. This fob is mega. I'm really getting used to watching vids on it."

That's all Sam needed to hear. Shifting into her most ingratiating marketing mode, she said, "You don't have to stop. We're simulcasting from the Q-Tech mystery location after the reveal."

"For real?"

Dean pulled her arm. "Sam, wait—"

She rolled out of his grip with practiced sibling ease. Turning to the stranger, she continued, "Yep. The HoloNet will stay online until it's all over. Maybe even the rest of the night. Spread the word."

"*Ultra*-mega! Thanks!" He switched his chat from the local group to a wide broadcast and soon his face appeared in the chat windows of every fob on the exhibit hall floor. "Hey, everybody. Tamblyn's crashing Q-Tech's after-party!" All around them, fobs tuned to Tamblyn's main feed in anticipation. 3D Maggies and Larrys bopped sprang to life on every HoloStage.

Sam finally let Dean drag her back to the tall table. "Are you insane?" he hissed at her. "We don't know where the party is!"

She grinned. "What's the matter? You were just bragging about how easy it would be to find out."

"Theoretically!"

"Theory's not that far from reality. I have faith in you three. You're the whiz kids." She smiled at them. "My turn to get some grub. Good luck. Make CC proud!" Sam waved and waltzed toward the front of the booth.

"French biscuits, she's so annoying."

"I'm told being annoying is a big sister's main job," said Wayne. "You could get back at her by—"

"No time for that," Mitch interrupted him. "How are we gonna highjack a BEAM and crash the party?"

Dean scratched the sides of his head. "I could mug a guy and steal his mystery case?"

"Expedient," said Wayne.

"But violent," added Mitch. "We'd get kicked out." He took his Jump!GO from his pocket and pried open the case. "How about we move jumpers around until we land on the BEAM frequency?"

"Worth a shot," said Dean. "Let's each modify our Jump!GOs with different jumpers."

They set to work. At the Q-Tech booth, Larry and Maggie donned portable mics and faced the crowd. Larry advanced to the edge of the dais, arms akimbo, and boomed dramatically in his TA voice, "Is everybody ready?"

"Yeeessss!"

"Heeeey!"
"Whoot!"

Maggie stepped up beside him, grinning mischievously. "Who's got a mystery case?" she said.

"Meeee!"
"I've got one!"
"Whoot!"

"Bet you're wondering what it's for," said Larry.

"A party!"
"It's a BEAM!"
"That guy already told us!"
"Whoot! Billy!"

In the far corner of the booth, Billy pumped his fists into the air and raised both thumbs up at the crowd. Larry covered his face with one hand.

Maggie shot Billy a disgusted look then said to the crowd, "But you don't know what *kind* of party. Or *where* it is."

"Only one person knows," said Larry. "Ladies and Gentleman, Christian Meadows!"

Christian's huge head appeared on the Q-Tech big screen above the booth, crowned in laser lights panning the dark room behind him. The crowd whooped and hollered. After appearing worn and unkempt earlier in the day, now Christian was meticulously coiffed, his features chiseled, and what little they could see of his neck and torso rippled, taut and tan, beneath a tight, collared shirt. Wayne paused to look up at the big screen and smacked his lips. "Mmm. Hello, Adonis."

"He ditched you, dude," Dean reminded him.

Wayne shrugged. "Was kind of mutual. He had problems. I'd go back."

"Guys, focus," said Mitch. "I'm out of jumpers. We need to try something else."

Dean snapped his fingers. "Your doom-stalking program. Isn't that tuned to find Christian?"

"Only if he's on the verge of going ballistic. It's been quiet all day. Mostly."

"Hand it over. Maybe I can make it find a BEAM instead."

Christian leaned closer to the camera and surveyed the crowd. "Hold up your cases, everyone," his deep voice rumbled out of the speakers.

Over two dozen hands, each holding a gold mystery case, shot up into the air.

"Wrap the strap around your write or put your case in a pocket. Whatever you do, keep it with you. It's both your invitation and your ride home. Now," he purred. "Are you all ready?"

"Stop teasing us!"
"Bring it!"

Out of the corner of his eye, Mitch caught a glimpse of Sam and CC trying to appear casual as they gawked up at Christian like everyone else. Sam noticed him. She cocked an eyebrow quizzically and tapped her watch. He felt a trickle of sweat roll down his back.

Christian smiled, supremely assured, and with an expansive wave, he said, "Good people of Convergence, welcome to the house of fun!" He held up a remote and pressed a button.

The gold boxes in people's hands ignited, and the glittering gold was overwhelmed by a burst of blue that spread out, up, and sideways into a column around each box's holder.

"Transport commencing," they all intoned simultaneously, all in the same deep modulation so much like Christian Meadows' own. The crowd gasped with amazement.

"We're out of time, Mitch," said Dean.

"No, wait. Maybe if I reverse the polarity—"

"The BEAMs are leaving, dude."

All around, one by one, the blue BEAM columns winked out of existence. "Crud puppet!" said Mitch. "We should've let you pound a guy. Hey, what happened to Wayne?"

"Right behind you," he said.

"Gah! Where'd you go?"

"Jumper shuffle failed, so I went low tech. I saw somebody with a golden case at the back of the line, trotted over, and took a picture of their BEAM's heads- up display before it disappeared." He showed them the picture and there, clear as day. were the party's coordinates.

"Score!" said Mitch. He opened a holo chat window and announced for all to hear, "We have capture!"

Dean leaned into the shot. "Arrr! The secret location is ours!" The crowd roared.

Wayne grabbed a HoloFob, tapped in the coordinates on his Jump!GO, and opened a plasma grid. Miniature versions of Mitch, Dean, and Wayne bobbed to life on the HoloStage of every fob as well as on the Tamblyn booth's big screen.

"Avast, ye hearties!" cried Mitch. "The party begins!"

They expanded the light hole and dove in. When they materialized in the midst of Christian's laser lights—the lone plasma grid among a forest of blue BEAMs— everyone in sight of Tamblyn's big screen or a HoloFob stage cheered.

One man in particular applauded their feat. Hallett lurked in the shadows at the edge of Tamblyn's booth. He'd been hiding in plain sight at the convention all day, keeping an eye on Meadows and Q-Tech from a distance, until he'd overheard CC Tamblyn's aide de camp challenge the "whiz kids" to crash Meadows' big soirée. He'd scribbled the coordinates onto a brochure almost as fast as the short one had tapped them into his gizmo, and now he was ready to execute his plan.

Hallett drew a portal of fire that opened into the coordinates on the brochure, adjusting its position until it landed near a dark corner. He crossed over and waited against the wall for Meadows to present himself. It'd be a fun night. Hallett was sure of it.

CHAPTER 27

Invasion

Maggie and Larry arrived via employee BEAMs some time later, after shutting down the Q-Tech booth for the night. The BEAMs landed near a controller rack in a dark, roped-off, "Employees-Only" area of a large room. "Transport complete," the smooth BEAM voice, so much like Christian's, intoned as their columns collapsed around them. Beyond the rope, the party was in full swing.

Larry headed to the rack as soon as he was freed, activated the diagnostic panel, and casually scrolled through the various system statuses. Maggie staggered out of her BEAM unit absolutely stunned by the brilliant sights in the ballroom. RMOR bands, their mylar strips dangling like reflective ribbons, bounced multi-colored lights across every surface and bestowed a trippy vibe on the festivities.

Strategically placed Q-Pods made the already cavernous room seem even bigger. Techno music pounded from the speakers. Several people danced, drinks in hand, in front of the DJ stand while smaller groups clumped around fun stations in and around the Q-Pods. Exotic locales cycled in the back walls of each Q-Pod as revelers surfed the world like channels on a monitor.

Maggie spotted the mayor and Billy, both encased in Billy's RMOR bubble, merrily chatting away on a bank above the gorge at Niagara Falls. Next to them, a Q-Pod portal had been locked on an actual beach and a full-blown cookout was in progress. Tiki torches lit up the shore, partygoers frolicked in the waves and sand, and the wonderful aroma of smoked meats and corn on the cob wafted into the room mixed with the heady scent of saltwater air.

"Alright, I'm impressed," Maggie said.

Larry grinned. "Not bad for a hotel. Guess you could call it the Dew Drop Inn."

"Hotel? With all the flashing lights, I thought we were in a club at Larimer Square."

"Too expensive to rent. Pollux's stunt cut our revenue, remember?"

"Oh, yeah."

"But we're not far away from Larimer. Take a gander out the window."

Maggie pressed her face against the glass. They were high enough up in the building for her to have a good view of downtown Denver. To the right, she could just make out the lights of Larimer Square five blocks away. Cars whizzed by below them on Fourteenth Street, pausing only for the light rail. And directly opposite the window, taking up most of the view, was the ginormous head of the forty-foot-tall Big Blue Bear, its face and paws pressed against the convention center's glass windows as it peeked into the second floor. "We're in the new hotel across the street? But they're not even done with this building yet."

"Which makes it perfect. The owner gets to give the electrical system and plumbing a workout, and we get an exclusive ballroom at the top of one of the newest buildings downtown for practically nothing."

"All of this... It's amazing. You guys outdid yourselves."

"I mostly just set up the racks and made sure the single-use BEAM units worked. Christian handled everything else. Did you know he used to DJ?"

"Get outta town!"

"Surprised me as well. Said that's how he paid for his undergrad. I'd have never guessed. He was so terse and invisible when he worked for Dr. Wilkins. Apparently, he's quite the music afficionado. Take a look behind you."

She turned around and for the first time noticed Christian on a dais wearing a headset. He was surrounded by portable speakers and sound equipment, clearly in charge of the ambient music. Next to the dais was yet another Q-Pod opened to what looked like a recording studio, its walls lined with oak-like acoustic panels and the band within running through sound checks. A handsome, glammed-out man stepped up to the microphone and Maggie gasped. "Is that Gary Childs and Sound Pirate?"

"Yup," said Larry.

"They're *on fire* right now. Why are they playing an office party?"

Larry chuckled. "Work's work. And somehow Christian knows them."

"You're messing with me."

"I'm totally serious. As soon as the Q-Pod opened onto their studio, Christian and Gary gabbed like it was old home week."

"My goodness, he's gorgeous. I think I'm going to faint."

"Don't, you'll miss out. I heard Sheelah's coming too. Along with Money Murphy, Justin Time, and a few other bands. All dialed up on the Q-Pod."

"Oh, this is too much. My RMOR is a disco ball, the mayor's talking to Billy of all people, there's a luau in the corner, and Christian's DJ'ing a music festival like 20 feet away... craziest party ever!"

"I think you mean *best* party ever."

Gary Childs walked to the edge of the Q-Pod and flashed a high sign at Christian. He dialed the techno music down with an expert fade and approached the microphone on the dais.

"Not your typical corporate party, right?"

"Yeeeeeaaaah!" a guy shouted from somewhere over near the mayor and Billy. For all Maggie knew, it *could* have been the mayor, but she had her doubts. *Oh, Billy.*

"In this room are just a few of the ways Q-Tech's products extend beyond the practical into the realm of entertainment. All of you here are witnesses to the future of fun. But enough marketing..." The crowd laughed along genially.

"It's my pleasure to introduce to you one my old friends, here with his new friends. From the comfort of their recording studio in San Diego, please welcome Colorado's own Gary Childs and Sound Pirate!"

Gary Childs prowled to the microphone stand at the edge of the Q-Pod. "Christian Meadows, everybody. He gave us our first break back in the day." He paused for the smattering of polite applause then, curling his fingers around the mic, said in a sultry voice, "Hit it."

Sound Pirate's drummer slammed into the opening beat of their latest hit "Pie City." The crowd erupted with considerably more enthusiastic applause as the party started up again in earnest.

Near the far edge of the "Employees Only" area, much to Maggie's surprise, a holographic projection of Gorgeous Gary sprang to life in mid-air. The light from the HoloStage revealed Mitch Campbell's face, partially obscured by his mass of brown curls. Dean Chambers bopped out of the shadows and danced beside the avatar. A pretty girl from the fringe of the roped-off area noticed Dean and joined in, and soon others from the fringe clapped and laughed, egging the duo on.

A chat stream floated into view, scrolling up the other side of the HoloStage. Wayne appeared behind Dean and the dancer, triumphantly waving a plate of Hawaiian barbecue. He stepped to the other side of the camera and held a short rib out for Mitch to take a bite.

"What's happening back there?" asked Larry. He glanced over his shoulder and smiled. "Ah. The Three Musketeers. I knew they'd find a way in."

Maggie giggled. "Think we ought to bust them?"

"Not at all. It's good press. They show off our gadgets, make them look fun and entertaining, all the while promoting their HoloNet as the 'Hot New Thang.' Works for everybody. I gotta check the other rack. Maybe you should go say hi?"

He stepped into the roped-off perimeter, away from the increasingly rowdy crowd, and headed toward the second rack. Maggie hung back too enjoying the 3D spectacle as well as the covert antics of Mitch and crew, the three of them as familiar to her as her own brothers. She crept up behind the trio until she was as close as she could get to the back of Mitch's head without him seeing her.

"What's soup, Campbell?"

"Gah!" Mitch nearly dropped the HoloFob, much to the amusement of the fringe crowd. "Maggie! Uh... Wayne won a mystery case. That's how we got in."

"Me?" Wayne raised an eyebrow. "Why not lie about Chambers?"

"You're more believable."

Dean gaped at him, wounded. "Thanks a lot, dude."

Maggie giggled. "You guys are idiots. I worked that station all day. I *know* you didn't win."

"Maybe while you were on break?" suggested Mitch hopefully.

"Don't worry, goofball," said Maggie. "I won't turn you in."

Mitch sighed, relieved. "Smile for the camera, then. We're live-casting to the HoloNet."

She stepped in front of Mitch's camera and a mini-Maggie appeared on the HoloStage. She raised her arms above her head. "Whoo! I'm Maggie! Buy Q-Tech stock!"

Dean jumped beside her. "HoloNet rocks!"

"BEAM units rule!"

"Jump!GO's cool! Number one!"

Dean jumped out of the view. Gary's avatar had aligned itself on the HoloStage close enough to Maggie's to make it seem like they were side by side. She aped his movements, pretending they were dancing together. The fringe group laughed in appreciation. The commenters on the scrolling chat went wild.

"Go, girl!"
"Dance, Pie City!"
"Kiss him! Kiss him!"

Maggie maneuvered until her avatar's face appeared to line up with the singer's. She puckered her lips and—

"What are you doing here?" Paul the Production Cop's big head replaced Gary's.

Maggie jerked back. "Yikes!"

He reached through the HoloStage and poked Mitch in the chest. "Employees *only*. Crashers not allowed."

"Watch it, pal," said Dean, knocking Paul's hand away from Mitch's chest.

"Not now, Paul," hissed Maggie. She mimed a camera and pointed at the chat stream, already filling up with irate comments.

"Take a hike, Paul!"
"Hey, mall cop, quit blocking the stage!"
"More Gary, less Paul!"
"Fight! Fight!"

Two fringe partiers moved into view of the camera, one pretending to be Mitch and the other Paul. The Paul-mimic wagged his finger angrily, then jabbed it into the chest the Mitch-stand-in. The two of them mimed a fist fight. Paul spun around, scowling, and they scrammed, taking the rest of the fringe group with them.

He turned back to the trio. "I know you guys," he said, practically spitting in disgust. "More frickin' Bische kids. You people are a menace. Who told you how to get here? Was it Billy?"

Like a genie, Billy appeared at Paul's side. "Hey, Mags. Guys. Mega party, huh?"

"You're in big trouble, Hoag." Paul shifted his attention to Billy and, true to form, jabbed his finger into Billy's chest.

"Chest poking. That's his power move," Wayne observed.

Billy nodded earnestly at Paul but dropped a hand low and made a waving motion at his friends. Maggie gave Mitch a push and she and the trio skulked away. Mitch restarted the holo feed, but Paul and Billy continued to distract from the fun, arguing loudly behind them.

"Who cares if other people sneak in?" said Billy.

"The boss, for one. They wouldn't be sneaking if you hadn't blabbed the location to the world."

"But it's a *party*, Paul. The more the merrier."

"It's supposed to be *exclusive*. For potential *customers—not* crashers and kids. Geez, look at this guy. Now, vagrants are getting in. Hey, beat it, buddy. Invited guests only."

"Step aside," a new voice said. Its flatness sent a shiver down Maggie's spine.

Who is that? The crasher sounded vaguely familiar and, amusingly, not the least bit intimidated by Paul. Sound Pirate switched to an older hit, "Extreme Entity," a louder, more rambunctious song. Maggie strained to listen to the mounting confrontation behind her. *Where have I heard that voice before?*

Paul persisted. "Back out the door or I call the cops."

"Paul," said Billy with more than a hint of warning, "I think it's that guy who was with the congressman,"

"Garbage. That guy was a soldier. This guy's a mess. Plus, he reeks."

A loud buzz from Mitch's phone drew Maggie's attention back to the party. "Mitch, are you getting a call?"

He waved it off. "Not exactly. It's a... diagnostic. Warns me about energy surges."

"From your HoloFob? Cool. You'd better check it. Looks like the feed's breaking up." The image of Gary and his band mates wavered.

Mitch squirmed. "It's fine. Been buzzing like that all day." He glanced over at Christian. "But false alarms, I guess. I think it's malfunctioning."

Dean and Wayne covered smiles. *Why are they laughing? And why's Mitch so embarrassed?*

Paul continued to harangue the crasher. "...so show me a gold case or hit the road."

"Don't press me, son," the man countered, his tone cold and dripping with disdain.

Mitch's phone buzzed again and again, adding a jerky strobe effect to Gary Child's gyrations.

"You gotta shut off the doom-stalker, dude," said Dean.

Mitch squinted at his phone, perplexed. "Guys... these readings look real."

Wayne stopped smiling. "Are they in the human electromagnetic range?"

"Yes," said Mitch. "But... they aren't Christian's. They're coming from someone else."

"What are you all talking about?" asked Maggie. Mitch didn't answer, just looked over her shoulder, alarmed.

Behind them, Billy had become more insistent. "Paul, seriously, it's the guy from the 'Kill Corner.' Back off."

"Kill Corner?" said Maggie. She turned around. His hair was askew, his uniform was rumpled with the fabric matted down by grease in some places, but his hard, angular face was the same, the ice-blue, slightly crazed eyes burned into her memory. "Oh, no! It's Major Asshole!"

"Hallett," breathed Mitch. "He's that gun-happy psycho."

Maggie did a double take. "How do you know about that?"

"Whoever you are, you aren't supposed to be here," said Paul, and before Billy could stop him, the production manager went to his signature move. He poked Hallett's chest and said, "Walk out, hobo, or crawl out."

That's when Hallett's icy blues began to glow. Maggie squeezed her own eyes shut, not believing what she was seeing, but when she opened them again two white stars glared down at Paul from Hallett's malicious face.

"Boy," he drawled, "I'll go when I please." He wrapped his hand around Paul's wrist, and it too began to glow, the brightness beginning at the cuff of his uniform jacket, then spreading to his fingers as he squeezed Paul's wrist.

Paul winced and tried to pull away, but Hallett wasn't inclined to let go. Through gritted teeth, Paul said, "Billy...run!" Then Hallett's hand burst into flames. Paul threw back his head and let loose an inhuman howl.

"Holy shit!" said Billy, but to his credit, he didn't abandon Paul. Instead, he grabbed the back of Paul's shirt, yanked hard, and ran. A trailing arc of fire from Hallett's fist followed them and Maggie watched in horror as it burned what remained of Paul's hand down to a stump. It would consume them both unless Billy acted fast.

"Billy, your belt!" she yelled. His RMOR was still latched around his waist. He activated it, but as the shield enclosed both him and Paul, it collided with Hallett's fire and exploded. The concussion flung Hallett back into the shadows and sent Billy and Paul flying across the room. They landed in a heap at the base of the DJ dais. The RMOR's dew drop cavity snapped and popped before the shield around them fizzled out.

A few curious heads turned toward the commotion, but most of the revelers didn't seem to notice. The band remained the most oblivious. Gary Childs continued to slink and strut while the Sound Pirates funkily played away. Larry and Christian, closer to the action, ran to Billy and Paul's aid.

Hallett didn't stay down long. Four flickering orbs rose from the floor, the shapes of flaming eyes and hands, and proceeded to float out of the darkness toward the dim, "Employees-Only" area lights. Jagged cracks appeared in the air beside him, and two near-duplicate Hallett's disgorged, paler than the original but no less sinister.

"Now I know what nightmare I'm having tonight," said Wayne.

Dean swallowed hard. "Mitch, please tell me your stalker app has a button to turn this guy off."

"I started one, but never finished. You guys razzed me so hard I ditched it."

"Then we'd better evacuate," said Maggie.

"I think I just did," said Wayne. "In my pants."

"Stop joking! Look, I'll trigger the BEAM rack's recall. That'll send everybody back to the Convention Center. Use your Jump!GOs and leave."

"Not without you," said Mitch.

"Don't worry. I've got this—"

"Mags!" Billy shouted from the base of the DJ dais. "Look out!"

She hadn't seen him appear, but there he was—one of Hallett's creepy clones seethed a few steps to her right, his hands aflame.

"Nobody's going anywhere," he said. He clenched his hands together and squeezed off two shots in rapid succession—one at the guys and the other at the rack.

Kablam! Kablam!

Maggie only had time to intercept one. Flipping on her RMOR, she dove in front of Mitch, Dean, and Wayne. Unlike Billy's, her shield managed to completely encase the trio before the bolt's impact. It shuddered under the blast, but the blueish-white encasement held firm and absorbed most of the energy from the blow.

The same could not be said for the rack. The other bolt hit it dead center and melted large segments of it into slag. "Now what are we going to do?" asked Mitch.

"There's two more racks," Maggie whispered, afraid the clone would overhear. "One near the luau and the other next to the Sound Pirates."

Kablam! Another energy blast, this time on the other side of the room. The music, which inexplicably had continued during the chaos, abruptly stopped.

"There goes the Sound Pirates," said Wayne. The Q-Pod smoldered, and Gary Child's bright recording studio had disappeared, though Maggie thought she could still make out the rack behind the smoke.

"There might still be a chance," she said. "Mitch and I will check it out while you and Dean jump to the luau. The Recall button is on the access panel. You can't miss it."

Dean nodded. "Let's just hope Major Asshole misses *us*."

The Hallett clone, briefly distracted by the Sound Pirates' demise, noticed the quartet still huddled behind Maggie's RMOR shield. "Hallett Prime says everyone stays. And if they won't stay, then everyone dies." He raised his fist again and pointed it their way.

"Go! Go!" yelled Maggie. The guys engaged their plasma grids.

A second later, she and Mitch fanned away smoke, but luckily it wasn't their bodies that had been singed. The Sound Pirates' rack still seemed intact. "Okay, we just need to find the RECALL button, then leap out of here and call the cops," she told Mitch.

"Got it."

Seemingly out of nowhere, Hallett's voice boomed. "Not happening, little lady. Everybody stays put."

She felt the heat of the energy bolt before she saw it and just barely managed to drag Mitch away from the rack before it hit.

Kablam!

"Eek!"

The steel cage melted, the support struts folding in on themselves like hot taffy. Another blast on the other side of the room told her the luau rack had gone too.

"This guy's insane," said Mitch.

Too true. And they were all trapped in this half-finished building with him. If only there was another way to trigger the BEAM units. But for the life of her, she couldn't think of how.

*****

Christian leaned back in his chair and propped his feet up on the sound board. The minute Gary had launched into his sexy-beast shtick, he'd begun to relax. Gary's sound had always had that effect on him. He didn't quite understand why and didn't really care. The music grooved, an old friend was in town, and for the first time in two weeks he could say without a doubt that he actually felt *good*.

Maybe I'll invite Gary and the band out after the party. It had been a while since he'd been out on the town. Bumping into Hirano earlier reminded him of that. He kind of felt like celebrating. It had been a harrowing few weeks, but now Pollux and Hallett were gone and Q-Tech was well on its way to prosperity. Already, he'd had more interest from potential customers and corporate contract offers today than he'd had the whole time he'd relied on Pollux. Tech Convergence was just what the company needed. Things were looking up.

Whomp!

The dais rocked. Something had slammed into it, hard. None of Gary's fans seemed to pay it much mind. Then again, their eyes were firmly fixed on his slick moves and the dynamite band. Christian got up from the chair and looked over the edge. Billy and Paul lay in a tangle at the base with Paul unconscious and Billy clearly dazed.

Wisps of smoke curled up from the sleeve of Paul's shirt. *That's odd*, he thought, but then he caught a whiff of charred meat, and suddenly his heart began to race. He jumped from the dais and landed next to Billy.

Larry slid beside him a second later, the cash bar's ice bucket in tow. He plunged the grisly stump of Paul's hand into the bucket and said, "Hoag, what *happened*?"

Billy sat up painfully and pointed toward the back of the room. "He did. Major Asshole."

"What?!" They all knew Maggie's nickname for Hallett, but Hallett was dead, shattered like glass. *No way he's here,* thought Christian. *He can't be.*

But as he squinted at the back wall, a familiar figure, huge and disheveled, rose from the floor like a grim shadow, eyes burning with the fire of a demon and palms as bright as supernovae.

"Trouble," said Larry.

"That's not possible," breathed Christian.

Hallett trained his demon eyes on Christian, and with an evil grin slowly advanced toward the dais. Sound Pirate's guitarist chose that moment to launch into an intricate, searing solo worthy of Prince Rogers. Just as his riffs hit their blistering peak, Hallett blasted the Q-Pod, plunging it into silence. "That's better," he said. Even the drunkest partiers had begun to take notice. They skittered out of Hallett's path like frightened rats.

"Christian, what's this about?" asked Larry as he wound an ice-packed napkin around Paul's stump.

"Long story."

Gut filled with dread, Christian stood up in front of Larry, hoping to distract Hallett long enough for Larry to tend to Paul. Arm outstretched, palm up, he summoned as much of the Aggressor's aura as he dared and shouted, "Hallett! Stop!"

The man grinned wider. "Surprised to see me, Meadows? I'll admit, your little love tap this morning stung. Cost me a soldier. Luckily, I've got a million more."

He paused and tore open the space on either side of him like it was brown paper. A near-exact duplicate of Hallett popped out of each tear—paler, though no less malevolent than the original—and fell into step beside him without missing a beat.

"Real trouble," said Larry.

Christian gawked at Hallett, horrified. *How is he doing this?*

[**He's lost his controller,**] Time Christian told him. [**He's destroyed his version of Time.**]

"We gotta get out of here," said Billy.

"As quickly as possible," added Larry. "If I can get to a rack, I can recall everyone's BEAMs."

Hallett overheard him. "Nobody's going anywhere. Not until Pollux's lapdog here gives me what I want, what he *promised* but then *denied* me. Secure the doors, boys," he ordered his goons.

The duplicates fanned out and pushed anyone near an exit into the center of the room. Then methodically, they blasted every door until the steel handles melted into useless blobs. Christian felt the fear in the room rise to a dangerous level. If he let it continue, everyone's fear would boil over into panic and more people would get hurt. But what could he do without exposing his abilities?

One goon peeled away and aimed his burning fists at Maggie. "Mags! Look out!" yelled Billy. He jumped up to intercept the duplicate, but Larry dragged him down. "Paul needs you. Take him to the hospital. I've got Maggie." He shoved his BEAM unit into Billy's hand.

"But—"

"No buts. Go!" He activated the unit, "BEAM, Denver Trauma Center," then sprinted across the floor toward Maggie.

The tell-tale blue column enveloped Billy and Paul. "Transport commencing."

The sound drew the second goon's attention . "Hey, no leaving," he said and drilled a stream of electricity at the column, but Billy and Paul winked out of existence before it hit. Larry streaked past him. "No running either!" he commanded, then fireball at Larry's head.

"No!" shouted Christian, and before he could stop himself, before any thoughts about the ramifications of his next action could overtake him, he unleashed a massive surge of power from his palm and intercepted the fireball mid-flight.

The two energy streams collided mere inches away from Larry's face, the concussion knocking him out of the goon's path too far away to save Maggie. Luckily, Billy's warning had been enough to alert her. She engaged her RMOR just in time to cover both herself and Campbell's crew, but not fast enough to include the rack. The blast hit the rack dead-center and within seconds, it listed to its side, then crumpled in half.

No one moved. Every guest stared at Christian and Hallett in fearful silence.

Christian could hear Larry breathing heavily behind him, but Larry wasn't afraid— he was angry. "You lied to me," he said,   his voice thick with betrayal.

"I can explain—"

"You'd better."

"—just not now."

Larry fought down his anger. "Timing's bad. But you owe me—"

"—and *everyone* here an explanation!" Hallett interrupted. The lights in his eyes and the flames in his hands dimmed as he took center stage, pointing an accusatory finger at Christian. "Why hide behind your fake 'technology'? Why not tell these people what your dew drops really do?"

Confused murmurs rose out of the crowd.

"Fake technology?"
"Oh my god, we've been poisoned."
"The BEAMs aren't safe. We'll turn into freaks like them!"

Christian could feel the waves of irrational panic flowing through the people around him. "Please, everyone," he said, patting the air and modulating his tone to convey calm. "This man is lying. He's not well. Q-Tech's products won't harm you."

"Doesn't seem so bad to me." A particularly tipsy guest staggered forward. "If lasers sprout from my fingers, I'm in."

"But look at him, man," countered a bearded, bleary-eyed guest. "He's radioactive and acting crazy. Meadows might be crazy too. Finger lasers are cool, brah, but they'll drive you nuts."

"I'm *not* crazy!" Hallett erupted. He ripped open a hole and dashed through it to the bearded guest's side "I assure you, stoner, I'm perfectly sane." A lick of fire escaped from his mouth and singed the edges of the guest's beard.

"Yah!" the man screeched. "Don't fry me, brah!"

Hallett sneered, then turned back to Christian. "I'm not angry about what happened this morning," he said, "although I have every right to be. I just want what Pollux promised. You *will* give me what I'm owed. Or I will cremate one person in this room every five minutes until you do, starting with Mr. 420 here."

Christian detected a subtle shift in the EM waves on either side of him, one near the luau and the other closer, by the smoldering remains of Sound Pirate's Q-Pod. Soon after, Wayne and Dean skidded to a stop at the luau's controller rack while Maggie and Campbell popped into view next to the music rack.

He could feel Maggie's determination to trigger the recall button like he could feel his own heartbeat, but their sudden appearance had caught Hallett's attention. "Not happening, little lady. Everybody stays put." He pointed his fist at Maggie to shoot.

Got to protect them. Christian projected a bubble toward Maggie, Campbell, and the rack, but Hallett's fireball was quicker. It landed solidly on the rack, melting it into goo. A second later, the luau rack suffered the same fate.

Hallett let loose a ragged laugh. "Whoo! Hit 'em all. And your bubble trick gave me a fine idea."

He gouged open another rift and stepped out of space beside Larry, glowing hand pressed against Larry's head.

"How's *this* for added incentive? Probably better than threatening that complete stranger. Four minutes, Meadows. Then it's bye-bye, Knight."

Christian couldn't believe it. *He can't be serious.* He reached into Hallett's brain waves, hoping for any sign that the man was bluffing. Intense hunger greeted him instead: raw, physical, and deadly. Hallett would do anything to satisfy it. Christian recoiled.

[**He has no version of Time. He's lost control. He'll burn all these people *and* you.**]

The realization shook him. He looked around the room at his frightened guests and all of the damage Hallett had done. The contrast between the fun mood when the party had started and now was stark. How had it come to this?

[*Your fault!*] the Others insisted

Not me. Pollux—

[*—who* you *called!*]

He wanted to deny it, but he knew they were right. He'd known Pollux was a bastard, more so than Hubert, but he'd never imagined the man could trap him. Never thought he'd bring in a psycho who'd completely destroy him.

"One minute, Meadows."

Now Pollux was dead, and Q-Tech was destroyed. Larry, Maggie, and these people might die too.

[*Because of you!*]

Shut up! Shut up!

"Time's up, Meadows," Hallett crowed. "Sorry, Knight, but I'm making an omelet and you just happen to be an egg." Hallett set his hand aflame and moved it toward Larry's head.

Christian felt something inside him break. The wall he'd built around his other selves fractured, and the carefully cultivated lock around his control snapped in two. He whipped out a tendril, wrapped it around Hallett's wrist, and stopped it in mid-air. "No, Hallett," he spoke in a fugue, his voice multiplied into a chorus of Christians. "No... you... won't."

His whole body ignited. Dozens of tendrils sprouted out of his torso, and he latched on to Hallett's goons and shorted them out of existence. "Aaaaargh!" Hallett doubled over in pain as each of his duplicates disappeared. Then, when only Hallett remained, Christian lifted him off the floor and flung him across the room, slamming him into the pod for Niagara Falls. The dew drop in the pod's control panel burst. Energy arced into Hallett and glued him to the pod's frame. "Gah! Gaaaaaaah!" he screamed over and over, until he crumpled to the ground. Wisps of smoke rose from his still form.

Christian wrapped his other tendrils around each of his guests. "BEAM, Recall," the chorus of Christians intoned and simultaneously, every BEAM unit sprang to life, including Maggie's. Blue columns enveloped the guests. Maggie shouted, "Wait, don't!" and banged on her column. She typed frantically on the heads-up display, but the unit would not open.

"Transport commencing," BEAM Christian said, and soon all around the room a cascade of diamond-blue columns collapsed in on themselves and winked out.

Only Campbell's crew and Larry remained, still tethered to Christian's tendrils. With a thought, Christian opened portals beside them. The Convention Center lobby popped into view.

"Christian, look!" called Larry. "You still need to—"

"Goodbye," said the chorus sadly.

The tendrils pushed Larry, Mitch, Dean, and Wayne through the portals, and the ballroom fell into silence. Christian wondered if he'd ever see Maggie or Larry again.

"Whew, that was some kick."

Startled, Christian swung around toward the Niagara pod. Hallett had pushed himself onto his knees. *He's alive!*

The major coughed and swayed as he sat back on his haunches, but a strong aura of energy emanated from the man, and Christian realized with increasing alarm what had happened. The arc from the dew drop hadn't fried Hallett. Somehow, he'd managed to absorb it.

"I must admit," he said, "I am impressed. Didn't think you had so much fight in you. You *could* use it to your advantage. Change the balance of power, rule the world." He straightened, growing stronger as he spoke. "But you waste it on high-priced toys and civil engineering. Boy, you've got no vision." His eyes blazed.

Christian understood Larry's warning now; he must have seen Hallett moving. The major was still very much a threat, but Christian didn't know what to do about it. *I just threw everything I had at this maniac. I've got nothing left.*

[**The dew drop drainer,**] said Time. [**Use it.**]

That's it! Christian had been so busy all day he'd forgotten about it, but there it was, still in his pocket. If he activated the device close enough to Hallett, it should stick to the bastard like a magnet and drain all his energy. He just needed to keep Hallett off balance, then maneuver him into position.

"I've got enough vision to know you're no better than *Bertrand*," he said. Christian sensed that Hallett's hatred of the congressman hadn't dissipated and that any mention of the man would unhinge him.

"Pollux was a self-important fool!" Hallett bellowed. He launched a stream of fireballs at Christian. The ploy had worked.

Christian raised his bubble, then snaked the device toward Hallett, wrapped in a tendril.

Hallett sagged when the device reached him, but before it could latch on, his eyes landed on the luau pod. Clumsily, he ripped open a portal and leapt through it to the pod. He smacked his hand against the dew drop cavity in the pod's control panel. Again, energy arced out of the cavity and Hallett sucked it in like a cool drink. The pod went dark, Hawaii disappeared, but Hallett's skin vibrated and glowed.

Christian lashed out at him over and over again, but the luau dew drop had completely renewed him. When a tendril got close, Hallett portaled to a different part of the room. Christian couldn't nail him down and soon Hallett began treating the attacks like a game.

"I feel fantastic, Meadows. I can run portals around you all night. But I gotta tell you, these dew drops are just snacks. What I want is a full meal."

"The store's closed, Hallett. I'm not selling you anything. With my friends gone, you've got nothing to bargain with."

"Maybe I've got one more card up my sleeve." He portaled to the bay window and opened a rift. Just inside of it was the head of the Big Blue Bear, its face still pressed against the Convention Center window. Hallett produced another pale copy of himself and told it, "Go raise hell, soldier."

The copy saluted and jumped through the rift onto the sculpture's head. The rift closed, but through the bay window, Christian saw the duplicate appear in the bear's eye socket.

Kablam! Kablam!

The sculpture rocked. Its ceramic paws pulled away from the second-floor window of the Convention Center and rained glass down onto the sidewalk below. Two more blasts freed the ceramic beast's feet, and soon the Big Blue Bear teetered into the middle of Fourteenth Street. It kicked cars, tore down a stop light, and crushed a falafel stand. It shuffled into the path of a light-rail train and casually knocked it off its tracks. Pedestrians scrambled out of its way only to find themselves in the path of hellfire shooting out the sculpture's eyes. Sirens blared in the distance. In less than five minutes, Hallett's duplicate had plunged Downtown Denver into chaos.

"Heh-heh. Hear that? My soldier's making a mess. Probably hurting lots of people. He can make that bear start tear down buildings, too, and it's all on you. You sent your party guests to 'safety'."

Hallett opened a portal to the Q-Tech warehouse. "How about you disarm the dew drop stash and let me take them all? As soon as you do, my soldier will come in to play."

Christian stared at the Big Blue Bear's slow parade of destruction. *I could short out the duplicate, but Hallett can make another one and who knows what kind of damage the new one will do?*

[Use the drainer. Portal it to him.]

"Come on, Meadows," Hallett drawled, "I've got the upper hand. Take the booby trap off the hopper, and I'll pick up my dinner and be on my merry way."

"Or maybe you can go straight to hell." Christian portaled to Hallett's side and smashed the drainer at the man's chest, but his aim wasn't perfect. Alerted to the attack, Hallett twisted away, and the device bounced to the floor.

"What's that?" he asked "Is that the shattering doodad? You're trying to kill me!" He jumped away from the device and lobbed a string of fireballs at it until it resembled a charcoal briquette.

"Take that, loser! *You* go to hell!" he yelled. Hallett's thoughts, already manic, edged out of the realm of anger into murderous rage. Christian knew without a doubt that he was out of time. The drainer had been his last hope. A fight with a deranged Hallett was a battle he couldn't win.

[Leave! Disappear! Before he kills us all!] begged the Others.

[Hold strong. He'll weaken, then you can negotiate,] reasoned Time.

But Christian was sick of it. Sick of not commanding his own destiny. Hubert had bullied him; Pollux had blackmailed him; even the dimensional versions of himself continually badgered him. Now, this insane asshole had threatened his friends, his livelihood, and was on the verge of killing him. "Enough!"

He wrapped his bubble around Hallett and propelled it so fast it broke through the bay window. They flew out over Fourteenth Street, and with a speed and fury he hadn't known he possessed, Christian pummeled Hallett's stupid, arrogant face until the major's head lolled to the side, senseless.

I can drop him now. Just let him plummet to the ground. It'd be no loss.

Just as he had the thought, a portal opened. Larry poked his head through the portal, but when he saw Christian's face, he recoiled. He'd seen the blood in Christian's eyes, and Christian didn't have to read his thoughts to know that Larry knew what he had been about to do. Larry's expression turned hard. Only then did Christian see the mishmash of parts tied to an RMOR belt in Larry's hand.

"No! Wait—" he began, but it was too late. Larry smacked the device onto Christian's bubble.

Hundreds—maybe thousands—of volts of electricity cascaded through his body. The last thing he saw before he blacked out was Hallett's eyes reopen and begin to glow.

CHAPTER 28

Shocked

Blue columns expanded on the floor of the main exhibit hall at the Convention Center. The Tech Convergence patrons still clustered around Tamblyn Tech's open bar and big screen cheered—until the BEAMs opened. The units' occupants ran out in terror. Some collapsed while others stumbled out, their cheeks wet with tears.

Maggie, who had been banging her fists on the front of her column, fell to the floor when it finally opened and landed at the feet of the mayor, who was newly discharged from his BEAM unit. "Larry! The guys!" she said as he leaned down to help her up. "They're still over there!"

Chithra Muraleekrishnan trotted to the mayor's side with her camera crew. "We're here with the mayor, back from the dazzling Quantum Technologies after-party. Mayor, the party looked fabulous on the Tamblyn Tech HoloNet. Tell us how you liked Niagara Falls?"

He looked at her like she was insane. "Didn't you see? There's a madman loose over there shooting lasers from his hands. I've got to call the police!" He rushed off.

Chithra watched him go, her eyebrows knitted together in confusion. "Sounds like the mayor had one too many cocktails. Let's find someone else. You, young lady." She motioned the cameraman to focus the shot on Maggie. "What did you think of the party?"

"Are you deaf? Didn't you hear the mayor? Go away!" Maggie turned her back on the increasingly puzzled Chithra and ran out to the lobby. She shook her BEAM. "Turn on, damn you. Why won't you activate?"

But shaking the unit didn't help and one look at the dew drop cavity told her why. The plasma shell had imploded, robbing the unit of its power source. "Christian, you bastard!" she yelled at the device. He must have shorted it out to keep her from coming back. "You need me!"

She closed her eyes and took a deep breath. "Calm down, Maggie. Just swap in the one from your RMOR," She checked the belt's dew drop cavity. "Grrr!" Its shell was inert and shriveled too. "No, no, no. The guys..."

"What about them?" Maggie whirled around. CC Tamblyn and Dean's sister Samantha had walked over from the Tamblyn booth. "You're Dean's classmate, right?" Sam continued. "You also work at Q-Tech." Maggie nodded curtly.

"Where are my interns?" CC demanded.

"They're trapped!" Maggie said. "Christian sent back the BEAMs, but they didn't have BEAMs and now Major Asshole's gonna kill Larry and burn the guys alive, and I can't stop it!"

"Whoa, whoa," said Sam. "Who's Major Asshole? You're not making sense."

"Actually, I think I—" CC began, but she stopped at the sight of four bright portals appearing on the opposite side of the Convention Center's glass doors. Mitch, Dean, Wayne, and Larry stumbled out of the lights into the middle of Fourteenth Street and late-evening traffic. Tires screeched against the pavement as drivers veered to avoid them.

"Thank god," breathed Maggie. She raced out of the lobby, Sam and CC fast on her heels. "Guys! I thought you all were dead!"

"So did we," said Mitch, breathless from dodging cars.

"Damn it, Christian!" Larry shook his fists as he looked at the top floor of the unfinished hotel across the street. Jagged, bright lights flashed inside the long bay window of the ballroom they'd just been ejected from. "He should have leveled with me weeks ago. We could have avoided all of this. Paul would still have a hand."

"Don't blame yourself," Maggie said. "He lied to us."

"That lie's about to get him killed."

"Let me guess," said CC. "Major Hallett crashed the party, provoked Meadows, and Meadows blew a gasket."

"Close," said Wayne. "But it's Hallett who blew a screw."

"What? Don't tell me Hallett's full of bees too?"

"Both fools ate dew drops," spat Larry, "and clearly, doing so drove Hallett insane. Christian saved us, but Hallett wants something that Christian won't give and now it's a fight to the death. Idiots!"

Screech!

The grind of metal upon metal interrupted Larry's diatribe. "What the—" Maggie began, but then the ground shifted under her feet and the sidewalk in front of the Convention Center buckled.

Beside them, the Big Blue Bear snapped out of its moorings and tottered away from the Convention Center. Its huge paws smashed windows and tore down electric lines as fireballs shot out of its eyes. Every step it took ripped huge chunks of concrete out of the street. A light-rail car picked a fight with it and lost. The crowd who'd gathered at the miraculous sight of portals appearing out of thin air ran for their lives.

"Scratch the old nightmare. This one's way worse," said Wayne.

"How is this happening?" said Maggie.

Kablam! "Heh-heh!"

"Did you hear that?" said Dean. "I think Major Hallett's in the bear!"

"He can't be," said Mitch. "I still see flashes in the ballroom. One of Hallett's duplicates must be inside the bear."

The sculpture continued to lurch forward, swatting cars, crushing food stands, and leaving a trail of destruction in its wake. The area quickly filled up with casualties.

"We've got to help get these people to shelter!" shouted CC.

Mitch, Wayne, and Dean fired up their Jump!GOs, targeting the Convention Center. Larry ran to the venue Q-Pod and did the same. Eventually everyone who'd been on the street had successfully been moved into the lobby. But the carnage to property and buildings outside of the Convention Center raged on.

Kablam! Kablam!

"This can't continue," said CC. "We need reinforcements." She took out her phone.

"The mayor already called the police," said Maggie.

"I know someone else with more firepower." She plugged her free ear and huddled close to the wall before making the phone call.

Kablam! Kablam!

"Reinforcements will take too long," Maggie said to Mitch.

"What's *your* plan, then?" asked Mitch.

"We use your Jump!GO to jump inside the bear."

"And do what when we get there?" Dean protested.

"Stop the duplicate, of course!" said Maggie.

"How?" asked Mitch. "He's lobbing fireballs. How do we beat that?"

"Throw water?" Wayne deadpanned.

"Or swing a crowbar," said Dean. "We grab one from the lab, jump into the bear behind him, and whack the duplicate upside the head."

"People!" Larry boomed in his classroom voice. Maggie and the guys clammed up. A commanding Larry was a force to be reckoned with.

He took a deep breath, then said, "Just... *think* for a change. Christian showed us what to do right before he activated the BEAMs. We need to short the bastard out. Not the duplicate, but Hallett himself. Do any of you understand why?"

Mitch answered first. "Because Hallett's the real problem, not the duplicate. If we short out the duplicate, Hallett will just make another one."

"Exactly, Campbell. We have to hit the source. And I think I know how. Maggie, give me your RMOR."

Maggie looked at her hand, startled to see that she was still gripping the belt. She handed it over. "It's useless. The dew drop's burned out."

"We've got another in the venue Q-Pod." Mitch opened a portal to the pod. Larry jumped in, removed the dew drop from the control panel, dodged a fire blast, and dove back through. Using his multi-tool, he pried the RMOR's circuit board from its casing and said to Mitch, "I'm gonna need your HoloFob too."

"Sure," said Mitch, handing it over.

They gathered around Larry as best they could in the tight space between the lobby and the building's outer alcove and watched with growing fascination as he re-configured the two gadgets. First, he connected them with one end of the RMOR's mylar strip, then fashioned a quick-release mechanism at the other end. He moved with a swiftness and surety that Maggie had grown accustomed to while working with him every day the past few months, but the experience of watching him work was new to everyone else. Tamblyn and the guys seemed suitably awed.

Even as Larry concentrated on the task, Maggie marveled that he still found a way to teach. "The mylar strip will be our trigger," he explained as he slipped it between the two halves of the jury-rigged device. "Right now, it's effectively separating the two energy sources. When I turn them on," he flipped both switches, "nothing happens. But when we get into crowbar-whacking range of Hallett, the plasma properties of each will be drawn to him and stick to him like a magnet."

"Oh, I get it!" said Maggie. "When you pull the quick-release, the power sources will clash and cause an overload."

"Exactly. But only in the contacting system. Hallett will get a jolt large enough to knock him out. We drag him back, tie him up, and wait for the cops or whoever Ms. Tamblyn's calling to show up."

"That's amazing, Larry," said Mitch. He stared at him as if he were truly seeing the man for the first time.

"And it took you all of five minutes to do it," said Wayne. "Impressive."

Larry tapped his head. "Thinking. It works."

Kablam! Bam! Boom!

The frequency of flashes had multiplied. A spectator near a window pointed at the sky. "Look! There's two more and they're floating!"

All eyes turned to the sky. A bluish-white bubble bobbed erratically above Fourteenth Street just outside the ballroom's bay window. Maggie spied Christian and Hallett in the bubble fighting. Christian seemed to have the upper hand.

"RMORs hover?" asked Mitch.

"That's not an RMOR," said Larry. "That's Christian's protective shield. Crap!"

"Welp, that throws a monkey wrench in our plan," said Dean. "We can't fly."

"We don't need to," said Mitch. "We can use Jump!GO's Short Range mode to open a light hole near them from here. Then all Larry has to do is lean into the hole, slap the short-circuiter on Hallett and drag him back.

"But we didn't count on them tussling inside of Christian's body shield,' said Maggie. "We'll wind up shorting out Christian too and they'll both fall."

"Serves him right," said Larry bitterly. Maggie looked at him appalled and he softened. "Don't worry. We'll catch them both. Christian's got to answer some questions and he can't do that if he's squashed."

Mitch and Wayne invoked their plasma grids, and within seconds, the group had front-row seats to Christian and Hallett's confrontation. Hallett's head lolled to the side as Christian landed blow after blow on it in rapid succession. Larry didn't like the crazed look in Christian's eyes. *He's going to beat him senseless then drop him. Time to end this.*

He leaned into the light hole. Christian turned his wild eyes toward him and shouted, "Wait!" but Larry ignored him. He slapped the device on the bubble and yanked the quick-release. Twin energy arcs encased the bubble then invaded it, zapping Christian and Hallett simultaneously. They writhed under the onslaught. The duplicate vanished from inside the bear. Without a puppet master, the sculpture toppled and landed hard on the light-rail tracks.

But then Hallett, who moments before had seemed on the verge of unconsciousness, raised his head and opened his eyes. The glow returned to them, and he smiled. The arc of energy that had incapacitated Christian switched direction and flowed into Hallett. Where Christian buckled under the assault, Hallett gloried in it. Soon the bubble shrank around them until it dissipated, and all that remained was the modified RMOR. Hallett clutched it to his palm and drained every last bit of energy from it.

As predicted, once Christian's bubble was gone, they fell. Wayne adjusted his light hole beneath Christian and dragged his limp body into the lobby. But Hallett, unperturbed by his descent, grinned at Larry and said, "Thanks for the charge," before opening a ragged hole in space and disappearing through it.

Christian woke up and pushed himself painfully into a sitting position. "I suppose this is a bad time to ask about my jacket," said Wayne.

Maggie ran over. "Christian! Are you okay?" He nodded groggily. "I'm glad," she continued. "I'm also pissed and so is Larry."

On cue Larry loped over and grabbed Christian by the lapels. "You were going to drop him!"

"Damn right. Why'd you stop me? I could have ended him and solved it all."

"Not like that! If you hadn't lied to us, Hallett would have never happened at all!"

A black SUV with tinted windows barreled through the intersection and came to a screeching halt at the lobby door. A woman and two men jumped out, guns drawn but pointed down. Tamblyn directed them toward the sculpture and the small crowd forming around Maggie, Christian, and Larry.

Maggie heard the woman say, "Disperse these people quietly." The two men with her worked the crowd while she and Tamblyn walked over to their little group.

"You're too late, Giganta. Bad guy's gone," said Dean.

"Always the bearer of good news, Lothar." To Christian, she said "Thoughts on where he went, Meadows?"

"He's hungry. And he doesn't understand about the dew drops. He thinks he needs more, so there's only one place he can go."

"He's outside of Q-Tech," said Mitch. He held up his phone to the woman, his tracking app on full display. "And from these readings on the doom-tracker, I... think he's about to blow."

CHAPTER 29

Release

Christian stood up and immediately felt light-headed. He leaned heavily against the Big Blue Bear's backside, fighting the urge to vomit.

CC Tamblyn looked over Campbell's shoulder at whatever app he had open on his phone. Apparently, it was an app that could track Hallett. He wondered how Campbell had gotten a hold of such a thing. *Was he working with the Agency? Could the app track me?*

"Campbell's not wrong," said Tamblyn. "It's not quite as bad as—" She paused and glanced in his direction, then back at Campbell's phone. *Guess that answered that question.* "But if Hallett slipped into a quantum overlap, it would do significant damage to Golden's warehouse sector."

"Perfect," said Agent Travers, sounding tired. "On the bright side, that means he'll go after the contents of the hopper and get zapped by your gizmo, right?" she said to Christian.

"Not exactly," Christian mumbled, blinking back a wave of vertigo. "Hallett fried it."

"What?! How'd you let that happen?"

Before he could answer, the mayor pushed past Marion and got in his face. "Meadows, you're fired! The contract between the city and Q-Tech is null and void as of right now. Whatever you did to that man to turn him into a lunatic, you're going to pay for it. That and all this damage." He spread his arms across the carnage left over from his and Hallett's battle.

Christian looked around for the first time since Wayne had brought him to the shelter of the bear. Fourteenth Street was littered with craters, crashed cars, and broken glass, and a few more feet away, a light-rail train lay overturned on the tracks. He breathed a sigh of relief at the lack of bodies. However, the large number of emergency vehicles parked next to the Convention Center gave him pause and more sirens blared in the distance. Were police cars headed their or ambulances? He couldn't tell. The desire to vomit intensified.

The mayor's loud tirade galvanized the sentiments of the crowd that had gathered in front of the lobby doors. Many of them had been guests at the disastrous after-party.

"The mayor's right!"
"That laser guy nearly killed me!"
"I'm completely traumatized!"
"You suck!"

"Get ready for court, Meadows!" yelled the mayor.

Travers stepped between him and Christian, badge in hand. "Agency, Mr. Reyna. I need you to move back. Now." She signaled to her closest co-worker, who was deep in conversation with a woman angrily gesturing at the remains of what must have been her car. The man excused himself and ran over. "Chuck, I told you to disperse these people," she said.

"Trying to, ma'am. The clean-up team will be here in five minutes."

Tamblyn touched Travers arm. "I don't think Meadows will last that long. These people are angry—we might be on the verge of a riot."

"On top of that, here comes the media," said Tamblyn's assistant. Chithra Muraleekrishnan and her cameraman were headed straight for them. "Now might be a good time to leave."

"Right. We need to regroup. Campbell, open a light hole to the machlab. Samantha, can you deal with Ms. Techline News?"

She nodded quickly, threw on a smile, and made a beeline toward the reporter. "Chithra, so glad I caught you. You've *got* to see our HoloFob footage from the Q-Tech party. It's amazing." She held up a HoloFob and steered Chithra back toward the Convention Center lobby.

"What's the machlab?" asked Maggie.

"It's our lab at Tamblyn Tech," Mitch answered.

Several grey and black SUVs bearing Agency decals arrived at the same time, parking so as to block off the intersection. "There's our cue," said Travers. Her fellow agent trotted off to greet the newcomers. "Time to go."

Campbell waved his Jump!GO. An azure grid appear with a light hole in the middle. Campbell expanded the hole and directed everyone into it.

Travers took Christian roughly by the elbow and pulled him through into a brand-spanking-new, state-of-the-art lab. She and Campbell's crew dispersed to workstations with a familiarity Christian found disturbing, while Maggie and Larry stood awkwardly in a corner, exchanging dubious glances. Their brain waves radiated confusion and frustration, but also anger. They avoided eye contact with him completely, a fact that made the already uncomfortable situation nearly unbearable. Christian wondered if he would have fared better with the Convention Center mob. Or if he could somehow slip away.

[*Yes! Leave! Let the Agency handle it!*]

The Others' suggestion was tempting. His palm itched to open a portal and disappear. But at that moment, Larry glared in his direction as if reading his mind, daring him to leave.

[*You don't owe him anything!*] the Others thundered.

[**They're wrong,**] countered Time.

Christian returned Larry's glare, but the itch left his palm. Rooted in shame, he stayed.

Tamblyn, arms crossed, stood behind Campbell as he opened what Christian assumed was the tracking app on his workstation monitor. "Where's Hallett now?" she asked.

"Somewhere inside Q-Tech. His energy output's more erratic."

"Great. Just great," muttered Travers. Like Larry and Maggie, she too, was becoming increasingly angry.

"We need eyes on him right now," said Tamblyn. Turning to Travers, she asked, "How's your clearance?"

"It's back. Hallett's shenanigans last night invalidated the gamma lock." She flicked on the room's central workstation and typed furiously. "Hirano, we're going to need your HoloFob."

"Sure. Let me know when you have the video link."

"Here you go." She clicked a button and Wayne's phone chirped.

A couple of seconds later, Wayne projected what looked like a holographic representation of the nearly empty Q-Tech parking lot.

Wayne zeroed in on the front door of the warehouse. The door's handle and lock appeared to have been burned off. "No sign of him near the entrance," he said.

"Keep switching feeds until you find him," Tamblyn demanded.

Just inside the dark alcove, Christian could see flashes reflected off the warehouse floor near the production side of the facility. "Wherever Hallett is, he's busy," said Wayne.

"How are you doing that?" asked Christian. Wayne and Travers ignored him. Campbell and Chambers looked at Tamblyn, but she pursed her lips and didn't reply.

"And why was it so easy?" demanded Larry. "You all act like you've done this before." He eyed them suspiciously.

"And what's with this Hallett tracking app?" asked Maggie. "It's like you guys planned to spy on him."

"Or had *already* been spying on Christian and Q-Tech," said Larry, "and their little app just happened to work for the major as well."

Wayne, focused on scanning the security feeds, remained impassive, but Campbell and Chambers could not hide their discomfort. Their brain patterns gave away their guilt. "That's exactly what you've been doing isn't it." said Christian. "You weren't tracking Hallett. You were spying on me."

"Okay fine. It's my fault," said Campbell.

"Not true, Mitch! Giganta—"

"Watch it, Chambers," said Tamblyn.

Maggie smacked her forehead. "*That's* how you knew about the major shooting at Christian. And why you've been asking me if things are okay at work. You've been spying on us. You knew about Christian all this time. And you said nothing! We're supposed to be friends!" She whacked Mitch's arm.

Larry shook his head. "Wow. That's terrible. Ms. Tamblyn... I'm shocked. You seemed honorable."

Tamblyn reared back, offended. "Now hold on, young man—"

"I would have never thought you'd condone corporate espionage," he said.

"Shut up!" Travers slammed her hand down on the bench top. Everyone, except Wayne who continued searching, froze.

She turned to Maggie and Larry. "Before you two get on your high horses, try to remember that your boss built Q-Tech by pawning off the side effects of an industrial accident as a stroke of genius. And I might add that he experienced that accident after having *stolen* the work Campbell, Chambers, and Hirano did, while in cahoots with his ex-boss, Hubert Wilkins. Wilkins, if you recall, is rotting in Supermax after having committed *treason* against the United States government."

She paused for a response, but Larry and Maggie, embarrassed, offered none. Everything the agent had said was true, and even Christian knew it was a waste of time to try to refute it.

"Keeping tabs on Meadows started way before he'd even had the *idea* to embezzle—yes, embezzle—Hubert Wilkin's money for his own little startup," she continued. "And honestly, neither of you have *any* clue at all about what's happened, what's happening now, and how it goes *way* beyond your butthurt feelings about Campbell keeping secrets or your petty concerns about 'corporate espionage.' We've got a loose cannon, full as a tick on raw plasma energy, and if he eats any more of Meadows' damned dew drops he's likely to take out three or four city blocks. *That's* our focus right now, people. Stay *focused*. Let's put our heads together and come up with a solution."

"Got him," said Wayne.

Everyone shifted their attention—gratefully—to the HoloStage floating above Wayne's phone.

"He's in a storage room, looks like, sucking dew drops out of Q-Pod packages. I'd have gone for the dew drop generator up front myself."

"He must think the hopper's still booby-trapped," said Travers. She turned to Christian. "What in the hell happened to your drainer?"

"You might start with an explanation of what this 'drainer' is," said Tamblyn, "and how Hallett got into his current so that you had to make one."

Christian gathered his thoughts. "Hallett and Congressman Pollux found out about my accident and blackmailed me into helping them steal minerals for Pollux's mining venture. Unbeknownst to the congressman, Hallett got a hold of some dew drops and ate them, hoping to acquire my... abilities to use for his personal gain. But the dew drops don't work for him the same way they work for me. The energy dissipates, and he needs more, which angers him. Last night, after I turned him and the congressman in to the Agency, he lost it and incinerated Pollux."

"What does that mean?" asked Maggie. "The congressman's dead?"

"Yup. Totally cremated," said Travers. "A pile of ashes in a box." Maggie looked appalled.

"Hallett's in the mailroom now, in case anyone cares," said Wayne. "He's started eating drops out of the shipping crates."

Travers nodded. "Wrap it up, Meadows."

"Agent Travers and I knew he'd come to the warehouse to steal all the dew drops, so I built a device to drain them out of his body and attached the device to the hopper. But he sent a clone instead of coming himself. The clone touched the hopper and shorted himself out. We didn't know it was a clone and so thought Hallett was dead. I pocketed the device—"

"Why?" asked Larry, his hostile gaze almost as discomforting as Travers'.

Christian looked away, knowing that once he said it out loud, the implications would be all anyone would think about. But what other choice did he have?

Reluctantly, he said, "I didn't want the Agency to study it or give them ideas about me. I'm different from Hallett, but they could adapt it. I couldn't take the chance. Hallett was dead, I thought, so it didn't matter. I unhooked it, went to Tech Convergence, and expected to smash it to pieces at the end of the day. Then Hallett showed up at the party. Once I pushed you all out, I tried to use it on him, but it fell off before it could do any damage, and he fried it with a fireball. When we fought, he realized he could absorb dew drops instead of eating them. Absorbing them makes him stronger, but like Campbell noticed, he's also more unstable."

"So how do we adjust?" asked Tamblyn.

Christian waited for his brain to chime in with an answer. Or for Time to come up with one. Hell, he was even open to a crazy take from the Others. Nothing came to him. He finally admitted. "I don't know."

Travers grimaced. "Not good enough."

"Geez, Marion, cut the guy a break," said Chambers. "Even Mitch needs a minute or two to flash up an answer."

"And if Christian had an idea, would we even have time to implement it?" wondered Mitch.

"Clock's ticking, folks," Wayne reminded them in his flat deadpan. "He's on the last shelf in the mailroom. And he's glowing so brightly it looks like the lights are on."

"I thought they were," said Maggie, her eyes wide with alarm.

Wayne shook his head slowly. "Nope."

Larry, uncharacteristically quiet, strode out of the corner and peered at Mitch's workstation. He highlighted a section of the tracking graph and clicked into it to drill down to the actual numbers. "Hmmph."

"Larry, what do you see?" Campbell asked.

He looked sideways at Christian and beckoned him over. "This pattern look familiar to you, Chief?"

Tentatively, Christian went to stand by his side. The pattern Larry pinpointed on the screen was indeed familiar. Christian's heart sank. "It's the MHD model for the new generator."

"Minus Maggie's stabilizing stick."

"No way." Maggie trotted to the workstation and skirted in front of Larry. "You're right," she breathed. "We've got what we need, then!"

"Explain," Tamblyn and Travers demanded simultaneously.

Larry turned around and said, "No time for a full explanation, but basically we've seen this happen before in the dew drop generator. Something in Hallett has caused a misalignment of his energetic pathways. Kind of like an electromagnetic stenosis. It's causing a pressure buildup disrupted by infusions from the plasma cells he's absorbing, but only when he actively sucks one in. Once he stops, the flow gets pinched in places, causing a disruption. We need to disrupt the disruption."

"I solved the problem in the generator by adding a magnetic stabilizer that cleared away the pressure buildups and distributed the energy evenly. Once it stabilized, the light packets separated, and the plasma shells coalesced around them. If we reverse the charge on the stabilizer, they'll dissipate. The energy should leak out evenly until he's empty. Problem solved."

Larry nodded. "The best part is we don't have to build anything new. We just need a matrix to drop the stabilizer in that will modify its charge."

"The Jump!Go ought to be able to handle that," said Mitch. "We just swap the jumpers around the mini-magna coils, flip the switch, and we're all set."

"But wouldn't Hallett just absorb the plasma from the unit the same way he absorbed the energy in the short-circuiter Larry made to knock him out?" asked Dean.

"The disruptor field will prevent that from happening," said Larry. "The short-circuiter was meant to overwhelm him, but this will stabilize and separate the light packets. He'll drain like a double-A battery."

"So, all we have to do is distract him long enough for you to take the stabilizer out of the hopper, attach it to a modified Jump!GO, and then someone's got to slap him with the device."

"How hard are the first two steps?" Travers asked.

"Hold on, there's a pre-step," said Maggie. "We need to turn off the generator and remove the dew drops before we start, else it will be just like when we first built it. We'll have our own mini-Hallett to contend with."

"I can reabsorb the excess dew drops in a few seconds," said Christian. "It shouldn't impact Larry's work time significantly. He's pretty fast."

Larry nodded modestly. "If you have an inversely polarized Jump!GO ready, shouldn't take more than five minutes for me to connect it to the stabilizer."

"Here, I did it while you guys were talking," said Mitch.

"Wow. Thanks, Campbell. Good work."

"No problem. Had to see if I could match your time cracking the shorter," he said with half a smile.

CC jumped in with a question. "If Larry's making the device, who's going to apply it?"

"I can," said Dean. "Hallett's about the same size as me and coked up on plasma balls, but I'm younger. I think I can take him."

"Actually, I think that's my job, too," said Larry. "As soon as the anti-stabilizer is ready, I can slam it on him."

"Why not Christian?"

Larry avoided looking at him again. "Too risky. Don't know if we'll need his 'abilities' or not, if this doesn't work. Best to keep our options open. Maggie, do you still have Pollux's box of RMORs at your desk?"

"Ugh, yes. Guess he won't be needing them."

"Right. You and Mitch string a protective perimeter around us with the belts, give us time to work."

"Good idea!"

Marion said, "I'll go too, to protect you all while Maggie and Mitch set up the perimeter. Maybe a couple of slugs from my sidearm will slow him down."

Chambers went to the tool pile and dug out a crowbar.

"What do you expect to do with that?"

"Element of surprise just in case your gun and the RMOR's don't work. Sometimes low tech is the way to go."

Marion cocked her sidearm. "Alright. Ready, people?"

"Ready!" said Larry.

Mitch started to invoke a plasma grid from his Jump!GO, but Christian was faster. He opened a portal that landed them within the shelter of the demo Q-Pod just across from the hopper. Flashes from the production side of the warehouse told them that Hallett was still making his way through the store of devices along the production line. Agent Travers unholstered her sidearm and placed herself between the hopper and the production side of the warehouse, waiting for Hallett's inevitable appearance.

Maggie crouched down, ran to her bench, and fetched the box of RMOR devices set to be shipped to Pollux. She ran back and helped Mitch string the belts together to form a protective ring around the hopper. Soon, Larry and Christian were surrounded by an RMOR shield. Hallett would likely absorb the shield, but it would take him time to do so, giving Larry more than a few seconds to get into position to apply the stabilizer.

Christian thrust his arms into the hopper, and in less than ten seconds, the dew drops were gone. Larry turned off the generator and set to dismantling the floor matrix to get at the stabilizer.

Larry worked as fast as he could to refactor the stabilizer, but he wasn't fast enough. For some reason, Christian thought Hallett would have to walk through the production area to get to them. He hadn't counted on him simply portaling into place.

The major appeared in front of Marion in a split-second. The incandescent glow of his skin made them immediately aware of his presence.

"Well, lookie here. I thought I'd have the dessert to myself, but I guess you all think I need to share."

Travers didn't waste time bantering. She unloaded her clip into him, but Hallett didn't so much as flinch. The bullets vaporized the minute they touched his body. Hallett laughed deep in his throat, then opened his mouth and breathed a stream of fire at Marion.

Mitch had seen it coming. He'd already expanded a light hole next to Travers and dragged her through it into their protective RMOR shield. Then Chambers appeared behind Hallett and, with a mighty swing, smacked the crowbar into his head. The blow caught the major by surprise, just as Chambers had guessed it would. "Ow!" He doubled over and staggered into the RMOR shield, but he recovered quickly. Grinning, he embraced the shield and absorbed its energy into his body. The shield began to shrink.

Chambers whacked him across the back with the crowbar. "Hey, psycho! Fight me! The energy's back here." He hit him again and again. Hallett ignored the younger man for the first couple of strokes, but became annoyed as the attacks continued. He flexed his back and suddenly the crowbar glowed.

"Aargh!" Dean yelped in pain. The crowbar stuck to Hallett's back, turned molten, then sloughed away.

Mitch worked his plasma grid magic again, but instead of dragging Dean into the RMOR, he pulled his friend all the way into the safety of the machlab. He returned for Travers and Maggie, but Maggie protested and fought to stay. "We can't just leave Larry and Christian! Stop!" He took her anyway, for which Christian was thankful. Finally, only he and Larry remained.

"So, not to rush you, Larry, but how's it coming?"

"Done. Feel free to portal out of here. I've got this."

"I'll open a portal, but only for you. Give me the device."

"Why? I know you won't use it. You were gonna *drop* him back at the Convention Center. Just cold-blooded kill him. I saw it in your eyes. You gonna try that now too?"

The shield around them decreased further. "Peekaboo! I'm coming to get you!" Hallett said, his face practically burning through what remained of the shield. He'd be in before they knew it.

"You're right. I lost it. But I'm better now."

"You lied. I can't trust you anymore. I've got no beef with this guy. For all I know, he's insane because of you. Just go. I'm on it. I'm stronger than Chambers. It'll be fine."

Christian didn't want to do it, but Larry had left him no choice. He mapped his brain waves into Larry's and aligned the TA's thoughts to his own. Christian held out his hand and said to him gently, "Thanks for giving me the device."

Larry smiled back, completely cooperative. "Sure thing, Chief," and handed him the stabilizer.

"I'm sorry, Larry. You were a good friend." Then Christian opened a portal and pushed him into the machlab just as the last of the RMOR shield evaporated away.

Hallett looked down on Christian, licking his lips. "Maybe I should start my dessert with you. I bet your dew drops taste the best of all."

"Guess you'll never find out." Before Hallett could see it, Christian latched on with a tendril and flipped the switch on Larry's device.

The effect spread through the tendril. Hallett's head snapped back and all the light and fire in his eyes, mouth, and hands, bulged near the edges. He opened his mouth wide and screamed—a terrible, pained, wrenching sound. Every orifice and pore expanded, releasing sharp streams of blazing-white light.

Christian withstood it as long as he could, holding onto Hallett with his tendril to ensure he was well and truly in the grip of the stabilizer. But soon, the disjointedness was overwhelming. He felt as he had the first day he'd met Hallett—fractured, splintering. The pressure in his gut built into nausea and the Others murmured non-stop. Finally, he couldn't take it anymore. His head went back, just as Hallett's had and the chorus of Christians cried out...

He was on his knees with his arms gripped around his stomach. The warehouse had disappeared, replaced by that same fuzzy-white room. Hallett stood across from him flailing.

"Aargh! Aargh! What happened?! What did you do?!"

Behind Hallett, his army of pale, fragile soldiers writhed in agony until one by one, they buckled and popped out like balloons. There were no shells to protect them. No Time version of Hallett to counsel them. He stood alone with his dimensionless brood. And as the inverse-stabilizer did its work, they faded and crinkled and burst into pieces. Amid the white fuzz, the pieces fluttered away, Hallett squirming in agony with each one.

Christian's side of the room was populated with the Others, and though their shells protected them, the carnage was no less. Some shells faded while others darkened. The dark shells, he reasoned, belonged to those versions of him whose existence had held the least probability. Still others, resigned to their fate, waved a final salute. "You are Prime," they said before fading away.

He felt the passing of each one, like a hot coal being pulled from his body. It wasn't pleasant, but his distress existed on a different plane from Hallett's. Whereas the major's duplicates were completely rent from existence, Christian sensed that his were merely being released. They and he registered a kind of relief, but sadness overwhelmed him too. Though he and they had been trapped in a kind of ultra-dimensional stasis, he'd grown accustomed to the company. Once the stabilizer pulled out the last ember, he'd be back to his original self—powerless, ordinary, and utterly alone.

"I'll go back to nothing," he said into the white void.

Young Time appeared before him. [**You were never nothing. Remember that when we are gone. You are most probable.**]

Hallett screamed again from across the room. "Stop! My soldiers! Make it stop!"

The departure of his duplicates and Christian's reflections accelerated. Fewer than twenty of Christian's shells remained. One shell in particular rocked to and fro. It was the Aggressor. He beat his fists against his shell, fighting the transition.

["*No! Release me! I can be Prime!*"] He pounded furiously against his shell, trying to breach it and take Christian's place. But the pull of his dimension was too strong. ["*Save me!*"] he pleaded with Christian, weeping. He spun down into a vortex and winked out.

Time morphed into his current self. [**"I will be with you until the end."**]

And as the last of the Others faded, Time turned to him in his shell and said, [**"I am you. You are Prime. You have friends and you are not alone."**]

He morphed into the old man, and then he was gone.

The jump space dissolved around Christian and he was back in the warehouse. Hallett, slack jawed and drooling, lay moaning on the floor. His eyes were vacant and his knees were drawn to his chest.

Christian had no strength to pity him. He looked up painfully from his own position on the floor. The door to the employee restroom was open, the mirror he had avoided these many months clearly visible. His reflection stared back at him, pale, shivering, and diminished. He did not see his perfect self nor any others staring back at him from out of his pores. Nevertheless, he could still hear the echo of Time in his head.

"I am Prime. I am not alone."

The whine of a Jump!GO cut through Hallett's moans.

CHAPTER 30

Aftermath

"What the—?" Larry whirled around. He was back at Tamblyn Tech in the place they called the machlab. The stabilizer was gone, and Christian was nowhere in sight. *Bastard! Damn him and his portals.*

Everyone but Mitch and Wayne had gathered around the HoloStage that floated above Wayne's phone. Larry rushed over. "Is Hallett still alive?"

"No idea," said the Agency woman, Travers. "They both just disappeared."

On the stage, the projected warehouse had been replaced by a cloud of static.

Larry cursed under his breath. "That's Christian's doing. He has no intention of using the stabilizer." He didn't want to say it aloud, but Christian had proved tonight that he was no paragon of virtue. "I think he's planning on killing Hallett instead."

"Not true!" said Maggie. "He activated it right after he portaled you away."

Mitch, at his workstation, said, "And from the doom-tracker's readings, they both seem to be alive."

Larry frowned, confused. "Then what's going on?"

"They're in jump space," said Wayne, gesturing toward his workstation.

Larry pinched his nose. "I can't keep up. Is jump space a thing I'm supposed to know?"

"It's what we call the pockets between the start of a light hole and its ending," explained Wayne. "Photon corridors, basically. We've only ever seen them when the trapping medium is refracted, but somehow Christian and Hallett fell into one as soon as he activated the stabilizer."

"The good news is the stabilizer's working," Mitch added. "The energy anomaly is steadily declining. Once it hits zero, they should both pop out."

"I want to be there when they do," said the agent. "Hallett's liable to scoot the moment his batteries run out." She loaded a new magazine into her gun. "I don't intend to let him."

"They've bottomed out," said Mitch. The static cloud cleared on the HoloStage. Christian, pale and shivering, had fallen to his knees while Hallett lay on his side, glassy-eyed and moaning.

"I don't think either of them are running anywhere," said Tamblyn.

"Open a portal!" urged Maggie. "They need help!"

Dean invoked a grid and expanded a light hole into the warehouse. Travers entered first, in a defensive position, gun at the ready. Christian lifted his head wearily as she approached. Hallett remained motionless on the floor.

Larry squeezed by her, ran to his bench, and retrieved his EMT bag and the first aid kit. When he dashed back, Maggie was sitting next to Christian, speaking to him quietly, her eyes concerned. Larry bypassed them and knelt beside the prostrate Hallett, hoping he'd find a pulse. After all of the awful things he'd just found out about Christian, he didn't want to add 'murderer' to the list.

Now that he was closer, Larry could see Hallett breathing and hear him mumbling incoherently in between ragged gasps. Relieved, he set up his portable monitor and attached leads to Hallett's chest and head. The major's vital signs seemed normal despite the heavy breathing, but the EEG waveforms that played across the monitor indicated his brain was a mess. *Man.* Larry hadn't enjoyed being a pawn in Hallett's game of cat and mouse, but whatever the major had done, he certainly didn't deserve to end up like this.

"Mission accomplished I take it," said Travers, looming over Christian.

"Yeah," he confirmed with a weak nod. "The stabilizer defused him... and me. That's what you wanted, I suppose."

"Perhaps. Looks like he suffered the worst of it," she said gesturing toward the major.

Larry unhooked the portable monitor. "His body's back to normal, but his brain is fried."

"Serves him right after all of the trouble he caused," said Maggie.

Larry shrugged. "Kind of feel sorry for the guy."

"He threatened to burn your head off!"

"I'm not saying he's a saint, but I can't believe he'd act that evil on his own. The dew drops must have driven him crazy."

Agent Travers shook her head. "He was more than halfway there before the dew drops, believe me. We've got evidence of war crimes, extortion, fraud. Seriously, he was never a good dude."

Hallett whimpered, then returned to mumbling. "Gone. Every... all... gone."

"That could have been you, Meadows," said Marion. And, then more quietly, "or me."

Now what did that mean? thought Larry.

"No," Christian answered. "We're not fortunate. He's just dumb. He destroyed his anchor. Killed his Time."

Travers turned to Christian, shocked. "Do you mean the controlling voice inside of us? The version of us that cycled through ages?"

"Yes," said Christian.

"But... that's insane."

Christian raised a tired eyebrow. "You said it yourself. He was halfway there."

Car doors slammed near the warehouse's front door and in walked Travers' co-worker, the guy who had shooed away the Convention Center crowd.

"Your ride's here," she said to Christian.

The agent made a beeline for Travers. "I brought a wagon and an ambulance just like you asked. Hoo, looks like the major took a beating."

"Something like that."

"He'll need medical attention," said Larry. "More psychological than physical, I'd bet."

Marion nodded. "The medical facilities at Supermax can handle it." Another agent propped open the door and let in two guys with a stretcher. They lifted Hallett onto it. His lips moved, but he made no sounds.

"What about him?" her buddy asked, pointing at Christian.

Travers locked eyes with Christian. "Ralph was pretty clear, Chuck."

Up until that moment, though tired from his ordeal, Christian had maintained a semblance of his standard, flat indifference. Now, however, to Larry's surprise, he dropped all pretense and said, "Please, Marion," with real distress. "Don't put me in the same cell as Hubert."

Travers threw back her head and laughed. "That *would* be a fate worse than death."

"Wait a minute," said Maggie. She stood up and confronted Travers. "You're taking him in jail?"

'It's okay, Maggie," said Christian. Still shivering, he pushed himself off the floor.

"No, it isn't!" she insisted. She stood up on her toes and got in Travers' face. "He defused the situation. He saved *everybody*, back at the hotel and here, Hallett included. He built a *good* company. We love it here. You can't lock him up!"

Agent Travers looked at Maggie kindly, if sadly. "You've got fire, Heinz. It does you credit. And you're right, Meadows' actions tonight will help his case, but the truth is, he's got a few things to answer for." Turning to Christian, she added, "The question now is where to keep him until his trial. Let me make a phone call."

"Thank you," said Christian, visibly relieved.

Her co-worker sighed impatiently. "What do we do with him until then?"

She looked around the facility, her eyes landing on the one conference room. "Lock him in there until I'm done."

Chuck grabbed Christian by the elbow and steered him toward their meeting space; suddenly Larry forgot about his anger at the lies, the endangerment, the betrayal. Everything Maggie had said was true. He *loved* working at Q-Tech, every minute of it, ever since that first day when Christian had given him a tour and tried to convince him to stay. Tonight, he had treated Christian badly, though he'd owed him so much. His cheeks flushed with shame.

"Wait," he called and trotted down the hall to intercept the agent. "He's cold. Let me bring him a blanket or his jacket."

"Whatever," said Chuck. "I'm still locking him up. Just bring it over."

Larry grabbed Christian's jacket and backpack from his office, then headed to the storage room. He hunted through the debris Hallett had generated until he found the thing he knew would make up for his own betrayal. He put it into the backpack, then rushed to the kitchen to supplement his find with water bottles and snacks. After that, he retrieved the first aid kit and his EMT bag from the warehouse floor and walked toward the conference room.

*****

Maggie watched mournfully as Agent Travers' partner led Christian away. She accepted what Travers had said, but she still didn't quite see how it was fair. *Saving everybody should mean something.* She just hoped the lady could make whoever Ralph was see that.

Mitch crossed the threshold from the machlab and came to stand by her side. "I'm really sorry, Maggie."

"So is Christian. He didn't mean for any of this to happen."

"Believe it or not, I know how he feels. It's horrible when the thing you created gets out of your control. People use it in ways you didn't expect, then it all goes sideways or worse."

"Is that what happened with the Jump!GOs?"

He nodded. "It was brutal, but we learned from it. Added controls and found more good uses for the technology. Now, it's not so bad. The same will happen for the dew drops eventually. You'll see."

"I hope so," Maggie said quietly. She looked around. The warehouse was trashed. Her internship too. "Now what am I gonna do?"

"Whatever you want."

CC Tamblyn had answered. Maggie hadn't realized she'd spoken out loud. She turned around, surprised to see Tamblyn, Dean, and Wayne crossing over from the machlab to join them.

"You've got a bright future ahead of you, young lady."

"How can I?" asked Maggie. "I worked for someone going to federal prison. His company doesn't exist anymore. The summer's been a waste."

"Glass half-empty, I see," Tamblyn replied.

"This whole experience goes on my transcript, and if it registers as a failure, that's it for me at Mines."

"Leland Hayman and I go way back. I'm sure I can work something out on your behalf. Q-Tech is likely not long for this world, but if you're interested we may be able to find a spot for you at Tamblyn Tech."

"Uh, wait a minute," said Dean. "Now that Tech Convergence happened, isn't our internship over?"

Tamblyn raised an eyebrow. "If you want it to be or, in your case, if *I* say it is."

Dean gulped. "I didn't mean to—"

"Relax, Chambers, just messing with you."

Dean sighed in relief.

"Actually, what tends to happen is successful interns get moved to junior technician spots, provided they decide they want to keep on working and their school schedule permits. I'm prepared to offer you all positions, Mr. Knight included. We're going to need the help if we're going to keep the momentum from today going."

Mitch grimaced. "After what happened tonight, do you still think people will trust the technology?"

"Campbell, I guarantee you, other companies will be chomping at the bit to be the new Q-Tech and prove they can implement light tech safer and better. It will be a feeding frenzy, most of them aimed at taking down Tamblyn's stake in the market— the one made possible by the work of you three. Everyone wants to fight the king. So, what do you all say? Feel up to the fight?"

"I'm in!" said Mitch excitedly.

"Wouldn't miss it," said Wayne.

"Me neither," added Dean. "I've got some ideas about how to expand the HoloNet. I was feeling kind of sad about leaving before I had a chance to try them out."

"Good to hear," said Tamblyn. "And you, Ms. Heinz? I'm told all of the shielding used tonight was developed by you. You could continue your work on it at my company if you like."

Maggie had been disappointed when she'd missed out on the Tamblyn internship. And even though she was happy when Larry had recommended her to Christian as an intern, she'd felt like she was settling for second best.

But creating the RMOR belt and working with Larry and Christian all summer had changed that. Trashed as it was, she looked around at the warehouse wistfully. "I don't know," she answered finally. "I really did like working here."

Just then, Larry trotted out of the kitchen and headed toward the conference room. Agent Travers intercepted him but spoke too quietly for anyone to overhear. Maggie noticed Tamblyn watching her and inexplicably felt embarrassed. "I'm sorry. Thank you for the offer. It's just been a weird night."

"Of course," Tamblyn said, patting her shoulder. "Just think about it. There's some time before the next semester. Anything could happen. Q-Tech might survive."

Turning to the guys, she said, "So, gentlemen? Have you given any thought to how the plasma grid might respond to the vacuum of space?"

They headed back across the threshold to the machlab. Travers' phone rang and she ended her conversation with Larry to answer it. He shook her hand, as if cementing a deal, then continued on to the conference room. Maggie wondered what they'd discussed and whether Larry would accept CC Tamblyn's offer of greener pastures. She also couldn't help but wonder how the RMOR would do in the vacuum of space.

*****

Christian sat at the front of the conference table, head in his hands, bleeding in places, feeling like crap. He very much did not want to go to prison, and even more than that, hated the prospect of being there with Hubert. The humiliation. The irritation. Either he or Hubert would be dead within a week.

The male agent opened the door and Larry walked in. Christian felt a pang of sorrow so deep he almost wept. He really needed a friend right then. It pained him to his core that Larry was no longer that friend.

Larry handed him his jacket, set his med kit on the table, and rolled over a chair. "Your hand's cut up," he said.

"I hadn't noticed."

"Bull."

"Well, maybe I need a band-aid."

"I'd say you needed more than one." Larry opened the med kit, found a disinfectant swab, and set to cleaning the wounds.

"Agent Travers stopped me on the way in here. She suggested I take charge of the company while you 'work your way through the judicial system.' "

"I guess that's Agency speak for 'rot in prison.' "

Larry sighed. "No doubt."

"Marion is a smart woman."

"You agree with her?"

"They'll shut Q-Tech down for good eventually, but until then... the team respects you. You're already a leader here."

"True, but I'm not you."

"I'm not me either. Not anymore. Who knows how long I'll be gone? I can't think of anyone else I'd trust to run the company while I 'work my way through the judicial system.' You're a good choice."

"And you're a good friend."

His eyes burned and Larry's faced blurred in Christian's vision. "I thought you were done with friendship?"

Larry shrugged. "I was, but I think I was wrong. Maggie kind of spelled out why."

"She's good at that."

Larry chuckled, then studied him. "How did it happen, Christian? And how in god's name did you survive?"

"It was a fluke. I reverse engineered Campbell's Canopy and turned his light holes into plasma balls. But for some reason it exploded, and the plasma balls got embedded inside of me. I didn't plan it, but once it happened, I didn't try fix it either. After a year of torture by Hubert, it seemed like a gift."

"Maybe it was."

Christian wiped his eyes and felt himself smile. "Only after I met Maggie and you."

Chuck opened the door. "Time to hit it."

Reluctantly, Christian followed Chuck to the van. Marion was waiting for him "Where are you taking me?" he asked her anxiously.

"My boss tried but couldn't swing a change tonight. It's still the Florence Supermax—"

Christian doubled over. He couldn't breathe. The news was worse than a punch to the gut.

"Hey! It's only temporary," Marion continued, pulling him up. "Listen to me. My boss will get you out, and the warden has orders to not put you with Hubert. It's a big facility. You probably won't even see him. And I'll do everything in my power to make sure they take *all* of your actions into account, not just the things Ralph wants them to think about. Got it?"

Christian nodded. "Thank you," he told her again.

Maggie threw her arms around his neck and kissed his cheek. "Thank you for saving my life."

"Just returning the favor, Maggie." She blushed.

"Excuse me. Gotta go," said Chuck. He loaded Christian into the van.

Larry pushed his way to the front of group, holding Christian's backpack. "Agent Travers, can he have some snacks? We missed dinner and it's a long drive to Cañon City."

"I don't see why not."

Chuck checked out the bag. It was crammed full of chocolate bars, chips, water, and bagels. "Almost makes me wish I was coming with you," he said, handing Christian the bag.

"Put our names on the visitor's list, wherever you land," said Larry. After a last wave from him and Maggie, Chuck shut the door and they were gone.

It won't be forever, he told himself. Even if they did wind up putting him together with Hubert, he'd survive it. He was certain. Because unlike his tormentor, he finally had something to live for. *You're not alone.*

His stomach growled, had been growling for some time, but for the first time in many hours he felt like eating. He opened the backpack to check the haul; the bagels smelled particularly good. It was dark in the van, the only lights being from other cars on the highway. But he remembered seeing an asiago bagel crammed to the side during Chuck's inspection.

He thrust his hand deep int the bag to retrieve it and felt something hard and metallic instead. *That's definitely not a bagel. I don't even think that's a water bottle.*

He scooped out the contents until he reached the metal and could not believe his eyes. There with a power pack, ready to go, was his original dew drop generator. One dew drop lay inside the cavity and with it a note from Larry. "It does what it should do now."

Tears filled his eyes. Would one be enough? It had been for Marion. The least he could do was try. He put the dew drop in his mouth, opened a water bottle, and upended it.

And suddenly, the light that had dimmed within him lit up again. What had been so painful before now felt warm, like a hug from an old friend. He closed his eyes and immediately saw them all: The Aggressor, scowling and angry as ever, and the Others spread out around him, staring out at him from their shells. For once, they were all silent. Time materialized in front of him. [**Hello, Prime.**]

Hello, old friend.

Looking at them all, he somehow knew they weren't trapped anymore. Just as Hallett had brought his reflections forward by violence into this dimension, Christian had the power to send the Others back to their own dimensions.

I can send you back, he told them. *Who wants to go?*

None of them replied.

Many shells still lay dark, dormant. Some appeared to be shorted out forever. One dew drop wasn't enough. But it would do.

Opening his eyes, Christian gathered the generator and food back into his backpack and put on his jacket. He pressed his palm against the door of the van and transformed it into a bluish-white, plasma swirl.

He could do it. Leave the country. Start over some place new, lay low until the heat around him and the whole crazy episode cooled down. He'd run away before, built a new identity before, knew the steps he'd have to take to do it again.

[**You'll always be running. Your past won't leave you. Your friends can't follow.**]

The plasma swirl of the portal was mesmerizing. He ached to jump through. But Marion's words came back to him. 'It's temporary,' she'd said. And Larry and Maggie had promised they would visit. Maybe it made no sense to run away.

Christian released the portal and settled in for the ride.

[**Your path is still the most probable,**] said Time.

Then let's take that path together.

ACKNOWLEDGEMENT

WRITING THE SECOND BOOK OF A SERIES might seem an easy feat to accomplish but can often present a significant challenge to the writer in maintaining continuity and momentum. Any success I had achieving either of these is due to the help of others. My continued thanks to JD Book Services for editing, Rick Magyar for yet another fantastic logo, and Lae Klinger plus Energy or matter © rolffimags/Depositphotos for overall cover design.

Thanks also to my wonderful family, Michael and Arthur. Your continued support, encouragement, and constructive criticism sustained me through the long months of writing.

And as always, thank you, Dear Reader, for taking another leap with Mitch and crew on this second Jump Light adventure. If you enjoy the book and have a moment to spare, I would really appreciate a short review. Your help in spreading the word is gratefully received.

Listen to the wisest of your inner voices.

AJ Kilgore
September 2020

ABOUT THE AUTHOR

AJ Kilgore's first words were "light" and "door". Her fascination with both has never ceased. She lives in Denver, the light of Colorado, but considers herself a citizen of the world.

COMING SOON

361

Jump Load

Prepare for the final leap! At last, Mitch Campbell and friends are on the path to success. The Jump Point technology is secure and theirs. But with that security comes questions about their mentor and alarming revelations about his and Mitch's past. In a whirlwind adventure that takes the Jump Point crew from the mountains of Colorado, to the steppes of Asia, out past the Kuiper belt and the edge of known space, Mitch must strive for more than security—before the future for his friends and mentor is lost.

Available, 2021.

For more information, visit Penny Candi Press:
https://pennycandi.com/books/jump-load/

www.ingramcontent.com/pod-product-compliance
Lightning Source LLC
Chambersburg PA
CBHW071149100726
47908CB00002B/305